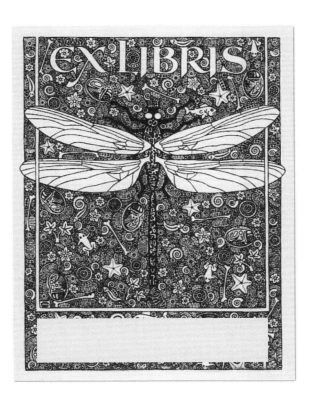

Other books by Ben Behunin

Remembering Isaac
Discovering Isaac
Becoming Isaac
Forget-Me-Notes
Borrowing Fire
Put A Cherry On Top
The Lost Art of Wooing Rabbits and Other Wild Hares
The Disciple of the Wind
How to Seduce a Sasquatch
Authentically Ruby

Ben's books are available from his website,
www.potterboy.com, www.amazon.com and
wherever above average books are sold.

SPLENDIDLY RUBY

The Acclaimed Matchmaker of Niederbipp

Book 2 in a series

by Ben Behunin

Splendidly Ruby
The Acclaimed Matchmaker of Niederbipp

Copyright © 2019 by Benjamin A. Behunin
All rights reserved. Manufactured in the United States of America

The contents of this book
may not be reproduced in any part or by
any means without written consent from the author
or Abendmahl Press except by a reviewer, or lecturer
who may quote passages in a review or lecture.

First printing, December 2019

Published by
Abendmahl Press
P.O. Box 581083
Salt Lake City, Utah 84158-1083

ISBN 978-0-9998516-0-9

Designed by Bert Compton and Ben Behunin
Illustrations by Preston Compton
Layout by Bert Compton
Editing by Laura Summerhays

To Nettie,
and our children,
Isaac and Eve.

Table of Contents

Prelude	391
Chapter 37, A New Day	393
Chapter 38, Challenging Personalities	401
Chapter 39, Reconciliation	409
Chapter 40, A New Start	419
Chapter 41, The Farm Stand	425
Chapter 42, Magnanimity	435
Chapter 43, Kryptonite	450
Chapter 44, Rhubarb and Humility	460
Chapter 45, The Economics of Socks	468
Chapter 46, Winged Messengers	480
Chapter 47, Bruised But Not Broken	487
Chapter 48, Discovery After Dark	500
Chapter 49, Some Fruits of Stillness	512
Chapter 50, Lessons in Free Enterprise	525
Chapter 51, Quiet Desperation	535
Chapter 52, The Thief	547
Chapter 53, Fugitive	558
Chapter 54, Of Flies and Worms	568
Chapter 55, A Time to Dance	588
Chapter 56, Balancing the World	602
Chapter 57, The Burdens of Imperfections	617
Chapter 58, The Proper Care and Feeding of Jerks	636
Chapter 59, Protopians, Unite!	648
Chapter 60, Impromptu Lessons in Gardening	660
Chapter 61, Right Place, Right Time	670
Chapter 62, Expiation	676
Chapter 63, Croissant Therapy	688

Chapter 64, Niederbipp's Liberty Fountain 700
Chapter 65, Searching for Joy 707
Chapter 66, Two Paths Home 716
Chapter 67, History and Cheese 733
Chapter 68, The First Key of Joy 745
Chapter 33, Illumination 754

Prelude

I began hearing about the farm up on Harmony Hill twenty-two years ago when the good people of Niederbipp began dropping in to have tea parties in my head. I've learned in that time that stories and the characters who inspire them are generally a jealous lot. They all want a piece of your time and attention, and if there's one thing they hate, it's waiting in line. But there was something different about Ruby. She was much more patient than the rest, sending up subtle smoke signals from her campfire every now and then just to remind me she was still waiting for me to share her story. And every once in a while I'd receive a surprise on my doorstep. Sometimes it was bowl of fresh berries. Other times it was a loaf of homemade bread. One time we opened the door to find a whole round of Lorenzo's coveted extra-sharp two-year-old Harmony Hill Bergkäse—still cool from the cheese cave. I shared it with my family and friends, and we all agreed it was delicious.

    The gifts were nice, but I began to realize that there were lots of strings attached, that those gifts were actually bribes to persuade me to share Ruby's story next. When I returned home from a week at the beach to find a pail of melted homemade strawberry ice cream on my porch, I knew I had neglected Ruby long enough.

    I began making trips to the farm a couple of years ago. I started dropping in every month or so. Then my visits became more frequent as I learned the rhythms of the farm, its nuances and quirks. Every now and then, Ruby and Lorenzo would invite me to help out with the laundry or to try my hand at grinding wheat into flour. And occasionally I'd stay late enough to hang out with the campers on the porch to play silly games as we took turns cranking Bessie. I never would have guessed that a farm could have so many lessons to share about life and love and joy. It feels like a creator must have designed every one of those two hundred acres to share some of the world's best kept secrets. And I am honored that Ruby and Lorenzo and the others so graciously shared those secrets with me.

I am a potter, but on my days off or when the pots are in the kiln, I get to be a writer. Man, I love those days! I enjoy few things more than wandering with a pen and my journal down the trail, through the woods, and out to the bench overlooking the orchard to listen to the wind as it whispers through the trees. I'll have to take you there sometime. It is truly a magical place. But until that day comes, I hope you'll enjoy these things I've been learning along the way.

Viva Niederbipp!
Ben Behunin

December 2019

CHAPTER 37

A New Day

Each morning when I open my eyes I say to myself: I, not events, have the power to make me happy or unhappy today. I can choose which it shall be. Yesterday is dead, tomorrow hasn't arrived yet. I have just one day, today, and I'm going to be happy in it.
—Groucho Marx

The blue light of morning was just beginning to illuminate the bunkhouse when Genevieve Patterson opened her eyes. Lost somewhere deep in the place between dreams and reality, it took her a moment to remember where she was. She listened to the soft breathing sounds of the other five women with whom she'd been forced to spend the last nine days here on this farm lost to time, deep in the backwoods of Pennsylvania—a million miles from the comforts she'd known in Manhattan.

Nine days! Could it really be only nine days? she wondered to herself, turning to look across the quiet room. Colorful patchwork quilts draped tranquil bodies atop simple bed frames and lumpy mattresses. So much had happened in those nine days that she was certain she could have written an entire book about it. But it wasn't a book she was after. Only ten thousand words, but still the longest article she had ever been assigned. She hadn't anticipated when she'd accepted the assignment that it would also require the most demanding and immersive research she had ever undertaken.

Only ten days earlier, Genevieve had arrived in Niederbipp with the intention of making a very short visit. Ruby Swarovski, the illustrious matchmaker of Niederbipp, had agreed to an interview request for the first time in more than twenty-five years. This story was going to change Genevieve's life—it would finally catapult her career in the direction she had always imagined. But the direction and the assignment she had anticipated were much different from the reality in which she now found herself.

She recalled that first morning, waking to the heckling cry of the rooster, wondering how everything had gone so quickly, terribly wrong. Her hopes of a quick escape from this backwater town had been so swiftly dashed. She knew it was something less than kidnapping, but still it felt reminiscent of an unsophisticated hostage situation—blackmail, at least. She'd heard of innocent bystanders being conscripted into unpleasant duties, but this was beyond belief—being forced to milk cows, cook for fourteen hungry campers, plow and plant fields, do laundry, and even make ice cream using bicycle-powered contraptions. It was simply too much, even for research purposes. But as she stared at the waxing light through the skylight above her, Genevieve recognized that somehow the farm had changed from a prison where she had to serve a five-month sentence into a place of unique understanding.

It had been only two days since her discussion with Matt—the oldest and perhaps the most brutally honest of the male recruits. He knew her secret, knew what was at stake for her here. He'd made it clear that he wasn't going to let her get in the way of his finding a wife. But he'd also brought to her attention that each of the other campers had at least as much riding on their experience here as she did. His words were firm and strong, but she was surprised by the underlying compassion and patience that accompanied them. Genevieve knew that Matt, perhaps more than any of the other recruits, had a whole lot of hope riding on this summer's adventure. Tired of being single, he dreamed of marriage and family. And at forty-three years old, his clock was ticking.

That discussion had surprised Genevieve. In the past week she had been teamed up with all six of the men for chores. In each case, she had found it remarkable to converse with men who actually wanted to be married—men who had made the commitment and sacrifice to step away from their lives and jobs for five whole months to work on this crazy farm in hopes of finding true love. She had given up on ever finding such a man, believing him to be a rare if not endangered species. And yet here were six of them—men who not only talked the talk but were willing to walk the walk by giving up a whole summer to the cause of love and matrimony.

But the men, Genevieve realized, were not alone in their desires for a loving, committed partnership. She turned her head again, looking over the five women who shared her bunkhouse. Each one of them was beautiful, talented, and remarkable in her own way. She knew that they, too, had made sacrifices to be here. They, too, were seeking a better life. They, too, were working hard, believing their work would pay off and that Ruby would reward them at the end of the summer with a worthwhile prize.

After only nine days, Genevieve felt an attachment to each of these women. The closeness and affection she felt toward each of them had been born in the fields as they labored together. But it was not until the events of the previous evening that things really changed. She rubbed the swollen lumps on her arm, remembering the attack. Wasps—hundreds of them—somewhere on the road to Tionesta. She smiled in spite of herself, remembering the ordeal: the broken bike chain, unintentionally kicking the wasps' nest, the mud that saved her from said wasps, and her time in the river trying to recover from all three. It had been traumatic, but it had also been undeniably cathartic. It was in that river, lying cold and nearly naked, that she had come to herself. Things had been so clear the night before. Now it felt less clear, somehow more distant. She yearned for that clarity now.

And then she found it. She found it immediately as she recalled the noble efforts of these women—as well as the men—who had left their comforts on a Sunday evening to go and search for her and bring her home.

She took a deep breath and let it go slowly, considering how this ragtag group of weirdos had somehow become friends—almost family. Genevieve had always wanted sisters, siblings, family. And here they were—eleven siblings somehow becoming more congruous in spite of all their differences. In just over a week they had come together, gelled, and taken on a shape and a form they never could have in their separate lives. She had never connected with any other group of people in this way.

It was easy to get caught up in the good feelings of all of that, swept away in the magic of this Shangri-La. But the reality of why she was here stung her like a delayed effect of wasp venom. She was, after all, a spy. A poseur. A mole. And after just over a week, she knew she had nothing that was worth publishing. How could she write about any of this in a convincing way? How could she convey Holly's sincere and innocent goodness without making her sound naive? How could she write about Spencer's addiction to sports without making him sound like a two-dimensional jerk? How could she write of her admiration for Susan and her ability to push past something as profoundly difficult as sexual abuse? It would be a betrayal of a delicate trust. And how could she write about Matt's undying hope for love and family without making him sound desperate? She went through each of the campers in her mind, hoping to find one that would enable her to begin writing something that the readers of the world could sink their teeth into. But as Genevieve considered each of them and their stories, she found it felt a little bit like stabbing them in the back. Their stories didn't belong to her, and to take them and use them to enhance her reputation as a writer not only felt disloyal, it felt weaselly. She had never had trouble writing an honest exposé or critical commentary, and she struggled to understand why this felt so different.

Her thoughts turned from the campers to Ruby and Lorenzo. She felt embarrassed and ashamed as she remembered the plans she had made on her flight to Pittsburgh. She had planned to quickly ascertain any obvious weaknesses in this fabled matchmaker of Niederbipp and then exploit those weaknesses to debunk Ruby's skills, making a mockery of her and the gullible, foolish people who came to the farm each year. Those plans, Genevieve now realized, had not only been mean-spirited and obnoxious, but they were also petty and ignorant. As she considered the sad reality of her plans, Genevieve found herself wondering how many other interviews she might have unfairly conducted and written up. Her words, she knew, had power. More than a million sets of eyes saw her articles in the magazine each month. Several social media platforms—with her tens of thousands of followers—provided an opportunity to sow her ideas even further and wider. At almost thirty years old, she had already accomplished nearly everything she had dreamed of. Nearly.

The one promising or otherwise noteworthy relationship of her life had ended several years before. Charlie Blackham had taken a job on the West Coast, while Genevieve had headed farther east. Despite all of their best efforts, their mutual promise to keep the fires of romance stoked had slowly faded as the demands of their jobs, along with the three-hour time difference, proved to be significant hurdles. Charlie had broken her heart, calling a few months in to tell her that he felt compelled to get to know a girl from his yoga class a little better. Genevieve had been tempted to catch the next flight to San Diego and remind him of the magic they shared. But with a business flight to Spain already on her immediate schedule, she decided against it. That decision proved to be her biggest regret to date. Charlie fell in love, got married, and regularly posted happy pictures to his social media accounts—including several recent pictures of his new baby boy.

Genevieve had never really wanted a child before she saw those pictures. It was the boy's eyes, she had told her therapist, that hit her envy button with an intense blow. Blue like his father's and every bit as charming, it was those pictures of that beautiful child that sent Genevieve back to therapy after a short hiatus. And like before, when she had lost Charlie, it had required nearly a dozen sessions for her to stop crying at just the thought of all that could have been hers. She'd drowned her sorrows in alcohol, work, and a new cat, hoping to quench the bitter fires of regret and jealousy. But even the best medication can only go so far to fill the void of a wounded heart. Surrounded by millions of people, Genevieve had never felt more alone in the city. She had been looking forward to the trip to Brussels as an opportunity to clear her mind.

She forced her eyes closed, trying to block out the growing light. Brussels, she knew, was a hundred million miles away from this farm. She did the math and realized she had missed it all. Even the interview with the cobbler in Milan would have been history and she'd be on her way back to JFK. Instead of basking for a week in Europe's most fashionable, star-studded glamour, she'd spent that week on a farm in the middle of nowhere, getting dirty, sunburned, and angry.

The change in her assignment had come as a brutal shock. Instead of lavish champagne parties that ran late into the morning hours, she'd had ice cream parties on the porch. Instead of donning her best gowns, she'd spent a week dressed in used farm duds. Instead of overwhelming her olfactory senses with the latest fragrances on the market, she'd been overwhelmed by the scent of labor and animals and farm. Instead of dancing and partying until dawn, she'd fallen asleep early, completely exhausted. Instead of squinting into the flashing lights of the paparazzi, she'd seen more stars than she ever knew existed in the night sky. But with her eyes squeezed shut, she realized that the things she'd experienced in the last nine days on the farm could be compared with nothing she'd ever experienced.

The last bits of her fingernail polish had finally fallen off somewhere between her wrestle with the wasps and the mud and the river. And she guessed it would be months before her next manicure. By then, she knew, they'd have to sand down the calluses on her hands and feet with an electric grinder. It had been more than a week since she'd put on makeup. And in that week, she was sure she'd inhaled more dirt and farm-scented stench than she had over the entire course of her life. It had been a week of firsts and more-than-I-evers, but she had to admit it wasn't all bad. There were new friends and ice cream and homemade bread and that strange sense of family that had developed among the campers.

As Genevieve compared this experience to the ten summers she'd spent at camp in the Adirondacks, she saw both similarities and differences. Those summers had also been full of a variety of activities, but never had she been asked to help with the cooking or even the laundry. In fact, she had learned quickly that by exercising a little attitude and an irritating whine, she didn't have to do anything she didn't want to do. While other campers made friends and worked on crafts, Genevieve usually had her nose in a book or took long naps or daydreamed of being anywhere else.

Her first morning on the farm she'd discovered that sitting out the day's activities was not an option here. That reality had been made clear over and over again with each daily chore or activity. Some of the machines wouldn't even respond to a half-hearted effort. The chores required two people, honest engagement, and full participation. But they brought a sense of meaning and accomplishment—something much more satisfying at the end of the day than a braided boondoggle lanyard.

She hadn't thought much about summer camp in the nearly fifteen years since she had last attended, but as she thought about it this morning, she found herself wondering how her lousy attitude and lack of participation might have kept her from fully experiencing camp. She had passed the time, but she'd made no long-lasting friendships as other kids had. She had met a few boys, but she'd had no teen romance as her bunkmates had. She read most of the books in the camp library, but she'd undergone no noticeable semblance of genuine self-discovery. She realized she had missed it. She had missed it all.

Genevieve watched through the skylight as the rooster roused on his perch, stretching his wings before cocking his head back and beginning his morning reveille. The women stirred, moaning and stretching in anticipation of the new day. As they dressed, Genevieve watched and listened to each of the ladies. One week in and they still wanted to be here, their outward attitudes reflecting their inner desires to improve their lives. She recognized that their attitudes were contagious, and for the first time since her arrival on the farm, she didn't fight it, choosing instead to embrace it.

She splashed cold water on her face and looked into the small mirror above the sink. The wasp stings still dotted her face and neck, but she smiled at herself as she once again remembered the events of the previous day. And as she left the bunkhouse to meet the new day, she was struck by a sense of freshness in all that surrounded her, as if she were seeing all of this for the first time. She watched as the men crossed the lawn to meet them, and she was struck by the truth of Sunday's sermon—that rock bottom might just be a reasonable place to begin building a sure foundation.

CHAPTER 38

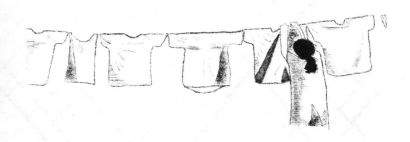

Challenging Personalities

Opportunity is missed by most people because it is dressed in overalls and looks like work.
—Thomas Edison

"I guess it's you and me today," James said, nodding to Genevieve with an early-morning smile, his hair a mess.

"And what is it we're doing again?" Genevieve asked, stifling a yawn.

"Laundry, remember?"

She nodded, but she didn't remember. "I'll go get the girls' basket if you get the boys'." She returned to the bunkhouse, gathering up the still-damp towels and odds and ends that hadn't quite made it into the basket. She walked through the long grass and climbed the gentle hill to the laundry house, where the door stood ajar. The boys' basket lay on the floor just inside the door, but James was not there. Tired and sore from yesterday's ride and pandemonium, Genevieve impatiently sat down on the stoop to wait for James. He arrived a few minutes later, out of breath from his jaunt to the big house, carrying another basket of clothes and dishcloths from the kitchen.

"Did you get the barrels loaded?" he asked.

"No, I was…waiting."

He looked disappointed, brushing past her. She stood and joined him, his hands moving in a frenzied speed as he sorted the lights and darks into their respective barrels. He quickly emptied both of the baskets he had brought with him and stood, impatiently watching as Genevieve slowly sorted out the women's laundry.

"If you want, you can grate the soap while I finish up," Genevieve said.

"I already grated the soap for this one. You can grate the soap for that one," he responded curtly.

"Oh, okay. I just thought maybe while I was…"

"Right—like how you sorted the laundry while I ran to the big house and got the basket?"

Genevieve bristled at his tone. "Is there a problem?"

"Yeah, there's a problem. If we don't get this moving, we're going to miss everyone on their way up to breakfast and then we'll have to hang up all the laundry by ourselves."

"It's not that big of a deal. We missed the help last week, and it only took…"

"I know. Ephraim told me you were slower than tar."

"He what?"

"Forget it," James said, grimacing. "Let's just hurry. I'm hungry and tired, and laundry has never been much fun for me."

"Oh, you think it's fun for me?"

"I didn't say that."

She shook her head. "Unbelievable."

"Wait. What is?" he asked, looking perturbed and surprised that this had been turned on him.

"Geesh. Just because you woke up on the wrong side of the bed doesn't mean you have to be jerk about it!"

"Me? I wasn't the one who was sitting around! You could have been sorting the laundry while I was busting my butt to get the other basket. You could have had the laundry sorted and the soap grated by the time I got back. Hell, we could have been pedaling the stupid machine by now, but you're still sorting. And you still have to grate the soap for *your* barrel."

"Wow! When did we start keeping score?"

"The minute I saw you sitting around when there was work to do!"

"So, this is all about me?" she asked incredulously, her voice getting louder.

"We have a job to do. Let's just do it and get this over with," he said, reaching for the bar of soap and the cheese grater, which he reluctantly began working over the barrel closer to her.

"Just give me that," she said, reaching for the soap and grater.

He pulled them back, flashing his angry eyes at her, but she didn't relent, stepping around the barrel to get closer. James responded by stepping back even further, and before either of them knew what was happening, a chase ensued.

"Give me the damn soap!" Genevieve said as she reached out to grab him, missing his shoulder by only an inch.

He responded with a menacing face and picked up the pace, running around the contraption a second time, taking this whole thing far more seriously than either of them could understand at that moment.

They had each circled the machine five times before Genevieve caught hold of his T-shirt collar and wrenched the soap and grater from his hands, scratching his neck and hands with her fingernails.

When he saw that he had lost the chase, he did what any self-respecting twelve-year-old boy would do and sloppily filled the barrels, purposely splashing the water over Genevieve's legs and shoes when he moved on to the second barrel.

Not wanting to be bettered by an immature, idiotic man, she responded by yanking the hose out of his hands and turning it on him, dousing his front with the cold water before he could respond. But respond he did, grabbing a waterlogged towel from the top of the barrel and throwing it at Genevieve. This served only to further enrage Genevieve, who turned the hose on James's face and head. James responded in turn, pulling more soggy laundry from the barrels and yelling loudly for her to stop being so unreasonable. Genevieve had never taken kindly to anyone calling her unreasonable. She continued to spray James in the chest and face with the hose as he continued to launch two days' worth of wet and dirty laundry at her. The mayhem continued until the barrels were empty and laundry was scattered across the small laundry-house floor. Upon discovering that he was out of ammunition, he charged the hose-wielding Genevieve as she continued her frontal assault with the water. Harsh words flew back and forth with the water as they wrestled for control of the hose.

"What in the Sam Hill is going on in here?" Ruby said, standing in the doorway of the laundry house, looking mad.

They stopped wrestling and looked up, but Genevieve continued to aim the water flowing from the hose at James's shoe.

"For the record, Ruby, I want you to know that she started this," James said, pointing at Genevieve.

Ruby looked things over quickly before looking back at James. "And I suppose she's also the cause of the laundry being all over the floor?"

"It was self-defense."

"Is that right?" Ruby responded, placing her hands on her hips. She stared at each of them before looking again at the floor, scattered with soggy laundry and soap bubbles. "Well, you forgot this one at the big house," she said, tossing James a towel. "And if you don't get this cleaned up and figure out how to work with each other before the end of breakfast, you two will be the first team this year to get to spend a full week working together."

"But…" Genevieve protested.

"The only butts here are the two of yours, which should be on those bike seats by now. I suggest you figure this out *now*—without any further argument or hostilities—or you'll spend the week doing all your chores in the Britches of Shame."

Genevieve looked around at the mess they'd made and was surprised by the smile that spontaneously spread across her face when she imagined how awkward it would be to spend even ten minutes sharing britches with a man she wanted to murder.

"This is ridiculous," James said in protest.

"You're absolutely right!" Ruby replied, shaking her head. "Two adults who can't even do the laundry. Absolutely ridiculous. Now, if you know what's good for you, it's time to accept your responsibilities and get your crap together. Breakfast will be ready long before you're finished. I better get back to Matt and Susan in the kitchen," she said, raising her crooked finger in front of her face. "This is supposed to be fun."

"This is definitely not fun!" James guffawed incredulously.

Ruby nodded. "Then you're definitely doing something wrong. One or both of you need an adjustment."

"Yeah, that's hilarious," James shot back.

Ruby put her hands on her hips again and looked at him very sternly. "James, you'd better figure this out now. If you think this is difficult now, you'll be crying after a couple of hours in the Britches of Shame. Swallow your pride. Get over yourself. And get back to work."

"What about her?" he asked defiantly, pointing at Genevieve.

"The same goes for both of you," Ruby said, turning to look at Genevieve.

James shook his head as water continued to splash into his waterlogged shoes. "This isn't fair. She wasn't even working. She's purposely trying to make me look bad. Don't you see?"

"What I see is two stubborn kids who've made a mess of things.

I see work that needs doin' and attitudes that need adjustin', and I see tempers that need a whole lotta modifyin'."

"Pfff," James said, shaking his head indignantly.

"You not seeing it, are you, James?"

"What am I supposed to see other than an impossible situation?"

"Really?" Ruby chided. "Impossible?"

"Actually it *is* pretty bad," Genevieve agreed.

"Of course it's bad—look at the mess the two of you have made," she agreed, her hands outstretched to the mayhem before her. "But why are you here?"

James rolled his eyes and shook his head.

"Why are you here, James?"

He let out a long breath. "Because I want to be married."

"What was that?" Ruby asked, lifting her hand to her ear.

"Because I want to be married," he responded a little louder.

"I can't hear you," she said playfully in a singsong voice that made Genevieve smile.

"Because I want to freakin' be married!" James said, almost shouting, anger in his voice.

"Yes, that's what I thought. That's why I chose you from a long list of men who applied to be here this year. Because you want to *freakin'* be married." She nodded, looking down at the laundry scattered across the floor before looking up at him again. "Passion, James, can be a beautiful thing. But it can also destroy you. Genevieve did not make you look bad this morning. You did."

He shook his head.

"You don't want to hear that?"

He forced out another deep breath.

"No, I suppose you wouldn't want to hear it. But it's true. Wanting to be married isn't enough is it?"

"What do you mean?" he asked after a moment of awkward silence.

"Simply wanting anything is rarely enough to obtain it. You have to work for it. You have to want it bad enough to change your life—to make room for it. You can't force a person to marry you and have any hope that it will last. You can't belittle a woman into being your wife and expect her to be happy with you. And you certainly can't fight through something as regularly occurring as laundry and hope to create a home filled with harmony and love. I don't know what happened here this morning to spur on this disaster, and I don't really care to know. But the negative energy that hit me before I even opened this door nearly knocked me over. The two of you created that energy. It didn't come from the laundry or the water or the soap. It came from you—both of you. And if you'll take an honest look at what transpired shortly before all this blew up, I have an educated hunch that you'll be able to see where you went wrong—each of you.

"If you haven't noticed by now, I'd like to encourage you to open your eyes a little wider and see the big picture. Laundry is part of the rhythm of life. It's one of those facts of life that none of us can avoid, at least not for long. Nor can we avoid the hours of work that go along with it." She looked up at the instructions written on the board above their heads.

"Good ol' Reverend Merton had it right, didn't he?" she asked pointing to the quote written across the bottom of the board. They turned and looked as she read: "*'Happiness is not a matter of intensity but of balance and order and rhythm and harmony.'* The rhythms of laundry come to most households in at least weekly intervals. Can you imagine how much harmony would be in your home if these sorts of shenanigans happened every time you attempted to empty the hamper?"

Genevieve stole a glance at James, who looked slightly more humble but still defiant.

"This," she motioned with her hands as if to signify the whole of the laundry operation, "is practice for the real thing. With any luck, you'll both be married soon. I've seen enough from both of you to suggest you need to seek other marital partners, but regardless of who each of you marry and how well you may be suited for each other, difficulties will arise. Passions will flare. Feelings will be hurt. Anger will boil.

Words will be said that you'll wish you could somehow take back. If you think marriage will be easier than doing laundry with any of your fellow campers, let me just spare you some ignorance and tell you now that you're wrong. Dead wrong.

"Now, let me suggest to each of you once again that you get over yourselves—that you forgive each other—that you recognize that you *both* had a part in creating this mess and you *both* are required to make it right. There are very few differences that cannot be reconciled, and laundry is certainly not one of those outliers." She took a deep breath and nodded to each of them. "Balance, order, rhythm, and harmony. Work on those, and your work here this summer will reward you handsomely. Neglect any of the above, and you'll be no better off than when you arrived. Any questions?" She looked from Genevieve to James, and they both shook their heads. "Good. Then I'll leave you to your work."

CHAPTER 39

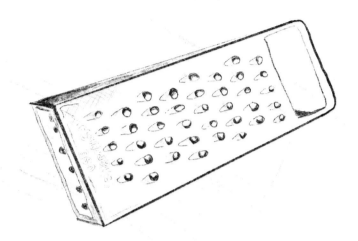

Reconciliation

Sometimes, carrying on, just carrying on, is the superhuman achievement.
—Albert Camus

Peace did not come quickly. Genevieve turned off the hose and hung it on the edge of the utility sink before gathering up armfuls of sopping, dirty laundry and placing it all back into the barrels, trying to avoid looking at or bumping into James, who was also obviously trying to avoid any entanglements. Without words, they navigated around each other as they took turns grating soap into the barrels and refilling them with water. James was already sitting on one old bike saddle when

Genevieve finished with the soap. He appeared every bit as impatient and sour as before, so Genevieve kept her mouth shut and sat down on the remaining seat. Her sitz bones were sore from yesterday's ride to Tionesta, and she winced as she settled onto the saddle. Remembering how difficult the rhythm of this machine had been for her and Ephraim to achieve just days before, she wondered how this could reasonably work without communicating with each other. But the idea of apologizing for something she didn't think was her fault felt disingenuous and forced. James was the one who came to this nonparty with a pissy attitude. He was the one who had seemed bent on keeping score in a game she didn't even know she was playing or by what rules the game was played. Sure, she had taunted him and sprayed him with water and called him a long list of unsavory names, but had her words and actions not been merited and made out of a response to his bad behavior? Could it not be considered self-defense? Whatever the answers to those questions, James was a brute. She was frustrated and still shaking from some fight-or-flight reaction that felt primitive and involuntary. But she had held her ground. She wasn't going to let a dumb, impatient, overgrown twelve-year-old ruin her day.

She reached for the handlebars of the old, tire-less bike to steady herself before pushing down on the pedals. But to her chagrin, the pedals moved only an inch or two before they stopped. She pushed with all her force, but they wouldn't budge.

"I already tried that," James admitted, looking quite defeated. "This stupid thing only works with two people—working together."

Genevieve nodded, taking in a big breath and pushing her wet hair over her shoulder.

"So what are we going to do about it?" he asked.

"You could start with apologizing for being such a rude, ignorant jerk."

James shook his head. "Me? Wow! You really *are* impossible."

"What the hell is that supposed to mean?"

"Really? Are you actually so oblivious that you don't even know how difficult you are to work with?"

"What? Where is this even coming from? You're not exactly a bundle of fun either. You're the one who started all of this."

"Really?" he asked, pointing to the dark red scratch marks that her fingernails had left on his hand. "I was just responding to your pissy little attitude. We were hoping your little disaster yesterday would soften you up a little bit, but you're just as big of a biddy as you were before."

"Wait right there!" she shouted, holding up her index finger, her eyes full of spit and fire. "Who the hell's *WE*?"

"The guys."

"Which ones?"

"All of us," he responded, looking away.

"Oh, so…what? You boys stay up late in your bunkhouse talking about me?"

"Don't flatter yourself. We talk about all the girls. Your name just keeps coming up as the one who's making life difficult for all of us. We've been trying to understand why you think you're so much better than the rest of us. I think that's why we all hoped yesterday would change things for you. Don't get me wrong—what Spencer did in ditching you was inexcusable. When we heard he'd found your bicycle abandoned on the side of the road, we were all concerned for your safety and well-being despite all the difficulty you've given each of us."

She looked both surprised and confused by that revelation. "Oh, and you boys are all Prince Charmings, right? This is ridiculous. You don't even know me."

"We've collectively seen enough to make some educated guesses," he responded confidently.

"Is that right?"

"Yep. And I'd be willing to bet we're right on."

She shook her head. "Ooh, this is rich. What have you geniuses come up with?"

"You really want to know?"

"Sure. Go ahead. It's obvious that we're going to be here a while, so why don't you just put it all out there. Give me the truth."

James laughed and shook his head. "I don't think you can handle the truth."

"Coward!" she chided.

"Really? Back to the name calling?"

"Prove me wrong."

"Fine! It's obvious to all of us that you were raised to believe you're a princess—possibly an only child; that you've never been told that you're wrong and would never accept that you were; that you probably had at least one pony along with a nanny and a housekeeper and a nose wiper. Most of us figured you spent your summers at a series of expensive summer camps for overprivileged rich kids and you spent your weekends and spare time prancing around your parents' country club."

Genevieve raised an eyebrow and laughed. "And your point is? I'm not going to apologize for my father's success or my family's lot in life. Is that really all you got?"

"Oh, no, I'm just getting started. We guessed that you had a total of two dates in high school and four in college; that your father paid some unsuspecting neighbor boy to take you to your prom; that you generally hate men, or at least find them worthless, as well as any women who threaten your hyperoverconfident level of self-worth. I personally imagined you to be the kind of woman that has one, maybe two, girlfriends tops, but your friendships with them are based only on gossip and a mutual appreciation for day spas and shopping, which may or may not continue to be funded at least in part by your father's expense card. We guessed that you have an inferiority complex which compels you to pride yourself on your ability to control, suppress, or otherwise manipulate anyone you feel shows any signs of weakness. Oh, and one of the guys guessed you drive an SUV that has never left the pavement. In short, we all agree that you're a poseur who's focused her efforts on her outward appearance to try to compensate for the shallowness of her soul."

Genevieve squirmed defensively. "Wow! So let me get this straight: ganging up to define me in the least complimentary ways possible somehow makes you boys…what, feel better about yourselves? Why are you telling me all of this?"

James laughed. "Because you asked, right? And because I'm tired and hungry and dripping wet thanks to you, and I'm not in any mood to be working with the woman we've all decided is the most difficult personality we've ever met."

"Well, at least you can take comfort in the fact that you're all equally moronic."

James guffawed and shook his head. "I told you you couldn't handle the truth. You have to resort to name-calling and insisting that you're somehow superior to everyone around you. The term *narcissist* comes to mind."

"Well, it takes one to know one."

James laughed. "Why are you here?"

"The same reason you are," she lied.

"Then why are you making it so difficult for the rest of us?"

She looked surprised. "What am I doing that's making life so difficult?"

He looked at her incredulously and shook his head.

"What?" she insisted. "What am I supposed to do to make you happy if all you boys are playing by some unpublished set of rules." She shook her head. "I can't believe I just said that. Since when is it my job to make you guys happy anyway?"

"I never said it was, but why do you insist on making our lives miserable?"

"Oh, and I suppose you think that working with you is some kind of privilege."

"I never said that. If we didn't know it before we arrived, I think we've all figured out that each of us is in need of at least a little work. I'm sure I'm probably not the easiest person to work with."

"There's an understatement. I don't even know why you're upset."

He stared at her for a moment before rolling his eyes and looking away.

"Oh, that's mature. I'm asking a serious question, and you brush it off like I'm some kind of idiot. How am I supposed to react to that? I can't read your mind. I have no idea what you're thinking or what you want from me. You mentioned at the bonfire the other night that you've had a lot of girls break your heart."

"Oh, so it's all about me now?" he responded defiantly.

"Oh, James," she said condescendingly, "it's always been all about you. I'll give you that women can be difficult at times, but there's usually a cause. Have you ever stopped to consider that part of your issues with women might be *you*?"

"So, you *are* making it about me. Is this retaliation for me being right?"

Genevieve shrugged. "James, I'm not going to lie and say you boys weren't probably right about some—maybe most—of your guesses about me. I've never pretended to be an easy person to work with. But something's different now. This past week—well, maybe mostly since yesterday when I was lying in that river—I've been thinking about what I want my life to look like five years from now. I want something different. I want to love and be loved. As much as I've tried to find fulfillment in living a successful single life, when I really look at it, I'll admit there's always been something missing. I don't know how to change that any more than you apparently know how to communicate without being an ornery jerk."

James looked at her and shook his head, obviously angry, but he didn't respond verbally.

"Look, you guys nailed it, okay. I am an only child, and yeah, my dad *did* in fact pay a kid in the neighborhood to take me to the prom. I found out about half way through the evening and ended up walking home, if that makes you feel any better. My dating experiences since then can be described as few and far between—thank you very much for digging up painful memories and throwing them in my face."

James pursed his lips and looked away, feeling embarrassed.

"Maybe my therapist is right," Genevieve continued. "That I'm still carrying some portion of shame and hurt from those painful experiences and a thousand other stupid things that shaped my attitude toward men and maybe life in general. I've probably held on to a lot of things I should have let go of a long time ago. We probably all have. I don't know what happened here today, and it's obvious that two people like you and me should never get married. Thank you for clearing up any questions that I might have had about that. But unless I missed something this last week, we still have to work with each other at least once a week for the next five months. And we're probably not going to be able to do that with any degree of success if we keep treating each other like we have this morning."

"I was waiting for an apology," he said after a long silence.

"*Really*? I thought we…"

"I suppose I've been waiting for way too long," he said, cutting her off. "My therapist told me on my last visit that she thought I was shaping every future relationship by carrying in my pocket every pain and negative emotion I've experienced in my past relationships."

Genevieve didn't know how to respond so she didn't.

"Maybe I'm not the easiest person to work with either," he finally said.

"Are you posing that as a statement or a question?" she asked after an awkward pause.

He shrugged. "We've all got baggage, don't we? A backpack full of rocks that weighs us down and keeps us from progressing. I've blamed my parents' divorce and the insensitivity of my past girlfriends for my lack of progress, but maybe you're right. Maybe I'm part of the problem." He shook his head. "I hate that!"

"Taking personal responsibility?"

He nodded. "It just feels so much better to blame everyone else, you know?"

"Yeah," Genevieve said, looking away.

"I overheard Matt talking about that the other night with Ephraim. He said something about finally coming to the point where he realized how fruitless it was to blame anyone else for his problems and for all the things he lacked. I didn't want to hear it, but I've been thinking about what he said ever since, realizing that I've probably been doing the same thing for years. I hate to admit it, but Gramps had it right."

"Gramps?"

"Oh, I mean Matt. We—the guys—we call him Gramps."

"Why?"

"Because we decided it was nicer than Bengay."

"What?" she laughed.

"Yeah, Spencer started teasing him the other night when we caught him rubbing his back with Bengay after that first day in the field. That guy is old—forty-three! That sounds so ancient, right? It was Spencer's idea to call him Gramps, and I guess it stuck." James snickered. "The dude carries a handkerchief in his back pocket, for crying out loud. I give the guy credit though. He's probably way too late to find a wife, but at least he's trying, right? You gotta give him that. If it doesn't work out, I suppose he'd make a good philosopher or...a librarian."

"I think he's nice and smart. We could probably all learn a lot from him."

James shrugged. "You must have done something to impress him too."

"Why do you say that?"

He looked a little sheepish. "When we were all talking about how difficult you are to work with the other night, the only thing he shared was one of those witty quotes he always has on the tip of his tongue—something about how we need to be kind because we're all carrying some unknown burden or fighting an unseen battle...or whatever."

Genevieve nodded thoughtfully, considering the simple truth and recognizing that the conversation she'd had with Matt on Friday must have coincided with this conversation he'd recently had with the other guys. "I guess it's true, isn't it?"

"What is?"

"I'm sure we've both heard that saying a thousand times, and, frankly, I've always thought it was a little cheesy. But I guess it feels different when you're on the receiving end of the compassion."

James nodded slowly, recognizing how right she was.

"Look," Genevieve started. "I've never been one to apologize—at least not first. I've always felt like it was weak, but whatever I did to make you upset with me this morning, I'm sorry."

"I'm sorry too," James said, looking like a young boy. "I've never been a morning person, and I'm sorry to take out my frustrations on you."

Genevieve nodded. "I think I got you back for that," she said, pointing to the scratches on his hands and neck. "It sounds cliché, but maybe…maybe we could start over, realizing we're both hotheaded and at least occasionally irrational."

James grimaced. "Yeah, that sounds reasonable. Where do you want to start?"

"Well, considering that we're both hungry and that everyone else is probably eating breakfast by now, we should probably get the laundry done so we can face them without feeling like we've been slacking on our chores."

He let out a long breath as if he'd been holding it all morning. "Maybe you're not as bad as the other guys suggested."

"No, actually I am," she said, trying to smile. "But I see now that it hasn't done me much good."

James looked surprised by her response before nodding knowingly. "I've always hated laundry. It's such a waste of time. I hope that someday I'll make enough money that I can hire someone to do it for me."

"Yeah, I totally get it. I never did my laundry until I went away for college, and even then I found it was easier to pay someone to do it for me."

"Seriously?"

"Yeah, well, it's nothing I'm exactly proud of. I just never considered it a life skill worth learning."

"And now?"

She laughed. "Maybe I had it wrong. Doing it this way, with teamwork and real physical exertion—maybe it has its virtues. Ask me again at the end of the summer."

CHAPTER 40

A New Start

*There's a crack... in everything.
That's how the light gets in.
—Leonard Cohen*

The breakfast dishes had long been washed and dried by the time James and Genevieve made their way to the big house after washing and hanging the laundry. But the feelings of anger and animosity that had existed that morning had been replaced with a shared sense of understanding, even friendship. As they had worked together as a team to make the washing machine function, they had also opened up to each other, sharing things neither of them had ever shared with anyone. And in that sharing, they were both surprised by the sense of compassion that formed between them as they recognized a common sense of fragility and humanity in each other. Genevieve had been more vulnerable than she'd ever allowed herself to be. And she recognized that in their shared vulnerability, a profound connection and alliance had formed—a connection that obviously surprised them both.

They found that Matt and Susan had left two bowls of oatmeal and a plate of scrambled eggs for them to share. It was all cold, and the oatmeal was lumpy. But their hunger kept them from being picky, and they ate together at the dining table, where several of their fellow campers were busy writing letters.

"We've been waiting for you guys to finish up so we can go to the farm stand," Crystal announced as she stuffed a sheet of paper into an envelope.

"What are we doing there?" James asked.

"I'm not sure. Something about cleaning it out and getting things ready for sales. I guess we begin taking shifts there on Wednesday."

"Wait, you mean like selling produce and stuff?" Genevieve asked.

"Uh, yeah, like it said in the paperwork, right? I guess that's one of the main sources of income for the farm. Pops said it's needing a new paint job and some minor repairs. I guess we'll see what that means," Crystal said.

Genevieve and James finished up their breakfast before taking their dishes into the kitchen. They found Matt and Susan just sliding the day's bread into the oven as Ruby watched.

"Well, look who's decided to join us!" Ruby said, wiping her hands on her apron. "I trust you two patched things up and figured it out?"

They looked at each other and smiled, nodding.

"Very good. That old washing machine has probably helped more than a few dozen kids learn how to communicate. I'm glad to see it still has its magic. We'll be heading down to the farm stand as soon as the bread's out of the oven. I'm sure Pops could use a hand gathering up supplies. And Spencer could probably use a hand fixing that bike of yours," Ruby said, nodding to Genevieve.

"Oh, are we riding bikes to the farm stand?" James asked.

"Yes. That's what the rest of the kids opted to do. The pickup truck will be filled with tools and supplies, so there won't be any room for passengers. Riding is always more fun than walking anyway, at least downhill. You missed the time for letter writing this morning, but there'll be time for that again this week. I'm sure I can trust you both to make yourselves useful before we leave?"

"Yeah, sure," James said, taking the dishes to the sink with Genevieve following close behind.

After drying the dishes, they helped Matt and Susan straighten up the kitchen before they all wandered out the front door. The pickup truck was being loaded with all sorts of tools and scraps of lumber. The four of them jumped into the parade, carrying additional tools and paint cans from one of the outbuildings at the back of the house. Those who weren't involved in loading the truck were lining up the bikes. All around them an unexplained buzz of excitement hummed, which was only intensified by the warmth of the sunny day.

Genevieve watched from a distance as Spencer and Ephraim worked on the bike she recognized as the one she'd ridden the day before. She was surprised by the sense of betrayal and disappointment she felt as she looked at Spencer, who was squatting next to the upside-down bike. His fingers were covered in grease, and he wore a black grease stripe across his cheek. Ephraim stood over him, his hands also greasy as he finessed a pair of pliers around the chain.

"Thanks for…this," she said, as she approached them. "Do you need any help?"

The men both looked up from their work. "Maybe. Have you ever worked on a bike before?" Ephraim asked.

"Uh, nope. Can't say that I ever have. You?"

"Yeah, but not since I was about fifteen. As it turns out, none of us have had much to do with bikes since we got our driver's licenses, so they called on the engineer to figure it out. I was just telling Spencer how beautifully simple and functional a bike is."

"I think that's engineer-speak for *greasy*," Spencer added, pulling his hands back from the chain to show her his blackened fingers.

"Sorry to cause so much trouble," Genevieve said sincerely.

"So am I," Spencer said, looking her in the eye. "Now that I have all my wits about me again, I want to apologize for ditching you yesterday. I'm not sure what got into me, but I was wrong. I'm really sorry. I'm honestly relieved that you're okay."

"Oh, thanks," she responded, surprised by his candidness and not knowing what else to say.

"I…I really blew it. I didn't sleep much last night, realizing how bad I messed up."

"Do you want me to give you guys some space?" Ephraim asked, looking up from the chain.

"No. Everybody needs to hear this," Spencer replied with a raised voice that seemed to catch everyone's attention. "What I did was really stupid and selfish and careless. I don't know how to express the level of my regret, but please forgive me for being an idiot. I'd love to promise you that it'll never happen again, but it's likely that you're going to think I'm an idiot again before the end of the summer. So let me just promise that I'm really going to try to work against my nature and be a better guy. I'm sorry."

"Thank you, Spencer. That's sweet. Apology accepted." She turned to see that the whole family had gathered around them and were listening. "I can't say I slept very well last night either," she said, loud enough for everyone to hear. "James informed me this morning over laundry that I've been an insensitive…what was the word you used?…biddy, I think." She heard one of the women gasp behind her.

"It's okay," Genevieve said, raising her hand. "I've been called worse. This past week has been the hardest week of my life, but I want to apologize for making it difficult for all of you. I know I didn't deserve the kindness each of you extended to me yesterday, but I am grateful for it—for each of you. Apparently I have a difficult personality—thank you, James, for pointing that out as spokesperson for the men." She watched as James squirmed. "I'm sure that my difficult personality has likely influenced my ability to form lasting friendships," she continued. "It's weird, but I realized this morning that after just one week I already feel closer to each of you than I do to any of my friends." She paused to look into each of their faces. "I just want to say thank you for your patience with me, and I invite you to tell me yourselves if you think I'm being a biddy."

She heard several of them snicker. "Okay—maybe not all at once," she laughed with them. "But I need honest, sincere friends more than I need agreeable ones who don't get in my face and call me out on my crap when they think I need it. I'm anxious for my next thirty years to be better than my last. So please, moving forward, if you see me being selfish or difficult or obnoxious, don't waste your observations by talking about me behind my back. I want to know. I want to hear about it."

She looked at each of the men. "You guys are obviously observant. I actually *am* an only child. And I probably do have some version of a princess complex. And okay, yeah, maybe I really *am* a biddy. But I don't want to be. I don't mean to be difficult or insensitive or, what was the word, James? *Manipulative*." She watched as each of the men looked away, obviously ashamed.

"Look, I want to be as happy as the next person, and I've seen enough in the last week to know I've been looking for happiness in all the wrong places and going about it in all the wrong ways. And I've seen enough to realize I need your help. I never would have thought that being stung by dozens of wasps and spending the afternoon looking like a swamp monster could be the best thing that ever happened to me, but today—right now—I feel like…maybe that's been the best thing that's ever happened to me. It woke me up to the reality that I was a…biddy, and I don't like that that's the way you've seen me—that that's the way I've been. I want to be better than that."

She paused again and looked around at each of them. "I'm sorry for making your first week here any more difficult than it needed to be. And I promise it's going to be different." She looked down at Spencer, who looked surprised by her honesty. "Would it be all right with all of you if we left last week in the past and tried to move on with a new day—with a new life?"

Ephraim smiled broadly. "I'm in."

"Me too," said Susan. Genevieve watched as the other eleven members of the family moved in closer, everyone either nodding their head or verbally agreeing to the proposal.

The distant alarm of the kitchen timer sounded, and Matt and Susan hurried off to pull the bread from the oven.

They returned a few minutes later with two picnic baskets. "We're ready when you are," Susan said, placing her basket in the bed of the pickup truck.

"Then we best be off," Pops said. If we get our work done early, there'll be time for fishing."

"What about ice cream?" asked Greg.

Ruby laughed. "If you insist, there'll be time for that too."

CHAPTER 41

The Farm Stand

A mediocre idea that generates enthusiasm will go further than a great idea that inspires no one.
—Mary Kay Ash

After giving the campers a head start to push their bikes to the top of the drive, Pops and Ruby followed close behind until they all reached the highway. Then Pops pulled the pickup truck to the front and encouraged them all to follow. They didn't drive far before he pulled over to the side of the road, where a whimsical patchwork of a shack stood next to an equally whimsical outhouse under the canopy of two tall maple trees.

"This is it?" Sonja asked, looking a little disappointed as she leaned her bike against one of the trees.

"What were you expecting?" Ruby asked.

"I'm not sure," she responded, taking a closer look.

"And we all have to do a shift here, right?" Rachael asked.

"No, you all *get* to spend one day a week here," Ruby said with a wink. "Starting Wednesday, you'll be on a rotation. One team at a time will spend a full day here—from 10 until 5. We'll keep this up six days a week until you all head home in October."

"And what are we going to sell?" Greg asked.

"You all get to decide that. It's different every year. We have plenty of eggs, but there's also flowers and cheese and cream, as well as a variety of fruits and vegetables as the summer progresses. Some kids have been more entrepreneurial than others and have also sold lemonade and crafts, even baskets," Ruby explained.

"And there's honey, too, at the end of summer," Pops added.

"Is it any fun?" Josh asked, looking at the farm stand with a rather sour expression.

"Well, that all depends on you," Ruby replied. "We have campers every year who say this was one of their favorite parts of the experience. But there are always those who never learn to love it."

"What's there to love?" Sonja asked.

"Again, that depends on you," Ruby responded. "Some kids like the interaction with the people who stop. Some kids enjoy having time to slow down where they can sit and think and read. Others enjoy having a chance to talk to their teammates one on one," she said, glancing at Genevieve.

"I think it would be a great place to sketch and do artwork," said Rachael.

"I was just thinking it would be a nice place to write poetry," added Holly.

"Yep, a place like this welcomes those kinds of activities and at least a hundred million more," Pops said as he approached the padlock and chain that held together the two sheets of colorful plywood that were the back doors. The campers parked their bikes and moved closer to the shack, curious if the inside were any better looking than the exterior. Pops entered the shack, unbolting the large rolling barn door that faced the highway, sliding it open before unlatching the wooden flaps that covered the windows. He encouraged the men to open the flaps and prop them open with the supports. As light flooded in from all directions, illuminating the colorful interior space, none of them were disappointed.

"Look at that," Crystal said, pointing to the layers upon layers of artwork on faded paper that had been stapled to the low ceiling. With all fourteen members of the family inside, the space was crowded but still somehow charming. Names and messages were scrawled or painted on the interior walls in dozens of colors.

"It reminds me of the walls of my favorite pizzeria when I was in college," Matt said.

"Yeah, I was just thinking the same thing," said Susan.

"So, where do we start?" Genevieve asked.

"That all depends on what you decide you want." Ruby pointed to a stack of sandwich boards leaning up against a wall. "Those will need some attention and refreshing. The exterior of the stand needs some love. And I'm guessing the outhouse could use some polishing. Each of you will be spending a significant amount of time here, so we encourage you to make it a place you want to be."

"So, we can do whatever we want with it?" Rachael asked.

"Short of burning it to the ground, yes," Pops replied, "though you wouldn't be the first to do that either."

"It's burned down before?" asked Spencer.

Pops smiled and nodded. "Back in '73. A particularly reckless prankster who got bored one afternoon in July thought he'd play a trick on his teammate and toss a string of firecrackers onto the roof of the outhouse while she was in it." Pops stopped to laugh for a minute. "The whole thing lit up like a bonfire and quickly spread to the farm stand too. They ran across the highway to fill buckets in the river, but they never had a chance. The whole thing was gone in just a minute or two."

"Do you have fire insurance?" James asked, looking up at the paper-covered ceiling as if he were considering potential fire-code violations and liabilities.

"Yes, it's called Arm and Hammer Insurance."

"I've never heard of it," James responded. "Is that a local company?"

Pops nodded, grabbing a dusty hammer from an old milk crate on the ground and handing it to James. "Very local. You mess with the stand, and it will be your arm and hammer rebuilding it."

The rest of the campers laughed.

Ruby took over. "This stand is tied directly to a significant portion of the farm's income. It allows us to pay property taxes, put gas in the truck, and buy whatever we can't raise or make ourselves. It enables us to upgrade the farm duds when they wear out and buy the tools we need to keep things going. We couldn't make it without it. We hope you'll find pleasure in the time you spend here, but we also hope you'll take your assignments seriously and professionally. With a little imagination and creativity, you'll find plenty of things that will make your time here rewarding and pleasurable, but we need you to remember that it's still work."

Pops joined back in. "I'll never forget those kids a few summers back who showed up at the farm in the middle of the afternoon with the news that they'd fallen asleep in the hammocks and woken up to find someone had stolen the cashbox."

Ruby nodded. "That was a little easier to swallow than the kids who foolishly traded the contents of the cashbox for a car."

"Wait, the farm stand earns that kind of money?" Holly asked.

Pops laughed. "Enough for a beater on a good day, but never enough to buy a two-year-old Honda. The warning *buyer beware* didn't even cross their minds. They figured they were just getting a good deal."

"But it wasn't?" Matt asked.

"Nope. Turns out the car had been stolen. Within just a few minutes of the transaction, the farm stand was swarmed by six cop cars from at least three counties. I think that's the only time any of our kids have ever been brought back to the farm with a police escort."

Many of the kids laughed.

"We tell you these things only to help you remember that paying attention to the money is a critical part of your job here," Ruby added. "When you personally know the people who have gathered the eggs and picked the fruits and vegetables—when you've done those things yourself—there's a different connection you make to the work and the land than if you simply buy those things from the grocery store. And when you have a chance to sell directly to the people who'll eat the apples or tomatoes you picked, there comes with it a unique sense of both pride and humility, being part of a chain that delivers nourishment from the Creator to the creation."

"That's right," Pops agreed. "I don't know if we've ever had a camper go home at the end of the summer who hasn't experienced a new and profound reverence for life and nature and the rhythms that tie us all together. It's a beautiful thing to watch every summer as kids begin to discover their true natures through recognizing their connections to all of creation."

"It sounds like you've been reading the writing on the walls," Susan said, looking up at the quotation that had been painted in a rainbow of colors on a board that hung just over the front doorway.

Pops grinned broadly. "Very observant." He lifted his finger and pointed to the overhead message before repeating it from memory. "'The earth's most profound wisdom comes to those who discover, then oft remember—with reverence and gratitude—their undimmable tie to all creation.'"

"Who said that?" Matt asked.

"Pops did," Ruby said as she wrapped her arm around her husband's waist. "That truth came to him fifty-seven years ago, right here on this spot. Of course, it was the old farm stand back then. That board there was one of the few things we were able to salvage from the fire. It's been hanging up there ever since, though I think it's been painted and repainted probably dozens of times over the years as different kids have taken it to heart."

"Every once in a while, if you're quiet enough and the Universe knows you're listening, it will drop into your mind a nugget of truth," Pops said humbly.

Genevieve looked up at Pops's quote and read it to herself as the rest of the campers filed out of the shack to unload the truck. The words were simple, but coming on the heels of her experience in the river, they felt profound. She'd never considered that she might share an undimmable tie to anything before yesterday, but in the stillness of the river, she'd made a connection to something much bigger than herself. She read the quote one more time before joining the rest of the campers in the day's work.

While the men were quick to take shovels and hoes to the overgrown weeds surrounding the shack, the women gathered together to take a closer look at the condition of the stand, the outhouse, and the sandwich boards. After looking over the available paint colors, Rachael got the women excited about the possibilities for the shack. She poured portions of three colors into a plastic cup and stirred them together to create a beautiful shade of orange. They soon were all busy with brushes and rollers, covering the weathered surfaces of the stand with bright stripes and swirls. Their enthusiasm proved to be premature in some areas where the flaking old paint had to be removed with a wire brush before the wood could accept a fresh layer. But their energy blossomed as they worked together to create something new out of the old shack. They even found joy in refurbishing the old, stinky outhouse by covering the top half with a thousand tiny moons in a variety of phases and the bottom half with playful flowers and vines.

After finishing with the weeds and landscaping, the men used tar to patch holes in the rusty corrugated steel roof. While they were up there, they also checked on the solar panel that ran the small minifridge inside the shack, clearing away leaves and dirt so the panel would work properly. As they swept out the shack's interior, a family of mice ran into the tall grass that grew on the adjacent hillside, and the men ran after them like little boys, wielding brooms and hooting and hollering as if they were chasing big game. In the rafters above the art-clad ceiling, they found two hammocks that required some minor repairs. While Matt and Ephraim worked at reweaving some of the frayed ropes and adding twine to make them stronger, Spencer and Josh discovered a Tarzan swing wrapped high around one of the branches of the overhead tree. Seconds later they were taking turns entertaining the gang with their youthful acrobatic shenanigans until they tipped over a pail of paint and were called back to work.

After an hour or so they all broke for lunch, making quick history of the fresh bread and berry preserves. A rock-skipping contest on the banks of the Allegheny on the other side of the highway distracted all of them and quickly turned into a refreshing and playful water fight. Then they were back to work, adding details to the new paint job and refreshing the old sandwich boards. After receiving permission to add a little paint to her bicycle, Rachael added stripes to the Schwinn's faded frame. When Susan saw what she was doing, she joined in, painting lightning bolts and rainbows to her own frame. The rest of the campers quickly followed suit, giving new, vibrant life to the old, rusty frames. James even painted the sidewalls of his tires with a couple of long, wiggly snakes that whimsically undulated as the wheels turned.

Time passed quickly as they worked and played, and even the most reserved among them found joy in their creative expressions.

"It feels like months since I was last in the office," James said as he dabbed white polka dots on his tires. "I can't believe it's only been a week."

"Do you miss it?" asked Holly.

He shook his head. "I really had no idea what I was getting myself into this summer, but I don't know if I've ever been this relaxed. I feel like a kid again. I think I could do this forever."

"Why don't you?" Ruby asked with a teasing smile.

James laughed.

"I'm serious," Ruby pressed.

"What? How?" he asked, looking very confused.

"What's stopping you?"

"Uh, you mean besides a boatload of student loans—and my job—and real life?"

"No offense, but that doesn't sound like much fun. Why'd you choose *that* life?" Ruby asked playfully.

Her question seemed to catch him off guard, and he wrestled with it for a moment as if it were the first time he'd ever considered it. "I guess I didn't know bicycle painter and rock skipper were viable professions."

"That's a shame. I think you may have missed your calling in life."

"Really?" he responded, straightening up and playing along.

"Sure. It would undoubtedly take some practice, but with a little passion, I'm certain you could find some success and happiness in whatever field you chose."

"Uh, thanks, but I think I've kind of chosen my path," he said, laughing. "I have a six-figure student loan to prove it."

Ruby nodded. "Do you enjoy it as much as this?"

James laughed nervously. "Practicing law?"

She nodded.

"Ruby, I'm an attorney."

"That's not what I asked."

He sat silent for a moment, not knowing how to respond. "This is just for fun. I have to work. I have debts and life to pay for."

"Of course you do. But if money wasn't part of the question, would you still choose to be a lawyer?"

"I'm not sure I understand the question. Isn't money part of everything—part of every decision we make?"

"I suppose it is," she said resignedly. "But I guess I still wonder why so many people go about chasing money when what often brings them the greatest happiness costs little or nothing at all. If we're not careful, James, our pursuit of money will leave us empty and unfulfilled."

He looked confused. "Okay, but in a world where we all need money, how do we keep that from happening?"

"Well, I'd say we each have to remember what makes us happy and we have to make the time to do those things often. You may not understand it now, but your life back home—as complicated as it may seem—will never be any easier." She took a moment to look at each of them, pausing to allow her words to have the greatest effect. "Soon, with any luck, you'll marry. And then the kids will come, and you'll feel pressure, both real and imagined, from your family and peers to work harder. If you're not careful, you'll become like many professionals who glorify busy-ness and become consumed with climbing corporate ladders. It may be too late for you, James—to become a professional bike painter or rock skipper, I mean—but someday, maybe twenty years down the road, when your teenaged son, full of passion and fire, tells you he wants to be an artist or a baker or a lion tamer, I hope you'll encourage him to try."

James nodded thoughtfully. "Does the world need more lion tamers?"

"The world needs more people with passion and fire coursing through their veins. No offense to your career choice, but the world certainly has enough professionals who chose their line of work based solely on their infatuation with a snug, secure income and the promise of an oversized but often soulless home in the suburbs."

"Ouch," he said, almost without thinking.

Ruby smiled and looked again into each of their faces. "We're all subject to the envy of money and the spoils of success. But if your eyes are open, you'll never have to look far to find people who have far less than you have now and yet spend more of their day smiling. There's not a lot of joy in poverty, but I've discovered that joy can also be difficult to find in poverty's opposite extremes."

She paused again to look into each of their faces. "If I could wish for you kids any level of success, I would wish for you to always have enough. Enough love. Enough to eat. Enough time to think and read and play and laugh. Enough space to breathe and dream and find yourselves. And enough courage to chase your crazy dreams no matter what people tell you. You're the only ones who'll know which path is right for you. And if you can find someone to love who knows the meaning of enough, and if the two of you can always remember that secret, you'll always be rich, regardless of what your bank statement says. And you'll always be happy."

Genevieve listened silently as she continued to dab blobs of paint onto her bicycle, allowing Ruby's words to echo off the walls of her head and heart. Her words were contrary to everything Genevieve had ever heard or thought or aspired to. And yet these simple words spoken from the mouth of the oldest woman she had ever met resonated within her. She had no reason to question their validity, because as she considered her home, her family, her parents' marriage, and her own job and aspirations, she felt the weight of Ruby's truth settle over her like a comforting blanket.

"We can't all be farmers and matchmakers," Susan said, pulling Genevieve from her thoughts.

"No, you're quite right," Ruby responded with a warm, disarming smile. "Pops and I would never want to persuade any of you to buy a farm or take up eccentric hobbies instead of returning to your homes and professions at the end of the summer. Our life on Harmony Hill has its perks, and the work we do gives our lives meaning and purpose. But each of you has a different voice inside your head and heart—a different calling—a different set of talents and passions. And it's a beautiful thing to know that you do. God paints the world in a broad and ever-expanding pallet, and as far as I've been able to tell, I believe He hopes we'll do the same."

She turned back to James, who'd returned to his painting. "Don't forget to play, James. In all your acquisition of ideas and education and experience, try to never pass up an opportunity to stop for a minute and skip a few rocks or splash in the river or color with a child. And don't you ever forget that the greatest joys will always be found in the smallest of packages."

CHAPTER 42

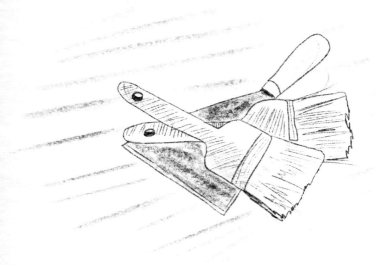

Magnanimity

Love cannot be expected to last forever unless it is continually fed with portions of love, the manifestation of esteem and admiration, the expressions of gratitude, and the consideration of unselfishness.
—Spencer W. Kimball

Though the road back to the farm was just as steep as it ever had been, Genevieve noticed that no one complained when they could pedal no farther and had to dismount and push their bikes the last quarter mile. The hills were covered in thick blankets of grasses and wildflowers, and without the sounds of traffic, the birds and insects sounded louder and more pleasing than any of them could ever remember.

"What's for dinner?" Josh asked as they neared the crest of the hill. "I'm starving."

"It's a surprise," Matt said, glancing at Susan to see if she had any ideas.

"I hope there's ice cream," said Spencer.

"There will be if we make it," Ephraim responded. "I'll volunteer for berry duty if anyone wants to join me."

"I'm in," said Holly.

"Me too," said Genevieve.

"Uh, don't we have to take down the laundry?" James responded, raining on the parade.

"Dang, that's right," Genevieve replied, looking disappointed.

"Well, maybe we could all help each other with all of the chores so we could have more time together on the porch," Holly suggested. "Who's on milking duty tonight?"

"We are," Josh said, nodding to Sonja.

"Could you use some help?" Holly asked.

They looked at each other and shrugged. "Sure," Josh replied.

"Greg and I will help with that," said Crystal.

Before they reached the top of the drive, they'd all made arrangements to divide and share the evening's work, making everyone feel needed. As Rachael and Spencer worked alongside Genevieve and James to take down the laundry, Genevieve was surprised how what had felt like such a chore that morning had somehow become almost fun. And the clothes were folded and put away much more quickly than anyone imagined. They all carried the spirit of goodwill with them to the berry patch, where Ephraim and Holly were happy to receive their help. A large bowl was quickly filled with strawberries, which they all accompanied back to the big house with a unified sense of accomplishment. They found Ruby in the kitchen with Matt and Susan, slicing bread, cheese, and salami, so they moved their attention to the dining hall. They were setting the table when Pops returned with the rest of the milkers from the barn and a couple of bottles of milk and cream.

After washing up, they all sat down at the table for a simple meal of cold sandwiches. After grace, Ruby spoke up from the end of the table. "Pops and I have been impressed with you kids. You seem to be learning the lessons of joy much faster than most campers do."

Pops nodded, his mouth full of food. "You kids are working together better than most kids do after several months of being together. Mom and I have been trying to figure out what's causing you all to gel so quickly, but we haven't been able to put our finger on it."

The campers looked at each other. "It seems like we all want to be here," Susan said as she scanned the faces of each of the campers, her eyes lingering for an extra awkward moment on Genevieve.

Genevieve nodded quickly, trying to brush off the awkwardness. "I'd like to give Holly the credit. She's always suggesting we help each other out with the chores."

Holly blushed. "This is the first time in my life that I've ever had anything like siblings. It's been fun to work together. I hope I'm not making a pest of myself."

"No, it's been great," said Greg. "It's amazing to me how much we can get done when we work together. And then there's still time for all the fun stuff. I don't know about you guys, but I can't remember a time when I've ever worked so well with a group of people. Most of my experiences in working with groups have actually been painfully awkward and even oppressive. I've been wondering why this is so different, but I'm not at all opposed to giving Holly the credit. She's a great team player."

Holly looked completely embarrassed to have so much attention directed toward her.

"Well, Holly, it sounds like we made a great decision in making an exception for you this summer."

"Exception?" Genevieve asked before she could stop herself.

"Yes, well, as you may have heard, we usually don't accept anyone under the age of twenty-four," Ruby responded.

"Yeah, I wondered about that," said Spencer. "Seems kind of random."

"It is, I suppose," Ruby admitted. "That was the age standard we inherited when we took over the farm. It seemed reasonable, so we haven't questioned it much. And we've made our share of exceptions over the years. We've tried to be open to unique circumstances. Holly's essay convinced us that she was both committed and mature enough to handle the rigors of farm life."

"We're glad to see you've accepted the challenge and are clearly stepping up as a leader," Pops added, smiling at Holly, who looked like she wanted to crawl under the table and hide. "As influential as one of you may be, we've been doing this long enough to know it takes more than one person to tip the scales toward magnanimity."

"Magna—what?" Ephraim asked, looking confused.

"Magnanimity. It's a great word, isn't it?" Pops said with a knowing smile.

"What does it mean?" Ephraim queried.

"Any guesses?" Pops asked.

They looked around before all eyes fell on Matt. He looked uncomfortable under their gazes. "Uh, magnanimity...I believe that's the state or condition of being of magnanimous."

"Oh, that explains everything," Ephraim responded sarcastically. Many of the campers laughed.

Matt, also laughing good-naturedly, continued. "Magnanimous is...acting from a place of generosity, of setting aside your own selfish desires to uplift or build up an individual or, in this case, a group. I think it means to step away from a *what's in it for me?* mentality and to pursue instead a path that will improve the common good."

"*Very good*," Pops said, nodding his approval. "I don't think I could have offered a better definition if I'd read it out of a dictionary. I'm guessing you may have encountered at least a few magnanimous people in your wanderings."

Matt nodded.

"What did you learn from them?"

Matt smiled thoughtfully. "I'm sure I've known several magnanimous people, but maybe one of the most profound examples was my neighbor Mr. Reeve. He kinda took me under his wing after my parents divorced. He was always hiring me to help him with projects in his yard and around his home. It wasn't till years later that I realized he probably didn't need my help as much as I needed him at a time when I didn't have any good male role models and was struggling with friends and confidence. He was the kind of person who just oozed love. You couldn't be around him without getting some of it on you. He was a great man."

Pops nodded. "I've often felt like magnanimity is one of the hallmarks of greatness. Your Mr. Reeve sounds like a fine example. Mom and I have done our best to encourage the development of magnanimity in each and every camper who spends the summer here. Heaven knows the world could certainly use more of it."

"That's probably true, but do you really think you can teach that kind of stuff in just five months?" asked Spencer doubtfully.

"Oh, I'll admit that it's far from the easiest sell," Pops responded. "I've been studying magnanimity since I first came to the farm, and I've come to the conclusion that it is much more of a lifetime pursuit than a one-time arrival. Everyone is capable of magnanimous efforts. But to become a truly magnanimous person not only requires conscious and sustained effort, but I'm also convinced it requires some touch of Providence."

"You mean like...*God*?" Spencer asked.

Pops nodded.

"Does everything always come back to that for you?"

"I suppose it does. All good roads lead to God eventually."

"Really? Surely you don't think that believers are the only ones who are capable of doing good in the world," Spencer challenged.

"No, of course not. But I do believe all good deeds are inspired by God, regardless of whether the doer recognizes or admits God's influence or not."

"So, you don't believe in random acts of kindness?" Spencer continued.

"No, of course I do. I just think they're far less random than you might believe," Pops responded. "Like I said, all good has a tie to God, either directly or indirectly. And I've found that when you make a conscious decision to invite God to be a part of your life, He is there—inspiring your mind, opening your heart and eyes to the needs of those around you, inviting you to be generous with your time and talents, encouraging you to become magnanimous."

"That might work in the backwoods of Pennsylvania, but in the dog-eat-dog world I come from, you'd be eaten in a New York minute," Spencer said, sounding more than a little braggadocious.

"That's exactly why we're glad you're here," Ruby responded.

Her response appeared to the take the wind out of his sails. "What do you mean?"

"The dogs have been eating well for far too long."

"Excuse me?"

"Spencer, why did you apply to be here this summer?"

"Because I..." he faded off.

"As I recall from your essay, you said you wanted to come to the farm before the last of your hope in marriage was completely eroded by the cynicism of the world."

Spencer nodded, looking suddenly humble.

"We don't pretend that we can change the world, Spencer. But if we can help you see past the end of your own nose, then the power of the farm and our work here can live on in you—in each of you." Ruby looked up and scanned the faces of all of the other campers before returning her gaze to Spencer. "We know that the principles we teach here on the farm are often contrary to the reality you live in, wherever you come from. These principles have remained the same over the course of the farm's three-hundred-year history, even as the outside world has continued to stray further and further away, following the whims of popularity and trending toward debauchery."

"Don't you ever feel like you're fighting a losing battle?" asked James.

"It wouldn't be hard to feel that way, but we decided years ago that the only battle we need to be concerned about is the one that's being fought within the hearts of the twelve kids that sit at this table each summer," responded Ruby.

"I'll always remember the rock climber we had here on the farm a few summers back," Pops said." He taught us something about climbing that has profound and direct implications for life in general. He told us that the first rule of rock climbing is to *never look anywhere you don't want to go*. There'll always be distractions, but if we can learn to focus our attention and efforts on what we want most, we can overcome any challenge and reach any goal."

Sonja shook her head. "I like what you're saying, but I feel like you guys missed the memo that we're all living in a dystopian world."

Ruby smiled. "We recognized years ago that we'll never stand a chance of living in a utopian world if there's not enough of us who believe that such a place is possible. Pops and I decided decades ago to join with a few other Protopians and see what we could do to try and turn things around."

"Protopian? I don't think that's even a word," James responded with a chortle.

"Just because you've never heard of it doesn't mean it's not real," Pops replied.

"Is that like a club you can join?" Crystal asked.

"You could say that," Ruby replied. "The more the merrier. There's room for everyone who believes the world could be better and is willing to help make it so."

"Mom's always looking for new recruits," Lorenzo added. "She says it's a bit like spreading leaven."

"Leaven? You mean like…yeast?" Susan asked.

"That's right," said Ruby. "Each of you has had a chance now to bake bread. Compared to the weight and mass of the other ingredients in bread, the leaven is small, but it makes all the difference in the world. Every summer—at least once without fail—one pair of kids get a little hasty and forgets to add the yeast to the dough. Without leaven, a loaf of bread looks and feels more like a brick than something you'd want to eat. Pops and I know that with only twelve campers coming here each summer, our progress at lifting the world around us is slow. But if we can send twelve magnanimous men and women back out into the world at the end of each summer, and they in turn create families that raise magnanimous children, the world is that much better for it."

Spencer smiled. "I'm sure you've probably noticed that the world is only growing darker in spite of all your efforts."

Ruby looked down the table at her husband and shook her head. "You can't be a true Protopian and dwell on the darkness," she said. "You gotta get up and do something every day to make the world a better, brighter place. And we believe that if more people made an effort at living a magnanimous life, even more people would want to join us. It's contagious, you know—even more contagious than selfishness and cynicism. You'll each have to decide what you'll do with the things you learn here, whether you put them to work or let them go at the end of the summer. Of course, we'll always remain hopeful that the experiences you have here will give you hope and encouragement and leave you believing you can be a leavening agent in the world you go home to. We know that it's difficult pushing against the tides of darkness and moral depravity, but Pops and I hope you can learn to seek out the good in others and add your goodness to theirs. We've learned over our combined eighteen decades that most people find what they're looking for. We hope you'll choose to look for light."

"And if you can't find the light, be the light so that others who are looking for hope can find it," Pops added.

"That's a lot of pressure," Holly admitted, looking unsure of herself.

"We won't deny that it is," replied Ruby. "It's difficult to stand up for what's right and true when the whole world seems to be either ignoring or mocking you. Knowing that you're on the right side of truth will help make that mocking tolerable, but it's hard to stand alone. In just one week, you've already learned the value of surrounding yourselves with people who can lift you and support you. In the next five months, we hope you'll consider how you might react when you go home and encounter people who need a lift and a support. It's a beautiful thing to be able to gather with like-minded folks who can support you. But learning to love and encourage those who need more of a lift than they are currently capable of giving back? That's what separates the average from the magnanimous."

"Isn't that also what makes you a sucker?" James asked.

Several others nodded as if his question were also theirs.

"If you're asking if it's possible to give too much and get burned, the answer is an absolute yes," said Ruby. "You will each encounter people who are parasitical in nature—who take and take without even a thought of giving back anything positive. You've undoubtedly already encountered some of those—people with insatiable appetites but without any thought of how their words and actions might affect the lives of those around them. And if you're honest with yourselves, you'll remember a time when you were like that too."

"Uh, no," James pushed back. "I don't think I've ever been like that."

"Oh, were you never a teenager?" Ruby asked with a twinkle of mischief in her eyes.

James thought for a moment before grimacing. "Maybe you're right."

She nodded knowingly. "We don't like to remember the times when we were our worst selves, but you'll likely get the chance someday when you find yourself harboring a herd of ungrateful teens in your own basement. Fortunately, most of us grow up and learn to give back to the world around us, but there will always be those who break the rules of maturation and common decency. Some of those will become your bosses and coworkers and neighbors, and with selfishness and arrogance, they will make your life unpleasant. It's possible that many of these folks can change and lead nonsociopathic lives, but it's important to note that change—if it's to be real and enduring—must come from within.

Love and compassion can and often do inspire a myriad of changes in ourselves and others. But you'll have to be wise as you decide how and where and with whom to share your compassion and love. Too many folks marry a service project, believing they can help change or fix their spouse, only to concede years later that the change they hoped for will never come."

Crystal shook her head. "That right there is basically the reason I'm here. My dad believed he could change my mom and help her overcome some of her psychoses. It was a nightmare for the whole family—still is, in fact. If that's what marriage is, I don't want to have any part of it."

"No, I don't suppose you would. And yet you're here," Ruby said, offering her a warm smile.

Crystal nodded. "I want to be hopeful that marriage can be better than what my parents had."

"Then I'd say you're off to a good start."

"Really?" she asked dubiously.

"Sure. You're being proactive. You've identified some of the problems you hope to avoid. You're experiencing healthy interactions with reasonably normal men. And you're making an effort to identify the attributes of a positive relationship. I'd say you're well on your way to a good life."

Crystal nodded again but didn't look convinced. "I guess I've always been happy that I'm more like my dad than my mom," she said after a moment. "But then I remember that he married my mom hoping he could fix her. I guess I worry that I'm doomed to do the same."

Ruby nodded. "That's a legitimate concern."

"So how do I make sure I avoid repeating history?"

"You recognize that you're a product of a dysfunctional marriage, and you never let that define you as a person or sabotage your hopes and dreams of a happy, healthy marriage. And you sort out the good things you learned at home and leave the rest behind."

Crystal nodded.

"That's a good place to start," Ruby added. "But our hope for each of you is that by the end of the summer, you will each have developed charity and magnanimity toward yourselves and others, as well as the ability to discern how to best use those virtues without getting burned." Spencer looked a little befuddled. "I thought I was just coming here to get a little help in the marriage department."

"Then you won't be disappointed," Pops responded.

"No?"

"Can you think of a marriage that couldn't benefit from a little magnanimity, charity, and discernment?"

The question seemed to catch Spencer off guard, but he shook his head after a moment's thought.

"The undeniable truth is that there is no relationship in life that could not benefit by all three," Ruby added. "And all of these virtues have been under attack by the forces of selfishness since the beginning of time. Selfishness, if left unchecked, has the potential power to destroy even the strongest relationships, leaving only sorrow and regret in its wake. You don't have to look very far to find proof of that truth. I have little doubt that each of you kids has been affected by its power in your families of origin, and I have little doubt that selfishness hasn't at least crimped some of your own romantic relationships. We are human; therefore we have a natural tendency to seek our own interests first, to take more than we give, and to choose the path of least resistance rather than the higher road. But what you kids have learned here on the farm in just a week is contrary to the natural tendencies we're born with. You've learned that it's more enjoyable to help each other with your chores so you can spend more time together. You've learned that there's really only one team here. You've learned that each of you is needed and important in making the whole farm work. You've learned the benefits that come from communicating, from accomplishing a task together, from seeing how each of your efforts are necessary to make things happen. All those things are clear here on the farm. They may become less clear when you return to your lives and jobs and homes. If you're not vigilant and mindful, you'll tend to fall back into the selfish patterns that have guided your life so far. If you're not careful, you'll forget the things you learned here, and you won't be any better off than when you came."

"It's like the story of the farmer down in Franklin County who taught his turkeys how to fly," Pops added.

"Wait, turkeys can fly?" James asked.

"Sure. They have wings and feathers, don't they? Most of them just lack the motivation and training. That's what this farmer found out anyway. With Thanksgiving coming up, he enrolled his whole flock of turkeys in a flight-training school, hoping the exercise would build up his turkeys' breast muscles as well as his profits."

"Flight-training school for turkeys?" Greg asked, looking amused. "Who taught them?"

"Well, eagles, of course. They're basically the best flyers out there, and this farmer wanted to make sure his turkeys received the best instruction available."

Susan smiled broadly. "So how'd it go?"

"Brilliantly. By the end of the course, the turkeys had all learned to soar and dive and glide on the wind. They had a wonderful time, and they were very pleased with themselves and their new skills. When class ended, they were each awarded a certificate of excellence, and then, after thanking the eagles for their wonderful flying lessons, they all walked home."

Many of the kids laughed, but a few of them looked bewildered.

"Wait," Spencer said, looking especially confused. "If they learned to fly, why'd they walk home?"

"That's the whole point of the story, genius," Josh muttered under his breath but loud enough for Spencer to hear.

Spencer laughed at himself. "Sorry, that was dumb."

"You're not the first to ask," Pops consoled. "Many of us can see the less-than-brilliant things that others do, but we generally have difficulty recognizing our own failings. Few of us take full advantage of the lessons we learn in life, and most of us have to repeat them again and again before we finally learn."

Many of the campers nodded.

"And the humility that comes from recognizing our own limitations and failings is often the doorway through which we connect with our spiritual selves," Ruby interjected.

"How's that?" asked Holly.

"Because the darkness of selfishness and the light of magnanimity and humility never inhabit the same place at the same time. All human growth and understanding is stunted by our natural propensity toward selfishness and its twin sister, pride," Ruby offered.

"Aren't we just talking in circles?" Josh mumbled through a mouthful of sandwich.

"Very perceptive, Josh," Ruby responded. "You have just identified the main reason why progress is slow. Rather than stretching beyond the confines of our natural borders, we get held up by repeating history again and again, making the same mistakes, failing to learn from either our own bungles or those of others."

"So how do we get off this crazy train?" asked Genevieve, recognizing the pattern in her own life.

Ruby smiled and let the question hang in the air as they each considered it and worked on their sandwiches.

"I'll take a stab at it," Matt finally said. "I feel like it has something to do with the quote over the doors in the bunkhouses."

"Wait, when were you in the girls' bunkhouse?" Sonja asked.

"I wasn't," Matt was quick to insist. "Genevieve and I compared notes yesterday."

"Hold up, what are we even talking about?" Spencer asked.

Josh turned to look at him. "You haven't seen the quote over the door in our bunkhouse?"

Spencer looked sheepish. "Are you talking about the one that says to turn off the lights when you leave?"

Josh shook his head. "That sign's on the side of the door, next to the light switch. We're talking about the big letters that are painted on the wall above the doorframe."

Spencer thought for a moment before shaking his head. "Nope, I guess I missed that."

"Dude, you've passed through that doorway at least fifty times in the last week. How could you not have seen it?

"Go easy on him," Pops said. "Many kids don't see it until it's brought to their attention, sometimes several months into the summer. Why don't you tell him what it says, Josh?"

Josh's eyes widened. "Uh...I've seen it, but I didn't know I'd be quizzed on it. I...I guess I didn't pay that much attention."

Pops smirked as the rest of the campers laughed. "Anyone else?" he asked, scanning the table.

Genevieve raised her hand trepidatiously.

"Yes?"

"I don't know it exactly, but it's something about how foolish it is to try to build a house without God's help."

"Not bad," said Pops. "An extra scoop of berries to the person who knows the whole verse." He scanned the group, his eyes falling on Matt, who was looking down at his sandwich. "Matt, you wanna give it a try?"

He looked up, clearly a little embarrassed. "'Except the Lord build the house, they labour in vain that build it.'"

"Impressive," Pops responded. "And for an extra scoop of ice cream to go with your berries, name the source."

Matt laughed. "I feel like I'm on Jeopardy."

"You are," Ruby said playfully, one eyebrow raised.

He shook his head. "It's from the Bible, from Psalms."

"Impressive. Yes, it's from the 127th Psalm. It was written by Solomon, probably as he was preparing to build the temple in Jerusalem."

"Huh, I thought it must have been written by David," Matt admitted, looking confused.

"Most of the Psalms were written by David, but he wasn't allowed to build the temple because of his dealings with Bathsheba and her husband."

"Wait, all of that was totally Greek to me," Spencer said, looking very confused.

"It's a long story for another day," Pops said. "Suffice it to say that King David missed the opportunity to build a temple because of some serious mistakes and personal failings. The people had to wait for a temple until his son Solomon was ready to build it. But whether you're talking about a temple or a humble shack, the idea behind the verse remains the same: without enlisting the help and direction of God, any efforts to improve our lives are little more than vain ambitions." Pops looked at Genevieve. "You asked how to get off the crazy train of repetition and lack of progress. There's your answer: enlist the help of God."

"Or better yet, hire Him to be your general contractor," Ruby added.

"Sounds expensive," Spencer joked.

"It is. It will cost you your pride and your defiance, but the results are guaranteed to be far beyond even your wildest dreams." Ruby looked into the faces of the campers on the right side of the table before shifting her gaze to those on the left. "The choice is always ours to make. We can continue to navigate our own lives and hope things will work out, or we can choose to exercise faith and invite God to lead the way to the destination he has in mind."

"Is the second way any easier?" Genevieve asked.

Ruby smiled warmly. "God's way never seems like the easiest way at first. But by going His way rather than taking the path of least resistance, you avoid going around in circles again and again, expecting things to go differently the third or thirtieth or three-hundredth time. You tell me what's easier."

Genevieve let out a long sigh as she considered Ruby's words. She had experienced the endless circle of attempts and failures that had left her feeling discontented and wanting something better, something more. "Okay, where do I sign up?"

Ruby laughed. "You already have."

CHAPTER 43

Kryptonite

What is to give light must first endure burning.
—Viktor Frankl

With the dinner dishes and the kitchen cleaned up, the campers poured out onto the front porch. The sense of unity that Ruby and Pops had identified earlier felt even stronger as they worked together to prepare the berries and load Bessie with all the makings for ice cream. Holly retreated into the music room and returned with the card file of games. She handed it to Crystal, who randomly drew a card form the middle of the stack.

"This one's called What's Your Kryptonite?" she said, looking up.

"What are the rules?" asked Rachael.

Crystal looked down at the card and read. "'The person sitting on Bessie will have exactly three minutes to identify and describe their kryptonite, or in other words, that thing, person, habit, or situation that causes them to lose their strength or resolve. Those who wish to pass rather than share have to pedal Bessie while singing their favorite *Sesame Street* song in a voice like they've been sucking helium.'" She looked up from the card with a smile. "This sounds more like confession than a game. Who came up with this one?"

"That would have to be Hillary Bernheisel," Ruby reported.

Crystal flipped the card over and found the initials HB written in pencil on the bottom corner, which she pointed out to Ruby.

Ruby nodded. "Hillary went on to become a therapist, and she focuses her attention on alleviating shame and overcoming personal weaknesses."

"You'll find her book, *Quelling Your Personal Kryptonite*, in our library in the self-help section," Pops added. "It's a good one. She was quite a character; married one, too. I think he was a professional bowler, right?" he asked, looking a little uncertain.

"He still is," Ruby confirmed. "They met the winter after Hillary's summer here. Her kryptonite, as I recall, was athletics of every kind." Ruby laughed. "She was terribly uncoordinated. Poor girl seemed to get hurt every other day or so. She holds the record for the most bruises ever received in a summer. We had to ground her from the bicycles until she practiced on the lawn for several weeks and was finally able to pedal to the cowshed without falling over. She'd been mocked most of her life for her lack of athleticism."

"So how'd she meet a bowler?" Rachael asked.

"Well, after she spent the summer on the farm and went back to grad school, she decided to join a bowling league to try and help herself further overcome her coordination challenges."

"So she went for bowling?" Spencer asked dubiously. "That sounds dangerous!"

Pops laughed out loud. "It was, but that was actually how she met her husband. She slipped on that glossy floor, and her ball landed a couple lanes over—on the poor guy's foot! Broke his toe just a week before a big tournament."

Spencer laughed and shook his head. *"And he still married her?"*

"Yep. They dropped by to visit us on their honeymoon a few years back," Pops responded. "He wanted to personally thank us for teaching her how to cook. I guess she took care of him while he was laid up with his toe, and they fell in love. They have a couple kids now, right, Mom?"

"Yep, a boy and a girl; Lorenzo and Ruby, actually. He stays home with the kids and bowls in the evenings, and Hillary teaches at the college in between seeing clients. We actually got a Christmas card from them last year with the whole family dressed up in bowling shirts with their names embroidered on their chests."

"That's right," Pops said. "Wasn't her husband holding the brightest green bowling ball you've ever seen with the word *Kryptonite* engraved on it?"

Ruby laughed. "You're thinking of their picture at the back of her book. That's the ball he's used to win several tournaments. Funny how things work out, isn't it?"

"It sure is," he agreed. "Do you think the kids are ready for this game?" Pops asked, looking concerned.

"I don't know why not. These kids seem to be ready for anything."

"I'm not saying you're wrong; it's just that we don't usually play this game until at least mid-June."

"Let's see how it goes," Ruby responded. "Who's first?"

Susan volunteered, and after identifying her kryptonite as shame, she went on to explain how shame had held her back from feeling worthy to date, to love, and certainly to marry. Josh lightened things up considerably by admitting that his kryptonite was women like Susan who were beautiful and smart but refused to acknowledge him, which had historically proven to be painfully awkward and resulted in his doing a series of stupid things, including last week's belly-flop contest.

He had everyone moaning in empathetic pain when he lifted his shirt to show the bruises that remained on the majority of his chest.

Genevieve surprised herself by admitting that her kryptonite was self-doubt, which manifested itself in her being fiercely competitive at work and in her life in general, making it difficult to make and keep close friendships and continually sabotaging any hopes she had for a love life. She recognized how easy it was to share these things with this group and may have continued if she hadn't noticed she was running out of time. Before dismounting, however, she thanked the other women who, by being honest about their own struggles, had allowed her to identify and work on her own.

Matt stunned everybody when he described his kryptonite as never feeling like he was smart enough, which had manifested itself in his withdrawing from friends and peers, indulging in regular binges of books and online wormholes, and depriving himself of sleep as he drank in as much trivia as he could hold before crashing into a mess of self-pity. He admitted that his father's lack of interest in him had initially spawned the mania, but he knew he was responsible for perpetuating it for so long.

Rachael admitted that her kryptonite was low self-esteem, which had kept her from believing in herself and her abilities. She admitted that she had sabotaged every potential love interest because she felt unattractive and figured they would eventually discover that for themselves and ditch her anyway. She recognized that her mother's constant nagging about her extra twenty pounds had left her feeling worthless and had taught her to focus on the superficial.

Spencer, after publicly apologizing once again for ditching Genevieve the day before, admitted that though sports were his business and passion, he was beginning to see how they were also his kryptonite, getting in the way of what he wanted most—marriage and a family.

Greg expressed gratitude to Susan for talking about shame and proceeded to be very open, admitting that his kryptonite was pornography, something he'd been introduced to as a child. It had left him constantly lacking in confidence and self-worth and had kept him from developing meaningful relationships with women. He acknowledged that his therapist and a twelve-step program had helped him finally kick the habit. But he knew that the scars ran deep. The far-reaching fingers of the addiction had left him worried that he might never be able to enjoy a close relationship with a woman. He also spoke of the satisfaction he experienced in participating with his therapist in antipornography outreach programs for kids in high school and expressed hope that his efforts would enable more kids to get help so they might enjoy normal relationships in adulthood.

Crystal admitted that she'd planned to sing "The People in Your Neighborhood" to avoid speaking about her kryptonite, but she had gained courage from Greg's heartfelt and honest disclosure. She recognized that pride had stood in the way of her making deep friendships, and she was determined to change. She spoke of growing up in the suburbs where the connections and professions of one's parents had determined far too much of their children's success. Because of her family's lower economic status and her father's job as a handyman, she had spent most of her life trying to hide the truth by pretending to be someone she wasn't. By the time she realized in her early twenties that she had only fooled herself, she had racked up huge credit-card debts and had nearly been driven to bankruptcy. She wept as she thanked Ruby for the handwritten note she'd sent her with last year's rejection letter, encouraging her to spend the year working on her debts and to apply again when she had things under control. It had been the challenge she needed, causing her to move back home with her father and take on three jobs, one of which was working part-time as his assistant. She had learned so much during that year, and she'd gained a better understanding of the financial challenges that had led to her parents' divorce. But she recognized that in spite of all the things she'd worked so hard to overcome, her pride and her disposition to be judgmental remained uncomfortably present.

Sonja mentioned that she was also tempted to sing rather than share, but she had pedaled only a few rotations before she opened up about her kryptonite—jealousy. She said she had identified it as her biggest hurdle to dating, recognizing that she couldn't get over the fact that every man she'd dated had dated someone before her. It kept her up at night and held her back from getting to know people better. She was jealous of roommates, her sisters, her mother, and nearly every woman she had ever met. She admitted that it was all she could do to keep herself from being jealous of each of the women here, their beauty, talents, and strengths being so much bigger and better than she believed hers to be. As the timer ran out, she stepped away from the bike and was quickly embraced by all the women.

While the women were still standing, James sat down on Bessie to keep the ice cream churning, but he didn't appear in any hurry to share his thoughts. When the women finally took their seats and encouraged him, James spoke about his kryptonite: faith, or rather his lack thereof. He'd wrestled with doubts for many years after his parents divorced, but he had felt something different here on the farm. He admitted he had arrived teetering on the edge of atheism, but from all that he had heard, felt, and experienced in the last week, he recognized that somewhere deep inside him there was a growing bit of hope that he'd long ago forgotten. He offered no promises and made no predictions, but he accepted that he may have overlooked some things in his nearly wholesale dismissal of all things mystical. He expressed gratitude for those who were honest enough to share their raw, unedited experiences and vulnerabilities, enabling him to do the same without hesitation.

Holly was quick to step forward after James returned to his chair. The kryptonite she wanted to talk about was her fear of failing. She acknowledged that she was young and inexperienced, but she admitted that her fear of failure had already held her back from a long list of things she regretted not pursuing. She had filled out her application to come to the farm several months before she actually sent it. She kept putting it off for fear that she would be rejected. She admitted she might never have sent it at all if she hadn't been pushed by her mother's best friend, who'd told her about the farm and her own experiences there.

She confessed that since her mother's terminal diagnosis, her fears had often felt debilitating, gripping her with all sorts of anxieties. She, too, expressed her appreciation for the openness and honesty that the group shared, and she thanked everyone for their support and kindness.

Ephraim moved forward with obvious hesitation when he realized he was the last of the campers to take a turn on Bessie. His kryptonite was shyness, he guessed, based on the long list of social phobias and anxieties he suffered from. He had consciously chosen his career as an engineer for its lack of direct involvement with people. He confessed that this past week had been one of the most difficult weeks of his life, leaving him constantly worried that he'd forget someone's name or say something stupid. Machines and computers, he admitted, were much more forgiving and predictable. He confessed that these games left him feeling exposed and vulnerable in ways he'd never allowed himself to be exposed before, but it was also meaningful and somehow comforting for him to be in a place where everyone seemed to be interested in overcoming personal challenges. Ephraim looked shocked when he returned to his seat and was quickly embraced by Holly, who held on to his neck long after his face had turned bright red.

With all the attention on Ephraim, the campers missed Pops taking a seat on Bessie's saddle. It was the first time the group had seen him there, and a hush fell over the porch as he began pedaling.

"You might think a man of my age has lived long enough to conquer his fears and overpower his kryptonite. I thought I had," he said, looking at Ruby with a look of intense love. He took a deep breath, and when he continued, his voice was not nearly as strong as it had been. "Ruby has been by my side for more than fifty-six years. We've worked together every day. We've always been there for each other. I don't remember what life was like before we…" He trailed off as tears rose above their dams and rolled down his cheeks.

The campers watched with silent intensity as Pops struggled to compose himself.

"My kryptonite tonight is also fear," he said, forcing a very unconvincing smile as he looked at Ruby. She shook her head and wiped away a tear of her own before standing and walking to her husband. They embraced and held each other for a long, quiet moment before turning to look at the campers, who were patiently anticipating an explanation.

Ruby lifted the hem of her apron and wiped her eyes before offering her warm signature smile. "Pops and I got some bad news this afternoon when we got home." She pulled a piece of paper from her apron pocket. "It's the lab results from a biopsy and some blood work I had done a couple of weeks ago. We knew there was always a possibility that this could be bad, but…" She straightened herself up and stood a little taller. "It still feels a little strange when it has your name on it."

Ruby turned and kissed Pops on the forehead, sending more tears spilling down his cheeks. She took a deep breath and began again. "I… uh, I have cancer."

An audible gasp was followed quickly by a rush of voices. Holly sprung from her seat and quickly moved in to embrace Ruby, burying her head in her neck. The swell of emotion consumed them all, and they all moved forward in a collective group hug, all fourteen members of this ragtag family feeling a sense of sorrow and tragedy coupled with concern and an outpouring of love. They held onto each other for a long time until Ruby spoke. "For crying out loud, the ice cream's melting."

No one felt like ice cream after that, but Ruby insisted that she wouldn't say any more until everyone had been served. The camper's faces were filled with questions and worry, but Pops scooped the ice cream into mismatched ceramic bowls while Ruby covered each serving with fresh berries and distributed the bowls to the each of the kids, kindly refusing to accept help.

"What do we need to know?" Matt asked when Ruby and Pops had sat back down on the wicker loveseat with their own big bowls of ice cream.

"You need to know that you kids will be the last graduates of the farm," Ruby said. "I know you probably have lots of questions— questions that may be difficult to ask. We welcome even the hard ones.

Maybe it'll be easiest if I tell you what we know." She gripped Lorenzo's free hand and smiled at him before turning back to the kids. "Nearly eleven years ago, doctors found a lump on my left breast. It turned out to be malignant. But they'd caught it early; it was still very small. Pops and I made the decision to just do the lumpectomy and get back to living our lives. I was already well past my prime, and we'd seen too many friends have their lives ripped apart by cancer and chemotherapy. In all honesty, we'd almost forgotten about it and probably would have completely if it hadn't been for a UTI I got a month ago. It had been so long since I'd been to the doctor that I didn't realize my doctor had retired several years ago and a young doctor had taken over his practice. He ordered some blood work just to get a baseline to work from. And I guess that's how they found it. Lymphoma, stage 4."

"That doesn't sound good," Susan spoke softly.

"Well, no, I suppose it's not. The letter I received today says I have six months to a year."

Genevieve shook her head. "I'm really sorry."

Ruby laughed. "Now don't go sayin' stuff like that. There's absolutely nothing to be sorry about. I'm at least three times older than most of you. I've lived a good, long life, and I've outlived all of my friends. The way I see it, this is a blessing. I have six to twelve months to put my house in order."

"I assume you'll need us all to leave so you can spend time with your family," James suggested solemnly.

Ruby laughed. "We have no family, other than the nearly seven hundred kids who've passed through here over the past fifty-six summers. You kids are the closest thing we have to family right now, and the last thing we'd want to do is send you all home. There's work to be done and things you need to learn. I've never had much patience for silly things like dying or being sick, and the last thing I'd want is thirteen people moping around feeling sorry for me. If you want to help me, just keep doin' what you're doin'. Life has always been too short for bellyachin' and whining, and now it's even more so. As far as I'm concerned, we move on just like we would have had I not received this letter today. I didn't want Pops to say anything, but I suppose we all have our kryptonite, don't we?

Many of the campers laughed nervously.

"Look, it's a waste of good ice cream to let it melt while we're being sad about this. I got at least six months and a fresh group of kids who need my help. I'm a stubborn old gal. Hell, I'll probably last closer to ten months or more. Pops can bury me in the orchard next spring when the snow thaws. I'm gonna be too busy to fit it into my schedule before then anyway."

Everyone laughed, dispelling the tension that had accumulated in the wake of Pops's kryptonite bomb. They ate their ice cream and laughed some more as they spoke of perspective and life and death and all the stuff in between that makes life worth living.

CHAPTER 44

Rhubarb and Humility

The life of every man is a diary in which he means to
write one story, and writes another;
and his humblest hour is when he compares the volume
as it is with what he vowed to make it.
—J. M. Barrie

The doleful mood that came with the revelation of Ruby's diagnosis was carried away in heavy hearts to the bunkhouses that evening. The overall atmosphere of the women's bunkhouse had never been so somber, as if the very timbers ached with the news. After showers and getting ready for bed, the women spoke softly about what this all meant for Ruby, Pops, and all of them—all those who had ever spent a summer on this farm and all those who had hoped they someday would.

Sleep came slowly to Genevieve, who watched the stars through the skylight long after the lights had been turned out. The shame she had felt earlier about her plans for exposing Ruby as some kind of fraud returned with increased discomfort. She knew she couldn't write an exposé on a dying woman, and neither did she want to. She recognized that after more than a week on the farm, she was no closer to knowing how her article might take shape. Ten thousand words had sounded somewhat daunting a week ago, but considering Ruby's fifty-six-year legacy as the matchmaker of Niederbipp, Genevieve wondered how an article of any length might possibly be enough to honor her and the legacy she would soon leave behind.

Because of the exclusive nature of her access to Ruby, Genevieve figured that many more people than the typical monthly readers would likely see this article. Her feeling of stress only rose when she recognized that Ruby's legacy of 523 successful marriages had undoubtedly affected thousands of individuals—spouses, children and grandchildren of those who spent time on the farm—people who would certainly have strong feelings and opinions about Ruby, the farm, and the myriad things they had gleaned from their experience. She would have to be both fair and honest, but she knew from what she had seen already that her writing would also have to be generous and kind, honoring the woman who had given so many years to positively impact the lives of so many. She couldn't think of any article she had written that carried as much weight and importance, and she realized this article would stretch her in many other ways as well.

Genevieve had often prided herself in the knowledge that her writing directly and indirectly supported the multibillion-dollar fashion industry. What she wrote and posted on her social media accounts could affect the choices of hundreds of thousands of individuals. But now, with Ruby's looming death in mind, what had felt so important for so many years suddenly felt superficial and shallow. Genevieve knew that what she wrote had the power to make or break a business, but she realized that Ruby's work could quietly change the lives of generations of individuals and families. There would always be another international fashion show on the horizon to write something about, some way to encourage the growth of the fashion industry by impressing young, persuadable women that they needed newer, better, more fashionable clothing, makeup, and accessories. But this was altogether different. This story had the potential to long outlast any fashion trend.

It felt like the rooster's morning call came just moments after she finally fell asleep, but Genevieve was surprised that she didn't feel as tired as she had on recent mornings. She rose from her bed with a new sense of urgency. If Ruby's days were indeed as numbered as she suggested, there was work to be done, things to learn, and a better understanding of the woman's work to be gained. But first there were chores that needed doing.

She found Ephraim waiting for her when she and the other women left the bunkhouse. The two of them they walked to the big house to begin their work in the kitchen.

"Good morning," Ruby said with a smile, looking up from a cookbook as they entered the kitchen.

"Good morning," Ephraim responded, sounding tired, his hair disheveled and sleep clinging to his eyes.

"What did you kids have in mind for breakfast?" Ruby asked.

"Do you have any suggestions?" Genevieve asked after quickly glancing at the tired Ephraim.

"I was just thinking about scones," Ruby said, pointing down at a recipe. "We have several cups of cut strawberries left over from last night. We could always freeze them until we get enough to make jam. But no team's made scones yet this year, and they're always a favorite."

"Sounds good to me," Ephraim said without much emotion.

Ruby handed Genevieve a long, narrow basket and led her and Ephraim out the back door of the kitchen and across the lawn to the edge of the woods, where huge, leafy plants grew.

"Is this a special kind of berry plant?" Ephraim asked.

Ruby laughed, pushing aside one of the giant leaves before stooping over to cut one of the long, red stalks hidden beneath the leafy canopy. "We call this *pie plant* in this neck of the woods. Most people call it rhubarb." She cut the leaf from the stem with a paring knife and threw the leaf onto the forest floor, handing the long, red-green stem to Genevieve, who placed it in the basket.

"We need four more of these," Ruby said, handing Ephraim the knife. He stooped down and cut four more stalks, quickly cutting off the enormous leaves and tossing them into the forest before handing the stalks to Genevieve.

As they walked back to the house, Ruby told them that the rhubarb plants on the farm had been brought to Niederbipp by the Zwahlens, the original homesteaders from Switzerland. These perennial plants had found their way into countless pies, scones, jams, and other creations over the farm's three-hundred-year history and were also responsible for winning many blue ribbons in pie contests far and wide.

After washing their hands and the rhubarb stalks, Ruby and Ephraim consulted the recipe and began pulling ingredients from the shelves: flour, salt, butter, sugar, buttermilk, baking powder, and vanilla. While Genevieve measured the ingredients into a big copper bowl, Ephraim sliced and diced the rhubarb into small pieces. Commenting that it looked similar to celery, he bit off a section from the stalk. Genevieve and Ruby both laughed as they watched his face scrunch up like he'd bitten into a lemon.

"I don't think it's ripe," he managed, his eyes watering. "Maybe we should make other plans for breakfast."

After teasing Ephraim and insisting it couldn't be that bad, Genevieve tried a piece herself and quickly spit it out, the tartness overwhelming her mouth.

"It'll be fine," Ruby reaffirmed. "Just keep chopping. If you're worried, you can make some oatmeal after we get these in the oven."

Following Ruby's instructions, they used a potato masher to mix the butter in with the dry ingredients. Then they added the buttermilk, vanilla, strawberries, and rhubarb, stirring it all together into a thick, clumpy batter. Using two sets of large spoons, they scooped blobs of the batter onto cookie sheets. It was clear that Ephraim and Genevieve were both way out of their element, but Ruby was patient and encouraging, telling them several times that there was really no wrong shape for a scone. Before the slid the trays into the oven, she instructed them to sprinkle the lumpy clumps of batter with sugar.

They set a timer and then got water boiling for the oatmeal, doubting their scones would be at all appetizing and knowing the rest of the campers would be arriving soon. The timer went off just as they finished cleaning up the island, and they pulled the scones from the oven, impressed with how beautiful they looked but worried everyone would be unimpressed with how they tasted. They were setting the table when those on milk duty came in from the barn with several bottles of milk and cream. When Ruby suggested they whip some of the cream to go with the scones, Ephraim and Genevieve were quick to agree, hoping a little whipped cream might go a long way in masking the sourness of the rhubarb.

The rest of the family arrived looking hungry and took their places at the table. Genevieve didn't hear the communal grace as she said her own silent prayer that the scones would somehow be palpable. But to her surprise, even without the cream, the taste was somehow sweet and pleasant. Ephraim smiled at her as he broke off a large piece of scone and popped it into his mouth. The only complaint people had was that there weren't enough for thirds.

"Can you tell me what happened to the rhubarb?" Genevieve asked Ruby when the rest of the family had left the dining hall to get on with the activities of the day.

"What would you like to know, dear?" Ruby asked.

"How could something so sour produce something so sweet?"

Ruby smiled and nodded, taking a seat on a tall stool. "I asked the same thing the first time I made this recipe. It's hard to believe, but that had to have been fifty-seven years ago. Millie Smurthwaite was quite a baker and loved using rhubarb."

"Why?" Ephraim asked, his face contorting much the same as it had when he'd first tasted it.

"Well, you seemed to enjoy the flavor once it was cooked."

"Yeah, but I never would have thought to put it in a scone, especially not after I'd tasted it. How do people come up with stuff like this?"

"I figure they were either starving or they were looking for a way to inject their food with symbolic meaning."

Genevieve and Ephraim looked at each other and then back to Ruby.

"My Jewish friend invited me to a Passover seder with his family a few years ago," Ephraim said. "We ate bitter herbs, but I don't remember rhubarb being part of it."

"No, I don't know if they have rhubarb in the Middle East, but I suppose rhubarb might share some symbolism with Jewish bitter herbs."

"How so?" asked Ephraim.

"The Jews eat bitter herbs at Passover to remind them of their historical captivity in Egypt. I don't believe I have any Jewish ancestry, but since coming to the farm, rhubarb has reminded me of finding peace and happiness amidst the trials and sorrows of life. Maybe that's why I thought of it this morning."

"You've been thinking about your diagnosis?" Genevieve asked soberly, almost afraid of the answer.

Ruby nodded. "I didn't sleep much last night, lying awake instead, thinking of all the things I hoped to do before I kick the bucket." She looked down at her wrinkled hands in her lap. "So much of this life is different than the way I hoped it would go," she admitted, looking up at both of them. "But somehow, since coming to the farm, I've always managed to find grace and happiness amid the disappointments. Last night as I lay staring up at the ceiling, I remembered my first night here. My aunt Millie, after feeding us all a hearty supper, rolled out several strawberry rhubarb pies and invited us all to eat a slice of what she called humble bumbler pie."

"I've heard of humble pie and also bumbleberry pie," Ephraim said. "Is that something similar?"

"I suppose it's probably a hybrid of the two. As I recall, she introduced us to the pie and the concept by saying that when we're humble enough to admit we've been bumbling, we can begin to make progress. But she also suggested a deeper symbolism in the pie's ingredients. The rhubarb, as you both found out earlier, is very sour by itself. Most people would probably prefer the sweetness of a strawberry any day of the week. But nobody gets a bowl of sweet strawberries every day of their life. And it's also true that few of us get a full bowl of chopped rhubarb every day. The trick to finding joy in the journey, Aunt Millie taught me, is to humbly take the sweet and the bitter together, to add the sugar of love, bake the mix between the layers of work and courage, and serve it up hot with a dollop of the cream of wholeheartedness."

Ephraim nodded thoughtfully. "I recognized last week that I've been bumbling for the last several years, hoping my lot would somehow magically change. I never realized that a lack of humility might have something to do with not being able to find the sweetness or getting past the hurt and disappointment of unfulfilled love."

Ruby pursed her lips and nodded. "Life has a strange and sometimes not-so-subtle way of teaching us the importance of finding the sweet among the bitter. I would have missed out on so many things if I'd blown off my aunt's invitation to come here. I was the rhubarb who needed the love my aunt offered before I could discover the sweetness I'd been missing."

"I assume you're referring to Pops?" Genevieve asked.

"Yes, but so much more. I really didn't know what living a wholehearted life meant before coming here. You might say I'd been so busy choking on the bitter that I'd never stopped to really experience all the sweetness that was around me. I learned that first summer that you take the sweet and the bitter together, like when you bite into a piece of strawberry rhubarb pie. If you took the time to separate the sweet chunks from the bitter, not only would you waste a lot of time, but you'd also miss out on the rich and complex flavor of the medley in each bite. I've learned in the past fifty-seven years that few of us could ever fully appreciate the sweet if we never experienced the bitter. But after tasting our share of the bitter, if we're at all smart about it, we'll do our best to dilute it by seeking out and surrounding ourselves with all that is sweet and good and lovely. I believe that's an essential part of the recipe of living a wholehearted life. The trick is to keep doing it again and again, day after day, year after year, finding joy in the journey until the journey is through."

"But what if you're not ready for the journey to end?" Genevieve asked timidly.

Ruby took a deep breath and let it out slowly. "Ready or not, here it comes," she said after a moment. "I asked Pops this morning what memories he wanted to make before my time is up." She smiled through tear-filled eyes. "He reminded me of the day we dropped my aunt and uncle off at the train station fifty-seven years ago, when they were headed off to Florida to spend their last days in the sunshine. As we stood on the platform, waiting for the train to pull away, Pops asked them if they had any parting advice. "Make good memories," Uncle Dan told us, "because there'll come a time when that's all you've got left." Pops reminded me that we always kept that advice. Our hearts are filled with the sweet memories of the past fifty-seven years. We've spent most of those years within a twenty-mile radius of the farm, but I can't say I have many regrets. I'm sure there have been many rhubarb days over that period of time, but they've been tempered by so many strawberry days that I can't imagine my life any sweeter."

Genevieve forced a smile, feeling uncertain about her own emotions and not knowing how else to respond. She had never been around a dying person before. The reality of it still felt distant somehow. Ruby was just as vibrant today as she had been the day before; only the fact that her days were now numbered had changed. But surely there would be things to learn from a woman who knew she was dying, different things than from a woman who thought she had all the time in the world.

CHAPTER 45

The Economics of Socks

If you wish to make an apple pie from scratch, you must first invent the universe.
—Carl Sagan

With the list of the day's chores still long, Ruby sent Ephraim and Genevieve to the cellar to grind the flour for the bread. Since she'd done this chore the week before and knew it was possible, Genevieve found the work significantly easier than it had been when she'd attempted it with Greg. They were nearly halfway through the task before Genevieve remembered that there was something here to learn that she had missed the last time. As she cranked, she scanned the walls, looking for the clue Ephraim had told her he'd found that had given him and Sonja the advantage of speed when they'd first used this contraption. She didn't see anything obvious and was just about to ask when she noticed his eyes resting on the floor joists above their heads. And there it was, just as he'd said:

WE ARE EACH OF US ANGELS WITH ONLY ONE WING, AND WE CAN ONLY FLY BY EMBRACING EACH OTHER.
–LUCIANO DE CRESCENZO

She read the words to herself as she continued to turn the hand crank, remembering how convinced she'd been that the two-person flour mill was nothing more than a broken piece of junk. But seeing this writing on the wall was a not-so-subtle dig to the independence she'd spent her life trying to defend. Though in her heart of hearts she had long hoped that marriage was in her future, that softer side of her had long been stifled as she'd fiercely played the role of an independent woman. How long had she convinced herself that she didn't need anybody in her life, least of all a man? But as she looked up at the simple calligraphy on the beam above her head, she wondered if her efforts at independence may have also kept her from more fully relishing life's joys.

Could embracing another human—a man in her case—make that big of a difference? Could it really be that easy? Her experience with this machine certainly seemed to suggest that it *was* that easy. But every one of the tasks on the farm had also supported the notion that two was better than one. And not just better, but possible, practical, attainable, and even fun. Things here on the farm, she knew, were somehow different than they were in the real world, where it felt like the game was every man or woman for themselves. On the farm, there was a sensible need for cooperation, teamwork, and synergism. Just the day before, she had learned from doing the laundry with James that keeping score was counterproductive and infuriating. But as she thought about it, she realized that every one of the tasks had the potential to go either way—to be a competition between rivals or a shared venture between allies. And the more she thought about it, the more she recognized the truth behind the quote on the floor joist.

Before she was even winded, the hand crank turned freely, and Genevieve looked at Ephraim with wide eyes, wondering if the mill really *was* broken.

"I guess we're done," he said, getting off his seat.

"No way! It took Greg and me way longer."

"Yeah, that's because you guys spent most of your time arguing."

"You know about that?"

He shrugged. "Girls aren't the only ones that stay up late talking."

"Hold on," she said, getting up from the seat. "What did he say?"

Ephraim smiled and shook his head as he stooped over to pick up the pail of flour they'd just produced. "Forget about it. We're moving on, right? It's a new day, a new week."

"Okay, but I'm still curious what he said!"

"Forget it, really. It's not a big deal." Ephraim looked like he wished he'd kept his mouth shut. "Last week was just practice for this week, right? That's the way I'd like to look at it. I mean, you and I didn't exactly *jell* in the laundry shack last week, but it's been much better today. I think everyone was worried yesterday when you and James took so long to do the laundry. Holly wanted to check on you, but Ruby asked her not to go—to let you guys figure it out on your own."

"James told me yesterday you all think I'm a biddy. Am I gonna get a chance to redeem myself?"

Ephraim smiled. "I guess that depends."

"On what?"

"Well, the day is still young. So far it's been good, but I'd guess there are a lot of things that could go wrong between now and sunset."

"So you're keeping score?"

"No," he said, backpedaling. "But I am trying to be observant. You know, like Ruby suggested in the paperwork."

Genevieve looked confused. "Remind me about that part."

"Oh, it was something about how important it is to go into this with our eyes wide open, ready to make objective observations instead of either judging quickly or closing our eyes to potential issues. I guess that rang true to me because I've recognized that not having my eyes fully open has been one of my problems during most of my failed attempts at dating."

"What do you mean?" Genevieve asked, motioning for the stairs.

They moved the conversation to the kitchen. Ruby was gone, but she'd written the recipe on the wall. Their limited experience gave them enough confidence to get started.

As Genevieve counted cups of flour and dumped them into the mixer, Ephraim recounted how Ruby had suggested in his interview that he may have been looking for the wrong things in the women he'd chosen to date over the last ten years. She had challenged him to focus his attention on a woman's character, talents, and personality rather than placing so much emphasis on her outward appearance.

The advice sounded obvious to Genevieve, but for Ephraim, it appeared to have been a revelation. He acknowledged the ego trips he'd gotten out of dating beautiful women, but in the days since the interview, he'd come to the conclusion that his thinking had been seriously flawed and had brought him only confusion and dejection. But he also recognized from being around the other men, particularly Matt, that he really needed to focus on becoming the kind of guy that a genuinely decent woman would want to be around. It had been a humbling and sobering realization that his dating life up to that point could be summed up as a disastrous, decade-long cringe comedy. But he admitted that for the first time in years, he was optimistic that things could change and that he could finally find the love of his life.

Ruby returned to the kitchen twenty minutes later as Genevieve and Ephraim were struggling to turn the dough out of the mixing bowl and onto the island. She watched them work for a moment and offered a few suggestions, but for the most part, she kept her hands out of it until all the dough was piled up in a big, sagging blob. Then Ruby helped them shape the dough into loaves and tuck the loaves into tins before she invited them to join her and Pops and the rest of the kids for the annual shearing of the sheep. Genevieve and Ephraim quickly draped the tins with clean dishtowels, as they'd been taught, and then they and Ruby hurried to catch up with the rest of the family behind the barn near the horse corral.

Rex, the farm dog, was in high spirits, excitedly corralling the sheep through the narrow gate while Pops instructed the campers to arrange the moveable fencing to make the temporary enclosure even smaller. The thirty sheep were bleating loudly, and everyone was in commotion. Genevieve didn't know how to respond or help, so she tried to just stay out of the way. The chaos and noise quickly calmed as Pops whistled for Rex to come to his side. The two of them walked to the head of the corral, where a big, black tarp had been stretched out over the ground and several strange-looking tools hung from the awning extending from the barn.

"Once a year our friends the sheep get a haircut," Pops explained, raising his hands to the kids to quiet everyone down. "This we do to make sure the sheep don't overheat in the summer sun and also because Mom uses their wool in the winter to knit the socks you kids wear, as well dozens of other pairs that she sells to help pay for the upkeep of the farm. Most of our sheep have been with us for many seasons and are accustomed to this annual haircut. Some even seem to enjoy it. The ewes—the lady sheep—are generally much friendlier than the five rams. They may all look like fairly docile creatures, but if you're not careful, you'll find out that the rams' horns aren't just hood ornaments."

"Are you saying they're dangerous?" James asked, looking concerned.

"Let's just say I wouldn't recommend getting in their way or makin' 'em mad. We've had a handful of minor incidents over the years, but usually only with those who tend to provoke them."

"Why don't you just get the kind of sheep that don't have horns?" asked Crystal.

"Good question," Ruby said, stepping in. "Does anyone have an answer for Crystal?"

They all looked at each other blankly.

"Uh, is it because you want to have lambs?" Spencer asked hesitantly.

Ruby smiled. "That's part of it. Several of the ewes will be dropping lambs in the next few weeks. That's always fun. Only the males in this breed have horns, and if we want our ewes to give us lambs, we're going to need to keep a few rams around. We've tried working with several varieties of sheep over the years, but a long time ago we decided to focus on the ones that are the best producers. We sold off all but these Rambouillet variety."

"What's so special about these?" Genevieve asked.

"Well, the great-great-grandparents of these sheep came from France. But I think they must have tangoed with the merino sheep in Spain, because they produce high yields of the softest wool. We'll get between ten and twelve pounds of wool from each of these sheep today."

"Is that a lot?" asked Holly

"Considering that five or six pair of socks can be made out of every pound of wool, I'd say it's pretty good," Ruby replied.

"Whoa, each sheep makes sixty pairs of socks?" Ephraim asked, looking very impressed.

Ruby smiled. "Unfortunately we haven't been able to train the sheep to make socks yet, but they do a fine job making wool. It takes many hours to clean, dye, and process the wool into yarn and then many more hours to turn the yarn into socks. You'll all have the opportunity to help with each step of the process."

"Wouldn't it just be cheaper and easier to buy socks?" James asked.

She shrugged. "It may be in the short term, but then we'd miss out on all the lessons that come from teaching the economics of socks."

"*The economics of socks?*" Susan asked amusedly.

Ruby nodded. "It's similar to the economics of gardening and the economics of milking cows and even the economics of raising chickens." She paused for a moment to allow her words to sink into their heads. "If the only thing we were concerned about was making sure we all have socks on our feet, then yes, it would certainly be easier to drive into town and pick up a few dozen socks at the department store. But this farm has always been about more than finding the cheapest or easiest way. There will come a time in your lives when the sink will get clogged or the car won't start or the lawn will need mowing. What will you do when that happens?"

"Call someone to fix it," James said without hesitation.

"You won't fix the problem yourself?" Ruby asked.

James laughed. "I went to school so I don't have waste my time getting my hands dirty with stuff like that."

Ruby smiled and nodded. "Then how will you teach your children to find solutions to their troubles?"

He thought for a moment. "I'll teach them to get an education so they can pay someone else to do it for them."

"That's certainly one way to do it, but I'm not convinced it's the best way."

James laughed. "So you're suggesting we need to each get our own sheep and make our own socks?"

"Not at all. But I am suggesting that it's beneficial for everyone to understand the nuts and bolts of the stuff we use every day. I've lived long enough to see each generation losing skills and know-how as they become richer than the generation that raised them. It takes about five or six hours of labor to make one pair of the socks we're all wearing today. For some of you, considering your regular hourly wage, I'm sure that would make the socks you're wearing right now worth thousands of dollars. But by sharing with you what goes into the things we use and eat and enjoy every day, Pops and I hope to impress upon your minds the beauty of the toil and the details of everything. We hope that by the end of the summer, you'll never look at an egg or a loaf of bread or a pair of socks with the same disregard you did before you came here."

"Okay, so socks start with the hair of these animals," James said rather impatiently. "What's the big value of knowing that?"

Ruby nodded, bending over to pick a blade of grass. She straightened back up and looked at that grass for a moment like she was examining a precious strand of pearls. Then she walked to James and handed him the blade.

"What's this?"

"I'll give you a hint: your socks didn't begin with the wool of the sheep."

He looked at the grass for a moment before looking up, a little more humble.

She bent down again and scooped up a handful of earth, taking his hand and letting the dirt fall into his cupped fingers. "The earth you stand on, the air you breathe, the sunshine that warms your day, and even the smallest raindrop, these are all part of your socks too. Next time you slide them on, think of all the elements that conspired to keep your toes warm and comfortable."

James swallowed hard, looking down at the blade of grass and the dirt in his hand.

She turned to look at the rest of them. "If you'll open your eyes to the details of your life, you'll see that you too are a piece of this earth, of this beautiful system of nuts and bolts and cogs that keeps things moving and progressing as our world spins day after day, traveling around the sun year after year.

"If you lose sight of who you are and begin to think of yourself as something more than a nut or a bolt, if ever you begin to believe your wealth or education or opportunities have made you superior to the nuts and bolts around you, I hope you will remember this," she said, pointing to the dirt in James's hand. "Your dance on this earth, whether short or long, will always be more meaningful if you can remember to be the best doggone nut you can be. With a touch of the hand of Providence, we spring from the earth like the grass and the flowers, and we will someday lie back down in the earth that gave us life. How we live these days of our brief dance makes all the difference. And the earlier we discover that we are each a small but important part of the whole, the more meaningful our lives will be and the more we'll respect every living thing around us." She took the blade of grass from James and walked to the sheep's pen, where she fed it to a fluffy ewe. "We are all part of the machine that is our universe. We can learn to respect it with reverence, or we can try to fight it and conquer it. But either way, you will someday become food for the worms. Those worms will till the dirt, which will nourish future generations, just as you and I are nourished every day by a thousand generations who lived before us."

"What you said there almost sounds like Buddhist philosophy," Matt suggested.

Ruby bobbed her head. "But if you look closely, you'll see that it is also Christian and Islamic and Hindu and Jewish and Mayan and Greek and Roman and Egyptian—you'll find these ideas in the truths of every people who have ever thoughtfully pondered the seasons of life and the meaning of our existence."

She walked back to James's side and put her arm around his waist. "I'm convinced that if we each spent more time thinking about our connection to the earth and to each other, there would be no room for greed or selfishness or discontent or even depression. We would see things as they really are. And we would see ourselves as we truly are—creations of God endowed with beauty and grace and unlimited goodness."

Ruby turned to Spencer. "If you'll take the time to slow down and truly watch and see and come to an understanding of these things—and then find a woman who shares that understanding—you'll not only be able to find marriage, you'll also be able to find joy and contentment within that marriage."

"You really believe that?" he asked.

"Absolutely. It's a simple recipe, but because of its simplicity, it's often disregarded as old-fashioned and outdated. Truth—real truth—transcends time and fashion. It's never reliant on the whims or trends of the day. And it's equally available to all of us."

Spencer shook his head doubtfully. "I want to believe what you're saying, but I've never been able to find the kinds of truths you're talking about."

"Then you've been looking in the wrong places," Ruby said without hesitation.

"How can you be so certain? How do you know I'm not broken and incapable of finding the kind of truth you're talking about?"

"Sometimes it's more a matter of not being broken enough," Ruby replied.

"Huh?" he asked, looking lost.

She took a deep breath and looked up at the nearby berm, where a bench stood under the shade of a tall tree. "Spencer, if you would, please run to that bench. On the ground, if you look closely, you'll find a few brown spheres, each the size of a small apple. Please bring me a handful of them."

He hurried off, scrambling up the berm, stooping to pick up several of the spheres Ruby promised he would find. He rushed back to the group.

"Does anybody know what these are?" Ruby asked, holding up one of the dirty-looking spheres.

"It looks like a rotten apple," Genevieve said.

"Yes, it does," Ruby said, motioning Genevieve to come closer. "But look inside." She handed her the strange fruit.

Finding a crack in the brownish-black skin, Genevieve peeled back the covering to reveal a dark, fibrous mass. "What's this?" she asked with an unpleasant face.

"Keep going. You're not there yet."

The others gathered around Genevieve as she pulled apart the damp fibers to reveal the buff-colored shell of a nut. She looked up, surprised. "It looks like a walnut."

"That's because it is. Pops and I planted that tree the year we took over the farm."

Pops nodded. "It was only about ten inches high at the time," he said, looking back at the tree, whose branches reached high into the sky and fanned out in all directions. "A lot of things change in fifty-six years."

"Yes," Ruby replied, turning her attention back to the nut. She picked it up out of Genevieve's hand and lifted it up so all of them could see it. "Nature offers us many lessons and metaphors. This one became meaningful to me my first summer on the farm." She looked at Pops before smiling. "Pride, I learned, always stands in our way of learning and growing. It forms a repelling shell around our hearts and heads. Aunt Millie taught me that we're capable of learning and growth only when we're meek and humble, when the shell of pride is removed and truth can penetrate our hearts and minds. Humility, as I've said before, is unfortunately not generally one of our natural tendencies. Just like the meat of a walnut cannot be enjoyed until the shell is cracked, most of us require a little cracking—a little humility before we're capable of understanding our potential."

Ruby handed the nut to Pops, who smiled and placed it squarely between his open palms before grunting as he added pressure. At the sound of a crack, the faces of the campers shone with surprise. He opened his hands to reveal the cracked shell and the white meat inside.

While some of the campers reached into Pops's hand to sample the meat, Spencer responded by tearing off the outer skin of another sphere and pulling out another whole nut. He attempted to copy what he'd seen Pops do, but no matter how loud his grunt or the effort of his force, he couldn't break the shell with his hands.

"All things in their due time," Pops said, reaching for the nut and quickly cracking it between his palms. The women laughed at Spencer's face, which showed an obvious sense of awe at Pops's strength. Spencer quickly reached for another sphere and repeated his actions, but once again he was denied. He grunted and cussed under his breath, but still the shell refused him entrance.

"Do you need help?" Pops asked.

Spencer shook his head and continued making noise, but with no recognizable progress. When he realized everyone was looking at him expectantly, he handed the nut to Pops, who quickly cracked it and offered the meat to the campers.

"Okay, what's the trick?" Spencer asked, looking very bugged.

Pops laughed out loud. "There's no trick. It's just a matter of being able to read the shell."

"What does it say?" Spencer asked.

Pops placed his thumb on Spencer's forehead and rubbed it back and forth. "It says this one's harder than some. It'll take some time, but it'll crack."

Many of the kids laughed.

"So, you're not going to tell me?" Spencer asked, ignoring the laughter and looking peeved.

Pops shook his head. "It'll have to wait for another day. We've got thirty sheep standing in line for haircuts, and I'm sure we'd all like to get them done before dinner."

Spencer forced a smile.

At the mention of dinner, Ephraim looked at Genevieve. "The bread! It's probably overflowing the pans by now."

They raced back to the house, leaving the barbers to their work.

CHAPTER 46

Winged Messengers

*Five enemies of peace inhabit with us –
avarice, ambition, envy, anger, and pride;
if these were to be banished, we should infallibly enjoy
perpetual peace.*
—Petrarch

Just as Ephraim had feared, the dough had grown high above the edges of the bread pans and overflowed. As he and Genevieve pulled the tins apart, the dough tore and flopped, making everything look scarred and uneven. They turned on the oven while they tried to tenderly coax the dough back into the pans, but they quickly saw that the more they messed with it, the worse it looked. After a few minutes, they gave up and slid the sorry-looking loaves into the oven. They wanted to be back with the rest of the family, but they knew that by the time they got to the shearing pen, they would quickly have to turn around and come back to pull the bread from the oven. So instead, they finished cleaning up the kitchen and brainstormed ideas for dinner.

Cooking three meals in a single day was more than either of them had ever fathomed. Neither of them had any expertise in the culinary arts, and they openly wished Ruby were there to offer suggestions and ideas. But it seemed Ruby was in no hurry to be back in the kitchen. After struggling to come up with anything that wouldn't require them to drive to the grocery store, they descended the stairs to the cellar, looking for inspiration.

They walked through the shelves lined with bottled fruits and vegetables, but they still couldn't come up with anything. They were about to give up when they came upon some bins in darkest, coldest part of the cellar. The old wooden bins were still half filled with potatoes and onions.

"Have you ever had raclette?" Genevieve asked.

"Raw what?"

"Raclette."

"No. What is it?"

"It's a Swiss dish. I've only had it once, but it seems like it would be pretty simple. It's made with boiled potatoes, and you pour melted cheese over the top."

Ephraim thought for a moment. "That's it? Just potatoes and cheese?"

"Yeah, and maybe some onions and pickles too."

"That's only four ingredients. I bet we could do that. Where do we start?"

They hurried back to the kitchen, where they grabbed a couple of pots to help them carry the items from the cellar. Genevieve directed Ephraim to select only the smallest potatoes. She sorted through the onions, trying to recall all the details of the memorable meal she had once eaten in a quaint restaurant in Lauterbrunnen, Switzerland, on her way home from Paris. They found a jar of mini dill pickles and selected a round of cheese that, based on Genevieve's memory, looked like it was about the right color.

The timer for the bread went off as they were ascending the stairs. They pulled out the loaf tins, surprised to find that the bread looked much better than they'd imagined, having somehow grown and healed while in the oven. They returned to the cellar after deciding on peanut butter and jam to top the bread for lunch. Genevieve taught Ephraim how to make peanut butter with the mortar and pestle. Wanting to serve up something original, they selected apricot, gooseberry, and cherry jams. After slicing five loaves of the warm bread, they packed picnic baskets with all the ingredients. Bringing a few blankets, they headed back to the barn to see how the campers were progressing with their work.

They were impressed to see that at least ten of the sheep had received haircuts and were grazing in the pasture while their fluffier friends awaited their turns. The campers were all involved in one task or another. Some held the sheep while Spencer used shears to cut away the thick fleece. Others busily pulled burrs and small twigs from the shorn fleeces before folding and rolling them up. Still others stuffed these bundles into cotton flour sacks, where they would stay until processing could take place.

Genevieve and Ephraim watched for a couple of minutes until they each found a place where they could get involved. There was a sense of community and camaraderie that existed as everybody worked side by side, and they made room for the extra help, teaching Genevieve and Ephraim how to accomplish the various tasks. It was dirty work, but no one complained as they learned skills none of them had ever needed before and would likely never need again.

As Susan took a turn at the shears and Spencer took a more supporting role, Genevieve was impressed that there was no gender delineation in this task. There was just work—work that was accomplished with everyone laboring together, side by side.

When Susan finished shearing the ewe, she handed the clippers to Pops, who turned them off. A group carried this latest batch of fleece to the table, where everyone made quick work of cleaning it. When it had been rolled together and stacked in a bag with the other fleece, Pops led all of the campers to an old water pump. They took turns pumping the water while a few campers at a time washed and rinsed their hands. A playful water fight ensued when Crystal accidentally splashed James's foot. The rest of the campers were quick to jump in, which left them all thoroughly soggy but refreshed.

A few campers had spread the picnic blankets onto the grass in the shade, but they quickly moved them into the sun when they all realized how chilled they were from the water fight. Ephraim and Genevieve presented lunch, which was well received. While the family took turns spreading peanut butter and jam on the fresh bread, they paused to listen as they were bombarded from above with a new sound that resembled the intermittent honks of a dozen airborne jalopies. Within seconds, they saw the source of the sound: a large flock of Canada geese, which flew in a V formation over the distant woods. The whole family stopped and watched as the birds approached, honking incessantly with each beat of their giant wings. The birds passed directly over the top of them, flying low and disappearing behind the trees long before their honks faded out.

"They sure are noisy," Greg said.

"Yeah, they are! They remind me of teenage girls," Josh said with a smile.

"Well, I was just thinking they remind me of junior high school boys trying to get the attention of the girls," Crystal responded.

"I think you're probably both right," Pops said.

"It seems like the noise they're making would be a disadvantage if there were hunters nearby."

"Yes, indeed, but hunting season doesn't begin until the fall," Pops explained. "And in the meantime, a whole lot of things are being communicated. There's probably a lot we can learn from the geese. I used to hunt them every December until about twenty years ago. One of our kids, an ornithologist, opened my eyes. Even though they're very tasty, I've never been able to raise my shotgun to shoot one after that."

"Because they're basically overgrown flying rats that will eat just about anything?" James asked.

Pops shook his head. "No. It's because I learned there's a lot more to them than their meat."

"I heard they mate for life," Matt said.

"That's true. I once saw a hunter hit one on the other side of the river. Its mate flew around in circles howling for nearly a half an hour. The hunter finally raised his gun and shot her too." Pops shook his head. "It was sad to watch—disturbing, really. That's when I knew my hunting days were over."

"But there's a lot more to Canada geese than just the fact that they mate for life," Ruby said.

"Like what?" asked Holly.

"Well, like the fact that they fly in a V formation. Do any of you know why?"

"Yeah," Ephraim responded. "I learned this in engineering school. It's about the physics of drag, right?"

Ruby nodded. "The first bird essentially cuts the wind for the others who follow."

"That doesn't seem fair," James said.

"Oh, it's more fair than you might think. They all take their turns at the front of the flock."

"So, what do you think they're saying to each other?" Rachael asked.

Josh laughed. "They're probably saying, "Are we there yet? How much farther? I have to go to the bathroom! Mom, Bruce is breathing my air and taking up my space!"

The others all laughed.

"I'm sure I probably guessed something similar until we learned better from Mary, the ornithologist Pops was referring to. She said the geese behind honk to give encouragement and reassurance to the leader. And as they each take a turn to be the leader, they also take a turn being a cheerleader."

There was silence among the campers for a moment as they each considered Ruby's words.

"It seems like maybe there's something we could learn from the geese," Ephraim said.

Ruby nodded, encouraging him to continue.

"I was just thinking about how my family might have been different if there'd been a little more encouraging instead of so much whining and teasing and complaining. I think my childhood home would have been an easier place to live if I'd heard motivation and support instead of sarcasm and negativity." He thought for a moment before continuing. "I think I could've done a lot better."

Many of the campers nodded slowly as his words sank in.

"Nature is a great teacher," Ruby responded. "I don't know if it takes any more effort to encourage and cheer than it does to complain and criticize. But while the first two have the ability to gladden hearts, the others only have power to demoralize and sow seeds of discontent."

"Did that ornithologist say how they discovered that the honks were positive affirmations?" Susan asked.

"Not exactly. I assume it would be difficult to translate goose language into English. But the fact that a flock sticks together—that they fly in formation and take turns leading and supporting each other for sometimes thousands of miles—that says something, doesn't it? To me, it speaks not just of loyalty and devotion. It also suggests a sense of love and affection."

"Do you really think animals can have those kinds of emotions?" Spencer asked dubiously.

Ruby nodded. "I'm not sure about all animals, but many of the animals I've observed on the farm exhibit an undeniable ability to express affection toward their own kind and others. It's a beautiful thing to find such affection in nonhuman life, but it's even more powerful to observe love and support developing among humans who recognize their differences but are still willing to cheer and support each other."

Ruby's words were met with the honks of two additional flocks of geese flying near each other over opposite sides of the farmyard. The campers paused and silently watched the V-shaped flocks as they passed noisily, heading in the same direction as the first.

"The earth and the universe are anxious to teach all those who are hungry for wisdom and understanding," Ruby said as the honks faded into the distance. "We each have to decide if we'll open our eyes and hearts to the lessons that come knocking at our doors or if we'll treat them as noise and shut them out. But for those who ask and are humbly anxious to listen and hear, the universe opens its mysteries and pours out all its secrets."

CHAPTER 47

Bruised But Not Broken

To reform a world, to reform a nation, no wise man will undertake; and all but foolish men know, that the only solid, though a far slower reformation, is what each begins and perfects on himself.
-Thomas Carlyle

A thoughtful discussion ensued as the campers worked their way through the bread and most of the jam and peanut butter. And though there were no articulated promises, each of them stood from the picnic blankets with an unspoken desire to do more and be more and support each other in more meaningful ways.

Genevieve and Ephraim gathered up the remnants of the picnic and folded the blankets as the others found their way back to their work. With dinner already planned, the KP staff decided to stick around rather than to head back to the kitchen right away. The other campers made room for them, and Genevieve soon found herself holding the shears while three of the other campers helped to secure the sheep. She was hesitant at first, but she quickly got the hang of things and picked up the pace, shearing a ewe, with the help of the others, in record time. While those who were assigned to cleaning the fleece gathered it up, Pops opened the gate of the corral and took hold of the twisted horn of the biggest ram. Spencer grabbed hold of the other horn, and the two men escorted the ram into the shade of the awning. The shearing crew looked on with trepidation.

Genevieve hesitated and tried to hand the shears to Rachael, but Rachael refused, a look of fear in her eyes. The ram was nearly twice the size of the ewe they had just sheared, and it was clear that he didn't like being controlled. Pops and Spencer held his horns tightly as he shook his head, trying to get loose. They positioned him as they had the others, sitting him down on his haunches. Moving the sheep into this position usually lulled them into quiet submission, but this ram wasn't having it. He continued to squirm as Genevieve reluctantly came closer with the shears. Susan, Rachael, Josh, and Ephraim each took control over one of the ram's legs, and Pops and Spencer let go of their grip on the animal's horns to make room. Genevieve switched on the shears and bent over to begin the haircut.

It happened quickly and without warning. Just as her head came down, the ram bucked his head backward, bonking Genevieve right between the eyes with his forehead. Already off balance, she fell on her butt, her nose gushing blood and her eyes watering so badly she couldn't see. Susan rushed to Genevieve's side, laying her down on the tarp while Rachael pulled Genevieve's fingers out of the death grip she had on the clippers. The ram, upon recognizing that two of his limbs had been freed and that the humans were distracted, wasted no time in getting to his feet. But before bolting back to the flock, he threw his head once more, ramming the blunt part of one horn into Spencer's groin.

Spencer folded in half, but on the way down, he landed a retaliatory punch to the ram's neck. The ram took off, rearing and kicking like a wild stallion and leaving a cloud of dust in his wake.

With the ram gone, the campers turned their attention to the wounded. Genevieve was crying, and Spencer was rolling in the dirt, clutching his crotch and stomach. The men gathered around Spencer while the women took care of Genevieve.

Ruby took off her apron and asked Holly to get it wet at the pump and, in the same breath, called out to Ephraim, telling him to run to the big house for ice. Holly returned quickly with the dripping wet apron. Ruby wrung it out and began clearing away the blood from Genevieve's face. Genevieve's nose was already swelling, and her eyes looked puffy. Ruby gingerly ran her fingers along Genevieve's nose until she seemed satisfied.

"The good news is it's not broken," she announced. "The bad news is that this probably won't be pretty." She looked over her shoulder. "Spencer, how are you?"

"Ugh," he groaned.

"Sounds like a couple of bruised marbles to me," she said, trying not to smile. "We'll get some ice on 'em as soon as Ephraim gets back." She turned her attention back to Genevieve, who had stopped crying but still lay on the ground, unable or unwilling to open her eyes.

"Do we need to go to the hospital?" Holly asked, looking very concerned.

Ruby shook her head. "Not for this. Open wounds, maybe, but not for a nosebleed and some bruised cojones. They'd just give us some ice packs and aspirin and send us home. We've got all that here."

Ephraim returned from the big house, winded and carrying a couple of clean dishrags and a copper bowl of ice. Several of the kids jumped in to help, making up ice packs. Genevieve winced as someone rested a cold pack on her nose and forehead, and she looked up through watering eyes into the concerned faces of Ruby and the other women.

"How are you feeling, dear?" Ruby asked, her face full of compassion and concern.

"Like my head is twice the size of normal."

Ruby nodded. "I'm sorry. I think I know how you feel. A similar thing happened to me the summer Pops and I took over the farm. I didn't ice it as well as I should have and ended up with two black eyes that lasted nearly a month."

"Does this happen often?" Susan asked.

"No, apparently only every fifty-seven years or so."

"With the same ram?" Holly asked.

Ruby laughed. "No. Rams only live about twenty years or so. It was Carlos's grandfather that got me. I was the only victim that time. Apparently the bloodline is growing increasingly aggressive." She looked over her shoulder at the men crowded around Spencer. "Gentlemen, why don't you help Spencer to his feet and take him to the bunkhouse. He's gonna need to rest for a while. Come back when you're done. We'll need your help carrying Genevieve to her bunk as well."

Genevieve's nosebleed had stopped by the time the men returned. Ruby had cleaned her up pretty well. But her eyes were swollen, and it felt like she had a nose full of gravel. The six remaining men, including Pops, linked arms to form a human stretcher and carry Genevieve to the women's bunkhouse. The women trailed close behind.

It was the first time the men had been in the women's bunkhouse, and they were both impressed and distracted by the layout of the beds and the mural on the wall.

"Ours doesn't have any art like that," James said, looking like he'd been cheated.

"Neither did ours," Crystal responded. "We painted that."

"Wait, you can do that?" Greg asked.

"As long as it goes back to a blank white canvas at the end of the summer, you can do whatever you want," Pops said as he escorted the men out of the bunkhouse after they'd deposited Genevieve on her bed.

When Genevieve was comfortable, Ruby left Holly in charge of looking after her and swept the rest of the women out the door to join the men back at the corral.

As her head continued pulsating with each beat of her heart, Genevieve asked Holly to find some ibuprofen. Holly moved quickly, returning from the bathroom less than a minute later with a few tablets and a cup of water. Holly kindly helped prop Genevieve up so she could swallow without making a mess. She took the cup back to the bathroom and returned with a damp washcloth to wash more dried blood and dust from Genevieve's arms and neck.

Genevieve was in too much pain to resist. It had been years since anyone had waited on her like this, and she recognized how nice it was to have someone care.

"How are you feeling?" Holly asked after a few minutes.

Genevieve peeked out from under the ice pack and saw the look of concern on Holly's face. "Honestly, I feel completely stupid," she said, closing her eyes again.

"Yeah. I'm sure it was a big surprise. I helped shear one of the other rams. He was feistier than the ewes for sure, but definitely not as aggressive as yours. I'm sorry," she said, laying her hand on top of Genevieve's forearm. "You probably feel like the world is conspiring against you."

Genevieve smiled. "That has crossed my mind, yes."

"Would you consider yourself accident prone?"

"I didn't until I came here. I mean, sure I stub my toes and end up with bruises in places I can't remember bumping, but nothing like being attacked by a swarm of angry wasps or being headbutted by a friggin' sheep. At this rate I'm going to look like hamburger by the end of the summer."

"Yeah, I guess this is probably a bit different from life in New York, right?"

Genevieve opened one eye again to look at Holly, whose look of concern had only grown. "You've never been to New York, have you?"

Holly shook her head. "My mom and I used to take virtual tours of the Metropolitan Museum of Art sometimes, and I've watched plenty of YouTube walking tours of Manhattan, but I've never actually been there. What's it like to live there?"

Realizing she wasn't going to get much rest, Genevieve set aside her desire to rest and her natural inclination to say something snarky and decided to be kind instead. "It's exciting and filled with new discoveries and millions of faces, and it's steeped in art and culture."

"Do you ever feel scared?"

"Of what?"

"Of…getting lost…or running out of money…or being mugged…or being involved in a terrorist attack?"

Genevieve shrugged. "I guess I've felt all of those fears at least a few times, but you can't let fear hold you back from experiencing the world, right? I mean, sure, there are things that could kill you, but being stung by wasps or headbutted by a sheep might be worse than death."

She was joking, of course, but no sooner than the words come out of her mouth, she remembered that Holly had recently lost her mother. "I'm sorry," Genevieve muttered. "That was a really stupid thing to say."

Holly looked down at her knees while Genevieve squirmed uncomfortably.

"I guess your own pain can feel like a really big deal until you consider someone else's. I'm sorry," Genevieve repeated.

"It's okay," Holly said after a moment. "It's still kind of raw, you know? My therapist told me that when you live with the fear of losing someone you love for more than a decade, it's nearly impossible for it not to affect you in unhealthy ways. I think about it way too much."

"Holly, your mom just died. You'd have to be completely insensitive to not be thinking about it, right?"

"Maybe. I just wish I could see past the end of the week, you know? See what my life is going to look like ten years down the road. If I could just see that everything's going to be okay, I think I'd feel a lot less anxious."

Genevieve nodded. "That's normal, right? I'm pretty sure everyone would like a sneak peek into their future. I know I would."

Holly nodded, but a look of uncertainty remained on her face. "Promise me you won't laugh?"

"Of course. What's up?"

"I have a strange recurring dream that I am walking along a forested path, enjoying all the beauty of nature. Then the path comes to a tall stone wall that runs to my left and right as far as the eye can see."

Genevieve smiled. "Is that wall about twenty feet high and super thick and solid? And do you feel compelled to find a way to somehow get over it?"

Holly looked surprised. "Yes, how did you know?"

Genevieve laughed. "I've had a similar dream probably dozens of times. What do you think it means?"

Her look of surprise only deepened. "My therapist said it was a common dream, but I've never talked to anyone else about it. When I was in college, I imagined that the wall was school—that monumental thing that was keeping me from seeing the rest of my life. I always hoped that as soon as I was done, I'd be able to see what was on the other side of the wall."

"But you couldn't?"

She shook her head. "Not nearly as much as I hoped. I dreamt just a couple of weeks ago, right after graduation, that I was standing on top of the wall, but I couldn't see very far."

"Yeah," Genevieve said, looking thoughtful. "Yeah, me neither. In one version of my dream, I'm somehow standing on top of the wall and all I can see is…" She faded out.

"It wasn't by any chance a beautiful courtyard and then another wall about forty feet away?" Holly asked.

Genevieve lifted the ice pack off her forehead and looked at Holly incredulously. "Yes, that's exactly what I saw, but it also looked like there was a series of walls that continued on and on until the horizon."

Holly shook her head. "This is crazy. That's exactly the way I remember it. What do you think it means?"

"I wish I knew. I used to wonder if maybe each of the walls represented a different decade of my life."

"Not anymore?"

Genevieve shook her head. "I'll be thirty soon, and I don't think I'm any closer to knowing what's on the other side of the second wall than I did when I stood on top of the first one. I've wondered recently if maybe it has less to do with time and more with who I am and what I want out of life."

"What do you mean?" Holly asked.

Genevieve laughed at herself. "I've never talked about this with anybody, and I've never considered myself an interpreter of dreams. But lately I've wondered if it has something to do with satisfaction and my desire to see something else—maybe something more."

Holly nodded slowly. "I like that. Metaphorically speaking, I know some people who seem to be content with hanging out all their life in that courtyard just beyond the first wall. And then there are others who seem to be insatiably curious about all that lies beyond the second wall. My mom was the kind of person who always wanted to know what was beyond the courtyard. I guess it must have rubbed off on me."

"Is that why you're here? Is that why you came to the farm this summer?"

Holly nodded. "Mom always felt like she was limited, like she could only go so far, like there was more to life than she'd been able to experience—more joy and hope and adventure."

"Yeah, okay, but let the me play the devil's advocate and suggest that there's also the potential for more frustration, failure, and disappointment," said Genevieve.

"Sure. That's the real decision, right? Do you move forward into the unknown or stay in the courtyard where you're comfortable? Every time I have the dream, I wake up worrying that I'm so curious about what's on the other side of the wall that I may not be fully enjoying the wonders of the courtyard. Does that make sense?"

Genevieve nodded. "So, what's your answer?"

"I have no idea. I like the idea of progress—of life getting better and better. That's the way my mom lived her life, but in the end, it felt like she was still discontented."

"Why do you think that is?"

"That's easy. She never found the love she was hoping for. She never married. Marriage was one of the biggest hopes of her life, and even on her deathbed, the fact that she'd never done it was one of her biggest disappointments. That was my mother's dying wish for me: that I'd find a happiness even greater than hers—that I'd find love and marriage and family."

"That's a lot of pressure—a lot to wish for. But wasn't she happy to have found some of that? I mean, adopting you must have brought her a whole bunch of happiness, right?"

"She often said that having me gave her life great meaning, but she admitted it was only a Band-Aid. Mom always believed there was more happiness than she'd been able to find—more satisfaction that she'd missed out on by not having a man in her life."

"Ugh! I don't know if I like that," Genevieve admitted.

"Which part?"

"The implication that her life was somehow less than complete without a man in it. I just don't know if that's true. We're more than that. I don't feel like I need a man to make me happy."

Holly nodded. "I get that, but isn't there a part of you that wants to be a mother?"

"Pfff," she said, lying back on her pillow and covering her eyes with the ice pack. "I guess I'd be lying if I said there wasn't some piece of me secretly hoping that kids are in my future, but I'm definitely not ready for any of that, especially not if it means being married to a stupid man."

Holly laughed. "Do you really think you'd marry a stupid man?"

"Are there any other options?" Genevieve asked with a smile. "It seems like most guys are selfish, ignorant, and self-obsessed."

"Okay…but couldn't they say the same thing about us?"

Genevieve thought for a moment before shaking her head and sighing. "How do any two people ever get married? It's kind of a miracle, right? To find two people who are either blind enough or dumb enough to believe life can somehow be better if they unite their selfishness and ignorance and make a go of it? It just seems so…unintelligible."

"And yet there are twelve of us here who want to believe it's possible to find a greater degree of happiness in marriage than in remaining single for the rest of our lives. It's crazy, right? It's almost like there's something in us—like whatever it is in other animals that gets triggered at some point and causes them to fly to the other side of the world or swim thousands of miles for love. I guess it's kind of like…hanging out in that courtyard. It's like I'm looking up at the wall and thinking, 'Life is pretty good here, but what if it's even better on the other side?' It's like I can choose to be happy and content as a successful, independent woman, or I can bet the farm and climb over the next wall to marriage and family."

"Okay, but if you're happy and content as a single person, why would you put it all on the line only to find out the garden on the other side is full of weeds and thorny brambles?"

Holly cracked a smile. "Is that why you're still single?"

"No! Yes! I don't know." Genevieve lifted the ice pack from her eyes, looking confused. "Don't get me wrong; men can be helpful and nice to have around sometimes, but it feels so…what's the word? Old-fashioned…cliché…*prehistoric* to suggest that the life of a woman can't be truly complete if she's not married to a man. I'm sorry, but I've just never really known a man who I believe could make my life better. I like my independence. I like the simplicity of it," she said as she had so many times before. But it felt different this time, almost empty and insincere. " If I ever decide to get married," she continued, "it's going to have to be a big improvement on what I've got now, and that's tough to compete with. Marriage seems messy and complicated and potentially disastrous."

"Okay, but couldn't it also be beautiful and fulfilling and satisfying? Isn't that hope what brought us all here to the farm?"

Genevieve didn't answer, knowing that her own true reasons for being here were quite different from Holly's reasons. "I don't know," she muttered, putting the soggy ice pack back on her face before she could say more than she knew she should. But when she closed her eyes, she imagined herself in the garden courtyard where her dreams had taken her so many times over the past decade. Before her stood the second wall, tall and imposing. And though she had tried so hard to find contentment in the garden, she felt an undeniable sense of curiosity about what was on the other side of the wall. Could it be that her aversion to the entanglements of love and marriage was keeping her from unfathomable joys on the other side? Was she somehow limiting herself and her potential happiness? Or was it more a case of protecting herself from the nightmares she'd witnessed other people experience? Whatever it was, she knew that even after witnessing those nightmare marriages, she still had some unreliable and perhaps unwelcome particle of hope that had kept her from being satisfied and content with her current life.

"Do you think it's possible to come back to the safety and comfort of the courtyard after you've climbed over the next wall?" Holly asked, interrupting Genevieve's thoughts.

"I'm not sure," she said after a moment of thought. "But it doesn't seem likely. Would you want to go back to the way things were before college?"

Holly laughed. "Absolutely not."

"Yeah, me neither. We've seen too much that's way better."

"So, do you think it's safe to assume that there's better things beyond *each* of the walls out there?"

Genevieve moved the ice pack onto her forehead so she could see Holly. "If we answered that question based solely on the happiness of Ruby and Pops, we'd have to at least guess that there are, right?"

"Even with cancer and the reality that Pops is going to be alone?" Holly asked.

"Yeah," Genevieve said after another moment of thought. "I can't really imagine what Pops is feeling, but wouldn't it be better to have someone to share that burden and sorrow with?"

"Yeah, but it's so sad. I can't even imagine spending fifty-seven years loving someone and then have to watch them fade away and die."

"Are you saying it's better to be single for fifty-seven years and then die alone?" Genevieve asked.

"Well, no. That sounds at least equally unpleasant. I know we don't get to choose the details, but…I just wish there was a way of securing a bright future full of mutual love and support without feeling completely vulnerable and exposed."

"Yeah," Genevieve said with a little laugh. "If you could figure that out and package it as a dietary supplement, you'd be a bazillionaire."

Holly nodded. "Yeah, I guess that's why we're all here, right?"

"Because we're looking for a supplement that will cure all our fears and inhibitions?" Genevieve joked.

"More or less."

"I don't mean to be a pessimistic cynic, but I'm pretty sure that pill doesn't exist."

"I'm not so sure it doesn't," Holly countered.

Genevieve looked to see if Holly was joking. "Are you saying you've discovered the miracle cure for all of life's ills?"

"Isn't it love? Or at least isn't that what love's supposed to be?"

Genevieve thought on it for a moment. She knew Holly was right. That is what love was *supposed* to be, at least in its purest form. But when had she ever witnessed love in its purest form? Sure, she had caught fading glimpses of real examples of warmth and tenderness from time to time. And some movies seemed to provide a picture of an ideal sort of love that felt less selfish than what reality provided. But those same Hollywood stars who appeared in these appealing films were often featured on the covers of the tabloids under devastating captions that revealed treachery and disillusionment. How could the light and hope of love be true if it were followed so closely by darkness?

Holly and Genevieve discussed their observations for some time, minutes turning into hours, with Holly occasionally switching out Genevieve's ice pack. Genevieve was surprised to find that at the tender age of twenty-two, Holly seemed to have developed a more mature and thoughtful understanding of love than she herself had, even with her nearly eight additional years of life and experience. Genevieve wondered if her slowness in coming to a better understanding of the topic might have been aggravated by her attitudes and the cynicism she'd developed over the past decade. It didn't take long for her to recognize that her work for the magazine had fed that cynicism. The rich and famous people she had interviewed and rubbed shoulders with over the years may have bigger homes and bank accounts than Holly ever would, but Genevieve recognized that most of them also lacked the clarity and awareness that Holly so simply and authentically expressed. Finding herself coveting the uncomplicated understanding of love that Holly espoused, Genevieve recognized that the edge of her own cynicism was beginning to melt away. And as she allowed her cynicism to fade, she was surprised by the rising tide of hope, optimism, and meekness that came lapping at the edges of her body, as ocean water had when she'd lain on inflatable floats many a calm summer's day at the beach.

CHAPTER 48

Discovery After Dark

*And into the forest I go,
to lose my mind and find my soul.*
—John Muir

The gentle sound of Holly's voice along with the peace that accompanied her words were so soothing that Genevieve faded off to sleep. And when she woke sometime later, she was alone. She pulled the dishtowel from eyes to find that the afternoon had faded into evening; the ice pack had melted into a dampness that encircled her head, neck, and shoulders.

As she lay there, looking up through the skylight, she was intrigued by a strange sense that something big had changed since she had closed her eyes. She ran her hands over the farm duds she was wearing and was surprised at how comfortable they felt, worn and faded by who knew how many women and summer suns. But there was something more, something deeper than her clothes. As she struggled to understand what it was, she realized that for the first time since coming to the farm, she did not feel even a hint of anger at the five months she was going to be held here against her will. Somehow, in the drowsiness of the afternoon's warm air, the last of her resistance had slipped out of her hands, head, and heart. But to her surprise, she felt no sense of loss. In the place of her resistance was something she couldn't quite understand. It was almost a relief that she wouldn't have to go back to her job, her apartment, and her life in New York for almost five more months! There was something here that she wanted—something she needed. And that need filled her with a strange and unexplainable sense of urgency.

She got off her bed and began walking to the bathroom but quickly had to stop, feeling dizzy. She sat down for a moment in a chair until the dizziness subsided. Then she walked the rest of the way to the sink. She barely recognized herself in the mirror. Her eyes were puffy, and it was already clear that despite the ice pack, she was not going to avoid two black eyes. She rinsed her face with cold water, stopping at the delicate point of contact where her forehead and nose met. A tender knot was tangible just beneath the surface of her skin, but she laughed to herself as she remembered the unfortunate connection of two thick heads. She gingerly dried her face and more thoroughly examined her reflection in the mirror, looking deeply into her own bloodshot eyes. She smiled at herself. Though her nose was swollen, it was still straight. And it looked as though gravity had taken hold of the purple eye shadow she had once worn in junior high and pulled it down to the swollen half-moons that hung under her eyes. It wasn't pretty, but she smiled again, grateful the cheeky ram hadn't broken her nose. And she smiled to herself again when she remembered that though her wounds were more visible, Spencer's were undoubtedly more painful.

At the front door of the bunkhouse, she slipped on her muckers. She had no idea what time it was, but she knew the group would eventually be getting hungry. She made her way to the big house, noticing that the day's laundry had already been pulled down and the chickens had been fed. Except for the sounds of animals and nature, the farm was quiet and still. She found Ephraim and Ruby in the kitchen and hurriedly jumped in, wanting to help.

"I'm sorry I'm late," she said, picking up a dishrag to dry a large ceramic bowl.

"We didn't expect to see you until breakfast," Ruby said, looking up from a big copper pot. "The kids loved your idea for raclette. It's a good thing Ephraim held a few potatoes back for you and Spencer, or they'd all have been eaten," she said, nodding at two plates on the island that had been covered with aluminum foil.

"Wait, dinner's over?"

Ruby laughed. "It's nearly eight. Dinner ended at least a half hour ago. I sent the rest of the family out to journal while we straightened things up in here."

"I'm sorry. I didn't mean to shirk my duties. How can I help?"

Ruby looked at Genevieve for a moment as if she were trying to determine how sincere she really was. When she seemed satisfied, she flicked Ephraim on the backside with her towel as he stood at the sink scrubbing the last of the trays. "Why don't you let Genevieve finish up?"

"I'm good. I'm almost done."

"I insist. Go get your journal and find a quiet place somewhere," Ruby said. "You have to take advantage of an evening like this one."

Ephraim dried his hands quickly and disappeared after looking quickly into Genevieve's swollen face.

Genevieve slipped into his place, applying elbow grease to the broiled cheese on the cookie sheet.

"How are you feeling, dear?" Ruby asked.

"A little foggy," she said, turning to look over her shoulder. "I'm not sure if that's from just waking up or if that stupid ram rattled my brain."

Ruby laughed. "Well, if it's any consolation, Carlos finally met his match. It took five of us to hold him down, but he's as naked as the rest of them now. He's back to grazing peacefully on the grass in the orchard. No one has to get that close to him again until next spring."

Genevieve nodded slowly as she remembered that Ruby's days on the farm were numbered. She wondered if Ruby would live long enough to witness the next shearing.

"So tell me," Ruby said, interrupting her thoughts, "how's your article coming?"

"Umm, it's not going so well, to be honest," Genevieve said humbly.

"Well, at least you can't say that your time here hasn't been exciting. Accidents are part of working on the farm, but you, my friend, have certainly had more than your share of excitement. In fact, you seem to be an excitement magnet."

Genevieve didn't know whether to laugh or cry. "It's been a rough couple of weeks."

"Yeah, and it's only been ten days," Ruby said, standing next to her at the sink and draping her arm over Genevieve's shoulder. "You're doing great. That's what I told Mrs. Galiveto. I said you're really starting to get the hang of things and are tackling your challenges with gusto. She seemed pleased."

"You spoke to Julia?" Genevieve asked, feeling a sudden pang of stress.

"Yes, just this afternoon?"

"What? Why?"

Ruby shrugged. "She called me. I didn't expect to hear from her for another couple of weeks, but she was just checking in. She seemed pleased to hear that you were doing well. I decided I wouldn't tell her about you getting headbutted by a sheep, but it seems it may be difficult to keep her from finding out."

"What do you mean?"

"She said one of her best photographers will be here tomorrow morning sometime to spend the day taking pictures of the farm."

"And you're going to let him?"

"Of course. It's part of the contract I signed with Mrs. Galiveto. We knew it was going to happen, we just didn't know when."

"Did she say who she was sending?"

"Yes. O'Brien Something-or-Other. Mrs. Galiveto said you two have rubbed shoulders before."

Genevieve let out a long, belabored breath. "Oh no. Patrick O'Brien?"

"Yeah, that's it. She said he'll be on his way back from a photo shoot in San Diego and was hoping to come a few weeks earlier than expected so he could move up some other plans. I didn't see how that would be a problem, but judging from your response, maybe it is."

Genevieve closed her eyes and shook her head. "Is there any place I can hide?"

"Uh, this is a two-hundred-acre farm. There are plenty of places to hide, but why do you ask?"

"Well, one, he's a beautiful man who's always been a bit of a distraction. I'm sure he'd blow my cover. And two, it's hard to hide two black eyes. Showing up in the pages of the magazine looking like a prizefighting country bumpkin will undoubtedly kill my social media status."

"Well, ding, dang, dong! I guess didn't consider any of that when I said yes. What are we going to do?"

"Maybe you could send me to Pittsburgh on an errand or something?"

Ruby nodded, looking distracted. "Or the farm stand. We were planning on opening tomorrow anyway. You could be gone all day without drawing unnecessary attention. I should have thought of that before."

"Are you sure Pittsburgh wouldn't be a better idea?" she asked hopefully.

Ruby laughed. "It's been at least a decade since the pickup truck has made it all the way to Pittsburgh. It might make it there, but definitely not back. And we'd be in world of hurt without the truck. We'll just assign you to be the first one to open the farm stand. Who would you like to work with tomorrow?"

"I have a choice?" she asked, looking surprised.

"Actually, it would probably make the most sense to send Spencer with you since I'm sure he won't be much good here on the farm. The poor boy can hardly walk. It's funny how things work out sometimes. The karma fairies tend to catch up with us when we least expect it. I know it's not kind, but I can't help but feel like what happened today was an ingenious stroke of poetic justice for him ditching you on Sunday."

Genevieve laughed out loud, and Ruby was quick to follow, both of them welcoming the comic relief into a relationship that had been short of levity from the beginning. The laughter continued for some time as they attempted to make plans for the morning. Though Genevieve had harbored no strong feelings of ill will toward Spencer, she admitted that Sunday's events had served as a clear message that good looks and a healthy income could not override an unchecked sports addiction and a profusion of self-centered behavior. She confessed he wasn't the first man she'd rubbed shoulders with who'd exhibited such unwelcome and unbecoming behaviors, but she acknowledged that the clear country air had opened her mind to the reality that such a man was not for her.

Wisdom, Ruby explained, often comes to those who are willing to open their hearts and minds and deeply breathe the country air. She expressed optimism that Spencer, if he were to try it, might come to the conclusion that his addictions and behavior would need to be altered in order to find the woman he was hoping for. And she admitted that in her many decades of matchmaking, she had never once met a camper who'd arrived at the farm fully ready for marriage. Instead, every one of the nearly seven hundred men and women who'd worked their way through a summer on the farm had eventually come to the same conclusion—that personal selfishness and pride were the biggest roadblocks to not only finding the spouse of their dreams but also to them becoming the spouse of someone else's dreams.

Genevieve and Ruby finished their plans for Genevieve and Spencer to tend the farm stand, where any unwanted interaction with the staff photographer could be avoided. With the rest of the campers enjoying an evening of personal time, Ruby asked Genevieve to drop off a plate of food to Spencer, who had been unable to walk to the big house for dinner.

A knock at the men's bunkhouse door was answered with a feeble "Come in." Genevieve pushed the door open but didn't enter, scanning a room that was configured much differently than the women's. Two towers of beds stacked three high stretched above the concrete floor, nearly touching the ceiling. It smelled like a locker room, and the air was musty and dank.

"Are you alive in here?" she asked.

"Barely," he responded, looking over the railing of one of the top bunks. "How are you?"

"Bruised but walking." She looked into the darkened space but stayed at the threshold. "I brought you some dinner."

"Oh, thanks. I'm starving. Can you bring it up?"

Genevieve laughed. "No, I'm pretty sure I can't. I'm afraid of heights. And besides, I'm not supposed to come in here. I'll just leave it here outside the door."

"Wait! I'll come down. I don't want the dog to beat me to it."

She waited and watched as he gingerly threw his leg over the end of the bed and slowly climbed down the stack, crossing the floor with a serious limp.

"None of the guys offered to trade bunks with you until you recovered?"

Spencer shrugged his bare, muscular shoulders. "Matt did, but I won the top bunk in an arm wrestle on our first day, and I'm not about to give it up."

"Even if you're in pain?"

"What doesn't kill you makes you stronger, right?"

"If you say so," she said, handing him his plate. "Ruby asked me to tell you that we'll be working together again tomorrow. We get to open the farm stand, which means we're on chicken duty too, collecting eggs to sell. I guess she figures we'll be useless around here so we might as well be doing something to help the farm, even if it's just sitting around most of the day."

"Wow, that sounds like all sorts of fun. I can't wait," he said sarcastically. "I swear, this summer's gonna kill me."

"If the sheep don't get to you first," Genevieve said, trying not to smile. "I better go. I'll see you in the morning."

Spencer thanked her for the dinner and sat down on the old chair on the small front porch to eat.

As she walked back to the women's bunkhouse, Genevieve was struck by the beauty of the farm as it was bathed in the warm, golden light of evening. Finding the bunkhouse empty, she remembered that Ruby had kicked Ephraim out of the kitchen to enjoy some quiet time with his journal. For the first time since she'd come to the farm, the thought of spending a little time in solitude was appealing. She quickly grabbed her sketchbook and a pen and stood on the bunkhouse's front porch wondering where to go. She considered the bench on the edge of the grainfield where she'd sat with Matt, but she decided instead to explore a different part of the farm. She had a rough idea where the orchard was even though she'd never seen it, and so she wandered off down a path that disappeared over a hill.

At the top of the hill, she saw that the path meandered along a fenced pasture and into a thick grove of tall trees. She was reluctant at first to follow the narrow path into the shady trees, but the birdsong in the grove summoned her on, and she walked quickly over the meandering trail. After a hundred yards or so of heavy shadows, she grateful when the golden light once again bathed the path in front of her. Around another bend, the view opened even wider as the path came to a bench that overlooked a beautiful orchard descending the gradual slope before her. Beyond the orchard, the view continued as the land rolled down to the river and across the valley dotted with farms and woods. She sat down on the bench, feeling a strange sense of awe settle over her. The air was scented with the fading blossoms of the fruit trees, the ground under the waxing canopy littered with white and pink petals.

She guessed that at least two hundred trees grew in those straight rows, their branches reaching toward the sky. She leaned against the back of the bench and looked out onto the landscape, wondering when she had ever seen anything as beautiful as this.

Light glimmered on the river below as it wove its way through the landscape like a silver thread. The world was silent except for the sounds of the birds and the gentle drone of the crickets. In that magical place, she had no thought of the day's events, which would certainly leave her feeling unattractive for several days, if not weeks, to come. She nestled against the back of the bench and felt something uneven on its surface. Turning to see what it was, she saw that the wood had been carved out to embed a small ceramic tile. She remembered the discussion on the front porch just a week earlier, when several of the campers had mentioned seeing tiles like this one on some of the other benches. She rubbed her fingers across the words carved into the clay: *Be still, and know that I am God.* She remembered her discussion with Matt as they'd ascended Harmony Hill after the ordeal on Sunday. *Be still, and know that I am God.* It remained a thought-provoking idea—one she had never considered before coming to the farm.

Genevieve thoughtfully turned back to the view before her, resting her back once again against the tile. So much had changed in the past ten days that nothing seemed the same. The world she knew had somehow gotten both bigger and smaller at the same time. Something was different—more beautiful—more approachable than she'd ever seen before. Had this been there all along? Had she somehow been ignoring all of this beauty, all of this peace, all of this sense of connection? Had she been so busy and self-absorbed that she'd missed it all?

Faith and spirituality had never played a significant role in her life. She had rarely attended church, and never two weeks in a row. And she had never, in all her travels, been to a place that felt so foreign. Here, so far out of her comfort zone, she recognized that she was feeling something different, something bigger, something new and exciting and full of… life and hope and awareness. She wrestled with this for a moment.

Looking down at her journal and pen in her hands, she struggled to imagine words that could be compelling enough to convey the depth and breadth of the beauty that engulfed her. But she knew that no human words in any language could express the contents of her heart right then. Indeed, the only expression that seemed even remotely appropriate was awe. And so she decided to just feel it. She set the journal and pen down on the bench next to her and opened her eyes and heart even wider to all the beauty that surrounded her. And as she did, she was filled with an even greater sense of the mystical.

The golden light waned after some time, and the shadows grew, washing the landscape with shades of blue and gray. The first stars began appearing as the crickets turned up the volume. Genevieve didn't want to leave, but the idea of walking back along the footpath in total darkness sounded even less appealing. Reluctantly she stood, picked up her things, and wandered in the direction of home.

The shadows cast by the grove of trees quickly obscured the path, and she felt reluctant to proceed, unsure of what she might encounter in the darkness. She paused at the edge of the shadows and imagined the reactions of the other campers if they had to call a second search party for her in less than a week. She shook her head, knowing she would have to carry on. She gritted her teeth and took a step into the darkness.

The snap of a twig under her foot sent a shiver down her spine and heightened her sense of fear. When it happened a second time, she picked up the pace. But the pace combined with the darkness did not work in her favor. Before she knew it, she was off the path, her feet crunching through old leaves and soft earth. She reached out her free hand, trying to grope her way, but she soon felt lost, unsure of which direction she should go in the near total darkness. Feeling panicked, she stopped to breathe, her heartbeat sounding in her ears like the galloping of a racehorse. She had to move. She had to get out of here.

After spinning around, frantically looking for the trail, she bolted toward what looked like a clearing in the trees. But she made it only a few paces when her shin hit something hard. She fell to forest floor in pain, her feet entangled in a fallen branch. She was too scared to even curse, and she bounced up as quickly as she could, ignoring the pain in her shin. After another few paces, however, she fell again, this time bruising a knee. Letting out a yelp of pain, she sat down on the ground and tried to calm herself. She knew she wasn't far, probably no more than a ten-minute walk from the bunkhouse, but she knew it was probably too far away for anyone to hear her yell. She'd have to get out of this herself.

Somehow after falling twice, she still had a hold of her journal. She was just about to lift herself off the forest floor when the feel of the journal in her hand caused her to pause. She remembered how a mere thirty minutes before, she had been too filled with awe and wonder to even begin writing. Her whole being had somehow buzzed with the same intensity of that beautiful golden light. But now it was gone, having been replaced with light's unpleasant opposites—darkness and confusion. She wanted out.

She turned quickly from side to side, looking for even the smallest hint of light that could offer hope and direction, but she saw nothing. Nothing, that is, until she looked up. There, hiding among the new spring leaves and branches, was a smattering of stars. Brighter than she remembered stars ever being, the glimmering dots of light felt like hope incarnate. She whispered a silent thank you to the universe as she stood, keeping her eyes on the tiny specks of light. After a minute or so, she looked around again and was surprised that the stars seemed to be reflecting off of something a little closer to the earth. At first she wondered if she'd stared too long at the stars and was seeing them everywhere. Was this a delayed aftereffect of being headbutted by and angry ram? But as the light continued to dance around her, she realized it was something else entirely. Fireflies!

It had been years since she had seen them on the shores of Lake Washington during those summers when she was a child. She remembered the magic of that first night as her father had taken her by the hand out into the yard, where the fireflies' magic was on display like a private miniature fireworks show. Tonight only a dozen or so alternated their short flickers of luminescence, but those tiny flashes offered all the hope Genevieve needed. She pushed on through the leaves and branches of the undergrowth until her feet found the clear, hard-packed dirt of the footpath.

The flashes of light continued, leading her carefully and hopefully along the path. She paused for a moment at the edge of the woods to watch even more fireflies dancing rhythmically in the clearing. She smiled to herself, her sense of awe only heightened by this ongoing display of nature's beauty. As she proceeded trepidatiously up the path, she considered the value of light. In Manhattan, where light was abundant and sometimes even overpowering, she had never much appreciated it. At times it had even been a nuisance, keeping her awake at night. But here on the farm, so far away from the light pollution of the city, light had a different meaning. Even these random and irregular tiny specks of light offered a sense of hope and happiness, and she noticed that her soul rejoiced with each glint from the fireflies or twinkle from the stars. By the time the women's bunkhouse was in view, Genevieve felt a closer connection to both heaven and earth than she'd ever felt before.

CHAPTER 49

Some Fruits of Stillness

Man is lost and is wandering in a jungle where real values have no meaning.
Real values can have meaning to man only when he steps on to the spiritual path,
a path where negative emotions have no use.
—Sai Baba

"What happened to you?" Crystal asked as Genevieve walked through the door of the bunkhouse. All eyes were on her, and the chatter of women's voices that she'd heard from a distance fell silent.

"Oh my gosh, are you okay?" Susan asked, getting up off her bed and rushing toward her.

In a moment, the women were gathered around Genevieve, asking her questions all at once as they pulled leaves and grass from her hair and clothes. When she didn't understand their concern, they whisked her into the bathroom to have a look in the mirror above the sink. She laughed at herself despite the fearsome picture before her. Her eyes were still swollen, and the coloring under her eyes had only grown darker. But now, after tripping around in the woods, her face was also smeared with dirt and mud. Her sweatshirt was also dirty, dark mud streaking across her chest. A clump of burrs hung from her elbow, and another clump clung to her socks. Her hands were also filthy, as was her right knee. Holly pointed out that a stream of dried blood ran from a dark wound on Genevieve's left shin down into her sock. And the cutoffs she was wearing were soiled, especially the seat. But to everyone's amazement, Genevieve was comforting everyone else, assuring them that she was fine—despite looking like she'd been hit by a Mack truck and dragged for miles.

After showering quickly in the tepid water, Genevieve found the women gathered together as if they were waiting for either an explanation or a bedtime story. As she looked into each of their worried faces, she once again assured them that she was fine, happy, and—though tired and a little sore—feeling better about life than she had in some time.

When it was obvious that they were still looking for an explanation, Genevieve's bedtime story began with her leading a quick barefoot excursion to the fields on the east side of the bunkhouse, where the fireflies were still dancing under the star-filled sky. For some of the women, this was the first time they'd seen fireflies, and they were in no hurry to return to the bunkhouse—until they noticed that the farm's mosquitos were also active. Like young girls at a slumber party, they raced back to the bunkhouse in their colorful pajamas and climbed into their beds, giddy and hyper.

While the women settled down and Genevieve turned out the lights were turned out, she told them about her evening. As she spoke, some of them brought up their experiences with the journaling Ruby had encouraged them to do. Soon everyone chimed in, talking about their time alone in the evening's beauty. They'd each found a quiet place to enjoy the peaceful, warm evening. They each expressed joy in the beauty they'd found. With the turn in the conversation from solo storytelling to collective sharing, it was easy for Genevieve to stop her own account before describing the details of the mystical things she'd experienced. Instead, she had them all in stitches when she recounted her walk home through the dark, possibly haunted, woods; her straying from the path; and her stumbling around as she groped her way home by the dim light of the stars and the playful encouragement of the fireflies.

The laughter and conversation faded slowly as four of the women drifted off to sleep one by one. Soon only Genevieve and Susan remained alert enough to converse in full sentences.

"I'm curious about something you said earlier," Susan said softly.

"About what?" Genevieve whispered back.

Susan paused before speaking again, and when she did speak, her voice was even quieter than before. "I guess I'm actually more curious about something you didn't say."

"Okay," Genevieve said, intrigued by where Susan was going.

Again Susan paused for a long time. "Did you…did you happen to… feel something tonight?"

Genevieve took a deep breath. "Are you asking if I felt something… mystical?" she asked, turning to face Susan in the next bed.

"Yes," Susan whispered.

"I think I did."

Susan, who'd been staring up at the stars through the skylight, turned to face Genevieve. "Do you think it might be…God?" she asked after another long silence.

"I…yeah, I guess it must have been something like that. You?"

Susan turned her head and looked back up into the stars. "I've been trying to decide all night. I definitely felt something."

"Go on," Genevieve said, encouraging her.

"What if there's a God?"

"What if there is?" Genevieve repeated.

"Well, if there is, then maybe a lot of things are different, aren't they?"

"Like what?"

"Like...pretty much everything, right? I mean, if there's a God, what we do, how we think, the way we treat people, the way we live and speak and...breathe, it all has a bigger purpose and meaning, doesn't it?"

"I've never thought about it like that, but, yeah, I guess it does. Is that a problem for you?"

"I don't know. I don't remember ever thinking about God before my uncle abused me. But after it happened, I had a really hard time imagining that somewhere there was a just, loving god figure who allowed dark things like sexual abuse to take place. I've spent most of my life being angry and hurt about that. I've been through years of therapy, trying to move past it. And then this happened tonight, and it's kind of turned everything on its head."

"What happened tonight?"

Susan took a deep breath, obviously reluctant to share.

Genevieve waited patiently, and a thought came to her. Maybe it would be easier for Susan to open the door a little wider if she could somehow feel less vulnerable. "Did it feel like...love?" Genevieve whispered.

Susan nodded, and even in the faint light of the bunkhouse, Genevieve could see that Susan's cheek was wet.

Susan wiped her face before she spoke again. "I didn't go looking for this. I didn't even know I wanted it. I was just minding my own business, writing in my journal, and it felt like it just dropped on top of me like...like the biggest, warmest patchwork quilt you could imagine."

Genevieve smiled. "I think I might know what you mean. As a child, I remember believing in God. I'm not sure if I ever really stopped or if I just stopped...caring."

Susan shook her head and turned over to face Genevieve. "What if he...she...what if God has been there the whole time and we've just been ignoring him—or her?"

"What if?" Genevieve asked, encouraging Susan to continue.

Susan shook her head. "I've been a skeptic for as long as I can remember. I never went so far as to claim to be an atheist, but I've certainly been agnostic…and apathetic. I just didn't care enough to…care. What if I've just been blind to it? What if…oh my God! What if there's something there just waiting for me to turn around and…what? Feel? Look? Open myself to the possibility? I've been going over this all night, and I just can't get past that feeling. It was just so…"

Genevieve waited. Susan wiped another tear from her face and shook her head.

"There's something about this farm…" Susan said, trailing off again. "I've felt it from the beginning; actually from the moment Pops stepped out of his pickup truck down at the bus station and welcomed us here with his big, hearty…Pops."

Genevieve nodded.

"And then walking down the drive that first day…oh my gosh! It just hit me over the head that something big was happening here." Her voice cracked at the last few words, and she wiped away another tear. "I wasn't sure then if I really wanted to know what it was. But now I feel it drawing me in, and it doesn't scare me anymore. It's crazy, but I feel like I'm finally where I'm supposed to be, like this is…home." She leaned up on her elbow. "Genevieve, I'm a freaking attorney. I bill out at over four hundred bucks an hour. I thought it would really bother me to take five months off, knowing how much that would cost me. But the crazy thing is, somehow I feel like my time is even more valuable *here*, where I'm pretending like I know how to shear sheep and plant potatoes. What the hell's happening to me?"

Genevieve smiled. "I'm not sure."

"But you know what I mean, right?"

"Yes," Genevieve admitted after a thoughtful moment. "I like to think of myself as smart and observant, but there's definitely something happening here that I don't understand. It's like some crazy bit of magic that's so over-the-top complicated that I can't even guess how the trick is being played."

"You're not saying you think Ruby and Pops are some sort of dark magicians, are you?"

"No...more like *light* magicians, if there is such a thing. But I'm not sure it's them alone."

"What do you mean?"

"You said it. I think it's the farm. It's like it's all around us—two hundred acres of some kind of magic."

Susan nodded. "But it's not just the farm."

"No?"

"The farm's just the beginning. It's the town, too. And the church. It's like this whole county is somehow on an elevated plane. I overheard a couple of tourists talking in the courtyard after church on Sunday. They were talking about looking for a place to buy so they could move here. It was almost like they'd discovered a utopia, and now that they knew such a place exists, they were never going to be happy with wherever they came from. I totally understood what they were talking about. I thought I had it pretty good in Raleigh. A nice home in a beautiful neighborhood. A good-paying job. I'm not sure what's gotten into me. I mean, we've been here...what? Ten days? And I'm ready to throw my old life away and reinvent myself as a Niederbippian when we finish up at the end of the summer—maybe open a cute little boutique down on the main street and live happily ever after. What the hell's wrong with me?"

Genevieve laughed quietly, not wanting to wake the others. "What's stopping you from doing just that?"

"Pfff. Reality? Responsibility? I spent three miserable years in law school, for crying out loud! I just paid off my student loans a couple of years ago. I can't just give that all up and fall off the map."

"Yeah, it sounds good for a minute, but that would be completely bonkers, right?"

"One hundred freakin' percent! I know that, but then I go sit on one of those benches and start thinking and dreaming—and all of a sudden, my tidy little world blows up with unlimited possibilities. It's like all the fear that's kept me living this boring, predictable life disappears and I think I can do anything, like I have no limits. It's maddening."

"But isn't it also liberating?"

"Sure, but I have no idea what to do with that much freedom and possibility. It feels like...it sounds silly, but it feels like I all of a sudden sprouted wings and can do anything, fly anywhere, be whatever the heck I want to be."

"That sounds pretty good. What's the problem?"

"The problem is, life doesn't work that way. Not for me. We're supposed to be responsible and practical. Pay our debts; put in our time; and then, if we're lucky and the stock market does everything it's supposed to do, we get to retire at sixty-five and spend the rest of our lives finally being happy and doing whatever the hell we want to do. That's twenty-nine years away for me! Twenty-nine freakin' years! That's almost as long as I've already lived! I didn't know I was signing up for this kind of torture when I went to school. I wanted to make to a difference in the world. I wanted to travel and find romance and eventually have a family. I wanted to be a mom and spend time with my kids at the park and throw fun birthday parties. I wanted to provide them with a home where they could laugh and learn and dream. But I'm not doing any of that. Instead, I'm trying to climb some crazy ladder, trying to make partner, making rich people richer, and working my freakin' brains out on this damn hamster wheel. And at the end of my twelve-hour days, I go home to my big, empty house feeling aimless and broken and exhausted, and I don't know how to get off this crazy train without derailing my whole life!"

"So, why did you come here this summer?"

Susan shook her head. "Because I got in! This was never on my agenda. I applied—totally on a whim—after my girlfriend recommended it. She spent a summer here eight years ago and loved it. She married a really great guy, and they just had their second baby. I really didn't expect to get in. I'm sure you know that hundreds of people apply every year. I knew it was a long shot. But I got the letter, and it just felt...right, I guess. I mean, it makes absolutely no sense that I'm here—maybe it doesn't make sense for any of us. But after only ten freakin' days, it feels like everything I've spent my whole life working for means nothing. Hell, I feel like I've gotten more insight after a couple of hours sitting on one of those damn benches than I have in the last twenty years of pretending I know what I'm doing."

"So…" Genevieve paused, looking for the right words. "Are you glad you came?"

Susan let out a long, exhaustive breath before collapsing back on her pillow. "These have been the best, hardest, most thought-provoking days of my entire life. And they've left me with a mixture of more clarity and confusion than I've ever had. And I'm frustrated that I don't know what to do with all this clarity and the confusion that it brings with it."

"You know you don't have to decide tonight, right? We still have almost five months to figure this out."

"Thank God. I can't even imagine having to go home tomorrow. As much as I'm sorry about Ruby's diagnosis, it would kill me if they decided to just send us all home at the end of the week. I've got so many things to figure out. And a big part of that is trying to understand what's going on here…what I've been feeling. I don't even like feelings! Emotions just get in the way. They're weak and vulnerable and totally unprofessional. I've guarded against them for as long as I can remember." She trailed off, shaking her head.

"But?"

She shook her head again. "But, damn it…there's something bigger going on here! I don't know if I'm ready to admit that I've been experiencing something transcendental, but I've very reluctantly resigned myself to the idea of it. And that changes a lot of things, doesn't it? It's like that quote over the door," she said pointing into the darkness. "I've built my entire house like a godless fortress, and now I'm looking at it and realizing it's really not that great of a house. It has way too many walls where there could be windows and doors."

"Susan, don't be so hard on yourself. You're a beautiful, successful woman. You have a lot to be proud of."

"Maybe, but in so many ways I envy Holly."

"What does she have to do with anything?"

"Are you kidding? She's the smart one. I thought she was going to be too young and naive to get any of this, but she's got a far better grasp on life than I do. I feel like I've wasted the last decade being cynical and apathetic."

"Okay, but hang on. You've got a whole life ahead of you," Genevieve said before she realized she was attempting to comfort herself as much as she was attempting to comfort Susan.

"Yeah, but what would you give to have an extra decade's worth of this kind of understanding? I have fourteen years on Holly—fourteen freakin' years—and I find myself looking at her several times a day, wishing I had half the wisdom she has."

"Okay, but you've got experience. That's at least as good as a little wisdom, isn't it?"

"I'm not so sure that it is anymore. I've paid a lot for that experience. I've paid…fourteen years of my life. And sure, I've learned a hell of a lot, but I certainly wouldn't consider myself as wise as Holly. She seems to have this innate intuition that helps her see things with X-ray vision and avoid all the *experience* I thought was so important. It's made me think a lot about all the time I've wasted trying to shelter my heart from vulnerable situations where, heaven forbid, I might actually *feel* something. It sucks to realize I've been a rebel without a cause and have only been holding myself back."

Genevieve nodded slowly, Susan's words bouncing around in her head as she internalized them. "So, what are you going to do?" she finally asked after wondering to herself how one might proceed from this place of unique understanding.

"I don't know," Susan admitted after a lengthy pause. "But I realized tonight while I sat on that bench by the pond that I've been concentrating so much on the defense that I've never much considered the possibilities of spending more thoughtful time on the offense."

"Hmm," Genevieve uttered almost involuntarily, feeling fatigued.

"What does that mean?"

"Ugh. That thing you said about your house having too many walls instead of windows and doors…maybe that's me too. I've found myself wondering since Sunday if maybe that's the only way we can have a transcendent connection—to open ourselves up to it. Or in my case," she said, laughing softly, "to be compelled to our knees so we can come to a place of humility. Hasn't that been your experience too? You were out of your comfort zone. We're all in a place of new experiences and people and vulnerabilities. Maybe stepping away from comfort is a critical part of the equation."

"I can see that. But what about tonight? What about the benches and those tiles? Do they fit with what you're saying?" Susan asked.

"I don't know, but it seems like they'd have to, right? Why else would there be twelve of those benches scattered around the farm? Isn't that why Ruby and Pops have encouraged us to take advantage of them during free time? How many times has Ruby told you that the writing's on the wall? Every time we turn around, the instructions are right there. Some are more subtle than others, but it's all there, right? *Be still, and know that I am God*. That sounds like instructions if you ask me."

"And don't forget that one over the doorway," Susan said, pointing into the darkness again. "I've read it at least two dozen times as I've passed under it. Do you think it can really be that simple? To let the Lord build your house…or your life…for you?"

"I don't know." Genevieve said with a little laugh. "Does that sound simple to you? Doesn't that mean giving up some control of your life?"

Susan nodded after a minute. "I guess it does, but compared to randomly throwing up walls and trying to slap on shingles without any blueprints. . . I guess that's what most of us do, right? But. . . it just feels like a mess. What if there's a better way?"

"Like what?"

"I don't know…like maybe being open to the idea that there might actually be a plan for our lives. That's what I was thinking about tonight when I sat down on that bench to write in my journal."

"What specifically were you thinking about?"

"Choices. I mean, people are obviously going to make their own choices. But what if there was a better, more informed way of making those choices? What if...what if there was a better design for our lives than just...winging it...hoping for the best. What if there is a God who actually cares what our lives look like? I mean, if there's a God and he—or she—created all of this and put it all in motion, do you think he or she might actually know the potential of what we could become? Do you think there's some blueprint of what this is all supposed to look like?"

"You mean like destiny or...fate?"

"I don't think so," Susan responded after a moment. "Fate and destiny suggest we have only very limited choices, like we're just puppets playing whatever role the puppet master wants. I can't imagine there being much purpose in a life like that. It just feels like...if there is a God who went to all the trouble to create all of this and put it into motion, it would make sense that there is a bigger purpose than just living aimlessly, suffering, and dying. He or she must have had some hope for us, some hope for how we'd use our time and what we'd do with the years between life and death."

"You thought about all of this tonight?" Genevieve asked incredulously.

"Yes and no. If I'm honest, I've been wondering about it for years. It just kind of bubbled up again tonight. I guess I found myself wondering if maybe there's some...*big picture,* for lack of a better term, some grand potential for what life could be. I guess I keep coming back to that quote over the door."

"What about it?"

"Well, speaking metaphorically, of course, what if this house I've been building for the last thirty-six years isn't supposed to look like an impenetrable fortress?"

"Do you feel like it does?"

"Yeah, unfortunately. I'm beginning to realize that I've spent way too much of my time and effort trying to protect myself. In the process, I've pushed a lot of people away. I hate being vulnerable. My therapist says it's common for survivors of abuse to put up walls to protect themselves from getting hurt again, but I'm beginning to recognize that those walls have also been a prison, keeping me from progressing and moving past all of that. After being here and feeling like I can open up, it makes me hopeful that there's something more—something bigger and better than I've allowed myself to believe. It feels like I've been stuck in a very small box and I'm finally able to stretch and dream bigger dreams than I've been able to in years. Tonight as I sat on that bench, both the thought on the tile and that quote over the door kept running through my mind. I've never been very comfortable around anything spiritual, at least not religious. I guess I've had too many well-meaning zealots try to thrust their gods upon me. But it's different here. I don't know… maybe it's because I'm open to it for the first time in my life, or maybe it's because it's just there, like a low-hanging fruit, inviting me to pick it. I want to know what's out there more than I can remember ever wanting to know anything before. If there's a God, what does he or she have to do with me?"

Genevieve nodded, feeling tired but curious. "Have you come up with an answer?" she whispered.

"I'm not sure. What about you? What happened to you tonight?"

"I don't know if I have words. I just sat down and looked out over the valley, and it just kind of happened, almost like I drifted off to sleep."

"But you weren't asleep, were you?"

"No. In fact I felt like I was more conscious and awake than I normally am."

"Yeah. For me, I was just watching the dragonflies doing their acrobatic stunts over the pond, and it was almost like I slipped into a parallel space where all my senses were heightened. And all of a sudden there was…light…almost like it was shining more through me than at me."

"I think I experienced something very similar."

"Do you know what it was?"

"I wasn't sure until just now, but maybe that's what God is, or some portion of him…or her. That's what the tile says, right? *Be still, and know that I am God.* Isn't that what happened to each of us?"

Susan took a deep breath and exhaled fully. "I don't remember ever being anything remotely like *still* before I came here, at least not on purpose."

"No?"

"For sure not. You know how it is. If we're not busy working, most of us are on our phones or answering emails or shopping on Amazon or checking social media. There's never any downtime. I think most of us are afraid of silence."

"You think so?" Genevieve managed through a yawn.

"Absolutely. I'm constantly thinking about billable hours, and if a quiet moment accidentally sneaks into my life, say, at a traffic light or something, I know just how to handle it."

"You reach for your phone?" Genevieve asked knowingly.

"Exactly. What are we so afraid of?"

Susan's question may have struck Genevieve as even more profound had she been more alert. But sleep was tugging at her brain, begging her to give in.

"I never could have imagined myself in a place where I'd be saying this, but I don't miss my phone," Genevieve managed, her eyes closed now.

"Neither do I. I've never been able to make such fast friends out of strangers. I've already shared more with you than I have with some of the friends I've been close to since college."

"Thank you for sharing," Genevieve mumbled as sleep finally overcame her.

CHAPTER 50

Lessons in Free Enterprise

*I am not a product of my circumstances.
I am a product of my decisions.
—Stephen Covey*

It was obvious the next morning that the rest of the campers were easily distracted by the dark blue and black patches of color that had settled quite confidently in the half-moons under Genevieve's eyes. After gathering eggs with Spencer, she went back to the bunkhouse and attempted to conceal the bruises with makeup. But since the sun had tanned her skin considerably over the previous ten days, her base was now the wrong shade and somehow made the bruising look even worse. She was just washing it the foundation off when Crystal surprised her and offered her a straw hat and insisted that she Genevieve borrow her mirrored, aviator-style sunglasses until the bruises subsided. Grateful for Crystal's unprecedented kindness, Genevieve accepted both hat and glasses and was pleased to find that they quickly and efficiently concealed all the conspicuous bruising.

At breakfast, Ruby stood at the end of the table and announced that today the teams would begin taking shifts at the farm stand. She explained that since Genevieve and Spencer had both been maimed by Carlos the ram and would therefore be less helpful on the farm, they would take the first shift at the stand. Interrupting the chatter that followed her announcement, Ruby also alerted the campers, almost as a sidenote, that a photographer would be dropping by sometime during the day to take photos for a story about Ruby and her lifetime accomplishments in the field of matchmaking.

Genevieve was surprised that no one asked questions about the photographer and that none of the women protested about being cosmetically unprepared for pictures. And so without any protest, life moved on. While Pops led the family in gathering up items for the farm stand, Ruby and the kitchen patrol got busy with the day's cooking.

A half hour later, with the pickup bed sparsely loaded with several dozen eggs, six quarts of cream, a few baskets of strawberries, a five-gallon bucket filled with wildflowers, and a few other supplies, Pops, Spencer, and Genevieve crowded into the cab for the drive down Harmony Hill to the freshly painted farm stand. As they drove, Pops explained that the campers who worked the stand generally followed the pickup truck on bicycles so they'd have transportation back to the farm when they sold out of produce. But because Spencer was presumably in no position to ride a bike, Pops said he'd plan on picking them up sometime between four and five o'clock that afternoon.

Eight to nine hours seemed like a very long time to sell what

Genevieve guessed was less than twenty dollars' worth of goods, but she didn't protest, happy to be away from the farm and the threat of Patrick O'Brien's menacing camera lens.

Pops helped them open the shack's doors and prop up the awnings on the three sides. He turned on the switch for the rooftop solar panel that ran the minifridge, suggesting that the cream would fetch a higher price if it were kept cool. The eggs, because they were fresh, would be fine on the counters, as would the berries and the flowers. He reminded them to keep an eye on the cashbox and suggested the day would go faster if they waited until it was actually lunchtime to eat the lunches Ruby had sent with them in the pail. Before returning back to the farm, Pops made suggestions for the best placement of the sandwich-board signs and pointed out the small shelf of books in case they got bored. Then he wished them luck and headed back to the farm to teach the rest of the campers how to make cheese.

"Well, this ought to be interesting," Genevieve said as she took a seat in one of the two creatively webbed lawn chairs.

Spencer laughed. "I'm not sure how you define interesting, but I beg to differ. I'm afraid this might be my definition of hell."

"Hell? Really? A relaxing day in the shade, playing shop? Didn't you ever have a lemonade stand as a kid?"

Spencer rolled his eyes before picking up a strawberry, pulling off the green leafy bits, and popping it into his mouth.

"Hey, you're eating the merchandise."

"You got a problem with that?" he challenged.

"Yeah. We're supposed to sell those. That's how we support the farm, right?"

He shrugged. "What's the point? Ruby will be dead in a few months, and I'm sure Pops will probably sell the farm and move to Florida. I don't know why they don't just send us home."

Genevieve felt her face and neck grow hot. "You're ready to just write all of this off and be done?"

"Like I said, what's the point?"

"Well, for me the point is that Ruby and Pops are still putting in a full effort. I feel like we should do the same."

"Oh, give it up! There's no way we're going to get the full experience this summer. They're just going through the motions because they don't have any other options. This is already way less than I expected."

"What did you expect?"

"More than this," he said, kicking the second lawn chair to the side before taking a seat in it. "I don't know why I signed up for this. It's been a total disaster."

"Wow!" Genevieve responded, unsure of what else to say.

"Oh, give me a break. You don't like it here any more than I do. You basically told me so yourself."

"Yeah, well, things have changed for me."

"Oh really?" he asked dubiously, laughing.

"Yeah. They have. It's definitely not how I expected to spend the summer, but I feel like my eyes and heart are open to this being a good experience."

"Bah! What about being bored? What about needing a beer? I don't know if you noticed, but things haven't gotten any more exciting here. And the closest beer is still almost twenty miles away—and now off-limits, thanks to you."

"Thanks to me?" She couldn't believe what she was hearing.

Spencer shook his head, looking like he was sorry he'd opened his mouth.

Genevieve wasn't ready to let him off the hook. "What's the hell is that supposed to mean? You ditched me on Sunday. I could have died, and no one would've known where to even begin looking for my body. I'm sorry to make you late to your first pitch, but you ditched me for a *game*—a *baseball* game, nonetheless. You really should get a life!"

"Oh, that's rich," he responded, any regret he felt for snapping at her vanishing. "If you haven't heard, sports is my life, or it was until I ended up in purgatory. I don't even know who I am anymore. I've got absolutely no way to even catch the highlights. I'm grounded like a teenager thanks to our little incident on Sunday, and now I can't even sit down without feeling like I got punched in the gut. I may not even be able to have kids."

"Then Carlos has done the world a great favor," Genevieve responded, her old self coming quickly to the surface. "The world would be better if self-centered people like you weren't allowed to breed."

"This is bull." He stood up quickly and walked out the front door, fuming mad. Genevieve was sure she would have done the same if he hadn't. She'd been around her share of arrogant men before, but his level of selfishness was astonishing. Spencer was a handsome, successful, passionate man, but under that thin veneer was a really big jerk. She watched as he crossed the highway and disappeared down the banks of the river.

"Good riddance," she muttered, still fuming that he'd been so contrite in front of everyone the day before but had flipped so completely when it was just them. Upset and disappointed, she looked at the books lined up on the shelf, hoping to find a distraction. They were mostly paperbacks that looked like they'd been read and reread by at least thirty years' worth of campers. She ran her fingers over them as she read their titles, pulling out a copy of Henry David Thoreau's *Walden*. She'd of course heard of the book but had never read it before. She set it aside for later when she'd run out of other things to do. She busied herself setting up the shop, assembling the craft-colored berry boxes and stowing the egg cartons on a shelf under the counter.

Traffic on the highway was very light, and after only a half hour, Genevieve found herself feeling bored. She had hoped that Spencer would return to put out the sandwich boards, but there didn't seem to be any sign of him. She considered crossing the highway so she could have a better view of the banks and see where he might have gone and what he was doing, but she quickly decided she really didn't care. She didn't need him or his arrogant attitude. She could handle this herself.

The sandwich boards were heavy, and despite the fresh coat of paint, the weathered wood was still rough. She did her best to handle the boards carefully, but she ended up with three slivers in her hands from the first sign and another two from the second. She had pulled out one of the slivers with her teeth and was working on a second when the sound of gravel under tires alerted her to the first customer of the morning. She looked up, smiling, trying to be cheerful. The driver's-side door of the white Land Rover opened after a moment, and a tall, handsome, *familiar* man stepped out carrying a map. Without warning, Genevieve began to sweat. In spite of her best efforts to avoid him, here he was, standing right in front of her: Patrick O'Brien.

It had been over two years since her first real encounter with Patrick, though she had admired him and his work since she'd become aware of him shortly after taking the job at the magazine. He was smart and dedicated to his craft, and his work showed it, often landing on the magazine's cover. She had seen for herself that models always seemed to enjoy working with him, and she'd witnessed that his easygoing nature and quick humor made him a magnet at after-parties and gatherings, where he was always surrounded by a crowd. But Genevieve was surprised to see, as he approached the shack, that in this setting he appeared to be anything but confident.

"Can you tell me—" he began. But those were the only words that made it out of his mouth before his forehead made contact with the edge of the wooden awning, causing him to drop everything in his hands.

"Son of a…" he said, biting his tongue and as he bent over to pick up his things, rubbing his noggin with his free hand.

"Ohhh! Are you okay!?" Genevieve responded quickly, leaning awkwardly over the counter while also trying to keep her distance.

"Ugh, it's already been one of those days," he muttered, gathering up his things from the gravel and standing up, one hand remaining on his forehead. "I feel like I've been driving around in circles since I got to Neiderbopp, trying to make sense of this stupid map. Can you believe there's no cell signal here?" He turned his phone over in his hand and shook his head. "And as luck would have it, I just cracked the damn screen."

"Oooh, sorry. But, yeah, it wouldn't work here anyway. You'd have to have a satellite phone to have any connection out here. We're farther off the beaten path than you might think."

He shook his head, looking down at the ruined screen. "I had no idea that places like this still exist, especially in America. It feels so primitive. How do people live around here?"

Genevieve grimaced, remembering her own first impressions of the town and its environs. "Well, it's not so bad, I…" But she caught herself, remembering that this was the man she was trying to avoid. No need to prolong the conversation and give him time to catch on to her identity behind the hat and sunglasses. "We get along okay. Is there something I can help you with?"

Looking up from his busted phone, he suddenly seemed to remember why he'd gotten out of his car in the first place. He approached the counter, ducking suspiciously as he passed under the awning. "I thought the guys at the rental agency were being a little dramatic, but maybe this place really is cursed."

"Cursed?"

"Yeah, well," he said, holding up his phone as if he were presenting evidence. He smiled a crooked smile, and Genevieve couldn't help but smile back, especially when she noticed an ugly, green goose egg protruding from his forehead. "Apparently they were just up here a week ago picking up a nearly identical Rover that some dim-witted chick filled up with gasoline instead of diesel and then ditched. Sounded like a real mess, having to rebuild the engine and everything," he said, gingerly touching his goose egg. "Anyway, I'm sorry to bother you with boring details," he said, looking down at the map. "I know I've gotta be close, but I can't find what I'm looking for."

"Well, maybe I can help," she responded, picking up the map and pretending she knew what she was doing.

"I'm looking for…" He paused to look down at a scratch pad that looked like it had been taken from a hotel. "Harmony Hill and a…Ruby and Lorenzo Swa-rov-ski."

"Oh yeah, the Swarovskis," she replied, playing along and handing the map back to him. "If you're coming from Niederbipp you just missed the turnoff. It's back up the road about a hundred yards. The Swarovskis live up on the top of Harmony Hill. You can't miss it. Their drive is just across from the phone booth."

"Phone booth?" he responded with a charming smile. "Where the hell am I? I haven't seen a phone booth in at least a decade."

"Yeah, well, that one's pretty special. It's supposed to be on the list of the most beautiful phone booths in America."

Patrick O'Brien smiled and nodded, looking at Genevieve a little closer before looking around and remembering he was at a produce stand. "Uh, what are you selling today?" he asked, looking around at the nearly empty counters.

"Um, well, it's still a little early in the season, but we have strawberries and some fresh cream and some eggs."

"Oh, well, uh…how about some of those strawberries?"

"You'd like to buy some?"

"Well sure, if they're for sale."

"Uh, yeah, they're for sale. How many would you like?"

"I don't know. How much are they?"

"Um," Genevieve responded, feeling stupid that she didn't know. "Uh, they're five dollars for a little box like this," she said holding up one of the small cardboard boxes she had assembled earlier.

"Wow, that sounds like a lot for strawberries!"

"Does it? I mean, yeah, these are pretty special. They're organic, you know, and they were just picked this morning by hand, plus they're pretty much the best strawberries in the whole county."

He took out his wallet and flipped it open before looking up. "Can you take a Visa?"

"Uh, no."

"PayPal?"

"Umm, no. I…sorry. Only cash."

"Okay," he said, looking back down at his wallet. "Do have change for a Ben Franklin?"

She reached for the cashbox, and in her nervousness knocked it off the counter, sending change jangling across the shack's floor. Forgetting the coins, she scrambled to pick up the bills and counted them as quickly as she could. "Um, you're the first customer of the day, and I've only got thirty bucks."

"Okay," Patrick said with a smile. "How much for the whole basket?"

"Um, well, how about fifty bucks?" she guessed after a quick calculation.

"Those must be some *really* good strawberries," he responded, looking up with wide eyes.

"They're the best, and they're super fresh. If you look close, you'll probably see there's still dew on them. Plus, they're handpicked!"

Patrick smiled playfully. "How else would you pick strawberries if not by hand?"

"Mostly robots," she said, making it up on the spot.

"Robots?" he asked dubiously. "Could a robot tell the difference between a green one and a red one?"

"That's exactly the problem with the ones you buy in the grocery stores. These guys are fresh, handpicked. And, as you can see, all of them are red and delicious. Here. Try one."

He accepted the berry and inspected it quickly before biting into it. He closed his eyes for a minute while he chewed, his mouth widening into a broad smile. "Okay, I'll take the whole basket. I didn't spend all of my per diem yesterday. What else have you got?"

She quickly looked around. "It looks like just the eggs and cream and flowers."

"Well, that's okay. Cream goes with strawberries, right?"

"Absolutely! I've got six quarts."

"And how much are those?"

"Oh," she said, taking a deep breath. "Uh, I think they're like…three bucks a piece."

"Are you new at this?" he asked, smiling bemusedly.

"Yep, first day," she said, forcing a smile. "Just kind of getting used to things, you know."

"Right. Well, I'm trying to make a good first impression. From what I hear, the Swa-rov-skis haven't allowed a photographer on their farm in a couple of decades. What would it cost to buy everything you've got?"

"Oh," she said, trying not to act too surprised while she looked around at all the produce. "Well, uh…" She looked down at the bill in his hands and tried to imagine Ruby's reaction when Patrick arrived at the farm with gifts purchased from her farm's own stand. "How about a hundred bucks even?"

Patrick laughed. "I have no doubt that I'm paying way too much for this, but you drive a hard bargain. That includes that bucket of wildflowers, I assume?"

"Yes, sir. All of 'em?"

"Yeah."

"And how about I help you load it all into your car."

"Sold," he said, slapping the hundred-dollar bill on the counter.

She put the money into the cashbox before helping Patrick load up the Rover. She tried hard not to smile, and it wasn't until she heard his car changing gears as it ascended Harmony Hill that she broke into laughter.

CHAPTER 51

Quiet Desperation

*Go as far as you can see; when you get there,
you'll be able to see farther.*
—Thomas Carlyle

With nothing left to sell, Genevieve gathered up the spilled change and organized it back into the cashbox as she wondered what to do with the rest of the day. Spencer was gone without a trace, so after sitting around for ten minutes with nothing to do, she made an executive decision to close down the shack for the day. With Patrick taking photos at the farm, she knew she couldn't go back there, but a relaxing day by the river sounded like a fine alternative.

Ten minutes later, with the shack secured, she walked across the highway carrying the lunches, Thoreau's *Walden* tucked under her arm.

Genevieve saw Spencer downriver a hundred yards or so. He was leaning against a shovel, chatting with a fisherman in hip boots. She didn't care to waste any time talking to him, but even though he'd been a jerk, she didn't feel like taking his lunch would even any score. She waved to him until he saw her, and then with exaggerated motions, she pulled out one of the sandwiches and set the lunch pail down on a large rock. Then she turned her back and walked upstream along the river she was beginning to know well.

The sun was warm and the day pleasant, and so she continued to walk, on past the beach where the campers had picnicked the week before and under the bridge where Matt had spotted her on Sunday. A shady spot on the far side of the bridge offered her a place to sit down and relax, and she was soon lounging in the crabgrass, diving into Thoreau's book.

The book's yellowing pages were dog-eared and underlined, and Genevieve found herself skipping from place to place throughout, following handwritten notes in the margins. She found Thoreau's writing charming, with his romanticized look at nature and simplicity, hard work and passionate living. She had heard many of the underlined quotes, those about living deliberately, sucking the marrow out of life, and marching to the beat of one's own drummer. But as she read them in this context, in this setting surrounded by wildness, the words felt unusually meaningful.

The setting of Walden Pond and the quaint cabin on the edge of the woods made her think of the bunkhouse, the pond, the garden, and the woods surrounding the farm. Thoreau's call for solitude and his attempts at creating a utopia for himself apart from the hustle and bustle of the larger community also reminded her of the farm and the simplicity and self-reliance Ruby and Pops championed. As she continued reading, she found herself wondering what would possess a man to leave the comforts of society and separate himself from the ease of civilization.

But for every question that arose in her mind, she considered the simple, modest beauty that Ruby and Pops had either engendered or perpetuated with the land they'd been stewards of for more than fifty years.

She peeled back the waxed paper from her sandwich and nibbled as she continued to read and consider the newfound charm of this place. In just under two weeks, she'd moved from loathing this godforsaken wasteland to learning to tolerate it, to beginning to recognize the beauty all around her. And it wasn't just the physical beauty. There was something more, something deeper, almost as if this place somehow had a soul, a spirit, an ethos.

She set the book to her side and finished her sandwich as she stared out at the sunlight reflecting off the river's rippled surface. It had been a decade since she had last attempted to write poetry, but the view before her combined with the strange feelings of contentment, conjured words and metaphors she'd never considered before. But with no writing instrument or notepad, she lay back in the grass and relaxed, trying to make a mental image of all that she was experiencing. *Is this what it means to live deliberately?* she wondered to herself. *Is this what Thoreau meant by sucking the marrow out of life?*

Another thought came to mind as she looked out on the beautiful nature, and she picked up the book again, flipping through several pages until she found what she was looking for, a black line forming a star in the margins next to an underlined sentence.

The mass of men lead lives of quiet desperation.

In the margin at the bottom of the page, she noticed some upside-down writing she had missed on her first perusal. She turned the book so she could read the words written in the same black ink as the star:

Protopians, unite! Down with mediocrity and apathy! Live passionately or die striving!

Genevieve smiled as she tried to imagine the quiet afternoon at the farm stand that could have possessed an idealistic camper to read Thoreau's book and respond in such a visceral way. She turned the book right side up and looked again at the starred and underlined passage. Flipping to the title page, she noted that the book was originally published in 1854. She did the math. More than 160 years had passed since Thoreau had made his observations, but she knew that the truths he'd discovered were still as true today as they'd been then. Quiet desperation was still claiming the hearts and lives of far too many.

She was about to set the book aside again when her eyes were drawn again to word *Protopians*. She remembered something of the conversation on Monday where Pops or Ruby or both had introduced the word to the campers. She even remembered James insisting it wasn't a real word. Now seeing it written in some stranger's hand only increased her curiosity. She remembered Pops connecting this word with another new word—*magnanimous*. Finding *Protopians* here, she wondered if she might find even more information about it. She flipped through the pages of the book, looking for any other mention of it, but after a quick perusal, she found nothing. She turned back to the handwritten note, wishing for a better understanding. Though the word was still new to her, its meaning, when she took a minute to look at it, seemed fairly clear. *Pro*, she knew, suggested forward motion in words like *proceed* or *progress*. And in the case of words like *pro-life*, it meant to be supportive of something or to throw one's weight or support behind a cause. She knew that *utopia* meant something like paradise. So combining *pro* and *utopia* into *Protopian* seemed to suggest a person who made conscious choices to work toward a better existence or society. It suggested optimism. It suggested searching out solutions to problems with a hope and desire to solve them. In spite of her natural inclination toward cynicism, Genevieve found this term and the ideas it engendered somehow hopeful, even empowering. And as with many of the other things she had encountered since coming to Niederbipp, she knew that understanding and appreciating this concept would require her to suspend her innate pessimistic disposition.

Protopians, unite!

She ran her finger over the word, wondering what Protopians were. Were they a group? A club? Or was is just an idea, an attitude, a philosophy? She guessed that Ruby and Pops knew more about it than they'd already shared, but she knew she would have to wait until the end of the day to ask.

The late morning sun was soon on Genevieve's face, and the patch of crabgrass was no longer comfortable. She got up and stretched her back and legs as she wondered how to spend the time before Pops came back to pick her and Spencer up. There was no sign of Spencer or the fisherman he'd been talking to—not that she really wanted to spend any time with him anyway. Figuring he had wandered farther downstream, she stooped back down and picked up her book and the rest of her lunch, deciding that a walk upriver would be a good way to spend a few hours.

The sun was warm on her back as she headed north along the pebbly banks of the river with no destination in mind. She paused for a moment to examine the skeleton of an old wooden rowboat, its sun-bleached ribs protruding from the gravely earth. But she continued on, looking for shade. A quarter mile upriver she came upon a bend where the trees grew tall on the high banks, sending their branches and shadows over the rounded river rocks. She was about to sit down on these cool rocks when she noticed a swing hanging from an outstretched tree limb. Wandering closer, she saw that the smooth but weathered surface of the wooden seat was heavily carved with names and symbols. One of these inscriptions stood out.

JAKE ♡ AMY

Genevieve stared at the hand-carved lettering for only a moment, but that moment was enough to change her mood, remembering all the negative feelings she had for Amy. She sat down on the carving, anxious to hide it from her view. It was hard to believe it had been less than two weeks since she had visited her old roommate and met her husband, the potter of Niederbipp. In a flash, she was flooded with difficult memories of receiving messages on her satellite phone, meeting the Swarovskis, and feeling like she was being kidnapped and forced to spend the summer in this backwoods wasteland. As she looked out on the river now, she was surprised by the strange feelings of embarrassment and even humor that these memories conjured. She recognized that she had overreacted, overthought, and generally made a mess of things that had turned out entirely differently than she'd anticipated.

As she ate her the last of her sandwich, she found herself wondering what the next few months would bring. She had always hated the unknown parts of her future. They had so often left her feeling anxious and unstable. To combat these anxieties when she traveled abroad on work assignments, she'd developed predictable routines and patterns. But this assignment had been entirely different. The unpredictability of what she'd be doing each day and who her work partner would be had kept her anxiety level high at first. But as she considered the different chores and the six men she'd be sharing those chores with for the next four and a half months, she decided that maybe she was up to the challenge. When she took into consideration all that she'd experienced so far—and had come through alive and well—she was surprised by a strange sense of relief that she had so much time left.

As far as her writing assignment was concerned, she still had no idea where to even begin. She laughed at herself when she remembered how she'd thought she could be in and out of here in just a few days and get back to her more urbane and classy assignments in Europe. She still knew nothing of the old woman's matchmaking skills, other than the evidence: the long list of people Ruby and Pops had referenced and the scrapbooks filled with wedding announcements in the library. Genevieve knew a thorough examination of these scrapbooks would likely yield additional insights. She wondered how she might contact those couples to inquire about their experiences on the farm. She wondered what they might say about their experiences here and what they might say about Ruby.

Remembering she was sitting on a swing, Genevieve did something she hadn't done in nearly two decades. She leaned her head back, looking up into the canopy above her head, then leaned back farther until her arms were stretched out entirely. The shift in her weight caused her feet to lift off the ground, and before she could stop herself, she began to swing. Higher and higher she rose as her legs moved with her arms to pump the swing back and forth with a long-neglected rhythm she hardly believed she could remember. Soon she was soaring over the pebbles, her shadow quickly appearing and disappearing just beyond the shade of the trees.

With the wind in her hair, she closed her eyes and smiled to herself as she remembered this euphoric sensation from her childhood. The simple pleasure she felt was so real and intense that she stayed and played in the memories of her childhood, when joys came easy and time was meaningless. She had just started wondering how long it had been since she'd sat on a swing when she realized she couldn't remember the last time she'd even seen a swing. It's not like she hung out in parks looking for fun, but not having swung in twenty years felt somehow criminal. As she started considering the possibilities of hanging a swing from the beams of her SoHo loft, the sound of a child's voice alerted her to the fact that she was not alone.

She stopped pumping her legs and dragged her shoes across the pebbles to slow herself down. Looking over her shoulder, Genevieve saw two women descending a walkway that had been cut into the steep riverbank, as well as a young girl who had beaten the adults to the river bottoms. Genevieve stood, suddenly feeling like she was trespassing.

The little pig-tailed girl raced across the gravel and threw herself, belly first, onto the freshly vacated swing. Her legs kicked up, flapping like fish thrown onto the banks, and she squealed with delight, smiling from ear to ear at Genevieve.

"Gracie, you have to take your turn," her mother said, chasing after her.

"She's okay. I've been swinging for the last half hour. I'm sure it's her turn," Genevieve replied as the winded mother approached.

The woman smiled at Genevieve. "Sorry. She's at a stage when she thinks all the world is hers, especially when her brother's not around to remind her who's boss."

"You have a son too?"

"Yeah. Eight years old. He's in school right now, so we thought we'd come for a picnic. Are you sure we're not disturbing you?"

"Yeah, I'm sure."

The woman looked at her for a moment. "I'm Molly," she said, extending her hand. "My husband and I run the grocery store in town. I don't think we've met."

"No, uh, no," she stammered as she glanced over Molly's shoulder and saw the second woman's unmistakable red hair.

"Genevieve Patterson?" the second woman said as she approached them.

"Uh, hey, Amy."

"You're the last person I expected to see here today," Amy replied.

Molly looked surprised. "You two know each other?"

"Yes," Amy responded. "This is the one I was talking to you about—you know, my roommate from college who's here for the summer to work on Ruby's farm."

"Oh, right!" Molly said with a grin.

"How's that working out for you?" Amy asked.

Genevieve shrugged. "I'll admit it was a rough start, but…it's not as bad as I thought it would be."

Amy looked at her a little closer. "Genevieve, you don't have black eyes, do you?"

Genevieve removed the dark glasses as Molly gasped.

"What happened to you?" asked Molly.

"Oh, just a little accident on the farm. I got headbutted by a sheep, if you need to know."

"Oh my gosh, I'm sorry," Molly responded as Amy obviously tried to keep from smiling. "Were you trying to milk her?"

"No, it was actually a ram. Apparently he didn't like being shorn, and, yeah, it didn't work out so well."

"I'm sorry," Molly repeated sympathetically.

"So, did they give you the day off?" Amy asked.

"No, uh, not exactly. I was working the farm stand, but I sold out early. So I've…just kind of been exploring."

Molly nodded as she turned to look up and down the banks. "Where's your partner? I thought you guys usually work in pairs."

Genevieve glanced at Amy, then Molly, then turned to look at the river. "It's a long story. Boring. Let's just say we're not exactly compatible." From the corner of her eye, she could see Amy's smirk.

"Oh, that's too bad," Molly said. "Sounds like it's been a rough year for Ruby so far. I didn't hear if they ever found that girl who went missing on Sunday."

"You heard about that?" Genevieve asked, honestly surprised.

"Yeah, Thomas and the mayor stopped by our house to see if Kai would be available to go search for her, but they never came back. We never heard if the search had been officially called off."

"They asked Jake too," Amy reported. "We waited to hear the bells, but they never rang."

"Bells?" Genevieve asked

"Yeah. Just the church bells," Amy explained. "Our husbands are both in the volunteer fire department, which gets called on sometimes for search and rescue. They use the church bells to summon all the volunteers. It's kind of a primitive system, but I guess they've been using it since long before telephones. I guess they found the girl they were looking for, huh?"

"Yeah, they did. So, do you girls come here often?" Genevieve asked, anxious to change the subject.

Molly smiled. "I ended up here on my first date with my husband just over eleven years ago." She turned to Amy. "Hey, wasn't your first date down here, too?"

"Well, kind of. Our first official date was actually a week later, but we got to know each other on this beach and this swing. It's kind of a magical place, isn't it?"

"I noticed your names were carved in the seat," Genevieve said, pointing at the swing that was moving back and forth as Gracie pushed it, her chest resting on the seat and covering most it.

"Oh, that's right," Amy responded with a little laugh. "Jake carved that into the seat for our first anniversary. He brought me down here to surprise me with a picnic and a ride on the swing, kind of bringing us back to where it all began."

"Oh, that's so…cute," Genevieve responded as she watched Amy bristle.

"I remember helping Kai set up that picnic for you and Jake. Seems like it was yesterday. Now look at you! What—seven years later? Beautiful! Happy! Very pregnant."

Amy smiled, placing her hands on her growing belly. "How nice of you to notice," she responded sarcastically. "It still doesn't seem real that this is finally happening to me."

"Oh, Jake didn't want kids?" Genevieve asked, not waiting for an answer before plowing on. "I guess that's pretty common with guys in our generation, right? It seems like most guys don't want to be tied down with kids. But it looks like you changed his mind."

Molly looked both confused and surprised by the frankness of Genevieve's words.

"Actually, we both wanted kids, and a lot sooner, but life doesn't always go the way you plan. I…we had fertility issues. It's been almost eight years since we got married, and it's hard to be patient when your best friends' kids are going to school and you're still trying to figure out how to carry a baby past the first trimester."

Genevieve suddenly felt like she'd put her foot in her mouth.

"After our last miscarriage, I was emotionally done," Amy continued, "but spending a weekend with Molly and Kai's kids convinced us to try again. I guess the fourth time was the charm."

"Oh...sorry, but that's so...great. When are you due?" Genevieve asked.

"August 12th."

"Wow! That's only like, three months away! Are you ready?"

Amy shrugged. "Ready or not. I don't know if you can really ever be ready. But we're very excited. We've been waiting for him for a long, long time."

"Oh, you're having a boy! Have you chosen a name?"

"Yes. Isaac Jacob."

"Sounds very...biblical," Genevieve responded. "Is that a family name?"

"Well, Jacob is obviously from his dad. And Isaac was the name of the potter who left the shop to Jake. Neither one of us actually ever met him before he passed away, but without him we never would have met."

"Wait, Jake didn't know Isaac, but he gave him the shop?"

"I know. It sounds crazy, right? We tell people Isaac was the greatest man neither one of us ever knew."

"We actually named our son after him too," Molly added. "Zane Isaac."

Genevieve looked surprised. "What did Isaac give *you*?"

Molly laughed. "A chance to meet my husband. Kai was a bit of a rootless tumbleweed until he stumbled into town. Isaac put him up and helped him believe in himself. If it weren't for Isaac, Kai would probably still be tumbling. But I'm sure you have more important things to do than listen to us go on about a man who's dead and gone."

"Actually, yeah, I...someone told me there's a library in town that has internet access. I was thinking I should probably check my emails. I'm sure my inbox is overflowing."

Molly looked at Amy before shaking her head. "It's Wednesday. I'm not sure if I'd recommend tangling with Roberta."

"Oh, I'm sure she'll be fine," Amy insisted.

"Who's Roberta?"

"I'm surprised Ruby hasn't warned you about her—Roberta Mancini?" Molly offered.

Genevieve shook her head.

"Well, she runs the library and has been known to make children *and* adults cry. She can be very cranky and…let's just say *extra*, if you know what I mean. You might want to wait for another day. I think she still has Thursdays off."

"Yeah, well, I'm not sure when I'll be able to get away from the farm again. I'll take my chances."

"Okay, well, don't say we didn't warn you."

"Can you tell me where the library is?"

Amy looked as if she were trying not to smile. "Just follow the path back to town. The library's between the church and the post office."

"Thanks," Genevieve said. "I guess I better get on my way."

"Toodle-oo!" Gracie said, her face scrunched up in a funny smile as her pigtails fluttered with her self-propelled swinging.

"Toodle-oo," Genevieve responded, smiling at the energetic child.

CHAPTER 52

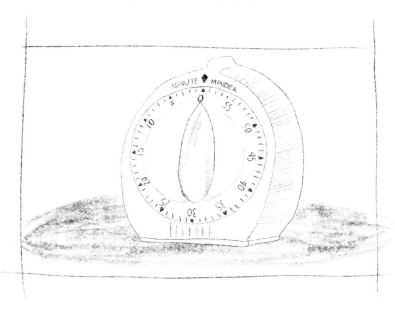

The Thief

A life spent making mistakes is not only more honorable, but more useful than a life spent doing nothing.
—George Bernard Shaw

Genevieve climbed the earthen stairs that had been cut into to the steep riverbank, making her way around first the roots and then the trunks of the trees. When she reached the top, she looked back to watch Molly spread a quilt over the graveled river bottoms as Amy reached into a colorful basket. Though the scene was pleasant, she turned away after a moment and marched up the trail toward town. Other than the recent picnics on the farm, Genevieve couldn't remember having had a picnic since her childhood. As she walked, she reasoned that life in the city didn't often provide many opportunities to waste time doing something as silly as taking one's lunch outside and calling it by another name. She couldn't see herself ever taking time away from work for such a frivolous activity. But the closer she got to town, the more she realized that the real issue wasn't time—it was that she didn't have anyone to enjoy an hour on a blanket with while consuming lunch. This truth surprised her, making her feel lonely and sad. She pushed it away, trying to remember her email passwords.

She stopped for a moment to catch her breath at a tall, stony monument on the river side of the highway. A slab of sandstone formed a bench at the base of the monument, offering Genevieve a place to rest and a view of the stony obelisk. Green and orange lichen and moss grew thick on the top of the monument. A shallow square alcove had been formed on the monument at about eye level, and round holes in the corners of the alcove suggested it might have once played host to a sign or plaque. Now stripped of an explanation, the monument felt more like a curiosity than anything else. She wondered why anyone would have gone to the trouble of building it and the bench. The bench. *The bench!*

She turned around and scanned the slab, not knowing exactly what she was looking for. It would have been easy to miss; she certainly hadn't seen it when she'd sat down. But hidden under a thin layer of lichen were carved the unmistakable words: *Be still, and know that I am God.*

She ran her thumb over the small carved letters before looking around for more clues as to why someone might have gone to all the trouble to stack stone upon stone to form a twelve-foot-tall edifice. From this vantage point, she could see just a sliver of the river as she looked to the east. And to the west, she could see the town of Niederbipp rising up the hillside. The highway ran north and south, and the four corners of the monument appeared to be nearly square with the cardinal directions.

She looked more closely at the stones of the monument, searching for any additional clues. The stones were well weathered, but they still showed the marks of being cut and fitted together without much mortar.

At the base of the lowest stone on the east side, she discovered what looked like two overlapping Vs, one pointing up and the other pointing down, along with a date: 1727.

Genevieve scanned the rest of the monument, looking for any additional clues. And that's when she found it, carved into the stone above the shallow alcove, about eight feet off the ground. It looked like a triangle from down below, but she could tell that there was more to the carving than she could plainly see. She walked closer, scaling the uneven surface of the monument until her nose was only inches away from the carving. Being careful not to lose her balance, she rested one knee on the edge of the alcove and traced her fingers over the lichen-encrusted carving. A three-inch triangle formed a frame around eight letters laid out similarly to those on an eye-exam chart. E Ben Ezer.

Realizing she was losing her grip, Genevieve jumped down from the monument but continued to examine the carving from the ground. She wondered if it might be the signature of a stone mason. She instinctively reached for her phone to snap a picture but remembered she didn't have it. She patted her pockets, looking for a scrap of paper and a pen or pencil, which she already knew she didn't have. So instead she stared at the carving, trying to memorize it. Without the plaque to explain the monument—or whatever it was—its meaning and purpose seemed to have been lost. But the three carvings she had found—the overlapping Vs, the date, and the letters in the triangle—left her curious. She wondered if the library might offer some answers.

The trail continued on the other side of the highway, cutting through grasses and woods before becoming wider. Eventually the dirt path gave way to cobblestone paving, similar to that Genevieve had seen in the center of town. She climbed the gently sloping hill, the old buildings rising before her, making her feel as though she were approaching a quaint European hamlet. For the first time since arriving in Niederbipp, she looked at the town before her and saw charm, beauty, and vibrancy. Somehow she had missed these attractive attributes in her first few visits. The main street was busy with shoppers and tourists. She considered taking a closer look at the shops, but the thought of an overflowing inbox kept her moving. She passed the post office and was soon standing in front of the public library, its window boxes filled with flowers that appeared far too bright to be real. Upon closer examination, she discovered they were a tacky mixture of silk and plastic haphazardly arranged in a strange hodgepodge, sun-faded poinsettias next to brilliant irises.

She pulled on the heavy door's handle, not knowing what to expect as she entered a small vestibule. She was immediately met with a gust of cool air and the scent of old books and stale perfume. The vestibule's internal door was propped open, and light bathed a large front desk surrounded by a narrow circular counter.

An elderly woman with a large silver beehive hairdo sat behind the counter, her oversized glasses reflecting the computer screen in front of her. She was playing solitaire and seemed to be quite engaged.

"Excuse me," Genevieve said after she had stood before the woman for at least thirty seconds without being acknowledged.

The woman raised her index finger as if to indicate that she needed a minute. Genevieve watched the slow progress of the game through the reflection in the woman's lenses. As she waited for a response, Genevieve noticed the woman's bright blouse, teal with fuchsia flowers, and a thick gold chain that disappeared into the chasm between her generous breasts. After another minute or so, the woman looked up.

"Welcome to the Niederbipp Semi-Public Library," she said in a saccharin voice. "How may I be of assistance?"

The woman's words and businesslike demeanor caught Genevieve off guard, but the introduction also left her curious. "Semi-public?"

"Excuse me?"

"You said *semi-public library*. I guess I don't know the term. What exactly does that mean?"

The woman rolled her eyes. "Public libraries are supported solely by the taxes of the people. This library is heavily subsidized by the Mancini Family Trust. I've always felt like it's important for visitors to know the generosity of the benevolent benefactors who both keep the lights on and properly catalog the collection."

"Oh, right," Genevieve replied, trying hard not to laugh at the woman's voice, which was dripping with an air of pomp and self-importance. "I've noticed the Mancini name around town. It sounds like a very prominent family."

"Indeed, *we are* quite prominent," she replied, pointing to the oversized lettering over an adjacent archway.

"The Roberta Mancini Romance Wing?" Genevieve asked.

The woman nodded proudly. "The lion's share of that collection is made up of books from my own personal collection—3,749 and counting."

"Wow, impressive," Genevieve replied, looking down at the woman's bejeweled fingers in search of a symbol of matrimony. "What does your husband think of your passion?"

"Husband? Pshaw! No man has ever proven himself worthy."

"But your ring?" Genevieve said, pointing to the big rock on the woman's chubby ring finger.

"Yes, well, a woman of my pedigree must do what she can to ward off any unsolicited affections from men of a lesser ilk. I see no ring on your finger. Should I assume you feel the same way about men?"

"Uh, absolutely," Genevieve responded, knowing it was probably useless to say anything contrary.

"Smart girl. Tell me, how I can help you today."

"I was hoping to use the computer. I understand you might have internet connection here?"

"On a limited basis, yes. The demand is often great, and of course we share a line between our phone and the computers, and so I will warn you that if the phone rings, you may be dropped at any time."

"Wait, are you saying it's a dial-up connection?"

"Yes, of course. The fiber opticals haven't made it to our county yet."

"Fiber opticals?" Genevieve asked, confused. "Oh, are you talking about fiber optics?"

"I've heard it both ways," the librarian said, reaching for a dingy plastic kitchen timer. She turned the knob before setting it on the counter in front of Genevieve. "You have only ten minutes. I suggest you use them wisely. Now if you'll excuse me, I have a pressing matter to attend to."

"Wait, I only have ten minutes?"

But the strange woman had already returned to her game. She pointed a bedazzled finger to an overhead sign:

> Computers are for the use of the patrons of the
> Niederbipp Semi-Public Library
> and are available in ten-minute allotments.
> If no one is waiting, you may return to the desk and
> request an additional ten-minute allotment.
> Thank you, The Management.

Genevieve had never paid much attention to how long it took her to log in to her email at work or home, but as she turned to look at the ancient computers, she knew this was going to take significantly longer. She hurried to the computer, turned it on, and waited several minutes for the monitor to wake up. With only three minutes left on her timer, she was staring at the pixilated screen of her magazine's homepage. She made her way to the employee log-in page and typed in her username and password. Thirty seconds later, the username and password screen reloaded. Apparently she had typed in something wrong. She tried again, and again the password was rejected.

The timer rang, and Genevieve got up and raced to the counter. The woman dramatically lifted one finger as she had before, encouraging Genevieve to be patient.

"Welcome to the Niederbipp Semi-Public Library. How may I assist you?" the librarian said, looking into Genevieve's face with a cheesy simulated smile as if she'd never seen her before.

"Uh, yeah. Can I have ten more minutes on my timer?"

"I don't know, *can* you?"

"Excuse me?"

"I believe the word you are lookin' for is *may*, as in, '*May I have ten more minutes on my timer*?' Is that what you meant to say?"

"Yes, yes!"

The woman blinked several times as if she were waiting for something else.

"Is there a problem?" Genevieve asked, trying not to sound impatient.

"The only problem I see is that you expressed no appreciation for our little English lesson and that you seem to think it is appropriate to ask for something without the customary and polite niceties of *please* and *thank you*. I'm not sure how things work where you come from, but around here we treat each other with respect, use proper English, and never forget our politeness. Oh, and we never wear our sunglasses indoors, where people might mistake our failure to remove them as impertinence or rudeness."

Genevieve stared at the difficult woman through her dark glasses, wondering if this was worth it. She took a deep breath and removed her sunglasses to begin anew the lengthy and infuriating process of getting what she came for.

The woman gasped when she saw Genevieve's black eyes. "You're a *brawler*, are you? I should have guessed, with your lack of manners."

"No, I am not a brawler!" Genevieve protested. "I had an accident… shearing sheep."

"Brawler! Fabricator! Delusional! Ingrate!" she replied, holding up a finger for each of the faults she had found in Genevieve.

"*Excuse me?*" Genevieve responded, raising her voice louder than she'd intended.

The woman lifted her other bedazzled hand, and with each additional adjective, she raised another finger. "Insubordinate! Defiant! Unruly! Disrespectful! Recalcitrant!"

"What? *Recalcitrant*? I've never…"

The librarian pulled on her gold chain, and a crucifix emerged from her bosom. Clutching it with one hand, she resumed using the other hand to punctuate each insult. "Questioning authority! Narcissistic! Ill mannered! Sassy!"

"This is ridiculous. I've decided I don't need to check my email."

"Volatile! Unstable! Fiery! Erratic! Temperamental!" the woman continued, her face turning red as she gripped the crucifix still tighter.

Genevieve shook her head, speechless for the first time in recent memory. She put her glasses back on and walked toward the door. But just as she passed the threshold, a very loud alarm sounded and bright lights flashed.

"Stop! Thief!" the obnoxious woman yelled, quickly getting to her feet and rushing to the corner of the desk.

"I didn't steal anything," Genevieve said, distracted when she noticed that the woman's garish blouse was actually a muumuu. She bit the inside of her cheek to keep herself from smiling as the woman pointed her finger at her as if it were a gun.

"Don't shoot!" Genevieve shouted, her hands raised as she gave in to the need to laugh. The siren and lights slowly faded back to silence.

"You think this is funny?"

"Umm, yes, I guess I do." She tried to erase her smile but failed.

"I'll have you know that library theft is a crime punishable by imprisonment in this county, a crime that robs entire communities of their right to good literature. I afraid I'm going to have to ask you to empty your pockets before you leave."

"You've got to be kidding me! I just told you I didn't steal anything!"

"Then you won't have any trouble emptying your pockets and proving your innocence, will you?"

Genevieve took a deep breath, lowering her hands. She turned her front pockets out and was reaching into the back pockets of her cutoff overalls and felt the book. She withdrew the book slowly.

"Aha! That looks an awful lot like a book to me, young lady!"

"No, I can explain. I got this from the farm stand. I'm sure it's been there for years. Look, it's marked up and dog eared." She flipped to the back of the book and saw what she didn't want to see—the official Niederbipp Semi-Public Library stamp along with an empty envelope that had been pasted inside the back cover. A round, white electronic patch like she'd seen on other library books was affixed to the back cover.

"Look, I didn't know this was a library book. I..."

"You also told me you didn't have any books in your pockets. You obviously don't know fiction from nonfiction. Hand over the book, Missy."

"No, I...there's been a mistake. This was part of the farm-stand collection. I swear I didn't steal it."

The woman shook her head. "Psychotic! Capricious! Thief!"

"How dare you?! You don't even know me. I didn't steal this book. I'm not a thief!"

"Hand it over, or I'll call the sheriff!"

"Fine!" she said, handing it across the counter to the woman. But just before the woman reached for it, Genevieve remembered the cash she had put in the book for safekeeping. She pulled it back, grazing the fingers of the woman's hand. The woman howled, clutching her hand to her chest, her eyes wild with rage. "Paper cut! You brute!" She howled again. "Paper cut! I'll need a transfusion. I'll need a tetanus shot! With filth like you, this will undoubtedly lead to a staph infection."

"Oh, give it a break," Genevieve muttered as she removed the cash and handed the book back to the woman. The woman snatched the book from her with her left hand, her right hand wrapped up in the ample muumuu. She hurried to the card file, where she quickly found the matching card.

"Aha! This was checked out to Adam Rawlings and was due back more than nine years ago!"

"Nine years ago! See! I told you I didn't steal it!"

"Then you're his accomplice. You're in cahoots with this vermin."

"What the hell are you talking about?" Genevieve shouted.

"Explosive! Hotheaded! Foul-mouthed! Vermin is as vermin does! I'll have you know that accomplices to rare-book theft can serve as much time as the perpetrators themselves."

"Rare books?" Genevieve responded loudly. "It's a freakin' trade paperback. I'm sure I could find an identical used copy on Amazon for less than a dollar."

"A dollar!" the librarian laughed out loud. "Ridiculous! Do you have any idea how much the overdue fine is for this book?"

"No, I have no idea," Genevieve responded impatiently.

The woman grabbed an oversized calculator from the desk and pushed several buttons before looking up. "It's $3,672."

"Oh, really? Is that all?"

The woman looked steamed. "I don't know who the heck you think you are, but if you think you can talk to me like you're the Queen of Sheba, you've got another think coming."

"What's that?" Genevieve challenged, her words dripping with sarcasm.

"What do you mean?"

"You said I had another think coming. I'm just waiting to hear what other nonsense is going to come out of your mouth."

The phone rang, distracting the woman. "You stay right there, missy," she demanded, pointing to Genevieve before walking to the far end of the big desk to pick up the phone. "Hello, Niederbipp Semi-Public Library. This is Roberta. How may I help you?" she said in a saccharine voice that didn't suggest even a hint of anger.

"Why, yes, we do have that book. I've read it myself several times," she replied.

Genevieve could hear the muffled excitement on the other end of the line.

"Yes, of course, Mrs. Nelson. I'd be happy to hold it for you. Of course. Yes, I'm here until five. Yes, yes, of course. See you soon."

She hung up the phone and, forgetting Genevieve, moved to the stacks in the Roberta Mancini Romance Wing in search of the book she was after.

Genevieve watched the odd muumuued woman disappear into the shelves, and she was just about to bolt when she remembered the book. She knew she could undoubtedly find one cheap on Amazon, but she didn't care. She wanted this one. And she'd certainly paid for it in harassment if not in dollars. Quickly and stealthily, she pushed open a small swinging gate that provided access to the space behind the desk. Dropping down to all fours, she rushed for Thoreau's *Walden*, slipped it into her back pocket, stood up, and turned to make her way back to the gate. She had nearly reached it when she noticed a small stack of books on the corner of the counter. The top book caught her attention: *A Short History of Niederbipp* by Thomas O. Kelly. The book's dark faux-leather cover looked worn and well loved. She picked the volume up from the pile and, without giving it much thought, bolted for the door.

CHAPTER 53

Fugitive

Our main business is not to see what lies dimly at a distance, but to do what lies clearly at hand.
—Thomas Carlyle

With alarms blaring and lights flashing, Genevieve broke out of the tension and the stale, musty scent of the library. She was back on the streets of Niederbipp, free of the madness. She ran for two full blocks before slowing down as she fell into an adrenaline-rich fit of laughter. As her conscience and imagination clicked into overdrive, Genevieve knew that the sheriff would soon be hot on her trail, looking for a troubled renegade woman sporting two black eyes, a straw hat, cutoff overalls, and mismatched socks. She'd be spending the rest of the week in the county jail until she could be bailed out by her father, who would have to fly in from Paris at great personal hardship to rescue his delinquent book-thieving daughter. She was contemplating where she could go to disappear when she remembered making her way back to the farm on Sunday by way of the river. Running parallel to the highway, the river would offer an alternative, more obscure way back to the farm stand. And today she was wearing appropriate footwear, so she wouldn't need to float.

The cry of a distant siren vaulted her into action, and she quickly retraced her steps, descending the gently sloping hillside trail and crossing the highway. For the second time in just over an hour, she stopped for a break at the stone obelisk, taking a seat on the sun-warmed stone that formed the bench.

The sun, now past its meridian, lit the face of the stone tower from an angle that made the carved stone above the alcove easier to see. E BEN EZER. What did it mean? She wished she would have also stolen one of the stubby pencils she'd seen on the library desk. Just then, she remembered the title of the book she'd been hiding in the belly flap of her overalls since she'd left the library. She wondered if it might offer some insight. She pulled it out, flipping through several pages before her eyes fell on a black-and-white photograph of the very monument in whose shadow she sat.

It was an old photograph of a man in a suit and a woman in a distinctive 1920s day dress standing next to an early-model car with enormous fenders. The dusty highway was on one side of the car, and the monument stood on the other.

A caption accompanied the photo: *Visitors to Niederbipp often stop by what has come to be known as the Engelhart Ebenezer, built in 1727 by brothers Abraham and Joshua Engelhart. Marked as the spot where the first settlers arrived in Niederbipp after crossing the Allegheny in search of religious freedom and peace, this monument was dedicated on May 3, 1727, exactly ten years after the cornerstone of the Niederbipp* chapel was set in place. Photograph by Andrew Carmichael, circa 1924 (see more on pages 223–27).

Genevieve was intrigued. She turned quickly to page 223 and began reading.

Engelhart Ebenezer
Erected in 1727 by Abraham and Joshua Engelhart.

Monuments like this one are found throughout America, marking places where wars were fought, people were born, events took place, and ideas were memorialized. The Engelhart Ebenezer is unique, however, for many reasons. This monument marks the location where Niederbipp's first inhabitants arrived (see the Schreyer Ferry section on page 27), and it played a spiritual and temporal role in the lives of early Niederbippians and has more recently experienced a revival of interest.

With ten years of farming on the western slopes of the Allegheny under their belts, early farmers had discovered the best times to plant their crops as well as the optimal times to begin their harvest. The oblong stone at the very top of the obelisk is said to be a traditional grinding stone given to another Engelhart brother, Johann, by a local Munsee Indian clan. Johann opened the first grain mill on this side of the Allegheny and often traded with the Indians. It is said that the shadow from this stone falls across the Planting Stone (the smaller stone at the top of the tower's southwest corner) at sunrise on the tenth day of May each spring and across the Harvest Stone (the smaller stone at the top of the tower's northwest corner) on the twenty-fifth day of September each fall. Though traditional Gregorian calendars were widely used at the time of the first settlers' arrival, this use of solar alignments was reportedly an acknowledgment of God's overarching hand in all things and an expression of gratitude for the earth's favorable place in the universe, which allows human life to be nurtured and sustained.

Genevieve looked up to the top of the monument and saw the elongated grinding stone protruding out of the pyramidal crown.

Curious, she stood and walked to the opposite side of the monument until she could see the smaller stones the book referred to. Seeing these stones and hearing of their meaning reminded her of visiting Stonehenge as a teenager. She had been impressed then with the size of the stones and with the diagrams at the visitors' center that explained the science behind the formation. Though this monument was far smaller, she was impressed that its builders had been alert enough to observe nature's alignments. She returned to the bench and continued reading.

Niederbipp's earliest settlers, including the Engelhart brothers, were faithful men and women who were quick to give God credit for the blessings they enjoyed, as symbolized in the monument itself. Carved into the keystone over the arched alcove on the north face is carved the word EBENEZER framed by a triangle. In an interview, Isaac Bingham, who ran Pottery Niederbipp (the local pottery shop on Zubergasse) and who is the son-in-law of the last Engelhart, suggested that many levels of meaning and understanding are associated with these symbols.

The triangle, according to Mr. Bingham, represents the unified work and purposes of the three members of the Godhead: Father, Son, and Holy Spirit.

The name Ebenezer has reference to the biblical story of the prophet Samuel, who, when the children of Israel were finally able to conquer the Philistines and claim the land they'd been promised, called for a large stone to be stood on its end at the center of their community. This he called Eben-ezer, a Hebrew phrase meaning stone of help, hoping that the following generations might never forget that they had come this far only by the help and strength of the arm of God.

According to Mr. Bingham, family tradition and history hold that the Engelhart brothers, with the building of this edifice, "hoped, like Samuel of old, to provide a similar physical reminder to those who lived within the monument's shadow—and to any who passed by—that it is only by God's help and hand that we are here and that life continues."

The bench at the base of the monument was not a part of the original edifice. Added in 1964, the bench was a gift to the people of Niederbipp by Isaac Bingham and the Engelhart Family Trust. The bench itself has a significant history and meaning.

Both 1727 (the year the tower was built) and 1964 (the year the bench was added) marked a decade after certain key events. The former came a decade after the first settlers arrived in Niederbipp. The latter was installed a decade after the passing of Isaac Bingham's wife, Lily Engelhart Bingham, and father-in-law, Henry Jakob Engelhart, the last two residents of Niederbipp who were direct descendants of those who built the monument.

Visitors to the Niederbipp Cemetery (see pages 237–42), adjacent to the Niederbipp Chapel, will find six ornate benches dedicated to the Engelhart family potters, who lived and worked at Pottery Niederbipp from the early eighteenth century until the passing of Henry Engelhart in 1954. According to town council meeting minutes, some members of the council were reluctant to allow Mr. Bingham to proceed with his desire to install a bench at the Engelhart Ebenezer site. The dissenters expressed concern that, given Mr. Bingham's association with the Engelharts, the bench might serve to honor one family over others that also contributed to the long, rich history and heritage of Niederbipp.

According to meeting minutes, Mr. Bingham was quick in his attempts to allay any concerns by clarifying that his desires were for a simple, unadorned bench that could offer a place of refuge and contemplation. This apparently did not sit well with some of the more outspoken members of the council, who quickly complicated the conversation by suggesting that if someone were to go to all the trouble of putting in a stone bench, it really ought to be ornately carved with flowers and vines. Others suggested that carvings of native birds, frogs, and fish should decorate the bench. Yet another group of individuals decided it would be a fitting place for a Ten Commandments monument.

Niederbipp town council meetings have a reputation for being quite lively, and this one was no exception. The council immediately divided into at least a dozen different factions, each claiming they had the best idea for the bench. When time for debate ran out, Council President

Julia Schneider suggested to those present that the following month's meeting would focus on the bench. Little did she know that arguments regarding the bench would consume the better part of the next five council meetings.

After patiently enduring so many inconclusive meetings on the matter, Mr. Bingham came to the meeting on October 6, 1964, with a different tactic. After respectfully addressing the council members and thanking them for their patience in working through the subject, he suggested that with many members of the community reaching retirement age, the time had come to consider what legacy the town's younger generations would inherit. After explaining that he had spent the previous five months considering legacy, he suggested that the most powerful legacy that could be left to the children of Niederbipp was the faith, conviction, and ideology of peace and brotherly love on which the town had been founded. This, he warned, could all be lost and forgotten without physical and spiritual reminders that subtly encouraged people to ask questions and seek answers about the better parts of themselves and the larger community.

Most of those in the Ten Commandments camp immediately agreed, believing Mr. Bingham was speaking about a monument that might include their desires. But he surprised them and everyone else by not ending there. Instead, he spoke about the beauty that comes from simplicity, and he suggested that honoring the natural beauty of the stone that God created might go further than complicating the purpose of the bench with a list of shalts and shalt-nots, which he suggested most people were fully aware of anyway.

When the council room erupted again into loud discussion and debate, council notes say that Mr. Bingham stood his ground as he cited Psalms 46:10 in such a calm and soothing whisper that everyone had to stop what they were doing, thinking, and saying in order to listen. "Be still, and know that I am God." By the third time he whispered it, there was such a silence in the room that all who were present could hear the mayor softly snoring behind his desk.

Council minutes note that everyone in attendance that evening was caught off guard by the calm peace that filled the very room that had been chaotic and loud just moments before. The arguing and contention that had accompanied so many of the prior council meetings did not return that evening. In the peaceful calm that followed, Mr. Bingham proposed that plans for the bench be allowed to move forward without any further delay and that the words Be still, and know that I am God be tastefully and discretely carved onto the bench without any fanfare or highlights, allowing visitors to find the phrase themselves. To the surprise of many, the council voted unanimously that evening to allow the project to move forward. And so it is that Mr. Bingham got his bench.

Two weeks after the meeting, stonemasons from Martin's Monument and Stone arrived from Warren with the large stone bench and set it in place without pomp or ceremony. Mr. Bingham's journal noted that only himself, Sam Gottlieb, Ruby and Lorenzo Swarovski, and Jerry and Beverly Sproodle were present to see the finishing touches placed on the stone and join him in a prayer of dedication.

I interviewed Mr. Bingham in December 1978 regarding the bench and the monument. He informed me that the bench represented the fulfillment of a dream he'd had in early 1964. In his dream, he said he was standing at the monument, watching as people rushed by on the highway, too busy to stop and consider how the hand of God had shaped their lives. The dream left him feeling compelled to do something about it. Shortly thereafter, he petitioned the town council with his proposal. Months later, when the bench was finally installed, he began spending his evenings cutting a path that would eventually meander from the town to the banks of the river, leading right past the monument that had nearly been reclaimed by nature and forgotten by history. By the time of the aforementioned interview, Mr. Bingham had singlehandedly cut more than seven miles of nature trails along the river. What began as one man's passion project now attracts the attention of many residents and a growing number of visitors.

Since the bench's placement at the monument in 1964, Mr. Bingham has constructed several others and added them along the trail, offering people comfortable places to consider where they fit among God's creations. He has crafted most of these benches out of wood so they can be installed without heavy machinery that can destroy the surrounding natural habitat. Each bench discretely displays a small tile created by Mr. Bingham with the words Be still, and know that I am God carved into its surface.

When asked what inspired him to put so much work into this project, Mr. Bingham became emotional as he spoke of finding his own connection with God again after neglecting it for so many years while pursuing education and fortune. It was not until he unintentionally arrived in Niederbipp that he began to recognize a need to reconnect with spirituality. He had just begun working at Pottery Niederbipp when he was asked to deliver some handmade tiles to a farm on Harmony Hill. It was there that he was introduced to Millie and George Smurthwaite.

Mr. Bingham learned that the tiles he'd delivered that day were destined to be used on the Denkbankli (traditional Swiss thinking benches) that Mr. Smurthwaite was building in his shop. It was on one of those benches, overlooking a freshly harvested field, that Mr. Bingham first felt an inclination to stay in Niederbipp. He often said that this decision was the second most important decision he ever made, the most important being to marry his wife, Lily.

On a subsequent visit to the farm, Mr. Bingham learned from the Smurthwaites that the tradition of the Denkbankli stretched back to the time when humans first began considering the purpose of life and their place in the universe. On that visit, while helping Mr. Smurthwaite place several of the new benches in locations across the farm, Mr. Bingham learned that much of the world's most beautiful music, art, and ideas were inspired on similar thinking benches scattered across the globe. Over the next several months, Mr. Bingham returned to the farm often, enjoying its peace and beauty and the wisdom and friendship that the Smurthwaites so kindly shared with him. And it was on that farm, while sitting on his favorite bench—the one overlooking the orchard—that Mr. Bingham sought God's council about marrying Lily. He said he "felt a small and peaceful voice from heaven telling [him] to proceed without delay." He proposed that evening and married Lily two weeks later on March 20, 1953. Unfortunately, she succumbed to an influenza epidemic that swept through the region less than a year later. But despite his sorrows and loss, Mr. Bingham maintained his faith and hope. His friendship with the Smurthwaites and later with Ruby and Lorenzo Swarovski—the current stewards of Harmony Hill Farm (see pages 241–46)—helped to sustain him. But he maintains that he became acquainted with God in the still, quiet moments he spent on the benches—those scattered across the secluded farm as well as those in the graveyard—considering his purpose in life.

In our aforementioned 1978 interview, Mr. Bingham explained that in spite of his desires to help people live more fulfilling lives, he had found that he lacked any significant power to instigate lasting change. He did note, however, that more often than not, individuals who spend dedicated time in expectant stillness find their own power to change. Mr. Bingham's work on the benches around Niederbipp has proven to be well timed. In years since that first bench was installed at the Engelhart Ebenezer, the young people of our nation and throughout the world have been swept into wars, drugs, sexual countercultures, and confusion of all kinds. He maintains that the only hope our world has for a peaceful future is for more people to have opportunities for reflection, contemplation, and spiritual connection like those available in our community.

Though the bronze plaque that once adorned the alcove of the Engelhart Ebenezer was stolen in the 1930s and presumably sold for scrap, the monument and the surrounding trails continue to fulfill the role that Mr. Bingham believes the tower's creators intended: to offer a place of peace where one might slow down, ask questions, and discover for oneself a connection to the divine.

Genevieve looked up from the book again to the monument that towered over her, its shadow growing longer across the weathered surface of the sandstone bench on which she sat. She reached out and touched the subtle carving, running her fingers over the letters.

BE STILL, AND KNOW THAT I AM GOD.

She took a moment to acknowledge the calm that filled her heart. And she remembered the same sense of calm she'd experienced just the night before on the bench overlooking the orchard. She wondered if that bench might be the same one that Mr. Bingham had visited so many years before. And she wondered how many people had sat on the orchard bench—or any of the other benches—and been filled with this unique sense of calm. This was a strange place. But she was learning that it was strange in a good way. The calm in her heart felt empowering and sustaining. It made her feel as if she could do anything, as if she had no limits, no fears that could hold her back, no challenges that could keep her down.

CHAPTER 54

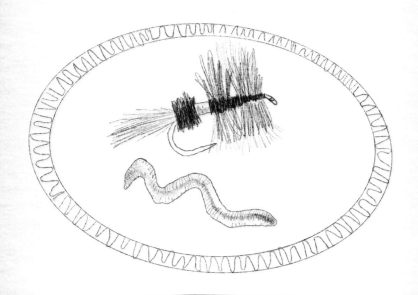

Of Flies and Worms

Correction does much, but encouragement does more.
—Johann Wolfgang von Goethe

The chime of the church bells rang out, and Genevieve counted them. One, two, three, four. Four o'clock! She suddenly remembered that Pops was supposed to meet them at the stand between four and five, and she wasn't certain how far away she was or how long it would take her to get there. She picked up the stolen books and headed back toward the river the way she'd come. She descended the earthen stairs of the riverbank and hurried past the swing, now vacant and waiting to do what swings do best.

Insects and birds and the crunch of gravel under her feet were the only sounds Genevieve heard as she rushed over the banks. She rounded a bend and saw the bridge a few hundred yards downriver. From there, she knew the farm stand was only another few hundred yards away.

As she strode up to the farm stand, she found Spencer sitting on a log, his back leaning against the shack. "Oh hey! What's up?" she said casually.

"You locked me out!" he replied.

"*What*? You expected me to stick around waiting for you after you abandoned me? I left you your lunch, which is way more than you did for me. Did you bring back the lunch pail?"

He lifted it up but didn't look at her. "Where'd you go?"

"I don't know why you care."

"Yeah, well, just because I don't really care doesn't mean I'm not curious," he said, turning to her with a charming smile. "I was hoping to put my fish in the fridge while we waited for Pops to get here. Do you have the key?"

"You went fishing?" she asked, checking her pockets before she remembered placing the key under a rock near the back door of the shack.

He nodded, lifting up a plastic bag filled with what looked like a dozen trout.

She laughed as she unlocked the back door. When the fish were in the minifridge, Genevieve followed Spencer back out into the sunlight, bringing a lawn chair with her. She sat down next to him, surprised by how tired and humble he looked.

"Wait, don't you have to have a fishing license to catch fish?"

"Well, yeah. Probably. I guess I didn't actually catch them."

"So…what? You just walked along the banks whistling, and they jumped into your bag?"

Spencer laughed, breaking the ice. "No, it was a lot better than that." He laughed again, turning to face her. "I'm sorry for being a jerk. I'm sorry I walked away and was an idiot."

She looked at him dubiously.

"What?" he asked. "Are you doubting my sincerity?"

"I guess I'm just waiting for the punchline."

He took a deep breath and let it out quickly through loose lips, creating a sound like a motor. "I'm sorry," he repeated. "I'm not good at any of this, least of all this," he said, motioning with his fingers to the space between them.

"Uh, you know that could mean many different things, right?"

"It could?"

"Sure. I could think of at least four different scenarios right off. You could be saying that you're not any good at communicating like you're an adult or that you're not any good at being a decent person or that you're not any good at *not* ditching the person you're supposed to work with or that you're not any good at treating women with respect."

He took another deep breath. "I guess maybe it's all of those things, isn't it?"

She nodded. "I'm not going to lie. You're a difficult personality, for sure—not that I'm perfect. But yeah, I think I could sum up our experience of working together as seriously disappointing."

He nodded and looked away. But he turned back and looked at her again after only a few seconds. "Do you think we could have a do-over?"

"Uh, isn't that what today was supposed to be?"

"Yeah, well, I obviously screwed up this one too."

"Yeah, you did. I don't get it, Spencer. I mean, yeah, I'm obviously flawed and…difficult to work with, according to James, who took it upon himself to speak for all of you men. But what's going on? Why are we so bad together?"

"I don't know," he said after giving it a moment's thought.

"No ideas?"

"Okay, if we're being honest, you remind me of my ex."

She waited for more, but nothing else came. "That's it?"

He smiled with pursed lips. "I think it must be the power you swing around."

"What?"

He held up his hand. "Obviously my problem, not yours. I…grew up with a strong single mother who left me with an aversion to strong women."

"Oh, I get it. You'd rather have a weak woman you can walk all over?"

"No, of course not. I…don't know what I want. That's probably part of the problem. Maybe it's *all* of the problem."

"Why did you come here this summer?"

"Because I felt like I was lost, like my life was going nowhere, and I was…tired of having every significant romantic relationship blow up on me."

"And you thought a summer on the funny farm would help you fix all of that?" she asked bemusedly.

"I don't know what I thought. I needed to do something different. My love life has been a series of disasters. I mean, meeting women has never been difficult for me, but things always end up exploding within the first few months."

"Do you know why?"

He shrugged. "You seem to be fairly observant, and you've been around me for almost two weeks. If you had to guess, what would you say my problem is?"

"I don't think I need to guess," she responded with a guffaw.

"Oh, really? Enlighten me."

She wondered if he were serious. "Okay, three things right off seem to be problematic: you're a short-tempered jerk, you seem to think that the world revolves around you, and you don't treat women well."

"Okay, that's probably a fair assessment based on my behavior here, but I guess I was wondering more about why you think things might have gone so poorly for me outside of this crazy town."

"Oh, are you suggesting that all this bad behavior is new for you?" she asked sarcastically.

"I don't know," he said, shaking his head. "I mean, I like to think of myself as a pretty patient and generous guy. I've always bought my girlfriends whatever they've wanted and taken them with me when I travel for work. That's good, right?"

"Are you asking if I think women just want to be pampered with lavish gifts and paraded around like exotic pets?"

He looked confused.

"Spencer, I don't know what the women you've been hanging out with want, but I would guess from our limited experience that you don't have much room in your life for them."

"What do you mean? I took my last girlfriend to Miami, Chicago, *and* LA, and we were only together for like two months."

"And how much time did you actually spend with her?"

"Tons of time."

"Really? What did you do?"

"Well, you know…she came with me to the stations. And she watched me work sometimes. You know, I got backstage passes to all the sports shows and a bunch of events."

"Oh yeah, that sounds like a lot of fun."

"Right?" he responded, not catching her sarcasm. "She got to meet all the stars: LeBron, the Williams sisters, Tom Brady, all of them."

"And was she impressed?"

"Who wouldn't be, right? I mean, who else gets access like that? I would've killed to get my picture taken with stars like them…I mean, back before I actually had access to people like that all the time. I thought she'd be super impressed, but she thought it was a total snooze. I didn't get her at all."

"What was she into?"

The question seemed to surprise him. He didn't have an immediate answer.

"Okay, here's an easier one: what was her favorite color?"

He looked uncertain.

"Favorite movie? Favorite music? Favorite book?"

"Oh, I know she liked Christian Louboutin shoes," he responded, proud he'd come up with one answer.

Genevieve laughed. "What woman doesn't? Did you know *one* unique thing about this girl?"

"Well, she was smokin' hot."

Genevieve rolled her eyes. "You really are hopeless."

"What?" he asked, looking clueless.

"Is that all you saw in her?"

"No, I mean…but that's important, right? I mean, hey, you've gotta be attracted to the person you're with, don't you?"

"Sure, but how shallow are you? I bet you didn't even know her birthday?"

"Uh…March, I think. She's a Sagittarius."

She shook her head. "Okay, there are at least two significant fails in that sentence."

He looked confused again.

"*One*, Sagittarius is in November and December. And *two*, March might be a birth *month*, but it's not a birth*day*!"

He shrugged. "What's the difference? She's gone anyway."

"Look, I know next to nothing about sports, but isn't that like saying there's no difference between LeBron James and Serena Williams."

"Pfff! No one would ever say that!"

"Spencer, if you're asking for my honest opinion about why things have turned out so poorly for you in the love department, I'd say it's pretty obvious."

"Oh really?" he said in a challenging tone. "Are you a therapist?"

"No, I'm a woman, and with almost thirty years' experience, I'd like to consider myself an expert."

"All right. Let's hear it," he said, cupping his hand to his ear.

"Okay. So, my experience with you is obviously limited, but I just have to say I'm underwhelmed. I mean, you have some of the things I find attractive in a man—you're good looking and well groomed. It looks like you take care of yourself. Those are good things."

"But?"

"I obviously don't know any of your exes, but I'd be willing to bet that if I interviewed them, they would all say that they found you to be a selfish, egotistical misogynist."

"Oh really? I bought them all sorts of stuff. How does that qualify me as selfish? I'm one of the most generous guys I know."

"Let me suggest that there's a difference between real generosity and playing fast and loose with your wallet."

"Oh yeah?" he asked challengingly.

"Why did you buy them stuff?"

"Because they wanted it. What can I say? I'm a generous guy."

She nodded. "Okay, but if you look a little deeper, I bet you were at least a little concerned about how you'd look if you said *no* to buying her that expensive Gucci purse, right? And you've got to admit that it's an ego trip for you, walking into those after-parties with a beautiful girl in a skimpy little cocktail dress and a pair of thousand-dollar shoes that you bought her, right?"

"What does that have to do with anything?" he asked defensively.

"I'm no generosity expert, but I'm guessing that at the root of what you call generosity, there's a big, fat piece of ego."

Again, he looked confused.

"I'm sure some women think having a sugar daddy to buy them pricey shoes and purses and then wine and dine them at the fanciest restaurants is a pretty great thing. But how shallow is that? I mean, I'm just shootin' from the hip, but shouldn't attraction be based on something that's beyond skin deep? I mean, surely there's got to be more to keeping two people together for fifty years than just physical attraction and the occasional shopping spree. You've seen the way Lorenzo looks at Ruby, right?"

He shook his head, looking blank. "I guess I never noticed."

"I've been watching them. There's not one fashionable thing in Ruby's entire wardrobe as far as I've seen, and if she ever had a figure, gravity got the best of it a long time ago. But it's obvious that Pops adores her and that they love each other and that their love is based on something much deeper than just physical attraction. Crystal said she saw them kissing the other day—and it wasn't just a peck."

"Yuck," he responded, screwing up his face.

"*Really*?"

"They're so old. Shouldn't they have gotten that out of their system by now? I can't even imagine them having…you don't think they…" he trailed off, looking disgusted at the mere thought of it.

"You know what? I hope they do!" she responded. "I hope they're passionate. I don't really care to think about the physiological details of how that works for old people. But my point is, a healthy, long-lasting marriage has got to be based on something deeper than physical attraction and expensive gifts."

"What kind of stuff are you thinking about?"

She shrugged. "Maybe I'm not talking about *stuff* at all. I don't know if I've ever thought about it until now, but maybe there's way more to a happy marriage than the stuff you see on the outside."

"Like what?"

"Oh, I don't know. I've heard stories about how things were when my parents were poor grad students, but by the time I was old enough to pay attention, they were already members of the country club and had a summer home on Lake Washington. We always had nice cars and toys and enough money to travel and do anything we wanted."

"That sounds like a pretty good life to me."

"Yeah, I know I should be more grateful. But I guess I've secretly always believed that marriage and family are supposed to be more than just looking good for the people you run into at Sunday brunch at the country club. On paper, my parents have all the stuff that's supposed to make you happy."

"They're not?"

Genevieve shook her head. "I don't think anyone would ever say they want a marriage like Ted and Sally Patterson's when they grow up. I know I don't. I'm not sure if they even talk to each other anymore. It's been years since they shared a bedroom. Mom drinks too much, and Dad's away too much. Like I said, it looks good from the outside, but if you peel back the shiny veneer, it's basically a loveless marriage of convenience. I'm sure they'd probably be divorced if they could figure out a way to split things up."

Spencer nodded thoughtfully. "So, in your mind, what's a good marriage supposed to look like?"

"I guess I've spent more time thinking about what I don't want my marriage to look like than what I do. I'm sure that thoughtful gifts can be a part of a healthy marriage, but I've watched my own father come home from trips with jewelry for my mom that felt like a sorry excuse for not being a better, more present husband. I think his *time* is what she really wanted. I think maybe that's what a real gift is—a part of yourself that you're willing to share with someone you love. No offense, but spending a day watching you work, with or without a bunch of famous athletes, sounds more like torture than quality time. But that's just me. I'm sure there are probably lots of girls who would think that's a good time, but I can't say I personally know any girl who would dig that."

"Really?" he asked, looking like he was sincerely surprised.

"Absolutely. What does she know about you at the end of the day other than that you know a lot of rich, famous athletes?"

He looked at her blankly.

"And maybe more importantly, what do you know about her? It's doubtful that you'll ever learn her favorite color or what makes her tick by filling her time and senses with everything that doesn't really matter and nothing that truly does."

"I make my living on what you're suggesting doesn't really matter," he said, sounding a little defensive.

"Then you'll have to work extra hard at making sure your next girlfriend feels like she's at least as important to you as watching replays and knowing stats. If you don't care enough to know *her* stats, what have you got?"

Spencer nodded slowly. "You're making this sound a lot more complicated than I imagined it would be."

"Why does it sound complicated?"

"I guess I just thought that...well, I guess I've always thought that

I could buy myself some points by taking my girlfriend shopping and introducing her to my friends. Sometimes it feels like girls are just so needy."

"Sometimes we are. And I'm sure that some are more needy than others. But would you really expect a girl to commit the rest of her life to you if you're more concerned about catching the game than making sure she's safe?"

"Well, it dep..." he began before he caught himself, realizing that her question was very specific to the situation between the two of them. "I...but what if it's my job?"

She smiled and shook her head.

"Look, if I don't have a job, how am I supposed to take care of a wife?"

"You may not ever need to worry about that."

"What? Why?" he asked, confused.

"Because not many women would marry a guy whose vows include, 'I promise to honor and cherish you in sickness and in health, as long as the game's not on or there aren't replays to watch.' That's not really love, right? It's like..." she searched for the right words. "It's like you'll show love when it's convenient for you, which is just...selfish."

"Wow, maybe you really are a therapist," he said, looking sincere.

"Nope, just a woman who likes to shoot straight and who's not afraid to call you an idiot if you deserve it."

"So how am supposed to get over this hurdle?"

"The *idiot* hurdle?"

"No, I mean, I work a lot. It's my passion. I get paid well, and the idea of spending less time at work is frankly really frightening to me. I could miss out on so much."

"Oh, I get it. So instead you're willing to give up on creating a relationship with a woman that could last a lifetime?"

"I guess that sounded pretty lame, didn't it?"

"Yep."

"So in your opinion, what do you think I should do?"

"I guess that all depends on what you want."

"Tell me what you're thinking."

"Well, I don't know much about football, but I would guess it's pretty tough to win the Super Bowl if you screw up the first five games of the season, right?"

"Not impossible, but I'd never bet on it," he responded after quick consideration.

"I guess I'm thinking it's gotta be kind of the same way with marriage. It seems like it would be almost impossible to have a strong marriage that lasts fifty-plus years if you didn't give it all you've got in the beginning and then keep striving throughout the whole marriage. I'm sure we both know people whose marriages fizzled out and died after just a couple of years. And then a bunch more fall apart when a midlife crisis hits or menopause begins or the kids leave home. The couple is just left wondering who that stranger is they've lived with for all these years."

Spencer nodded. "So how do you keep any of those scenarios from happening?"

"I don't know if there's only one answer. I'm sure it's probably different for every couple. But I'd guess that communication plays a big role in all cases. And it seems like you'd have to make a continual, conscious effort to look outside of yourself and consider the needs of your partner."

"Yeah, that sounds like a lot of work."

"You didn't expect a good marriage to be a cakewalk, did you?"

"I can't say I've seen a lot of positive examples of awesome marriages. I guess I've just thought that focusing on finding a woman who shares some of my interests would be a good place to start."

"Okay, sure, but can you imagine spending fifty years with someone if your only commonality were that you like the same wine or that you spend three hours a day working out or even that you both root for the same team?"

"I've seen marriages based on less than that."

"Yeah, but were they lasting marriages? I mean, what happens after a year or two when you realize you don't have as much in common as you thought you did before the lust wore off and the credit-card bills arrived?"

"You're a cynic, aren't you?" Spencer suggested.

"Probably. It just seems like a lot of things change for people after they've been married a year or two."

He nodded but looked unconvinced. "Like what?"

"Well, I'm sure we both have single friends who work out for a couple of hours each day. But I don't think I know one married person with kids who has time for more than a thirty-minute jog, and it seems like that's more to clear their heads than to actually get a workout."

Spencer shook his head. "Yeah, I've seen a lot of married people let themselves go. It's really sad."

"That's one way to look at it, but maybe it's because a lot of married people realize there's more to life than stroking their egos and pretending they're still twenty years old. I don't want to admit it any more than you do, but the truth is, we're both aging out of our prime. In my business, I'm starting to feel like the old lady when I go to fashion shows and realize there aren't many models older than thirty. And the few who are spend a mint on silicone and Botox to keep up the facade of youth and beauty."

"Are you saying you'd rather just let the clock roll over you?"

She shook her head but didn't answer for a moment. "I guess I'm starting to recognize that trying to outrun it is pointless. No woman ever wants to admit it, but it seems like if you want a healthy marriage and couple of kids, you have to be willing to give up your size 6 and sacrifice a lot of freedom of movement."

"Oh boy, you're making marriage sound really attractive!" he said sarcastically.

She nodded. "Ya know, before I came here, I used to tell myself that marriage is for people who don't have a better plan."

"You've changed your mind?" he asked dubiously.

"I don't know if it's changed or just…evolved."

"What's the difference?"

"I don't know. Maybe evolving takes longer."

"Uh, yeah. I don't know if you noticed, but we've been here less than two weeks. I'm not really a science guy, but last I checked that's hardly enough time for evolution."

She nodded thoughtfully. "I think maybe it's been evolving for a couple of years and I just haven't really taken the time to acknowledge it until now."

"What kind of evolution are we talking about?"

"Evolution in what I want in life. My dreams. The realities I'm willing to accept."

"It sounds like you're giving in."

"I don't know—maybe I am. I guess I'm tired of pretending that I know what I'm doing. Being here, unhitching my wagon from the world I've lived in for the last seven years—it's given me a lot of time to think and recognize that I don't really have things figured out as well as I thought I did."

"What don't you have figured out?"

"Like independence, for one. I used to think independence was something I needed to defend tooth and nail. But looking back to just two weeks ago, that picture I'd drawn of myself as a career woman with all the glamour I thought was so important, it just feels shallow…lonely. I really can't believe I'm admitting this, especially to an insensitive guy like you. I mean, I love my job. It's the job I always wanted, and it's been awesome. Really, really awesome."

"But?"

"But it's not real." She closed her eyes and shook her head. "None of it's real. And if I'm honest, you've helped me recognize some of that."

"Me? How?"

"By holding up a mirror and helping me see how shallow our lives have been."

"Excuse me?"

"Oh, come on. I mean, you're a beautiful man, but there's not a lot of depth behind your charming smile and chiseled muscles."

"What the hell are you talking about?"

"I'm talking about how you spent a thousand dollars to buy a girl a pair of shoes without knowing anything about her other than the fact that she's hot. If I had to guess, I'd say you probably met her and most of your past girlfriends at either a nightclub or on an app like Tinder or Hookuplandia, right?"

He nodded, looking surprised.

"Have you ever thought about that time, twenty years down the road, when your teenage son asks you where you met his mom? And then you have to tell him you were looking for a one-night stand but she was so hot it lasted longer than you thought? So you hung around for five or six years until you realized she no longer looked as hot as she did when she was twenty-four and you were drunk and horny and an idiot?"

"Is there a point to this, or are you just trying to make me feel bad?"

"I guess I'm trying to say that it sounds like you're the kind of guy who's been searching for an orchid in a huge field of dandelions. But your ego and self-centeredness have kept you from recognizing where you are and that it's nobody's fault but your own that you can't find what you're looking for. And I guess I'm also suggesting that unless something big changes in your outlook or performance, the most you'll ever end up with is a bouquet of wilted dandelions."

He looked at her strangely. "Have you been talking to Thomas?"

"Thomas who?"

"Thomas, you know. The priest guy."

"Not since that first Sunday, why?"

He looked at her closely, almost as if he were looking for any hint of insincerity or deception. "I ran into him after I left this morning. Did you know he's a fisherman?"

"No."

"Yeah, he's a really good one—a fly-fisherman. Even ties his own flies."

"Really? So is he the one who caught all those fish?" she asked, pointing to the minifridge.

"Yeah, and about fifty more. He let most of them go. He only kept the ones he caught in the last hour."

"You were with him all day?"

"Pretty much. He's a really cool guy. He knows at least a little bit about everything, and he is full of surprises."

"Like what?"

"Well, he was engaged once."

"You mean to be married?" she asked incredulously.

"Yeah, to be married. But it was a serious tragedy. She was with some friends, and they drove off an icy road and drowned in the river back in the early eighties."

"That's horrible! Is that why he became a priest?"

"No. He was a priest before he came to Niederbipp. His first assignment was to a small town upriver. He made some stupid mistakes that made his congregation and the rest of the community hate him, so they tied him up, threw him into a rowboat, and sent him downriver."

"Seriously?"

"That's what he said. I guess he washed up on the riverbanks near Niederbipp and was taken in by some potter named Isaac."

"Isaac? Was it Isaac Bingham?"

"Yeah, I think so. You know him?" Spencer asked, looking surprised.

"No. I just read a little bit about him in this book," she said, pulling the book from inside the belly flap of her cutoff overalls.

He took the book, reading the cover. "Where'd you get this?"

"The library in town."

"You have a Niederbipp library card?"

"Well, no, not exactly."

"So how did you get this book then?" he asked suspiciously.

"Don't worry about it. It's a long, boring story. What do you know about Isaac Bingham?"

"Not that much. I guess he was one of Thomas's best friends, but he died a while back."

"Yeah, a friend of mine—I think her husband took Isaac's place when he died. He's the potter now, anyway."

"Yeah, that's what Thomas said. It's Jack or something, isn't it?"

"Jake, I think. But I've only met him once."

Spencer looked back at the cover of the book. "Thomas O. Kelly," he said, pointing to the name on the book's cover. "Do you think that's the same Thomas as the priest guy?"

"I don't know," she said, taking a closer look and recognizing the potential. "Does it say anything about the author at the back of the book?"

Spencer flipped open the back cover and leafed through the last few pages until he saw a short paragraph under the heading *About the Author*. He read it aloud:

Thomas O'Sullivan Kelly, originally from Boston, MA, has made Niederbipp his home for the last ten years. Before arriving in Niederbipp, Thomas studied at St. Vincent Seminary in Latrobe, PA. After a short stint as a parish priest in Codham, PA, Thomas made the decision to walk away from ecclesiastical duties and focus instead on nonclerical forms of ministering. His passion for history and his desire to share what he's learned prompted the writing of this book. Pulled from the town's archives, as well as from the hearts and minds of its residents through hundreds of hours of interviews, this short history offers its readers the most comprehensive history of Niederbipp ever compiled in one place. Thomas hopes that as they study these pages, readers might come to love the unique town and its residents as much as he does.

"Sounds like the same Thomas to me," Genevieve suggested.

"Yeah," he responded as he flipped through the pages of the book, stopping briefly at several of the old photographs to take a closer look.

"Why did you ask if I'd been talking to him?"

"Oh, just a few of the things he was saying today sounded similar."

"Like what?"

"Do you know much about fishing?"

"Do I look like the kind of girl who'd know much about fishing?" she asked, laughing.

"Yeah, no," he said after looking her over quickly.

"Why do you ask?"

"I've never fished before, but I've seen people do it. But I've never seen anyone fish the way he does."

"Fly-fishing? That's where you whip your fly back and forth, right?"

"Yes, but Thomas also uses worms."

"Is that normal?"

"No. Even he admitted it isn't. Get this: the guy catches fish with his flies, but before he lets 'em go, he sticks a worm in their mouths and thanks them. He says, 'I'll see you again when you get a little bit bigger. Go, be free, and eat well.'"

"What?" she asked, laughing.

"Yeah! Crazy, huh?"

"Did he say why he does that?"

"Yeah. He says he feels so bad about deceiving the fish with his artificial flies that he decided he was going to thank them by giving them something real to eat for their troubles."

"Seriously?" she laughed again.

"Yeah. He said he's been doing it for years, that it just feels like good karma or something. Most days he doesn't keep any fish at all. He just catches them, feeds them worms, and lets them go. He kept me busy all day digging for worms," Spencer said, showing Genevieve the blisters on his hands.

She smiled but looked confused. "So wait. How did that remind you of anything I just said?"

"It's the worms. Well, and the flies too, I guess."

"What?"

"Thomas said fishing was a lot like dating and courtship."

"Oh really? Because you can spend your whole life doing it and not catch anything?"

"Ha! That's exactly what I said. No, he said that most fishing is about deception and trickery. Real flies offer fish nourishment that keeps them going. Artificial flies offer zero nourishment, and the fish usually end up on someone's dinner plate."

"And that's like dating…how?"

"Well, think about it. I can't tell you how many girls I've met who look pretty awesome at the club but turn out to be totally artificial fakes. I'm sure it's probably the same for you and guys, right?"

"Well, actually…yeah. I mean, it feels like the analogy is a bit of a stretch, but I can see it."

"Thomas said that he's known a lot of people who've married and later realized they were clueless about who their partner really was."

"Did he offer any suggestions about how to avoid that scenario?"

"Only that it's important to keep your eyes wide open when you're dating."

"That seems obvious."

"Yeah, but how often have you ignored it? I know I have. Sometimes when you're in the middle of a romance, your senses get dulled. I dated a girl a few years back. Man, I thought she was the one. She was beautiful and smart and…the full package deal. I was so whooped that I missed a lot of warning signs. Just a few weeks after we started dating, she started talking about getting married and moving in with me. And she wanted more and more of my time. I was just going along with it, not really sure about her but also not sure how to slow things down. I had a couple of friends telling me to put on the brakes, but of course I didn't want to listen. You never do when things are going well for you, right? She was saying all the right things and totally makin' me think she loved me. She was this close to moving in with me."

"But?"

"But my buddies intervened, thank God. They saw all sorts of things I didn't see, like that she was needy and manipulative. I was so naive. They finally came to me with an ultimatum—either slow things down with Shayla and pull my head out of my butt, or they were done being my friends."

"So what happened?"

"Well, for some reason I listened. She totally freaked out when I told her I needed some time and space to think. She unfriended me on

Facebook that night and blocked my phone calls and texts even though I had just bought her a new phone and paid for a two-year contract. It went from hot to ice cold so fast, it created a hurricane that blew my world apart. That was almost three years ago, and I'm still skittish about trusting women."

"Sorry."

He shrugged. "I'm sure whatever Thomas said sounded way better than how I explained it, but since I've been hooked by an artificial fly before, it made a ton of sense to me."

"So you turned around and became an artificial fly yourself?"

"What do you mean?"

"Don't you see we're back to the same place we started? Instead of giving a woman your time and being sincerely interested in her, you give her whatever time's left over and make her think you really care by faking her out with expensive gifts."

He smiled lamely. "Hey, it works."

"No it doesn't. If it did, you wouldn't be here. You'd be married and have a couple of kids by now. You'd be living a real dream instead of some fake one."

"Ouch!" he responded, clutching his heart.

"Maybe Thomas has it right."

"Which part?"

"If you're gonna attract a woman with your outer charms, you better be able to offer her something real to back it up. None of this inviting-her-for-a-bike-ride-and-then-ditching-her-when-she's-too-slow nonsense."

"Hey, I'm sorry, okay? Are you ever gonna let me live that down?"

"The question is, are *you* ever gonna *decide* to live it down? Your performance this morning suggested to me you might not be capable of better behavior."

He nodded slowly. "I understand why you would feel that way, and I'm sorry."

She looked at him. He looked sincere, but she wasn't about to trust him further than she could spit without seeing some serious changes. "I've got an idea."

"Okay?"

"I'm sure it's obvious to both of us that we would never marry each other or even date."

He nodded.

"So what do you say we just cut the crap and try to be honest friends? You can tell me when I'm out of line, and I will do the same for you. We can help each other see whatever we might be naturally clueless about."

"So are you suggesting we kind of treat each other like siblings?"

"Yeah, I guess I am. I'm an only child, so I'm not really sure what that means. But it might be fun, as long as I can call you an idiot when you deserve it."

He laughed. "Can I do the same for you?"

"Okay," she agreed after giving it a moment of thought. "Let's be real or die trying."

CHAPTER 55

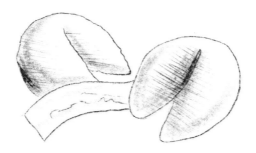

A Time to Dance

> Life should not be a journey to the grave with the intention of arriving safely in a pretty and well preserved body, but rather to skid in broadside in a cloud of smoke, thoroughly used up, totally worn out, and loudly proclaiming, "Wow! What a Ride!"
> —Hunter S. Thompson

Pops arrived in the pickup a few minutes after Genevieve and Spencer had sealed their pact with a handshake. He seemed pleased with Spencer's bagful of trout and even more pleased to hear that they had sold all the goods at the farm stand, making at least twice as much money as he'd expected. Genevieve decided there was no use in pointing out that she alone had sold the goods after Spencer had abandoned her, and so she kept it to herself.

The smell of basil and garlic hit them before they could open the door to big house, and they found Matt and Susan in the kitchen working on dinner. While Spencer and Ruby rinsed the trout and got them ready for the freezer, Genevieve made her way to the bunkhouse. There she found Holly and Crystal writing letters and Sonja napping, her journal open on her chest and a pleasant smile on her dozing face.

Genevieve grabbed her own journal and went to find a vacant bench. She wanted to write down her thoughts about Thomas's book while they were still fresh. The words and thoughts poured out of her as she described her feelings surrounding the benches' origins. She wrote of the unique feelings of peace she'd already experienced at the farm benches and of her desire to spend more time in contemplation. She had filled nearly four pages when she heard the distant sound of the dinner bell. Reluctant to put her writing aside, she made her way back to the big house.

Most of the campers had already found their seats around the table by the time she arrived, and Ephraim was enthusiastically passing around the jar of Wisdom Cookies. Pops and Ruby made their way to the ends of the table, and they all bowed their heads for grace.

As the family passed around the bowls filled with fresh pasta, pesto sauce, and salad, Ephraim broke into the first Wisdom Cookie and read the slip of paper aloud: "'Opportunity is missed by most people because it is dressed in overalls and looks like work.'"

"Amen to that!" Pops said.

"Who said that?" asked Crystal.

All eyes turned to Matt, the resident quote collector, who looked reluctant to say. Finally he declared, "Come on, guys, this is an easy one."

No one seemed to have any ideas.

"Thomas Edison, right?" Matt asked Ruby.

"Very good. Mr. Edison certainly knew a lot about finding opportunities buried deep under piles of work and experimentation. And if we're honest with ourselves, that's usually where we find our opportunities too."

Several heads nodded.

"I've got one," Sonja said, pulling a strip of paper from her cookie. "'Following the path of least resistance is what makes rivers and men crooked.'"

"That almost sounds like Thoreau," Susan offered, "but I don't think it is."

"No, Thoreau's words were similar, but that one come from Aunt Ann," Ruby said.

"Anonymous?" Rachael asked, laughing.

"The one and only."

"This is a good one," Greg said, holding the strip of paper closer to his face. "'Indeed, man wishes to be happy even when he so lives as to make happiness impossible.'"

"Whoa! Who said that?" asked Josh.

Matt shrugged, his mouth full of pasta. "Sounds a bit like C. S. Lewis," he managed.

"Yes, it does, but I believe that's Saint Augustine," Pops suggested when no one had a better answer.

"Read that one again," Spencer said from across the table.

"'Indeed, man wishes to be happy even when he so lives as to make happiness impossible,'" Greg repeated.

Spencer nodded slowly, stealing a glance at Genevieve.

"So, I've been curious how the photo shoot went," Genevieve said, feeling a need to change the subject.

"Oh, just peachy," Ruby said. "He was in and out of here in just a couple of hours—said he'd be back another time to see how things were progressing. By the way, Mr. O'Brien was kind enough to bring us a large basket of strawberries, among several other gifts. You wouldn't happen to know anything about that, would you?"

Genevieve soon had them all laughing as she recounted how Patrick O'Brien had stopped by the farm stand, hit his head on the awning, cracked the screen on his phone, and then let her talk him into buying all the merchandise.

"I recognized the basket right away," Ruby said in a fit of laughter. "I had a hard time keeping a straight face, and then the cream and the eggs and the flowers from my own garden..." She laughed so hard that the rest of the family couldn't help but join her. "Have you ever considered a career in sales?" Ruby asked through her tears.

The sunny spirit of the evening continued as the family finished dinner and split up the evening chores, some going with Pops to the cowshed to help with the evening milking while the rest gathered in the kitchen, either helping with the dishes or preparing Patrick O'Brien's gift of strawberries and cream for dessert. The evening was darker than most, storm clouds rolling quickly across the sky. A loud thunderclap startled everyone in the kitchen, and before Pops and the rest of the campers returned from the barn, huge raindrops began to fall, making loud popping sounds on the roof and the kitchen's overhead skylight.

Ruby, mischievously smiling, insisted that the kitchen crew follow her to the porch with the dessert and dishes. She kicked off her shoes and stood at the top of the painted stairs. There she closed her eyes, stretched her arms out to her side, and breathed deeply as the rain splashed on her bare feet. Genevieve noticed that several of the campers were smiling as they watched the old woman behaving more like a child. The childlike wonder and happiness on the old woman's face were inspiring, even contagious. Tossing aside her natural inclination to avoid spontaneous behavior, Genevieve walked to the edge of the stairs and mimicked the matriarch. The other campers followed, taking in the sounds and scents of the storm, their eyes closed, helping them focus on their auditory and olfactory senses.

But their solemn stance didn't last long. At the joyful sound of a playful squeal, they opened their eyes to find Ruby dancing on the lawn, her face already wet and shiny in the magical light of the storm. Rex, the farm dog, appeared out of nowhere and raced around Ruby in a chaotic circle, howling like his ancestor wolves. The campers watched in wonder from the porch until Holly pushed through the crowd. She joined Ruby on the lawn, and the two danced to a tune only they could hear.

A second dancer was all it took to get the party started. The campers rushed the yard, carrying Genevieve with them down the stairs and onto the lawn, giant raindrops quickly soaking them to all to the bone. Pops and the others came rushing from the barn, and the front yard quickly turned into the most glorious dance hall any of them had ever seen. Ephraim ran back to the house and turned on the porch's festoon lights, illuminating the yard with magic. Rain, lightning, and thunder enveloped the dancers as the water ran like rivers from their hair and clothes and faces. Genevieve looked around and noticed that all of them, even Spencer, were smiling broadly and seemed to be enjoying themselves in the spontaneous act of joyous frivolity. The dancing continued as the water accumulated, soaking the lawn so thoroughly that a generous splash echoed each dancing step. Laughter filled the air, overpowering even the rolling thunder and Rex's howls, as campers danced around with childlike abandon.

Genevieve looked into the faces of each of the campers, smiling to herself as she watched them interacting with each other, splashing and dancing like they didn't care at all how silly they might look. But even with rain dripping off her face, Genevieve could tell from a distance that there was a different emotion on Holly's face—a subtle but definite sadness.

"Are you okay?" Genevieve spoke softly after making her way stealthily to Holly's side, being careful not to draw the others' attention.

Holly forced a smile. "Just missing my mom. We used to do this all the time," she said, a sob catching in her throat.

"You were lucky," Genevieve said, out of breath. "This is my very first rain dance, unless getting caught in the rain between the subway and my apartment qualifies. But that wasn't any fun, so I don't think it counts."

Holly nodded. "Sometimes you don't realize how lucky you are to have crazy parents until it's too late." She forced another smile, her eyes filled with loss. "Thanks for caring."

"Oh…sure," Genevieve said, surprised by an unfamiliar pulse of emotion. Another crash of thunder sounded, this time directly over their heads.

"That was from Mom," Holly said, pointing to the sky before turning her face up and opening her mouth to catch raindrops.

The rain dance continued for ten more glorious minutes. When all the campers were thoroughly waterlogged and soggy, Ruby sent Ephraim and Crystal to the wardrobes in the dining hall for towels while she carefully dismantled the few parts of her updo that hadn't already fallen. Genevieve watched as Ruby amassed a handful of bobby pins, allowing her long silver hair to fall over her shoulders and down her back. With her hair down, Ruby looked at least two decades younger. Genevieve wondered if Patrick O'Brien's photographs had captured anything as powerful as the old woman who stood before her now, dripping wet, her whole soul smiling.

"May I have this dance?" Pops asked from behind Ruby, tapping her on the shoulder.

"I thought you'd never ask," Ruby responded, smiling impossibly wider, her eyes reflecting a hundred sparkles from the porch's lights. She handed Genevieve a handful of bobby pins and took Pops's hand, resting her other hand on his waist. And just when the campers thought they'd seen every possible surprise Pops and Ruby had to offer, Pops led out in a rather slow but skilled tango step, Ruby following his every move as if they'd been dancing for years.

Greg, inspired by what he saw, quickly slipped away. He returned to the porch seconds later with a guitar. Without missing a beat, he lit out with a beautiful Spanish-sounding guitar solo. After listening for a moment, Rachael disappeared into the house and reemerged with a tambourine, adding a little spice as she played off Greg's beat and tempo. With the skill of well-trained dancers, Pops and Ruby entertained the campers, who all gawked at the elderly couple and their near-flawless complementary movements. It was so beautiful and captivating that no one noticed when the rain slowed and then stopped.

A loud round of applause rang out as Pops dipped Ruby, holding her inches above the lawn and kissing her with a passion usually exhibited only by much younger men. Pops staggered enough to make everyone worry they'd fall, but he found his footing and returned his bride safely to her feet before they both took a bow. Again the applause and whistles rang out across the yard, even Rex adding his loud *woof* of approval.

The campers followed Pops and Ruby up the stairs and onto the porch.

"Where did you learn to play like that?" Pops asked, patting Greg on the shoulder.

"The question is, where did you two learn to dance like that?" was Greg's rejoinder.

"We ought to have something to show for fifty-six winters on the farm," Ruby said, flipping her silver mane over her shoulder. "Pops and I took night classes at a studio in Warren for several winters after we got married. And we've tried to keep up the skills to entertain you kids."

"You look like you're naturals," Rachael said.

"Yep, we are," Pops responded. "It only took three months to learn how to dance like that...only three months and...fifty-six years."

Everyone laughed.

"Do you ever teach?" Susan asked.

"We do—but only our kids, as long as they want to learn."

"I'm in," said Genevieve. "And after talking to Spencer today about his goals in life, I bet he'd be in too. Anyone else?"

James shook his head. "My body wasn't made for dancing."

"Sounds like a cop-out to me," Genevieve teased.

"Whatever it takes. Why do you think I learned how to play the piano?"

"That got you out of dancing?" Josh asked.

"Sure, it's hard to dance with a woman when there's a Steinway between the two of you. My mom used to always say that some people are made to dance and the rest of us are made to either appreciate them or laugh at them."

"Bah!" Pops roared. "Dancing skills can make up for a multitude of weaknesses. I predict that if you find the right woman, she'll make a dancer out of you yet."

James only laughed.

They all gathered on the porch, bundled up in towels and sitting shoulder to shoulder to keep warm. But some still shivered as Matt and Susan dished up bowls of strawberries and cream.

"Can we do this again tomorrow night?" Josh asked. Many campers smiled or nodded their approval.

"I'm glad you enjoyed it as much as I did, but I'm afraid not," Ruby responded, surprising them all. "It's been a glorious evening, but I think it would be foolish to suggest we could ever repeat it."

"Why not?" Josh asked, sounding surprised and looking a little hurt.

"Because there's only one today, and until further notice, we get only one chance at it, just as we'll have only one chance at tomorrow. But I think you should all congratulate yourselves on the fact that you did it right tonight. You are here, present and all in, living for the moment and making that moment count for something worth remembering. Tonight, I dare say, you've used your time as God intended—you are using it to find joy."

"So...can we find some of this same kind of joy tomorrow night?" Josh asked timidly.

Ruby smiled. "I think that's a better question. The answer, of course, is entirely up to each of you. The opportunity to find joy will likely present itself. We each get to decide if we'll take that opportunity by being present or if we'll choose something else."

"I've been hearing for years about the importance of being present," Susan said, "but I think I've spent too much of my life dreaming or worrying about the future rather than focusing on the now. I know what you're saying is true, but I'm having a hard time imagining how I'm going to apply it back in my normal life. It seems like time is somehow more meaningful here on the farm."

"Yeah, why is it so different here?" Greg asked. "It's like time slowed down and I can do things and think about things I've never had time for at home."

"That's something we hear every summer," Ruby responded. "But believe it or not, we don't have even one more minute in our days here in Niederbipp than you do back home."

"So what's the difference?" Crystal asked. "I've felt it too. I'd guess we all have."

The rest of the campers nodded their heads.

"The easy answer is that each of you is out of your comfort zone," Pops said. "You've awoken from a long slumber to the reality that life is bigger than the little world you've been living and working in."

"So why hasn't this ever happened to me before?" Susan asked. "I've traveled out of my comfort zone dozens of times. Nothing like this has ever happened before."

"Okay, but when was the last time you traveled without your phone, without your laptop, without at least minimal connection to the internet?" Pops asked.

"Never," Susan responded after only a moment's thought.

"And because of that, you've never truly been present," Pops continued. "Every year—for the past twenty years, anyway—we hear something similar from all of you kids. It usually takes about three days or so for you campers to recognize that their dependence on their phones has inhibited their ability to see, feel and connect with the world around them. Even the most extreme technology addicts stop shaking after about a week. And when they do, it's like they become suddenly aware of the real world all around them. They start making art and writing poetry, looking into the night sky, and taking the time to get to know the people around them for the first time in years. It's like they wake up from a deep hibernation and look around and see that life in the real world is way more colorful and interesting than they imagined. You can't do that if you spend most of your waking day in front of a screen. You miss it all, living on a parallel plane—in an alternative reality—and ignoring what's right in front of you. Every fall, we get at least one of the same kind of letter. It's always from a kid who's just completed a summer on the farm. They tell us they went home and *met someone*. Well, it turns out in many cases that they'd already worked around or known this person for years without truly seeing them."

"And many more of our kids come to the conclusion over the course of the summer that they've totally missed their calling in life, and they go home and do something totally different, finding happiness in their work for the first time in their lives," Ruby reported.

"That's frightening," James responded. "I'm still paying for law school. I can't imagine jumping ship and doing something else after graduating from Duke. It's one of the top ten law schools in the nation, you know."

"Not that it matters, but my law school was too," Susan reported, "and I have to admit I've found myself wondering since about the fifth day I got here how the heck I'm going to make it as an attorney until retirement."

"My point, if you missed it," Ruby interjected, "is that you don't have to decide your future right now. Sure, it doesn't hurt to be conscious of the fact that the future is there, just beyond the horizon. Keeping the future in mind can stop you from being entirely stupid in the present and messing up what you've worked so hard to achieve in the past. But it's so important to live *this* moment and make it full and real and meaningful. I hope you all recognized this evening that great magic comes naturally when we respond to life with spontaneity. Too many of us worry about how we'll look or what people will think, and we hold back from playing and experiencing all the joys life has to offer."

"Yeah, I never could have done this at home," James said, laughing to himself.

"Why not?" asked Pops.

"Are you kidding? Decorum, for one. I don't think anyone would pay a thousand dollars an hour to an attorney who dances in the rain."

"Dude, you bill out at a thousand bones an hour?" Ephraim asked.

"Not yet, but I hope to someday soon. That's what I'm saying—I wouldn't expect anybody to be willing to pay me that much if they saw me dancing around like I didn't have better sense."

"Then I'm glad we caught it all on video," Pops responded. "Blackmailing you is gonna be sweet!"

"Wait, what?" James said, his smile quickly fading.

"Relax," Ruby said, hushing the laughter of the other campers. "What you said there, James, is an example of the attitude I worry about."

"Huh?"

"To my knowledge, dancing in the rain and engaging in good, clean fun has never kept anyone from achieving their goals in life. On the other hand, sitting on the porch and watching while everyone else dances in the rain because you're worried about what clients think is sad at the very least and, even worse, potentially damning."

"Pfff, damning? Really?"

"Not in the burning-in-hell sense, but I would argue that it certainly is damning to your ability to progress," Ruby responded. "Even overpaid lawyers can benefit from unbunching the knots in their expensive undies and inviting the magic of the moment into their lives. You can't do that if you take yourself too seriously. And you certainly can't do that if you're so concerned with what people think of you that you forget to be true to the playful child within you."

"But what about maturity, respectability and acting your age?" James challenged.

Ruby smiled. "There is a time and a place for everything, but in my humble opinion, life is much better when you can experience joy every day. If being a stiff brings you joy, by all means continue. But Pops and I decided a long time ago that we'd rather die of laughter than ulcers, and we'd rather spend whatever time we have left scattering sunshine and pixie dust than bellyachin' about our pains and sorrows. I wouldn't suggest it's the perfect life for everybody, but it gets us out of the bed in the morning and keeps us going all day, which is more than I can say for most of the folks our age."

"That's because most of the folks our age are pushing up daisies," Pops said, laughing.

Ruby nodded. "But you gotta be above ground to enjoy the pretty parts of those daisies. And taking the time to dance and play and seize the magic of the moment—that's the only way I know to keep life worth living. Ol' Ben Franklin said that some people die at twenty-five and aren't buried until they're seventy-five. Those are generally the ones, if I may be so bold, who are more concerned about *decorum* than they are about squeezing the magic out of every moment. I'm sure there are plenty of women, James, who will be impressed with your ability to earn big money, but if you're not careful, I'm afraid you'll find, as have so many before you, that money has very limited buying power in the happiness department."

"So you really don't think we could re-create this, huh?" Josh asked. Apparently he'd missed the last few minutes of discussion and was still stuck on his original question.

Ruby laughed. "Josh, by tomorrow the magic we experienced tonight will be history. It will live on in memory. But there's nothing you or I could do to duplicate all the elements that conspired to create tonight. We could spend all day making plans to re-create the details and events that took place here, but then we'd be left comparing the two evenings. And I'm afraid we'd be very disappointed with the results. Comparison has been known to steal the joy away from too many magical moments. And I'm afraid that trying to plan a repeat of this evening's activities would not only squash spontaneity, it would also certainly put an end to the magic that accompanies it. I take my advice from Uncle Ralph, who used to suggest that we should write it on our hearts that every day is the best day of the year."

"Uncle Ralph?" Matt asked. "As in Ralph Waldo Emerson?"

"Do you know of any other?" Ruby asked, smiling. "He had it right, I think. How would our lives be different if we went to bed each night thinking, 'Boy, I can't wait for tomorrow—it's going to be the best day of the year'? Can you imagine waking up to each new day with that idea in your heart?"

The campers laughed as they considered the idea.

"It would certainly change the way we face the world, wouldn't it?" Ruby continued. "I'd say we'd be far less concerned about the past and would focus our efforts on making each day and our current situations the very best they could be. What's that poem you always share with the kids?" she asked, turning to Pops.

"'Gather ye rosebuds while ye may'?" Pops asked.

"No, the other one."

"Uh, 'Two roads diverged in a yellow wood'?"

"No, the Longfellow one."

"Oh right," Pops said, looking like he was trying to remember.

Trust no Future, howe'er pleasant!
  Let the dead Past bury its dead!
Act,—act in the living Present!
  Heart within, and God o'erhead!

Lives of great men all remind us
  We can make our lives sublime,
And, departing, leave behind us
  Footprints on the sands of time;

Footprints, that perhaps another,
  Sailing o'er life's solemn main,
A forlorn and shipwrecked brother,
  Seeing, shall take heart again.

Let us, then, be up and doing,
  With a heart for any fate;
Still achieving, still pursuing
  Learn to labor and to wait.

"That's the one," Ruby responded. "All we can do is act in the living present, to labor and to wait on whatever is to come. The magic of this evening happened because we were all willing participants and we each allowed it to unfold naturally. We all contributed to the magic. Unfortunately, Josh, you could never re-create this evening and have it be any better than it has been. But if you are present and fully engage yourself, the magic will always surround you. You might think that few activities could be quite so immersive as dancing in the rain. And maybe you'd be right. But I'd like to suggest that tonight would have been very different if any one of you had chosen to stay here on the porch where it was dry—or, heaven forbid, if we'd had a Wi-Fi connection to distract you. Remember that. Magic will never be far from you if you'll remember what it feels like to be spontaneous, to be willing to step out of your comfort zone, to laugh at yourself and with others."

"It's true," Holly said. "I forgot until this evening that my mother taught me that very lesson. It was good to remember."

Ruby nodded. "It's always good to remember, but unfortunately, it's one of the easiest things to forget. For those who fully engage, spontaneously or otherwise, the road of life is full of magical surprises that will keep things interesting, unpredictable, and fun."

CHAPTER 56

Balancing the World

Perfection is achieved, not when there is nothing more to add, but when there is nothing left to take away.
—Antoine de Saint-Exupéry

Genevieve woke the next morning with the thoughts and themes of the evening's discussion still in her head. The women, after showering and getting ready for bed, had continued to talk about the ideas of being present, avoiding comparisons, and finding the magic that every day offers.

With deeply heartfelt emotion that had been triggered by the evening's rain dance, Holly had shared with the other women some of the things she had learned from her mother about finding joy and making whatever time was left count for something good. Her explanation and description of her mother's love left them all in tears, while also offering a perspective that none of them, in their young and healthy states, had ever considered. By the time sleep overcame them, they were united in a shared determination to make sure that whatever time Ruby had left, it would be filled with as much magic as they could possibly muster.

After listening to the rooster cry out his third rousing reveille, Genevieve rolled out of bed and found her way to the bathroom to wash her face. She couldn't help but cringe when she looked in the mirror and saw that the black patches under her eyes had begun to turn a sickly shade of green. A fleeting sense of anger pulsed in her veins, but she quickly squelched it, searching for something else to focus on instead. Her nose was the obvious choice. Though it was still swollen and tender, it wasn't broken and was still in the middle of her face. And so rather than feeling sorry for herself, she smiled and chose to be grateful.

A handwritten note taped to the upper corner of the mirror caught her attention, and she smiled again as she read it.

<blockquote>Write it on your heart that today is the best day of the year!</blockquote>

She looked at the mirror over the second sink and saw that a note had also been posted there:

<blockquote>Find Magic Today!</blockquote>

The messages were short and simple, but they were directly tied to the meaningful discussions from the day before. Genevieve noticed that they shared a common word: today. After spending the last seven years of her life constantly working toward ever-looming deadlines, the concept of *today* had always been inextricably tied to the targets of tomorrow. In thirteen days, she'd made exactly zero progress on her current article assignment, but in this moment, she didn't care. For the first time in recent memory, she made the conscious decision that today was more important than any distant deadline.

With these thoughts in her head, Genevieve got dressed and was just about to walk out the door with the others when Susan stopped and pointed at the sign above the doorframe. "I've been thinking about this since last night," she said, "and I'm guessing this might have something big to do with the magic we're looking for." She paused, giving Genevieve and the others a chance to read it.

EXCEPT THE LORD BUILD THE HOUSE, THEY LABOUR IN VAIN THAT BUILD IT.

"Do me a favor and think about this today as you're working," Susan continued. "I'd be interested in hearing your thoughts about it."

Though this wasn't the first time Genevieve had seen it or even considered it, it felt like there was something new about it today, some bit of gravitas that felt meaningful, even powerful. As she passed through the portal, a feeling washed over her that whatever the day brought forth, it was going to be important.

"I guess it's you and me today," Matt said with a lazy smile, stepping away from the other men who had come to find their partners for the day. "I think Pops is already waiting for us at the milk shed."

As they wandered down the path to the barn, they heard the cows before they saw them. The deep tones of their bells rang out as Matt and Genevieve crested the earthen berm. Genevieve stopped at the fence for a moment and watched the cattle; they looked almost heroic as they surveyed the farmyard before sauntering off to the stalls.

"I heard Pops whistling as he walked past our bunkhouse about thirty minutes ago. He'd got to be around here somewhere," Matt said as they entered the barn, expecting to find him waiting for them. But Pops was nowhere to be found. They prepared the water and feed for the cows, who filed into their stalls like trained pets. While they waited for Pops, Matt washed the cows' udders, and Genevieve, with caution based on experience, secured the tails of the four happy cows and turned the crank to get them out of swatting range.

After a moment, they heard Pops intermittently whistling a happy tune. It sounded like he was near the back of the barn, but he didn't seem to be in any hurry to join them. After waiting nearly five more minutes, Matt went looking for him, Genevieve following close behind.

A door near the stalls opened into a clean room with a cement floor, the back window bathing the room in soft morning light. A large copper cauldron sat up on sturdy legs in the middle of the room, and shelves full of round, wooden barrel-like things lined one wall. Against the opposite wall stood a narrow stainless-steel table. Above it, a series of curious wooden contraptions extended from the wall on ratchets.

They might have explored the place a little more were it not for the joyful sounds of Pops's whistling, which drew them to the window. They spotted the old man outside, and they held their breath when they saw what he was up to. He was standing on a wooden stool, holding a stone with both hands, his arms extended over his head toward the top of a tall, unwieldy-looking stack of stones.

Silently, they stepped closer to the window. Looking out past an old bench, they saw that Pops and the stack were positioned in what looked like a large, triangular sandbox that was framed with rough-cut lumber and filled with small, colorful gravel. The tower of stones had as its base a roundish boulder that was at least three feet across and close to eighteen inches tall. On top of this stone was a series of many others in various sizes, ascending haphazardly in an impossibly unnatural configuration, almost defying gravity and looking as if it might fall at any moment.

"What is he doing? Genevieve asked, looking confused as they watched Pops teetering on his toes atop the stool, reaching out with a stone the size of a grapefruit.

"I think he's balancing the world."

"Is that really a thing?" she asked, chuckling.

"I think so. I watched a man doing it one morning on top of a cliff in the Himalayas. And I've also seen stacks like that along trails and rivers."

"You're not talking about cairns, are you? We had those at summer camp when I was a kid, but they were nothing like this. Those were just piles of rocks. This looks more like…art."

Matt nodded, keeping his eyes on Pops as he struggled. After a minute or so, they watched him close his eyes as if he were expending all his concentration on balancing the stone. After several tiny adjustments, he slowly moved his hands away from the stone, leaving it there in a state of impossibly precarious balance. He opened his eyes, and looking satisfied, jumped off his stool to observe his work.

"Amazing," Matt said, smiling broadly as he looked out at the unique sculptural form before them.

They watched as Pops stood there, his eyes glued to the top stone as if he were waiting for something to happen.

"Look!" Matt whispered, pointing to the top of the stack. The tip of the rock Pops had just balanced suddenly began to glow.

"What's going on?" Genevieve asked, leaning in, her nose nearly touching the glass. They watched as Pops closed his eyes and breathed deeply, his barrel chest filling with air.

"It's the sun! It's rising on the rocks," Matt said, almost reverently. "It was the same way with the guy in Nepal. Watch!"

They both looked on as the sunlight descended down the face of the top rock rather quickly, lighting it up like a streetlamp. The light continued to move downward, chasing away the shadows from the second rock as well. In less than a minute, the sunlight had moved down to illuminate the third rock. As they watched, a second bit of magic began: steam began rising from the sun-drenched rocks, still damp from the evening's storm.

"This is amazing!" Genevieve whispered.

"Yeah!" Matt agreed.

"What were you saying about balancing the world?"

"I wondered if it might have been lost in translation, but the guy I watched in Nepal said something about it being his calling to build monuments like this to inspire people to seek balance in their lives."

Genevieve nodded thoughtfully. "Do you think that's what Pops is doing?"

"I don't know, but it looks like it could be the same idea, right?"

She nodded, accidentally hitting the glass with her forehead and causing the whole windowpane to vibrate loudly.

Pops looked up, alerted by the disturbance, and smiled when he saw them standing at the window. He motioned for them to come, which they were quick to do. They walked outside and across the yard until they came to the bench adjacent to the gravel-strewn triangle.

"Good morning," Pops said, his smiling face awash in warm yellow light.

"Good morning," Matt responded, distracted by the unique beauty of the gestural sculpture, which almost seemed to be dancing.

"Tell us what you were doing," Genevieve said.

"Oh, this? I was just…resetting the balance of the world," he said in a matter-of-fact tone.

She glanced at Matt before turning to look up at the undulating pillar rising at least two feet above her head. "That looks really difficult."

"It can be," Pops admitted with a shrug. "Of course, it's a bit different every time. I've been working at it for as long as I've been on the farm. Some days I feel like I've almost mastered it, and then there are days that feel like a total disaster."

"Wait, you do this every day?" she asked, looking surprised.

"No, sometimes the stones stay up for several days, and sometimes they have to be reset a couple of times in a single day. I reckon last night's wind and rain probably knocked 'em over this time."

Genevieve glanced again at the pile of rocks. "So," she paused, wondering how to ask her question without sounding ignorant. "Forgive me, but if they're just going to fall down, wouldn't it make more sense to glue them together so you don't have to keep doing this?"

Pops smiled but shook his head, motioning to the nearby bench. They all sat down, facing the stacked stones. "I've heard that this tradition has been part of the farm since the time Johann Zwahlen crossed the Allegheny and began homesteading here on Harmony Hill. Legend has it that before he and his family even laid the foundations of their home or began clearing the woods to plant crops, Johann drove his wagon back down to the old ferry crossing and, along with his sons and daughters, gathered up twelve stones to bring back to the farm. I was told fifty-seven years ago that these are the very stones they gathered."

"But why would they go to so much trouble to go down to the river?" Matt asked. "We cleared lots of stones from the fields last week that looked a lot like these."

Pops nodded. "I remember wondering that myself the first time I heard the story, but like many of the things on the farm, you have to look a little deeper to discover there's much more to understand."

Genevieve nodded, her mind suddenly kicking into gear as she looked at the triangle and the stones piled up in front of her. "Wait… this…this is an Ebenezer, isn't it?"

Pops looked surprised. "Yes, it is. What do you know about Ebenezers?"

She smiled cautiously. "Not much. Yesterday, after I sold all the stuff at the farm stand I…I went on a walk and discovered the Engelhart Ebenezer."

"Excellent. And what were you able to learn about it?"

"Umm…" She paused, knowing she couldn't truthfully say much without incriminating herself but also knowing it was likely too late to avoid it. "I…read something about it in a book that that priest guy, Thomas, wrote."

Pops nodded. "Thomas's book is one of the most read books in the farm's library…but…I thought you borrowed that book last week," he responded, looking at Matt.

"Yeah, I did. I was reading it last night as a matter of fact. Fascinating read. But I haven't seen any mention of Ebenezers yet."

Pops turned back to Genevieve, looking confused. "I thought we had only one copy of Thomas's book."

"Okay, okay," she said, waving her hands. "It's a long story, but I borrowed the book from the Niederbipp Semi-Public Library yesterday."

"You went to the library *yesterday*?" Pops asked, looking either surprised or alarmed.

"Yeah, well, I...was curious...and okay, I'll be honest—I was also hoping to check my email. But I didn't get that far."

"Wait, let me rephrase my question: You went to the library *on a Wednesday*?" Pops asked slowly. "Didn't anyone warn you about Roberta Mancini?"

"Well, yeah, but I didn't think it could be as bad as they said. That woman, she's a..." Genevieve stopped short, having difficulty coming up with an appropriate word.

"She's a monster!" Pops said, finishing her sentence. "She's made dozens of our kids cry over the years. I'm surprised she let you check out a book without seven forms of ID and a blood sample."

"Uh, yeah, about that..."

Pops chuckled. "You didn't check the book out, did you?"

"Nooo, not in the traditional sense. I just...borrowed it. I would have tried, but she was just so awful. She accused me of stealing a book I'd borrowed from the box in the farm stand—said it was nine years overdue and that I owed something like $3,000 in late fees."

Pops laughed. "Of course she did. You'll probably need to return that book before she sends the sheriff to find you. I'm sure she has it all on video. You don't want to cross her. She's very particular and incredibly vindictive. I wouldn't be surprised if she hasn't already drawn up a wanted poster with your picture on it."

Genevieve nodded. "I'll take it back as soon as I can."

"I think I may send you down today. Roberta has Thursdays off, and I'd like to avoid any trouble."

"Okay, sure," Genevieve responded nervously. "Do you want me to go now?"

"No, there'll be time for that later. Right now I'd like you to tell me what you know about Ebenezers."

"Oh, umm, well, if I remember right, after some people won a war, didn't some guy...I forget his name, but I think he got some people to stand a big rock up on its end so that everyone who saw it would remember that God had protected them in battle. I think Ebenezer means *rock of help* or something like that, right?"

"Impressive memory, especially for a book thief," Pops admitted. "You might also remember that the guy you referred to was a prophet—Samuel."

"Yeah, that's it. But..." She looked confused. "Does that story have something to do with *these* rocks?"

Pops nodded. "Rocks have played a significant role in many faith traditions. Adam and Eve, Abraham, Moses, even Mohammed—they all used rocks in some way to honor God. And hundreds of years before Samuel set up his Ebenezer, another prophet—Joshua—used rocks to help his people remember God. Do you know that story too?"

Genevieve and Matt shook their heads.

"It's a story that was at least forty years in the making. It started with Moses leading the children of Israel out of Egypt. God intended for them to inherit the land of Canaan, but to make a long story shorter, they chickened out. Even after they'd walked through the Red Sea and escaped hundreds of years of enslavement, some of them actually said they'd rather go back to slavery than face an unknown future. So instead of accepting the blessings God had to give them, they mutinied. They began worshipping idols and rebelling against the very God who'd just saved them. And because of that rebellion, God let them wander around in the wilderness for forty years until all the rebels had died and a new generation was ready to listen and obey.

"When God told the people it was finally time to enter the promised land, they were pretty excited until they found out it was on the other side of the river Jordan. Of course, these were desert folk, and swimming wasn't really in their repertoire of skills."

"They had to swim across a river?" Genevieve asked, thinking of the depth of the Allegheny and the strength of its current.

"Fortunately for them, no. Joshua led the people to the river's edge, and as soon as the feet of the men who were carrying the ark of the covenant touched the water, the river miraculously divided. Just like Moses had done forty years earlier at the Red Sea, Joshua led the children of Israel through the river on dry ground. And as he did, he asked one man from each of Israel's twelve tribes to pick up a stone and carry it to the other side. At their first camp across the river, Joshua brought the rocks together and stacked them up so that everyone who saw them for the next several generations would ask questions about them and come to know the miracles of God's grace."

Matt nodded as he looked at Pops's Ebenezer. "It sounds like that must have been a story Johann Zwahlen didn't want his children to forget."

"Yes, I've thought that very thing hundreds of times as I've come here in search of balance. There's something special about these stones—some sacred connection to meaning and purpose and history."

"Don't get me wrong," Genevieve interjected. "I can imagine the skill that's required to build something like this. But you must have spent hundreds of hours stacking these rocks over the years, and they just keep falling over. What's the point?"

Pops laughed. "If it were only about the rocks, it would have been better for me to take them back to the river years ago. But you can learn things from this search for balance that would be difficult to learn any other way."

She looked at the stack of rocks for a moment before turning back to Pops. "Like what?"

Pops looked thoughtful. When he spoke again, it was nearly a whisper. "Almost anybody can stack one rock on top of another, but in order to stack twelve stones, you need to slow down, to concentrate, and to focus all your senses and energy. It makes me think a little differently about the purposes of life and my place in the world. And if I'm mindful and sincere, rebalancing these stones always becomes an exercise in meditation and a pathway to inspiration."

"Okay...but doesn't it frustrate you when it all comes tumbling down without warning?"

The old man nodded. "It did in the beginning, and I've certainly lost my share of fingernails when I haven't been paying attention. But I've learned that these stones and the balance I find here are really a metaphor for life.—learning to reset the fragile balance of life over and over again. It takes practice and patience, and just when you think you have it figured out it surprises you. It's a perpetual exercise in humility, persistence and self-control. They may be a little heavy and clunky, but these stones are my rosary. This is my place of prayer and my temple for meditation. I understand how it may seem like a silly use of time to you, but I've found more insight and inspiration while restacking these stones than I have doing anything else. The balance may never last for long, but it's helped me to keep in mind that life itself is fragile and constantly changing. There are endless treasures to be gained in the pursuit of balance—so much to learn about ourselves and others in the perpetual process of seeking balance, finding it, losing it, and going in search for it all over again."

"Does any of this ever get easier?" she asked humbly.

"I wish I could say that it does. But usually just about the time you think you're starting to figure things out, the universe decides it needs to keep you humble by tossing you a curveball or smacking you upside the head with a two-by-four. Whether you manage to dodge the trouble or you take it head on, life regularly requires at least minor rebalancing."

Genevieve nodded, knowing he was right.

"I don't believe God ever intended for man to slump into an angle of repose on a cushy couch and stay comfortable for the rest of his life. We simply weren't designed to be stagnant or lethargic. We've got big brains and strong hearts and things to do and learn. Most of us aren't even aware of the fact that this spaceship we're traveling on is spinning at over a thousand miles an hour while traveling sixty-seven thousand miles an hour as it orbits the sun year after year. *Sixty-seven thousand miles an hour!* Something happens inside your brain when you start realizing things like that. And by the time you're my age and have seen it all, it's impossible not to acknowledge that all of life is propped up by the very hand of God. These," he said, extending his hand to the rocks and the place on which they stood, "these have kept me grounded and helped me remember that it's only by his grace that I'm here today—that I've come this far only with his help and blessings."

Genevieve looked at the stones differently than she had just moments before.

"And the triangle...I assume that has meaning also," Matt suggested, interrupting Genevieve's thoughts.

"Oh yes, on many different levels. But for me, the most important of them all is that it symbolizes the united efforts of the only constant in the entire universe: Father, Son, and Holy Ghost," he said, pointing to each of the corners."

"Does everything around here have a mystical connection?" Genevieve asked.

Pops chuckled. "You almost sound disappointed."

She shook her head. "It's just...new for me, that's all. I don't think I ever would have guessed that a triangle is somehow related to anything spiritual."

Pops nodded solemnly. "The world you cut your teeth on is much different from the world I knew as a young person. I grew up understanding that there were spiritual connections in all things. It seems as though your generation is generally more interested in avoiding even the mention of anything spiritual. We weren't embarrassed or afraid of acknowledging God's hand in our lives. We pledged allegiance to the flag as one nation under God. Sometimes we even prayed in our schools and public meetings. Today it seems that out of political correctness and fear of offending a vocal minority, anything that even attempts to recognize God's hand in the world is immediately scrubbed. Miracles are called coincidences. Grace is called luck. And even faith has been demoted to superstition. It makes me wonder if God feels like he's being constantly uninvited from the very world he created."

"I understand what you're saying, but it seems like religion's made more of a mess of things over the years than offering any real salvation," Genevieve said.

"Ahh yes, cynicism comes easy when you look at the history of the world and the role of religion in it. But if you'll dig a little deeper and spend a little time in meditation and expectant stillness, I believe you'll find that the *darkness* of history has nothing to do with God and everything to do with the pride, greed, and selfishness of man. And if you'll open your mind and heart even further, I believe you'll find that God's united purposes revolve around us finding joy."

Genevieve nodded thoughtfully. "So…joy…is that like the magic Ruby was talking about last night?"

Pops chuckled. "Not only is it *like* the magic, joy *is* the magic she was referring to. You kids seem to have discovered that secret much quicker than most. Mom and I were just saying last night how this group's general unselfishness, curiosity, and intuition are enabling you all to learn the farm's lessons much more rapidly than normal. It's hard to believe it's only the second week. You've already discovered things that many groups don't learn until their final month. Some kids don't learn them at all."

Matt smiled. "And here I thought I was just coming to a matchmaker so I could finally figure out how to get married."

"Is there anything you've learned so far that you don't think would help you have a better marriage?" Pops asked.

"No," Matt responded humbly after taking a moment to think about it.

"Ruby, like every Harmony Hill matchmaker before her, owes her success to what you kids call *old-school* truths and standards. We've never concerned ourselves with trends and fashions that change with the seasons and the winds. The traditions of this farm and the things that generations of kids have learned here is that good marriages— those that last and inspire others and pass on great attributes to the next generation—are the marriages that focus on things far deeper than surface niceties and glossy facades."

Feeling a sudden pang of guilt upon hearing those words, Genevieve tuned out. Surface niceties and glossy facades were her business. And as uncomfortable as Pops's words made her feel, she couldn't argue. Nothing real could be said in defense of the work she'd chosen to do— the work she'd prided herself on doing. She tried to shake it off, tried to push it away, but it was a truth that stung deeply. She could hear Pops talking, but the words were no longer discernible as she felt her attention weaving and dodging and reeling as if she were lost in a drunken stupor.

And then suddenly, feeling a touch on her shoulder, she was back. She looked down at Matt's hand nudging her softly like he was trying to subtly get her attention.

"...if things slow down the way the doctor says is inevitable," Pops was saying, "we'll need more of your help to make it through the summer. I hope I can rely on you both to keep going strong," Pops said.

"Of course," Matt replied. "I'm all in. What about you, Genevieve?"

"Sorry, I got lost there for a minute. What were you saying?"

"Pops was just saying he's gonna need our help if things go south with Ruby's health. You're in, right?"

"Oh...yeah, of course. We were actually just talking about that in the girl's bunkhouse last night," Genevieve stammered, trying to recover. "We're all on board to make this time count." She rested her hand on top of Pops's large, farm-worn hand. "I'm sorry. This has got to be really tough for you."

He pursed his lips and forced a smile, placing his other hand on top of hers. "We've always known this time would eventually come, but that hardly makes it any easier. It's been difficult focusing on the present when we're surrounded by signs that say the end is near."

"Are those the concerns that brought you down here so early this morning?" Matt asked.

Pops looked surprised, but he nodded.

"I woke up early, too, and I heard you whistling as you walked down from the big house. I'm sorry you and Ruby are facing...this," he said awkwardly.

The old man nodded again. "Sometimes when it feels like things are falling apart, balancing these stones brings as much comfort as anything else. I can't imagine not being able to come here, not being able to sit on this bench, not being able to do my best to reset the balance of the world each time these stones fall..."

"But you'll stay here, won't you?" Genevieve asked.

She watched his face as a tear ran down his cheek. He let out a long, heavy sigh. "I don't know where else I'd go, but I can't imagine life here without Ruby." He swallowed a sob, obviously trying to hang on to his emotions. "The problem is that everything around here is made for two. I realized this morning that I won't even be able to do the laundry without her." He took in several long breaths as if he were trying to swallow the tears before they escaped. "Thank you for your compassion," he said softly after a moment.

Genevieve and Matt both nodded.

Pops reached into the pocket of his overalls, pulled out a big red handkerchief, and wiped his eyes and nose. "We've got milking to do, don't we?"

"Yes," Matt said. "The cows are ready and waiting."

"Thank you. Maybe you kids could help me with something else this morning."

"Sure," Matt replied. "What's up?"

"I was hoping to teach y'all how to make cheese yesterday, but the photographer's visit changed everything. How would you feel about being my assistants today?"

"Uh, I'm not sure how much help we'll be," Matt responded, glancing at Genevieve, "but we'll be happy to do what we can."

"Ahh, thanks!" Pops said, cracking a generous smile. "I know it's cheesy, but you guys are grate."

CHAPTER 57

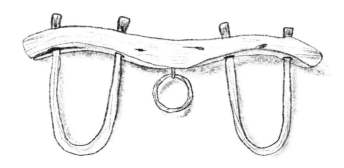

The Burdens of Imperfections

In the middle of every difficulty lies opportunity.
—Albert Einstein

After milking, instead of having them skim the cream off the top or funnel the milk down the pipe to the Hagen farm as they'd done in the past, Pops instructed Matt and Genevieve to carry the tall milk cans to the creamery. Then, after rinsing and drying the oversized copper cauldron in the middle of the room, they emptied the contents of the milk cans into it and covered it with a big metal lid. Then they rinsed the cans and headed up to the big house to join the others for breakfast.

They found most of the campers sitting at the table when they arrived, but it was obvious that something was amiss. Instead of engaging in the normal banter, the campers were quiet. They seemed to be focusing their attention on a conversation taking place in the kitchen. A gray haze hung over the dining hall and was accompanied by an undeniable scent that landed somewhere on the spectrum between mesquite and burnt offering.

"What's going on?" Matt asked softly as he and Genevieve approached the table.

Ephraim looked up, putting his finger to his lips and shaking his head.

Genevieve and Matt sat down, listening with the others to the muffled voices emanating from the kitchen.

"Is everything okay?" Genevieve whispered.

Holly shook her head and looked a little worried. "When we got here about ten minutes ago, they were yelling at each other."

"Who's in there?"

"James and Crystal."

Genevieve grimaced, remembering her experience with James and the laundry on Monday. "It doesn't look like it's going very well," she said softly, looking up at the smoke.

Holly shook her head. "The smoke alarm went off shortly after we got here. Ephraim and Greg went to check it out, but Ruby beat them to it. She pushed them out of the kitchen and closed the door."

"I did catch a glimpse of them," Greg whispered, looking a little frightened. "They were both covered in pancake batter and had fire in their eyes."

Pops sat down at the end of the table and rather nonchalantly began to read his book without offering any commentary on the situation.

"So what's happening now?" Matt asked.

"We're not sure," Holly replied. "Ruby came in and shut them up, but there was some pretty harsh language getting thrown around before that."

Genevieve tried not to smile. "James is kind of a hothead, isn't he?"

Holly nodded. "But I think he might have met his match. Crystal wasn't stepping down. She gave it right back."

"Good for her," Genevieve responded.

Ephraim jumped in. "Yeah, except for Ruby sent them back down to the cellar to grind more flour and they just kept going at each other. We could hear them from up here. Ruby's been pretty loud herself, trying to get them to shut up. She sounds pretty upset."

Genevieve glanced at Matt before scanning the rest of the campers' faces.

They all jumped as the kitchen door flew open, smacking the wall with a loud crack. Ruby came into the dining hall carrying a large platter of scrambled eggs. She was followed by a humble-looking Crystal, who carried a big plate of pancakes. Crystal avoided eye contact with any of the campers as she set down the pancakes and took a seat. James trailed behind, obviously peeved and also avoiding eye contact as he put down a platter of bacon and sat as far away from Crystal as he could.

"Good morning, Mom," Pops said to Ruby, who was now seated at the end of the table opposite him. "Are you well?"

Ruby let out a long, loud breath of air. "I've been better, dear. How are you?"

"Good. The cheese lessons are ready to commence this morning. Would you like to teach them or should I?"

"You should. I've got some lessons of my own to teach in the kitchen. James and Crystal have graciously volunteered for kitchen duty for the next several days and will be needing some remedial lessons on etiquette and…what's the word? Ah yes—*decorum*."

Genevieve watched as Pops's lips curved up ever so slightly into a smile. "Very well," he said. "I'll say grace to start off our respective lessons with a little help from someone far more patient and wise than any of us."

"We certainly need it," Ruby replied, closing her eyes and pursing her lips as if she were keeping herself from saying anything she might regret.

Pops's prayer was short, and after the platters of food were passed around the table, he drew everyone's attention to some implements that hung on the wall over the kitchen's pass-through window. "There comes a time every year for another lesson that we hope will become a consequential and beneficial part of your lives. You all have had the opportunity to witness the power of cooperative efforts in the various chores here on the farm, but the origin story of these dual-effort contraptions began with that one there."

"Are you talking about the yoke?" Greg asked.

"Yes. Each of you learned through experience the functions of a yoke as you worked the fields last week. This particular yoke was retired almost seventy years ago, when the Smurthwaites sold the oxen and began contracting the planting and harvesting of the grain to folks who use tractors. This yoke was hung here in the dining hall to remind us all every day of the power that comes from working together. All of the machines on the farm, if you haven't noticed, are based on this principle. Some of you have likely tried to figure out work-arounds so you wouldn't have to work with your partner. And I'm sure as you've tried to independently plow your own row, you've come to the realization that you're not nearly as strong as you thought you were.

"Some campers in years past have accused us of trying to break their wills. Mom and I prefer to think of it as a redirection of energies. Independence has an inherent and undeniable beauty, but there is and always will be more power and longevity in cooperation and partnership. In the process of learning to work together, we all discover that sacrifice is required in order to obtain something of greater value. In a marriage scenario, the beauty of independence must be sacrificed in order to obtain the power unleashed through cooperation. There are always those who bemoan the loss of independence. But even the most ardent independents, after experiencing the change in energy and strength they gain through companionship, recognize that the beauty they sacrifice is nothing compared to the beauty they gain. Unfortunately, few of us can ever come to that knowledge and understanding without first committing to live companionably. It becomes a test of faith.

"As many of you have already observed, reminders of the farm's lessons are all around us. Some of these are subtle, some are less so," Pops said, pointing to the yoke. "But they are all there to help us learn, remember, and rediscover truths that have the power to set us free."

"As an elementary school teacher," Ruby interjected, "I learned that our ability to obtain knowledge is directly tied to the principle of repetition. That's why we practice our times tables thousands of times in the third grade—so that by the time we advance to algebra and calculus, multiplication has become second nature to us. If we neglect practicing the basics, or we avoid learning them altogether, we miss out on the ability to advance our learning and gain deeper understanding. When things have been challenging between Pops and me, that yoke has reminded me many times that I'd much rather be trudging through the challenges of life with him than trying to slog through life's challenges on my own. If we'll regularly remember the lessons we learn out in the fields as we struggle to pull the harrow and planters, we'll be much less critical and more grateful to have someone with whom we can share the burdens of our imperfections. Our hope for each of you is that over the years you might learn—regardless of how inflated your self-esteem is—that although you won't reach perfection on our own, you can come closer to any lofty goal with someone near your side to encourage you and strengthen you."

"That's like the quote on the beam above the flour mill," Holly said.

Ruby nodded. "'We are each of us angels with only one wing, and we can only fly by embracing each other.' Those of you who discovered that secret early found a truth that helped you avoid many frustrations. And if you'll keep that secret in mind and apply it to every challenge you encounter, I believe you'll discover that life can be far more fulfilling with a little help from your friends than it ever can be on your own."

"And what about that ring in the middle?" Matt asked, pointing to the iron ring that hung between the yoke's two wooden neck loops. "Does that have symbolic meaning also?"

Ruby smiled down the table at Pops. "Would you like to answer that one, dear?"

Pops shook his head. "And take away all the fun of them figuring it out for themselves?"

"Yes, I suppose you're right."

"Wait…you're just going to leave us hanging?" Greg asked.

Pops smiled. "It's often better to plant a question in the fertile soil of an open mind than to drop a ready-made answer on the dinner table of indifference."

Greg looked confused.

"What Pops is saying," Ruby explained, "is that personal answers you come up with after you've got a little skin in the game will likely be more meaningful than anything we can share with you."

Greg nodded thoughtfully.

The conversation continued through breakfast, and Genevieve was impressed that Ruby and Pops said very little that might publicly shame James and Crystal or even suggest reasons they would be spending the next few days working together rather than participating in the regular rotations. And though Genevieve sensed a general curiosity about the matter, no one was nosy enough to ask.

The season's first lesson in cheese making began shortly after breakfast. Pops led the group of ten campers to the cowshed and through the door to the creamery behind the stalls. After a quick walkthrough tour, Pops handed an enormous enameled pot to Matt and a basket of rubber gloves to Genevieve and led them all out the back door to a patch of tall, leafy plants.

"Our first task is to pick these nettles," Pops said, reaching for Genevieve's basket, "but before you do that…"

Ephraim didn't wait for further instructions and jumped right in to the task, picking a leaf off the tall stems. He jumped back immediately, dropping the leaf and shaking his hand in pain. "Oh brother," Pops said, quickly stepping to the far side of the nettle patch, where he squatted and picked a large leaf off a plant that grew close to the ground. He took the leaf to Ephraim, who had already started to dance around in pain while the other kids slowly backed away.

"Give me your hand," Pops said.

"Why? What are you doing?" Ephraim whined.

"I'm trying to save you some pain. Hold still."

Ephraim looked like he was anything but convinced.

"Look, I can't help you if you don't trust me."

Reluctantly, Ephraim stuck out his hand as the rest of the kids watched closely. Red bumps had already begun to rise from the top of his hand, and he continued to writhe around like his hand was on fire.

Pops moved quickly, handing the leaf to Ephraim and reaching into the big enameled pot he'd given Matt. He pulled out a roll of duct tape.

"You're taping a leaf to my hand?" Ephraim asked incredulously.

"Only if you want me to," Pops said, laughing. He ripped off a six-inch length of tape and took Ephraim's hand in his, placing the tape over the bumps. After a moment, he ripped the tape off and immediately applied it again.

"What are you doing?" Susan asked.

"Pulling out the hairs."

"Yeah, I was thinking his hands were looking a little gorilla-like," Spencer joked.

Pops smiled. "I was talking about the hairs from the nettle. Each leaf has hundreds of tiny hairs, and each of them can cause some discomfort."

"Discomfort? My skin is on fire!"

"Oh, we're almost done." He patted the tape onto Ephraim's hand again and pulled it off, repeating the action several more times until the tape was no longer sticky. Then he took the second leaf from Ephraim and rubbed it over the bumps, compressing and massaging it with his thumbs. "This is called wooly lamb's ear," Pops said, turning to the others. "It's nature's antidote to nettles."

"Is it still burning?" Susan asked Ephraim.

"Actually, only a little," he said, looking down at his hand and then at Pops. "How do you know how to do stuff like that?"

Pops smiled. "You learn stuff working on a farm. Running into the hospital for stuff like this is a poor use of time, especially when nature usually provides its own remedies."

"Like duct tape!" Spencer said.

"Yep. And wooly lamb's ear. It's nature's Band-Aid. We have it growing in several places around the farm so you never have to be far from the medicine cabinet. It will clot bleeding, and it's naturally antibacterial and anti-inflammatory. It helps wounds heal much faster than any kind of man-made Band-Aid. And on top of that, it's arguably one of the softest plants in the world."

Matt stooped over and plucked one of the blue-gray leaves from the plant, rubbing it between his thumb and fingers before passing it on to the others.

"I'm confused. What does this little horticulture lesson have to do with cheese anyway?" Susan asked, looking a little confused.

"Have you ever heard of rennet?" Pops asked, looking up from Ephraim's hand.

"No, I don't think so."

"It's an enzyme that curdles milk, which is necessary to make cheese. Traditionally rennet is derived from the stomach lining of an unweaned calf or lamb, but fortunately it's also found in stinging nettle, which is abundant—and which no one ever seems to miss if you harvest a lot of it. It takes some work to do it this way, and it obviously has its hazards. But I'd rather let the calves and lambs live to fight another day."

"Thank you," Susan said. "I assume there's probably a safer way to pick these leaves?"

"I was just getting to that when Ephraim jumped the gun. The rubber gloves there do a fine job in keeping you safe, but they only work when you wear them. Please be careful. We had one camper fall into a patch of nettles when he tripped chasing a Frisbee a few years back. That was painful to watch. And never, under any circumstance, should you ever, ever accept a dare to use these leaves for toilet paper."

Several of the campers chuckled.

"You laugh, but it's been done before, less than ten years ago, and I'm afraid all the wooly lamb's ear on the farm was not enough to bring him relief. That one had to go to the hospital, and we nearly had him castrated to keep him from muddying up the gene pool."

All of the campers laughed.

"You can put the nettle leaves in the big pot, and then we'll need to boil them for a half hour or so."

After Pops offered the campers a quick demonstration on proper nettle harvesting, they donned the long rubber gloves and got to work, making quick work of the tall, leafy plants. The pot was soon filled with leaves, and Pops instructed Genevieve to cover the leaves with water and Matt and Josh to set the pot on top of a propane burner to boil.

Taking advantage of the thirty-minute boiling time, Pops continued the creamery tour. Near the back door, he showed the campers a winch that, when cranked clockwise, opened a hatch in the floor, exposing a hidden stone staircase that descended into darkness. He flipped a light switch and led the group down into the dimly lit cheese cave. The temperature here was at least thirty degrees cooler than upstairs, which they all realized by the time their feet hit the stony floor. Wooden racks lined each of the stone walls, and a freestanding rack in the middle offered even more organized space for aging cheese. As the campers' eyes adjusted to the low light, they could see that many of the wooden boards that crisscrossed the racks were occupied by butter-colored cheese wheels.

"By the end of the summer, most of these shelves will be filled," Pops said. "Though with only four dairy cows, we don't make anywhere near the amount of cheese this farm once produced. But the cheese from Harmony Hill used to consistently win awards at festivals all over the Eastern Seaboard and received four stars from the International Society of Fromage Bon Vivants." He pointed to the nearest stone wall, where a bundle of faded blue ribbons hung on a hook next to a shelf containing a half dozen trophies in various sizes.

"What kind of cheese do you make here?" Holly asked.

"Usually hard cheese that we age for up to two years. You've already tasted some of the newer cheeses, but would you like to try some of the really good stuff?"

"Sure," Holly responded.

Pops seemed pleased. He walked to one shadowy corner of the cave; the light from the two bare bulbs hanging from the ceiling barely reached it. He slid out one of the boards from the aging rack and plucked one of the small yellow wheels from the shelf. The cheese was slightly bigger than a hockey puck and looked like it had a skin as thick as leather. Pops walked to a small wooden table where a few cheese boards were stacked. With a shiny-bladed knife, Pops cut through the cheese wheel, dividing it in half before cutting several very thin slices from one of the halves. After cutting away the rind, he slid the board toward the campers, inviting any of them to try it.

"Wow, that's amazing," Matt said immediately after popping a slice into his mouth. "That might be the best cheese I've ever tasted."

Spencer, smacking his lips rather loudly several times and pulling a funny face, left all of them laughing with his response: "Uh, yeah. Uh, maybe it would be better with wine. You don't happen to have a Cabernet hiding down here, do you?"

"No, but we might still have some ginger ale that the kids bottled last year," Pops said. He turned around and looked on the floor under some of the racks. Locating several quart-sized canning jars filled with amber liquid, he picked up one and brought it back to the table. He loosened the ring and used the back of the cheese knife to pry up the lid, breaking the seal with a pop. Immediately, small bubbles formed and began rising from the bottom of the jar. "Anyone want to give it a try?" Pops asked, lifting the jar off the table.

"Why not?" Genevieve said, stepping forward. She took the jar in her hands and brought it to her nose, sniffing it quickly before lifting it to her lips and tipping it back. She closed her eyes and let the cool liquid fill her mouth and run down her throat, swallowing a couple of times before setting the jar back on the table.

She coughed and sputtered and cleared her throat before smiling. "It's really strong—and spicy," she responded, reaching for a piece of cheese.

"The way a good ginger ale oughta be," Pops replied, encouraging the others to try it. "This recipe is almost two hundred years old. It's the original recipe that was bottled for more than a century at Meyers Apothecary and Brewery down by the old spring near the river."

"I was just reading about that in Thomas's book last night," Matt said.

Pops nodded. "The oral history of the farm includes a story about Martin Meyers, one of the great-grandsons of the man who invented the recipe. Martin was to be the heir to the family business, but he met a girl from South Carolina here on the farm. Apparently the Meyer family didn't approve of the relationship, and so Martin and Molly eloped. They ended up moving down south and starting a ginger ale company that's still in business today—Blenheim Ginger Ale."

"Are you kidding?" Greg asked, stepping forward to the table. "They make the best ginger ale ever." He took a swig from the jar. "This has got to be the same recipe," he said, taking another swig before setting down the jar and wiping his mouth with the back of his hand. "If it weren't for Blenheim, I might still be drinking Jack Daniels. Do you share the recipe?"

"Of course," Pops responded.

Several others stepped forward to taste both the cheese and the ginger ale.

"Do you ever make other flavors of cheese?" Sonja asked after trying a small slice.

"We've been known to make all sorts of varieties. What did you have in mind?"

"Well, uh, maybe something like Velveeta or American?"

Pops blinked several times as if he were waiting for the punchline, but it didn't come. "Hmm, nope, we don't," he said, sliding the cheese board away from her. "This is a probably a little sharper than you're used to. It would be a shame to throw around a prized two-year-old Allegheny Bergkäse when your pallet is more accustomed to nacho or string cheese."

"Whoa! You know how to make string cheese?" Sonja asked. "I love string cheese."

"Yeah, well, maybe we'll have to make some of those someday soon."

For the next twenty minutes, Pops led the group around the cheese cave, pointing out different features, including one rack that was inscribed with hundreds of carved signatures and dates, some from as far back as the 1820s. He explained how the thick stone walls of the cave helped maintain its year-round temperature of fifty-two degrees Fahrenheit without any electrical refrigeration. It had historically been used to cache the cheeses from several local farms.

When Pops realized many of the campers were getting cold, he wrapped the remnants of the two-year-old cheese wheel in a piece of cheesecloth and slid it his pocket before leading them back into the light of the creamery. The pot on the burner was bubbling away, and Pops took a giant spoon and stirred the contents. Then, lifting out the fluid-filled spoon, he blew on it until he could stick his pinky into it. He swished his finger back and forth several times. "Looks like it needs another five minutes. Let's get everything ready while we wait."

After they all put on hairnets, they washed their hands and their arms up to their elbows. Then Pops showed them how to use cheesecloth to line six of the small barrel-like wooden molds that stood on shelves along one wall. When he was satisfied with the boiled nettle leaves, Pops turned off the burner and had Matt and Spencer put on leather gloves, take the hot pot by the handles, and tip its liquid through a cheesecloth-draped funnel into a heavy cast-iron pot that they'd brought up from the cave. Similar in color to herbal tea and smelling earthy like grass or compost, the liquid cooled quickly against the chilled metal.

Pops ladled a scoop into a small copper creamer that had been used as a measuring device for six or seven generations. Then he had the campers gather around as he stirred the rennet into the milk that had been waiting in the copper cauldron. Within a minute, the milk began to thicken. Pops quickly added a handful of table salt and continued stirring until the milk began sticking to the giant wooden paddle.

"This seems like a very imprecise science," Susan suggested.

Pops nodded. "People have been making cheese far longer than they've known how to write. Recipes can be helpful in the beginning, but there's something magical that happens when you reach the point that you're not beholden to a recipe and can simply feel your way through whatever it is you're creating. The longer I've lived, the more I've recognized that there are only a few things that need to be honored with hard-and-fast rules. Your marriage vows and your personal integrity are, of course, two of those. But for most everything else, there's plenty of room to expand and be creative. Some of my favorite cheeses have been created by kids like you who've been willing to set aside their fear of being wrong and try new things."

"Like what kinds of cheeses?" asked Sonja.

"Like apricot scallion or sun-dried tomato bacon or blueberry chive."

"You can do that?" Sonja asked.

"Sure. If all you've ever had is American cheese, your mind could be blown with all the possibilities."

"But how do you know if it will work or not?" Sonja asked. "I'd be afraid of messing things up and wasting all that milk."

"Fear is a funny thing," Pops responded with a smile. "It's a little bit like a German shepherd that's been trained to attack. If it senses you're afraid and you turn and run when it growls, it will likely chase you down and knock you over. If, on the other hand, you approach it with respect but nonchalance, it will leave you alone and allow you to pass by without giving you any trouble."

Sonja nodded thoughtfully. "What about honey and figs?"

Pops smiled. "Oooh, I'd be happy to try that one. Each of you is welcome and encouraged to try new things. If you're concerned about it being a flop, ask your partner for the day what he or she thinks, and listen to the answer. You will likely get a better answer from your partner alone than you would if you asked all thirteen of the other folks on the farm and thereby accidentally succumb to what I call *death by committee*. Far too many would-be incredible ideas are driven to an early grave by naysayers and haters."

"What about garlic and fennel?" Sonja asked.

"I think that sounds like a winner," Pops replied.

"Hold up! I hate fennel," Spencer said. "It tastes like black licorice. Blahh!"

"Thank you, Spencer, for providing that perfectly timed critique—and fine example of naysaying."

Spencer shrank a little as all eyes turned to look at him.

"The simple fact is that you'll never be able to make even a single choice that makes everyone happy. From the time we're just kids, we learn to listen to the voices all around us, voices that say we're not good enough or smart enough or good looking enough. And though each of us is born a dreamer with unlimited possibilities, we all spend too much time listening to the nonsense both inside and outside of our heads. And the dreams get squashed and the haters win—and the world is a darker, uglier place because of it. So make your garlic-and-fennel cheese. Spencer might not even try it, but I'm betting Ephraim or Matt or Genevieve will. And who knows? The very same cheese that you might not have made if you'd listened to a negative voice, well, it may turn out to be someone's favorite cheese in the entire world."

"Okay, but what if it really is bad?" Sonja asked.

Pops shrugged. "Then you learn. You make a mental note, and you move on to the next big idea. There's no shame in sticking with the ideas that are tried and true, but in order to stretch and learn and grow, it's necessary for us to reach beyond what's comfortable and common. None of us will hit home runs with everything we do. But one good failure can often give us a hundred ideas about how we can make our next try better. Cookies-and-cream cheddar may not be a great idea, but gingersnap-cayenne cheddar might be a real hit. You lose only if you stay home, if you don't put in an honest effort to try, if you don't get back up and dust yourself off and go again every time you get the wind knocked out of you."

"And here I thought I was just coming to the farm to learn about marriage," Ephraim said.

Matt laughed. "I just thinking that very thing. As it turns out, most of the things we've been learning on the farm have applications to marriage, right?"

"I've noticed that too," Susan said. "Before I came here, I never considered that doing laundry or gardening could share a connection to or be a metaphor for some aspect of marriage."

"You don't have to look far around here for connections," Pops replied. "Every activity on the farm is designed to help you discover where you need to work on yourself so you can be ready for marriage. But a marriage is only as strong and vibrant as the sum of its parts. Unless a marriage begins with two individuals who are mature and mentally, spiritually, and emotionally healthy, there will be stress on the union."

"When I got here, I thought I was ready for marriage," Ephraim responded.

"And what do you think now?" Holly asked.

"Now I wonder if I'll ever be ready. It's a lot more work than I expected."

"Our goal is not to intimidate you but to stretch and prepare you," Pops said. "One camper a few years back said it's a bit like jogging with weights on your ankles in preparation for a big race—it helps you get ready, but you wouldn't wear the weights on race day. Very few of you will go home, get married, and milk four cows for the rest of your lives. Even fewer of you will ever have to grind flour with a two-person grinder or do your laundry in tandem. But each of you will have to learn how to work closely with your spouse. And you'll each need to be sensitive to the duties and chores your spouse will spend their days doing, whether that's bringing home the bacon or cooking it."

The discussion continued for twenty minutes or so until Pops drew them back to the cauldron in the middle of the room. He dunked his pinky in, and everyone was surprised to see the surface of the milk break; it had changed from a liquid to a semisolid. At this, he instructed Matt and Genevieve to bring a couple of tools that were hanging on the wall above the sink: a long, blunt-ended metal sword and a strange harp-like tool with a shape that mirrored the cauldron's. Matt carried the sword to the cauldron, and Pops demonstrated the art of cutting curd into one-inch squares. He sliced a grid across the semisolid surface and then deepened the grid by going over it again, this time pressing the sword all the way down to the rounded bottom of the cauldron. When he was satisfied, he reached for the harp tool in Genevieve's hand. Its frame was crossed with twenty horizontal wires about one inch apart. This he inserted into the chunky soup along the far side, slowly drawing the tool toward him. When it reached him, he lifted it out, walked ninety degrees around the cauldron, and repeated the same motion. This procedure, he explained, allowed the curd and the whey to separate from each other.

Pops instructed Matt and Genevieve to rinse the tools and hang them back on the hooks above the sink while he checked the cheesecloth in the minibarrels to make sure they were properly lined. Then, with the campers standing around the cauldron, Pops instructed them all to reach into the big pot and gather up the curd into round balls. Some were reluctant at first, allowing the more daring to get in and give it a try. The curds were firm and could easily be packed into snowball-like globes. Within a couple of minutes, most of the solids had been gathered up and placed into one of the six cheesecloth-lined minibarrels. Pops used a long-handled strainer to scoop the last of the butter-colored curds out of the watery whey and encouraged everyone to try a piece.

"It almost tastes like mozzarella," Sonja observed. "What makes it taste so strong later?"

"Oh, just the same magic that changes a sassy young lass like you into a salty, mature specimen like Ruby."

Sonja laughed nervously.

Pops smiled as he looked at the rest of the campers. "There's a difference of more than two decades between Holly and Matt, our youngest and oldest campers. Twenty years may sound like a long time, but the older you get, the more you'll come to recognize that time and age are simply illusions. Other than having a few more aches and pains, Matt probably doesn't feel like he's even one day older than twenty-three."

"Are you kidding? Most days I still feel like I'm eighteen," Matt admitted. "How did you know?"

"Because most days I still think I'm about twenty-one. My body doesn't move as fast as it used to, and sometimes when I look in the mirror I think, *What the heck happened?* But I don't know many happy people my age who like to think of themselves as geezers. If we're honest, we like to think that we can be compared to good, mature cheese, that a similar fermentation process is taking place in each of us and making us better and richer and more flavorful."

"You and Ruby are definitely the youngest older people I've ever met," Matt said.

Many of the campers nodded.

"Thank you," Pops responded. "When you're happy and healthy, your age becomes far less relevant than it would be if you were unhappy and your health were shot. We've been lucky," he said, folding the cheesecloth over the curds in the first barrel. He placed a round wooden board over the barrel before carrying the whole thing to the stainless-steel table near the ratchet-lined wall. They watched as he manipulated a dark and seasoned ratchet, placing it on top of the round piece of wood covering the barrel.

"Whoa," Ephraim said, stepping forward. "I get what this is! This is a pivotal compression apparatus, right?"

Pops laughed. "If you're asking if this pushes down on the curd to help expel the whey, then, yes, you're right."

Ephraim nodded, looking at the simple configuration of the framework, following with his eyes the lines of the old wooden armature as he deciphered its functionality. "It seems like the pivotal compression would work best with a little weight on this end here," Ephraim said, pointing to the outstretched lever that sat at about chest level.

"Smart kid. You'll find that the brick in the windowsill there will do the trick," Pops said, pointing as he walked back to the next barrel. The campers followed Pops's instructions, and soon all six barrels were lined up on the table, slowly oozing whey into a trough that angled slightly downward and dripped into a pail.

"What a great design," Ephraim said. "Simple yet efficient."

Pops nodded. "There are undoubtedly more modern ways to make cheese, but I'm not sure any of them produce better-tasting cheeses than we do with old-school equipment and techniques that have been going strong for three hundred years."

"Yeah, I like the idea that newer isn't always better," Matt said smugly.

"Yes, but we must not delay making progress, regardless of our age," Pops responded. "I mentioned that Mom and I have been lucky to have so many years of health and happiness. It's been a beautiful life, but even the best lives come to an end. You never know how many years you'll have, and so it's better not to procrastinate living it the best you can."

Matt nodded, looking a little more humble.

"So what do we do now?" Sonja asked.

"Now we clean up. The curds will sit under pressure until this evening's milking. The whey will go to feed the pigs, and the rest of you will kindly help Ephraim and Holly get things ready to open the farm stand for the day."

"Should we sell some cheese?" Ephraim asked.

"That's up to all of you. Now that we've started more cheese to add to the cave, I don't mind letting some go. The cheeses you made this morning won't be ready for at least a few months and won't be their best for a couple of years."

"Will the farm be around by then?" Spencer asked and then immediately wished he hadn't.

"You never know," Pops said, pursing his lips. "You never know."

CHAPTER 58

The Proper Care and Feeding of Jerks

It is only with the heart that one can see rightly; what is essential is invisible to the eye.
—Antoine de Saint-Exupéry

After instructing Sonja and Greg to fill the milk cans with the whey and feed it to the pigs, Pops left Matt and Genevieve in charge of cleaning up the creamery. He helped the rest of the campers gather up items for the farm stand. They pulled two cheese wheels up from the cave—one sharp, one mild—and took them out to the pickup truck. Matt used the hose attached to the sink faucet to rinse the cauldron and the cement floor, and after the milk cans were returned, Genevieve washed them out.

"What time do you think it is?" Matt asked, drying his hands on a rag.

"I was just wondering the same thing. I don't think it's even ten yet."

Matt nodded. "It feels like it's been a productive day already."

"Yeah, what do you want to do with the rest of it?"

"I don't know. I was thinking I'd like to read more of Thomas's book. It's pretty fascinating."

Genevieve nodded. "Yeah, well, I have to go take my copy back to the library."

"Oh, that's right! I forgot about that."

"Do you…maybe…want to come with me?"

"Sure," he responded, shrugging his shoulders. "And maybe you could show me that Ebenezer you were talking about earlier."

"Okay. If we left right away, we could be back by lunch."

"Are you sure you're feeling up to another bike ride? That last one didn't go so well."

Genevieve smiled. "I think I'll take my chances. My black eyes are slowly fading, and I'm not getting anywhere near the same attention I was getting before. I feel like I'm overdue for my next misadventure."

After stopping at the women's bunkhouse to pick up the library book, they arrived at the big house just as the pickup truck, loaded with items for the farm stand, pulled away from its parking place under the cottonwood tree. They watched as Ephraim and Holly followed behind on their bicycles, making it nearly to the top of the steep, bumpy drive before dismounting and walking the last thirty feet. Matt and Genevieve turned to get their own bikes from the shed when they noticed Ruby on the front porch. She was sitting alone with a book in her lap. As they approached, they could hear the muffled sounds of murmuring emanating though the screen door.

"It doesn't sound like it's going well in the kitchen," Matt said under his breath.

Ruby looked up and shook her head. "It's not." She smiled. "Some nuts are harder to crack than others. I'm sure they both hate me now, but in ten years, when they're both married and dealing with kids and work and the stresses of marriage, they'll look back on today and be grateful for a little extra training."

"Wouldn't it be better to separate them?" Matt asked. "I know James is a bit of a hothead."

"And so is Crystal," Ruby responded. "Who would've thunk that the preschool teacher and the lawyer would have so much in common?"

"You think this is a problem of too many similarities?" Genevieve asked, looking surprised. .

"Absolutely. They're both fiercely independent, hotheaded, and passionate."

"So…why is it a good idea to keep them working together for any longer than necessary?" Genevieve asked.

"*Necessary* is an interesting term," Ruby responded with a slight grin and a twinkle in her eye. "I don't usually discuss other campers' challenges, but I sense your sincere desire to understand. I will say that if I had to guess, I believe they both missed out on some critical lessons in their childhoods. Working and playing well with others would be on the top of that list of missed lessons. I'd guess they're both used to being the alpha in most relationships. When confronted with another alpha who's used to winning and believes yielding is a sign of weakness, both of them are obviously unprepared."

"So that's why you're making them work together for a few days?" Genevieve asked. "Are you trying to break their wills?"

Ruby shook her head. "I'm hoping to give them a chance to recognize their own brokenness."

Genevieve glanced at Matt, who looked as confused as she felt.

A door slammed in the background, and the loud sounds of stomping echoed through the front hallway before the screen door flew open. James aggressively approached Ruby, so angry that he didn't seem to notice that Matt and Genevieve were even there.

"This is ridiculous," he roared. "She's impossible."

Ruby nodded, smiling slightly and looking attentive.

"I can't do this anymore."

"So what are you going to do?"

"I want out. I'm done. I've given it my best shot, and I've come to the conclusion that I've been sold a bill of goods. There's not a woman here who's even capable of being competent. I've already wasted two weeks of my life, and I've got nothing to show for it. This is absolute bullshit."

Ruby nodded calmly, unshaken by either his words or his temperament. "I'm sorry to hear that. It sounds like you have some things to work through."

He shook his head, fuming. "I'm leaving. I told you last week that I'm not going to put up with this crap. Do you realize that I bill out at over five hundred dollars an hour?"

"Yes, I believe we're all aware of that," Ruby responded. "I'm sure you reviewed the contract you signed before you arrived here. That contract, as I'm sure you're aware, is binding. You would not be the first to attempt to argue to the contrary. I'm quite glad for you that your time is as valuable as you believe it is, but according to page three, paragraph six, you have agreed to stay here on the farm and give your best efforts until the fifteenth of October."

James raised himself to his full height and put his hands on his hips before closing his eyes and taking a deep breath. "Can I buy out my contract?"

Ruby laughed. "What, and set the whole farm in commotion? I don't think you realize what you're asking. This farm was designed to have six men and six women working it every summer. If you left, one woman would always be without a partner and all of us would suffer. I'm sorry, but the contract you signed was designed to protect all fourteen of us as well as the farm itself. No amount of money would make it acceptable to put all of this at risk."

He shook his head, a growing fire raging behind his eyes. "Are you suggesting that my only way out of this is for me to make life so difficult for everyone that you kick me out?"

"No," Ruby said calmly. "I'm suggesting that you man up, accept your responsibilities, and put aside your natural inclination to be a selfish son-of-a-gun."

He ran his fingers through his hair and began pacing back and forth across the porch, looking like it was all he could do to keep himself from kicking the furniture and screaming at the injustice of his reality. "Is there nothing I can do?"

"Of course. There's a lot you can do. I suggest you start with baking some bread because in less than a couple of hours, thirteen hungry people will be waiting for their lunch—lunch that you and Crystal are in charge of providing today and for the next few days."

"I feel like I'm in prison, like you're holding me captive against my will and making me work without pay for the sake of torturing me."

Ruby smiled calmly. "James, you are certainly not the first to feel the way you do. And in all honesty, I am sorry you feel that way. But when you agreed to work on the farm and signed on the dotted line, you agreed to put aside a portion of your own will and take on a greater concern and obligation toward the common good. I understand that sacrificing your will can be uncomfortable, even painful at times. Pops and I both experienced some of these same emotions when we were here as campers. You may not understand the reasons for all of this now, but you will twenty years down the road. You'll be married and dealing with your first teenagers, who will be filled with the same fire and spit that you have, and you'll look back on this time and be grateful that you stuck it out. Spending five months on this farm will teach you many things that will help you face the challenges in your future. If you'll open your heart and mind, you'll see that changing your attitude and developing the ability to look outside of yourself will go an awfully long way to secure for yourself a brighter and happier future. You cannot know the truths of which I speak until you've put your heart into it."

"Pfff, this is insane," he fumed, turning his back to her and hurrying down the stairs. Ruby, Matt, and Genevieve watched as he ran to the bike shed and pulled out one of the old bikes, noisily knocking over several others in the process. He didn't say another word as he threw his leg over the seat and peddled across the lawn. They watched him struggling up the steep drive until they all turned around at the sound of the screen door closing. Crystal had come out. It was obvious that she too was upset; she looked as though she'd been crying.

"I can't do this," Crystal said as she approached Ruby.

The old woman nodded. "It's tough sometimes, isn't it?"

Crystal looked surprised by Ruby's response. "It's more than just tough. It's impossible. He's such a jerk."

"I'll give you that, but shame on you."

"What? Me?" she asked, totally surprised.

Ruby nodded and looked up into Crystal's face. "You took the bait."

"What do you mean?" she asked defensively.

"Yes, James is a jerk, but you're not exactly a pleasant picnic on a sunny day either."

Crystal glared at her, speechless.

"Look, there has never been a pancake so thin that it doesn't have two sides. I was not present for the majority of your...*discussion* this morning, but I heard enough to know that your response only added fuel to his fire."

"We can't work together. He's impossible. Just ask her," Crystal contended, pointing to Genevieve.

"This doesn't have anything to do with Genevieve. I'll give you that James is not easy, but then neither are you. Isn't that why you're here?"

Crystal exhaled rather loudly, falling into a chair in front of Ruby. "Am I ever going to be able to find a guy who's not a total jerk?"

Ruby smiled but shook her head. "It's doubtful."

"Wait! Seriously?"

"Crystal, how many jerks have you dated?"

"All of them! Seven...eight. I don't know anymore. They're all bad."

"Really? All of them? You seemed to have gotten along quite well with him," Ruby said, pointing to Matt, who seemed to be suddenly uncomfortable.

"Yeah, well—no offense, Matt—" she said, turning to acknowledge him before responding to Ruby, "but he's only like five years younger than my dad."

"That may be true, but I would say you know at least one guy who's not a jerk. And Pops…I know him pretty well. He's not a jerk either. That's two right off the top of our heads. What about the rest of the guys here on the farm?"

Crystal shook her head. "I guess they're not terrible. I mean, none of them are really my type, and I'm sure I could find a few things that really bug me about each one of them if I had to."

Ruby nodded. "Do you think you could also find some really good things about each of them?"

Crystal looked at her blankly.

"I'd like to suggest that you start looking at the men you meet with different eyes. Few if any of them are going to be perfect. All of them will require some training and patience. But if you'll open your heart, I have no doubt you'll be able to see the good in each of them."

"Pfff," she muttered, shaking her head.

"You don't believe me?"

"Not really. If I open my heart, I'm only going to get hurt."

Ruby nodded. "Whenever the heart is open, the potential for pain and sorrow always exists. But you cannot close your heart without shutting out the potential for joy and love and magic."

"So what am I supposed to do? Just throw my heart wide open to get trampled on?"

"Well, no. I wouldn't suggest that's the best way either. The hinges on your heart, as is the case with everyone, are lubed with trust."

"Right! But if no one's trustworthy, you can't just force a heart to open."

"That's true. But building an impenetrable razor-wire fence around your heart will make it quite impossible for anyone to get close enough to even attempt to add a little lube to the creaky hinges. There's a fine balance between protecting yourself and allowing yourself to be vulnerable. And unfortunately for all humans, fear often keeps us from dropping our weapons of defense and learning to open ourselves to the trust and love required to fuel every human heart. You've been hurt. That's part of growing up. That's part of learning and developing and life itself. You have a heart, therefore you're vulnerable to pain and sorrow. But if it's fed correctly and nurtured over time, the same heart that's full of inherent weakness can grow wings, not only enabling it to fly but also to embrace everyone around it with love and affection. And you would be surprised what happens to even the most hardened jerk who is wrapped in the wings of a heart filled with love."

Crystal shook her head. "Do you really think a guy like James is capable of change?"

Ruby smiled and nodded. "Change is rarely easy, especially where the heart is concerned. I've come to believe that upon arrival in mortality, the heart of every human is filled with love. And then it is subjected to the perils of life. Unkind words, loss, tragedy, and broken trust—among a long list of other hazards—slowly shrink the love in our hearts, allowing fear to fill the void. But fear, I believe, is an antilove venom, which, if left to its own devices, erodes all of our natural tendencies to love and be loved. Being a jerk is often a symptom of a fear-filled heart—a manifestation of a heart that's been bruised or broken and is in need of therapy. The funny thing about most jerks is that instead of being open to healing, they tend to set traps and snares around themselves, anxious to prove that they can't trust anyone. And when some unsuspecting person takes the bait and becomes caught in the jerk's snare, that person become a victim of the jerk's venom and retaliation."

"So...what am I supposed to do?" Crystal asked. "It's like James has land mines and snares all around him. It's like he's just waiting to pounce."

Ruby laughed. "It seems that way, doesn't it?"

"So why don't you just let him go? We'd all be happier without his negativity."

"We might, but what about him? I'll admit he's going to be a tougher nut to crack than most, but I believe we're up for the challenge."

"But why is that my responsibility? I didn't come here to try to fix the jerks of the world."

"No, you all came here to prepare yourself for marriage. And there isn't a marriage in this world that couldn't benefit from jerk-taming skills. Pops and I knew James wouldn't be easy when we read his application, but we knew he needed to be here. It's good for all of us to not only witness the proper care and taming of a jerk but also to participate in it."

"But it could ruin the summer for everyone!" Crystal protested. "Are you willing to put that all at risk?"

Ruby smiled calmly. "You should know that in the fifty-six years we've been running this farm, not once have we brought anyone here who we thought would be perfectly easy to work with."

This revelation appeared to surprise Crystal. "So why do you do this?" she stammered.

"Because Pops and I felt the call. Fifty-seven years ago, as our summer on the farm came to a close, we both felt a desire to stick around, to help other people, and to do what we could to change the direction of as many marriages as possible."

"Doesn't that feel completely impractical and maddening?" Crystal asked after a moment of reflection.

Ruby nodded. "We'd have to be both blind and foolish not to notice the many obstacles to achieving a happy marriage. But we've never felt like we could walk away and do nothing when the world is reeling and children are suffering due to the choices of those who don't nurture life's most important relationships. We both knew we were completely underqualified to do what we were being asked to do, but neither of us could let go of the desire to help. Fortunately, we realized very quickly— once we committed—that the answers to our toughest questions were all around us. The farm, the chores, the animals, the gentle whispers we heard as we sought out the wisdom of heaven—these all became our teachers. That wisdom has whispered answers as we've considered each spring which applicants to accept for the summer. And I'll admit that many times I've questioned the wisdom we've received, especially when things go poorly like they have this morning. But I've learned over and over again to put my faith in those whispers. They have never let me down. By the end of each summer, the wrinkles of doubt have always been ironed out, and twelve more lives have been set on a course that, if followed, will hopefully lead to joy."

Crystal nodded slowly. "So what's the answer to this situation?"

"Pardon me?"

"How do I...how can I work with a jerk like James?"

"Are you asking how to avoid the snares and land mines that surround James, or are you asking me how to deal with your own emotions that get in the way of your being able to communicate with him?"

"Maybe both," Crystal admitted.

"I don't know."

"*You don't?*"

Ruby shook her head. "There are very few one-size-fits-all answers in life."

"So what am I supposed to do?"

"Well, I'll give you the same answer my Aunt Millie gave me right here on this porch fifty-seven years ago. I came to her, upset and ready to quit when I couldn't find a way to work with an immature, pigheaded boy named Lorenzo Swarovski. He refused to cooperate with me in the kitchen and made me so mad I wanted to kill him with the meat cleaver and bury him the backyard."

Crystal smiled, her eyes wide open. "*What?* You had similar problems with Pops?"

"He was a real jerk, and I was a hotheaded, self-righteous spitfire with my cranky pants hitched up way too high."

"But something obviously worked out pretty well. That must have been some kind of amazing answer she gave you, huh?"

"Actually, she didn't give me any answer at all."

"So...how was that helpful?"

"I wondered the same thing at first. But she did much better than giving me an answer. She told me where to find the answers to every question. She sent me out to find a Fragenbank."

"A frog what?" she asked, looking very confused.

"A Fragenbank—that's the German term for *question bench*, sometimes known as a Denkbank, or *thinking bench*."

"I read about those yesterday in Thomas's book." Genevieve reported. "Those are the benches all around the farm, right?"

Ruby nodded. "There's no question that exists or has yet to be asked that doesn't have an answer. And while your generation usually goes first to the internet in search of answers, untold numbers of generations before you have sought wisdom from the Creator who set all of this in motion. I don't know what the answer is for you, but I do know that God knows. And His answer will be far better than any answer I could possibly give you. Go and ask. And if no answer comes right away, be still and wait for the answer to come."

"Uh, do you mean right now?"

"Have you got something better to do?"

"Well, I'm supposed to be getting lunch ready."

Ruby nodded. "Yes, but I doubt if you'll be able to make much progress on the flour grinder without James."

"Yeah, and everyone will blame me when they're hungry."

"Oh, I doubt there's a camper here who's not still burping up the burned breakfast you two fed them. There are more important things than three square meals a day. No one will starve from missing a meal if your answer's slow in coming, or if James continues to be difficult."

"I was kind of hoping for an easier answer," Crystal admitted.

Ruby smiled. "Any answer I could offer would be limited and insufficient. I believe you will know the answer when you hear it. It will resonate in your heart like it has always been there. Now go and find a place where you can hear God's voice speak to you."

Crystal nodded slowly. She moved to the edge of her seat and looked intently at Ruby. "Are you sure this is going to work?"

"I have fifty-seven years of experience riding on it. You may not like all the answers you receive, but the truth, if you'll accept it as it comes, will always set you free."

CHAPTER 59

Protopians, Unite!

True godliness does not turn men out of the world, but enables them to live better in it and excites their endeavors to mend it.
—William Penn

They watched in silence as Crystal removed her apron, descended the stairs of the porch, and walked off toward the lake. Genevieve considered suggesting that Crystal try the bench near the orchard, but she held back, remembering how easy it was to get lost.

"What can I do for you two?" Ruby asked, interrupting Genevieve's thoughts.

"Oh, uh, Pops told me I should take this book back to the library while that crazy lady isn't working."

"Ahh, you've met our Roberta Mancini, eh?" Ruby replied.

"Yeah, yesterday. It's kind of a long story, but I *borrowed* a book that Pops insisted I get back right away."

"Yes, he mentioned that. And are you two going together?"

"If that's okay with you," Matt responded. "Genevieve was going to show me the Ebenezer."

"That sounds like a fun outing. Do you mind picking some things up from the grocery store while you're in town? In all the commotion this morning, I realized I forgot to send the list with Pops."

"Uh, sure. Will everything fit on our bikes?" Matt asked.

"You should be able to handle it if you take bikes with baskets on the handlebars. I'll go grab the list."

She walked into the house, and Matt went to the bike shed to untangle the bikes that James had knocked over. The bikes with the baskets were deep inside the pile, and Matt was sweating by the time he'd freed the first one. Genevieve joined him in the tug-of-war after Ruby returned and handed her the shopping list and some cash.

Matt and Genevieve waved to the old woman as they rolled across the shaded grass and began the slow ascent up the steep drive.

"Did you understand that bit about answers that Ruby was talking about—that part about the benches?" Matt asked as they neared the summit.

"I think so. I'm sure I wouldn't have when I first got here, but. . .there's something going on here, isn't there?"

Matt nodded. "It sounds like you might've come to appreciate the farm a little differently than you did last week."

"You think so?"

"Am I wrong?" he asked as they reached the road.

"No," she responded, feeling a little out of breath. "I know this is going to sound weird after last week, but I really want to be here."

Matt nodded, looking off into the valley below. "That is a big change. Your article must be going really well, huh?"

"Actually, it's not going at all. This is the first time in my short writing career that I don't even know where to begin. So much of it's personal, right? I mean, how could I possibly write about what we just saw down there without making James look like a total jerk? I mean, of course I'm change the names anyway. The real problem is that I'm not sure how to capture Ruby's wisdom and understanding and write it in a way that our audience will believe."

"You don't seem to have much faith in your audience."

That truth hit her like a cheap shot to the stomach. She shook her head after thinking a moment. Not knowing how else to respond, she walked away from Matt, pushing her bike.

"I'm sorry. Did I offend you?" he asked, catching up to her.

"No, it's just…it's just hard to hear the truth about the career I always thought I wanted."

"Whoa! *Thought* you wanted? What are you thinking?"

"Well, maybe I'm…confused," she said, stepping over the center bar of her bike and pushing off.

"Are you running away from this conversation?" he asked as she pedaled away.

"I don't know," she called over her shoulder when she was already thirty feet gone.

Matt smiled. Then he threw his leg over his seat and followed her, keeping a healthy distance so she could have space to think and breathe. As they rolled down Harmony Hill, Genevieve tried to understand why his question about her audience was so difficult to answer. It wasn't the first time this week she'd wondered about her reading audience and the reactions they might have if they could see her now, so far from the glitz and glam of the world she'd promoted—the world that now felt so far away and disconnected.

She slowed down at a curve, hoping Matt would catch up to her, but he seemed reluctant, staying back fifty feet and giving her plenty of space. At the next curve, she stopped completely and looked back. She didn't want things to be weird between them, but she was worried that they already were. He came to a stop fifty feet up the hill and leaned forward over his handlebars like he was inspecting his tire.

"Matt!" she yelled, trying to get his attention.

He looked up but not directly at her, playfully scanning the hills and bushes as if he were trying to figure out where her voice had come from.

"Matt! Knock it off!" she yelled out, then she laughed as he pretended to finally see her.

"Are you talking to me?" he asked.

"Yes. Get down here."

"Is that an order?"

She laughed out loud. "Yes! Now!"

He nodded and got back on his seat, coasting quickly down the last fifty feet before slamming on his brakes and joyfully sliding into a power skid like a twelve-year-old boy.

"You want a piece of me?" he asked, looking tough.

"I'm not sure. Why are you being weird?"

"Me? You started it! I was just thinking that's the way you wanted to play."

She rolled her eyes and looked at him incredulously.

"Okay, sorry. I don't know how to respond," he said. "My question obviously made you uncomfortable, and your reaction surprised me. So then I wasn't sure if you wanted me to try to be your friend or if you just wanted me to stay back and give you space."

She looked at him for a moment, unsure how to respond. "Can you be my friend for a minute?"

"Uh, sure. Are you talking about the *listening* kind of friend or the *advice* kind of friend?"

Again she wasn't sure how to answer. "This is awkward. Can you just shut up and follow me for a minute?"

"All right, the s*hut up and follow me* kind of friend. Sure. Where are we going?"

She couldn't help but laugh at the goofy, confused face he was pulling. "Just shut up and follow me, would you?"

"As you wish."

"Shut up! Just follow me!"

He smiled and nodded. She pulled away, happy to see this playful, goofy side of him. They coasted down the rest of the of hill, Matt following close behind. After checking for traffic on the quiet highway, she continued on, crossing the road, hugging the wide shoulder on the far side. She pedaled for several minutes without looking back, trying to figure out the route she'd taken along the riverbank the day before. She was looking up at the town of Niederbipp when she accidentally drifted off the edge of the road, nearly crashing in the gravel. She came to a stop, her heart pounding.

Matt pulled up alongside her, still on the road. "Sorry, was I supposed to follow that more precisely? You know, come off the pavement and look like I was about to eat gravel for lunch? 'Cause I could go back if you want and try it again."

"You were also supposed to shut up," she responded without thinking.

"Right. Sorry." He looked straight ahead, but Genevieve could see that he was trying not to smile. "What's that up there?" he asked, pointing thirty feet ahead to the stone tower rising over the tops of the scrubby brushwood.

"Oh, that's the Engelhart Ebenezer I wanted to show you."

"So, you didn't accidentally coast off the highway and almost crash and burn?"

"Well…no…I did, but the Ebenezer is where I wanted to go."

Matt shook his head. "You really should be more careful, considering your track record."

"Hey, I don't remember giving you permission to speak," she responded, slugging him playfully in the arm.

"Ouch," he feigned. "I don't like this game."

"Yeah, well, let's get to the Ebenezer and then we can play a different game."

"Can I choose the game this time?"

"That depends on what you want to play."

"How about that we just sit down and talk to each other like adults."

"That doesn't sound like very much fun," she responded playfully.

"Maybe not. But I'm trying to figure out what's going on in your head, and you're not making it very easy."

She didn't respond verbally, getting off her bike and pushing it back onto the shoulder of the road. Matt followed her until they came to a patch of gravel directly in front of the monument. They put down their kickstands and turned to look up at the stony structure that rose above them.

"There's something special about this place, isn't there?" he asked softly after a moment.

She nodded. "You feel it too?"

"Yeah," he responded, motioning to the bench. He walked to its edge, leaning over to run his fingers over the carving she'd discovered the day before. "Hey, it's the same as the tiles on the farm benches."

"I know."

He looked from the bench to the monument. "The bench looks like it's newer than the tower," he said, pointing. "What do you know about this?"

"It's probably easier to just read it," she responded, turning around to retrieve Thomas's book from her bike basket. She flipped through until she landed on the pages she'd read the day before. She handed him the book, and he quickly patted his pockets like he was looking for something. "Uh, I don't have my glasses. Do you mind reading?"

"You wear glasses?"

"Umm, just for reading."

"That's right, I almost forgot that you're an old man."

"Ouch," he replied, opening the book. He squinted at the words for a moment and then handed the book back to her. "Yeah, well, I guess maybe I am an old man."

She smiled and took the book back, reading the full description of the Engelhart Ebenezer before looking up.

"That's it?" Matt asked.

"Yeah, why?"

"Did you read the part in the book about the Schreyer Ferry that was mentioned there?"

"No. Why?"

"I was just reading about it last night." He reached for the book, turning back to the beginning until he came to the page he wanted. He squinted, shaking his head before handing the book back to Genevieve. "Sorry, do you mind reading it?"

"Sure," she responded, accepting the book. Matt sat down to listen, and she joined him on the bench.

The Schreyer Ferry

In the autumn of 1716, the earliest settlers of what would become New Niederbipp arrived in Pennsylvania. Lured by the promise of fertile farmland and freedom to practice their Quaker faith, 207 souls left their homes in southern Germany and Switzerland and made their way to Marseille, France, before crossing the Atlantic on two ships, the Meridian and the St. Blasien.

Arriving first in Philadelphia, these religious refugees were immediately concerned that their hopes for a brighter future might go unfulfilled. Philadelphia, the City of Brotherly Love, founded by Quaker leader William Penn in 1682, had become embroiled in conflicts and moral canker. Penn's Holy Experiment, that of providing a space where people of all faiths might live together in peace and harmony, had been corrupted by greedy men and women. Penn himself had left the colony more than a decade earlier to return to England with his family. Without his leadership, the once peaceful city succumbed to many of the common challenges and growing pains of life on this new colonial frontier.

Disappointed but not undaunted, the men and women who would become the Niederbippians continued their search for a better world for themselves and their families. They purchased wagons, animals, and provisions and pushed westward from Philadelphia, taking refuge for the winter among the Amish of Lancaster County.

Before the snow had fully melted in the spring of 1717, the New Niederbippians continued west, following the spiritual direction many of them had received in visions and dreams. Making friends with local bands of Lenape and Munsee Indians, the New Niederbippians wove their way through the woods of eastern and central Pennsylvania, searching for the right place to put down their roots. Upon arriving at the eastern edge of the Allegheny River, many of the refugees felt that they were getting close to their new home. But records indicate that they remained unsettled as they explored the area. For several days, many considered building a settlement on the eastern side of the river. But scouts crossed the river in a dugout canoe to survey the land on the other side and returned with glowing reports; it was decided that they would keep going. That decision proved to be fortuitous for many reasons.

The river itself was, of course, the first challenge to overcome. Deep and cold with spring runoff, the river was a formidable border separating the settlers from their dreams. Without bridges or boats, they knew they would have to come up with creative solutions. All of the settlers, including the children, got involved in looking for a way to safely reach their new home. They collectively and individually sought heavenly help in finding the right course. They sent scouts north and south to search for an easy or shallow passage. What they discovered instead was what the group later considered to be the first of many miracles.

About a mile upstream from camp, they found hemp growing wild and thick. They harvested it and turned it into rope. Then they felled trees and lashed them together with the new rope, forming a raft big enough to hold a few people. They braided together heavy guidelines and built landings on each side of the river to keep the ferry from running aground once it was loaded and sitting low in the water.

After several failed attempts at propelling the ferry across the river with poles and paddles, Bethany Schreyer, a young girl of twelve, came up with a better answer. After watching her brother playing with his toy top, she was inspired with a creative solution to the propulsion problem. Her father, a blacksmith, recruited several other craftsmen, and together they put the idea to work. They secured the ferry to a long loop of rope, which they stretched tight across the river, attaching either end to wooden spindles secured to trees near each landing. They wrapped a second cord around the eastern spindle. This second cord they attached to a team of oxen. When the team walked up and down a path parallel to the river, the ferry was smoothly conveyed back and forth across the river without anyone incurring rope burns.

On the afternoon of May 2, 1717, the first eighteen settlers were ferried across the Allegheny to what would eventually become New Niederbipp. The ferry continued operating for several days, until all 226 settlers—including the nineteen babies who had been born since the group had arrived in the New World—had crossed over with their families, livestock, and goods.

According to journal records, a prayer meeting was held on the banks of the river May 7, 1717, the day the last settlers made the crossing (near what is now known as the Engelhart Ebenezer; see pages 37 and 223–39). They sang hymns of praise, and they freed a large granite stone from the riverbank, sledged it up the hill, and laid it as the cornerstone of the Niederbipp Chapel (see pages 287–93).

The ferry was never used again. Heavy rainfall two days later caused the river to swell precipitously, and it washed away the ferry and both of the landings, as well as any remnants of the camp on the eastern side of the river. The loss of the ferry effectively cut off Niederbipp's contact with the outside world for several decades, allowing the settlers to focus their attentions and efforts on community building. They avoided many of the challenges and social vices that plagued other *frontier settlements, which helped them to preserve their faith, families, and community.*

Genevieve looked up from the book to find Matt staring at the grinding stone atop the Engelhart Ebenezer.

"Everything around here really does have a tie to spirituality," Matt said.

Genevieve shrugged. "Yeah, I'm noticing that too."

"What do you think about it?"

She considered the question for a moment, reluctant to share openly without knowing what he was thinking. "I guess it's...new to me. How about you?"

Matt turned to face her. "I guess I find it really...old-fashioned but also charming, maybe even refreshing. I mean, it seems like the whole world is becoming a godless wreck, and then there's this little island of hope and faith out here in the middle of the Pennsylvania Wilds that doesn't seem to care what the rest of the world is doing. It's like it's just going to go right on believing in the spiritual principles it was founded on and not let anything get in its way."

"I can't tell if you think that's good or bad."

"No, I think it's really...brave. I mean, when was the last time you saw a bench that was built for the purpose of inspiring people to slow down and think and reconnect with anything spiritual? It feels like most of the world is hell bent on scrubbing even the mention of God from the record. And then here's this town that was settled by religious refugees, and it welcomes everyone to come and see that life can be different, that faith isn't dead, that people can live in harmony with each other and nature. It's like they didn't get the memo around here that the world is falling apart, so they've collectively decided to build and maintain a utopia."

"Protopians, unite!" Genevieve said, raising her fist.

Matt smiled but looked confused. "Protopians? You mean like what Ruby was talking about on Monday?"

Genevieve nodded slowly. "In the margins of a book I found at the farm stand yesterday, someone had written 'Protopians, unite!' I like the idea of it, don't you? The idea of working and uniting for a better world?"

"Protopians, unite!" he yelled, raising his fist zealously to the sky. "It feels empowering and maybe a little bit cheesy," he said with a smile. "Did your book say anything else about it?"

"Yeah, something about purging apathy and mediocrity and swearing to live passionately or die trying."

Matt smiled. "Sounds like the founders of this town," he said, pointing to Thomas's book. "Actually, it also sounds like Ruby and Pops and most of the people we've met around here, doesn't it?"

Genevieve nodded.

"What would it be like to live in a place like this where God was invited to play a significant role in your life rather than being uninvited and swept out of sight?"

She laughed. "I don't think we need to wonder. It would be a lot like this."

Matt smiled and nodded. "But what would it be like to live here? I mean for more than just five months?"

"Are you thinking about taking up residency?" she asked playfully.

"Maybe. I don't have a practice to go back to, and people have teeth no matter where you go. If they need a dentist, I'd consider it."

"Seriously?"

He shrugged. "This is as nice a place as any I've been to before. It might be a tough place to meet women, especially at my *advanced age*," he said, nudging her shoulder, "but I think I could live here."

"Do you think they even have dentists in such a small town?"

"I don't know. There's only one way to find out," he said, getting to his feet.

"What, you're just gonna go walk through the streets of Niederbipp looking for a dental office?"

"Do you have a better idea?"

"Well, no. It just seems so…spontaneous."

"That's kind of the way I fly. I figure I'll be here for another four and a half months. I might as well use my spare time for something good, right? Wanna come with me?"

"Sure, but what are you gonna do? Just walk through the door and see if they need an assistant dentist?"

"Maybe. We don't even know if there is a dentist here yet. Maybe I'll have to open my own office. Come on. Let's go."

CHAPTER 60

Impromptu Lessons in Gardening

All I have seen teaches me to trust the Creator for all I have not seen.
—Ralph Waldo Emerson

Matt led the way, pushing his bike across the highway and up the footpath on the other side. Genevieve watched him from behind. Though his hair was thinning on the crown of his head, he still stood tall and his shoulders were broad. And she noticed that in spite of his natural humility, there was a confidence about him that was...charming. She had never considered herself a spontaneous person and had long had an aversion to surprises. But somehow this jaunt felt different, almost adventurous, filling her mind with a sense of curiosity at what might lay ahead.

They parked their bikes at the first bike stand they came to, which sat at the edge of Hauptstrasse, Niederbipp's cobblestoned main street.

"We don't have a lock," Genevieve said as she looked around nervously, wondering if it would be safe to leave the bikes in such a public area.

"Nope, but I don't think anyone's going to want to steal a couple of fifty-year-old bikes with handlebar baskets that look like they were painted by bohemians. If someone does take them, they probably need them worse than we do. Come on. They'll be fine."

"So where are we going?" she asked, hurrying to catch up with him after grabbing her library book. "Are you just planning to walk through the streets looking for a dentist office?"

He smiled. "I guess we probably have the time to do that, but I was actually thinking it might be more effective to just ask someone for directions."

"Really?"

"Have you got a better idea?"

"Well, no. It's just...I didn't think guys asked for directions."

"Wow, that sounds like a huge generalization!"

She shrugged. "It's definitely not something my dad would ever do. I remember him driving around for hours looking for places rather than just asking directions. It drove my mom crazy."

Matt laughed. "I've never thought that was a very effective way to find anything. Plus, you miss out on talking to people."

"Wait, you also like talking to people?"

He turned to her and smiled. "You look surprised. Is that a problem?"

"No, it's just a different approach than I'm used to."

"So what do you do when you're lost or you're not sure where you're going?"

"I usually reach for my iPhone and have Siri help me."

Matt smiled again. "And what if you don't have a phone?"

"I don't know. I don't remember the last time I was without my phone—before I came here, that is."

"Yeah, I guess fifteen years really is a big difference—you probably had a phone in high school."

"Sixth grade, actually. I wanted one in third grade, but my mom made me wait."

Matt shook his head. "When I was in the sixth grade, I was still building forts and climbing trees. The only person I knew who owned a mobile phone was this rich doctor across the street who had a phone the size of a brick with a big antenna on top. I didn't get my first cell phone until I was almost thirty. Maybe it's old school, but even now I'd much rather stop a stranger and ask for directions than rely on technology."

"You're not afraid of them giving you bad information or mugging you or thinking that you're trying to panhandle?"

He laughed. "*Really?*"

"Yeah, they could be dangerous."

"Okay, but it's more likely that they're friendly and knowledgeable and happy to share what they know. Take that lady for example," he said pointing across the street to an elderly woman walking with a cane. "I'd bet she knows everything about this whole town."

"Yeah, or she could have a switch blade in her purse and know how to use it."

He shook his head but smiled as he walked toward the old woman. "Excuse me, miss?" he called out to her.

Genevieve watched as the old woman stopped and turned to look up into Matt's face. "Are you talking to me?" she asked in a charming accent.

"Yes, hi!"

"Why, I haven't been called *miss* in sixty years," she said with a gracious smile. "What can I help you with?"

"My friend and I," Matt said, motioning to Genevieve, "are looking for a dentist. Do you happen to know where we could find one?"

Genevieve walked a little closer but still kept her distance.

"Oh yes, of course," the woman said, raising her cane and pointing up the perpendicular street. "Dr. Cummings's office is just up the street on the right, in the big white bungalow. And you're in luck. He only works two days a week anymore—Tuesdays and Thursdays—so he'll be in the office today. Do you have a toothache?"

Matt glanced at Genevieve and smiled before turning back to the old woman. "No, uhh…actually, I'm also a dentist and thought maybe he could use an assistant. I—we—we're both working on the Swarovskis' farm this summer, and I thought maybe I'd stay on when the summer's over."

The old woman smiled. "Niederbipp got its hooks in you, did it?"

"Yes," Matt replied. "It's a charming town, isn't it? Have you been here long?"

"Seems like only a few years, but it's probably closer to a hundred."

"Your accent—you sound like you might be from…Germany?" he suggested, a little hesitation in his voice.

"Yes," she said, looking up into Matt's face with a bright smile. "You've been there?"

He nodded. "Only once, but my friend has been many times," he said, motioning to Genevieve.

Genevieve stepped forward. "Only three or four times, and mostly just Berlin."

The woman nodded, looking at Genevieve a little closer. "Didn't we speak on Sunday in the graveyard?"

Genevieve looked at the woman again, recognizing her as the woman with the gumdrops. "Oh right. I wondered how I knew you."

The old woman smiled at Genevieve, showing off her big white teeth. "It looks as though you've taken some of my advice to heart."

"Huh?" Genevieve responded.

"What advice was that?" Matt asked.

"I suggested she stop worrying about the younger, unripened boys and focus instead on the men who are seasoned but still have enough hair to someday turn into silver foxes."

Matt laughed. "Is that right?"

"That's what I told her."

"I don't recall…" Genevieve blushed and lost her train of thought. The old woman reached into her purse and handed her a purple gumdrop.

"Well, I think that's great advice," Matt responded. "If you don't mind, keep spreading advice like that around. I need all the help I can get."

The old woman smiled. "My name's Hildegard," she said, extending her wrinkled hand to Matt.

"It's a real pleasure. I'm Matthew Owens, but please call me Matt."

The old woman nodded, a mischievous look in her eyes. "I know that neither of you asked for advice, but I've never let that stop me, especially when I run into Ruby's kids. It takes a village, you know?"

Matt turned to Genevieve and smiled a goofy smile that nearly made her laugh.

"Ninety-eight years of living has convinced me that love is always far less complicated than we make it. But I've noticed that if you'll get out of the way, if you'll stop guarding against getting hurt—if you'll let yourself believe—love will grow and blossom spontaneously in directions you never could have considered." She pointed her crooked finger at Genevieve's chest. "It's in you. Get out of your own way. Open your eyes to the beauty that's inside. And when you've learned to love yourself, then loving others becomes easy."

"That's a relief," Matt replied, letting out a long breath as if he'd been holding it for some time. "I thought you were going to tell me to just hurry up and get married already."

"I'd guess that a handsome middle-aged man like you probably gets that a lot."

"You have no idea," Matt replied. "But I'm sure you get it too, right?" he asked, turning to Genevieve.

Genevieve nodded slowly, realizing once again that the old woman was quite different than she'd expected. She realized that she too had been bracing for the dreaded lecture that many older people were often quick to offer when they discovered she was single. She hadn't realized until that last sentence that Hildegard wasn't asking why she wasn't married. And she was left wondering how this woman could have known that self-love and self-worth had always been a challenge for her.

Matt apparently had similar thoughts, but he put them into words: "How did you know I've struggled with loving myself?"

Hildegard smiled at both of them. "Lucky guess."

"No, really—do I have *Poor Self-Esteem* written across my forehead?"

Hildegard moved her glasses to the end of her nose and stepped forward to take a closer look. "I'd say no more than most of us."

"I guess that's a relief," Matt said, turning to Genevieve.

"There aren't many of us who don't struggle with some challenge to our self-esteem—even those men and women who believe they're God's gift to humanity. I'm convinced we all love ourselves less than we should. We all have difficulty overlooking our faults and weaknesses and recognizing all that is good, bright, and beautiful within us."

Matt looked at Genevieve then turned back to Hildegard. "Are you clairvoyant or something?"

She shook her head. "I'm just a ninety-eight-year-old woman who's seen it all—and I can't help but open my big mouth and share what I've learned along the way."

"Are you married?" Matt asked.

"Why? Are you looking for a date?" she asked with a teasing smile.

Matt blushed, looking flustered.

"My husband was killed in the war, which means I've been alone for more than seventy years," she responded as the smile faded from her face. "That's given me a lot of time to stick my nose into other people's business." She turned to look down the perpendicular street again, where people were shopping and milling about.

"Most people don't see how similar we are to each other. We all yearn for love, but we spend far too much time not loving ourselves. We obsess about our looks or our weight or our hairlines, overthinking almost everything. We believe we're not smart enough, talented enough, or good looking enough for anyone to love us. We don't even know how to take a compliment; talking people out of the kindnesses they share with us rather than graciously accepting them as tokens of friendship."

Matt and Genevieve nodded slowly, both of them recognizing the truth she spoke.

"Tell me," she said, waiting for both of them to look her in the eyes. "How different would your life be if you could gather up all the minutes you've spent putting yourself down and instead could use that time to laugh and learn and play—just like you did before you grew up and lost your sense of curiosity and invincibility? What would you try if you weren't afraid of making a fool of yourself if you failed? What would you tell your six-year-old self if you could go back and give yourself a bit of advice about life and love and happiness?"

Hildegard turned to Genevieve and looked into her face. "I've often wondered what might happen if every woman could learn to love herself. I'm convinced we'd be happy with our wardrobes and bra sizes and the laugh lines around our eyes and mouths. Our time could be so much better spent reading and thinking and playing instead of fretting, distressing, and being depressed. We're all hard on each other, but most of us are far harder on ourselves, using our limited time and effort beating ourselves up rather than improving our lives."

"Hey, I have lots of regrets, but there's nothing any of us can do to change the past," Matt replied.

"No, there isn't," Hildegard said, turning back to Matt, "and you'll likely carry those regrets until the day you die."

"Oh, that's really comforting," Genevieve responded sarcastically, wondering where all of this was going.

"What most people don't realize is that many regrets are tools in disguise," the old woman said.

"What kind of tools?" Matt asked.

"Tools of torture," Genevieve answered cynically, forming her hand into a claw and threatening Matt with it before breaking into laughter.

Hildegard smiled. "Unfortunately, they often become that, don't they? But they don't need to be. Regrets can be tools for learning and tools for construction and tools for gardening— tools for so many others useful purposes."

"Gardening?" Genevieve asked.

Hildegard nodded. "Surely Ruby's taught you this, hasn't she?"

Matt and Genevieve looked at each other, but both of them appeared to be confused.

"You've planted a garden, I presume?"

"Yeah, that was the first thing we did last week. It's actually growing really well," Matt reported.

Hildegard nodded. "It sounds like you've been watching it."

"Yeah, just about every time I walk past it. And I've already worked in it twice."

Hildegard nodded again. "Does either of you remember what the garden looked like before you began working it?

Matt looked at Genevieve. "I do. It was a mess—completely overgrown with weeds."

"And what does it look like now?"

"Oh, it's really nice," Genevieve said. "It's organized into sections, and there aren't any weeds at all."

"No weeds?"

"Well, there are—new ones every day. But a team goes through the whole garden every morning and pulls them out," Matt replied.

"Is that effective?"

"I guess. I mean, it has to be done every day, but, yeah, it seems to be working well."

Hildegard nodded. "What if you didn't pull any weeds for a week? What if you waited a whole month? What do you think it would look like if you waited until the end of the summer?"

They looked at each other. "Then the garden would probably look like it did when we first got here. It hadn't been weeded in several months and was total chaos," Matt suggested.

"Hmmm. Isn't it funny how we recognize the value of weeding our gardens but don't take the same care of our own souls?"

Genevieve looked confused.

"Instead of digging out the weeds and tossing them onto the dung heap of history," Hildegard continued, "we tend to fertilize those weeds with our thoughts and fears and frets. And with our minds and hearts occupied with fertilizing the weeds, we don't nurture the lovely parts of our gardens. I suppose we shouldn't be surprised that the flowers and fruits of love and faith get crowded out."

Matt nodded solemnly. "But how do you forget the weeds after focusing on them for so many years?"

"It's not likely you will if they're under your nose all the time. They certainly can't stay, continuing to rob attention and sunlight and nutrients. They've got to go. And when they're gone, you must be vigilant to make sure they don't take root again and sprout up in unattended corners."

"Okay, but how do you get them out in the first place?" Genevieve asked. "Is there weed killer for stuff like that?"

"Yes, but I'm quite sure it can't be applied by ourselves alone."

Matt and Genevieve looked at each other blankly before turning back to the old woman.

"Are you talking about…faith?" Matt asked.

Hildegard tapped her nose and smiled warmly. "It's strange, isn't it, that the Creator of the entire universe could have interest in us—in our struggles and worries, in our desires and dreams?"

"You really believe that's true?" Genevieve asked.

"Oh, I've doubted it many times over the years, but every time I find myself in my proverbial garden feeling overwhelmed and disheartened, I eventually sense God standing near the fence, waiting to be invited in."

Matt nodded. "I want to believe that's true…"

"Then you're in good company. Even those who walked and talked with Jesus learned that though the spirit may be willing, the flesh is often weak. For most of us, there's no shortcut to faith. It requires desire and sacrifice and work."

Matt glanced quickly at Genevieve. "We were just saying earlier that it seems like everything has a spiritual connection around here."

Hildegard smiled. "Everything has a spiritual connection everywhere."

"But why is it so much more apparent here?" Genevieve asked.

"Niederbipp is an unusual place, but I believe that wherever God is remembered and invited, the clouds of apathy and indifference part, allowing the sunbeams of faith and understanding to shine more brightly."

"The sunbeams that make a garden...grow," Matt replied thoughtfully.

Hildegard nodded. "If you'll look—if you'll open your heart—you'll recognize that the entire universe is stitched together with the invisible strings of God's love and grace. The next time you stand in your garden, overwhelmed by the work and the weeds, invite Him in."

"That feels a little intimidating," Matt responded. "I'm not sure I want the Creator of the universe to see the mess I've made of my garden."

"You don't think he already knows?" Hildegard asked with a teasing smile.

Matt smiled and shook his head. "Yeah, that feels a little embarrassing—and, like I said, intimidating."

"Oh, don't be intimidated. I'm convinced He's seen it all. And still He's there, waiting to be invited in—waiting to be allowed to shower your garden with light and grace and love."

"You know," Matt laughed, "when I asked you for directions, I didn't expect an answer like this."

Hildegard smiled. "I think that's the way it works for most important questions; we always get more than we ask for. And I've noticed that if we keep the conversation going, there's always more to learn and share."

CHAPTER 61

Right Place, Right Time

Important encounters are planned by the souls long before the bodies see each other.
—Paulo Coelho

Dr. Cummings's dental office was right where the Hildegard said it would be, and it was a stone's throw away from both the library and the bus station. As they passed the quiet station, they both agreed it felt as though they'd been in Niederbipp much longer than two weeks. With Matt already knowing most of her secrets, and knowing she could trust him, she shared with him the events of her first day in town: driving in from Pittsburgh, putting the wrong fuel in the gas tank of her rented Land Rover, and feeling like she was being kidnapped by the Swarovskis when she learned she'd be spending far more time here than she'd ever imagined.

In front of the dental office—an old Craftsman-style bungalow—stood a tall sycamore that shaded the grassy front yard and the front porch, which was in need of some paint and love. A paper note taped to the front door said that the office was closed for lunch until one o'clock. Matt and Genevieve considered going to the library first, but the old rocking chairs on the porch distracted them. They soon found that the time was quickly spent as Genevieve continued her story. And as she did, she recognized a strange sense of lightness that came as she downloaded the details of her secret; somehow sharing more of her story with Matt lifted an unseen burden.

She was grateful he would listen and even more grateful that as she exposed her own vulnerabilities, Matt seemed unflinching and steady. Her ability to share and his willingness to listen encouraged the conversation to continue, neither of them seeming anxious for it to end when the big white Buick pulled up in front of the office. They watched silently as an old, balding man got out of the driver's side and walked around to the passenger side to open the door for a white-haired woman. He reached in and took her hand and helped her to her feet. Together they shuffled up the walk, leaning on each other and moving quite slowly.

"Good afternoon," Matt said as they approached the front steps, startling them.

"Oh, hello," the man replied.

"I don't think the doctor's in yet," Genevieve offered, "but you're welcome to join us on the porch to wait for him."

"That would be nice," replied the elderly woman, flashing her gray-blue eyes and smiling with lipstick that was slightly crooked.

Matt jumped from his seat, quick to offer assistance to the couple as they attempted to pull themselves up the front steps with joints and limbs that seemed to be less than cooperative. Genevieve followed Matt's lead, offering her hand to steady the woman's trembling arm. Matt and

Genevieve sat the couple down in the rocking chairs before sitting down opposite them on a faded porch swing.

"Lovely day, isn't it?" the old man offered.

"Yes, I don't know if it can get any better than this," Matt replied.

"Then you haven't been here in October, have you?" asked the woman.

"No…no, I haven't," Matt said.

"Oh, the autumns here are just splendid." She pointed her crooked, bony finger out at the yard. "The whole street is paved with gold," she said.

Matt turned to see that sycamores lined the street, their branches crisscrossing in the middle to form a dappled green tunnel. "I guess we'll have to come back then. I wouldn't want to miss that."

"No, you definitely shouldn't miss that," she replied.

"Where are you kids from?" the old man asked.

"I'm from New York," Genevieve said.

"Well, then you know the magic of autumn in the Adirondacks," said the old man.

"Uh, no…I…I don't. I'm actually from the city."

"Oh, that's a shame," said the old woman. "We've traveled to the mountains many times to fill our memories with beauty before the winter comes. Isn't that right, dear?"

He nodded. "If you think Niederbipp is beautiful, the Adirondacks in mid-October…ahh, what can you say?"

"Perfection. That's all you can say. Perfection," the woman repeated.

"And what about you, son? What part of God's green earth are you from?" the man asked, looking at Matt.

"Oh, kind of all over, actually. I've lived in eight states and fourteen countries."

"Military?" the man asked.

"No, uh, I just haven't found the place I'm supposed to be. And part of the travel was for Dentists Without Borders."

"You're a dentist?" the man asked, looking surprised.

"Yes, I am. I have been for almost nineteen years."

"Where's your practice?"

"Oh, well…I don't have one right now. I've decided to take the summer off. I—I mean Genevieve and I—we're both spending the summer up at the Swarovskis' farm."

"Oh, you're such a handsome couple. I thought you were married," the woman said, smiling.

"Uh, no," Matt replied, laughing nervously. "No, Genevieve's far too smart to get tangled up with a vagabond like me. Nope, we're just here for a little help in the romance department."

"Then I wish you luck—both of you," said the old man. "It's been close to sixty years since Patsy here proposed to me."

"Sixty-seven," Patsy responded, correcting him.

"*And you actually proposed to him?*" Genevieve responded enthusiastically.

"You bet. Barney was a little *slow on the draw*, if you know what I mean. I was tired of waiting for him to get up the nerve to ask me, so I made it easy on him."

"She's been making it easy for me ever since," Barney replied. "Best decision I never made. I've been following her around ever since."

"Oh, I think we make a pretty good team," Patsy said, patting Barney's hand as he sat and rocked in the chair next to hers.

The old man nodded.

"Do you folks live here in Niederbipp?" Matt asked.

"Yes, right here in the thick of it," Patsy responded. "We raised our five kids here. Great town. And this has been a great house, hasn't it dear?"

"Yes, ma'am," Barney said. "The best."

"Wait—this is your house?" Genevieve asked, looking confused.

"And our office," Patsy said, nodding her head. "We've been here since we finished dental school a hundred and fifty years ago.

"I'm the dentist; she's the boss," Barney said with a matter-of-fact air.

"Oh, I thought you were patients," Matt said, laughing.

"No, no, we were just coming back from lunch," Barney said. "Every Thursday we split a chicken alfredo down at Robintino's. That's been our standing date since—well, since we stopped driving all the way to Warren to go bowling every Friday night."

"And you're still doing dental work?" Matt asked, looking at the old man's shaky hands.

"Of course. I'm not sure what else to do. People keep calling and needing work done, and I'm the only dentist for thirty miles. I'd like to spend more time fishing, but I still put in twelve hours a week—Tuesdays and Thursdays from nine to four, with an hour break for lunch."

Matt nodded. "Have you ever considered taking on an assistant?"

"Oh sure. I'd like to, but most dentists these days are looking for six figures and a town that has more than one decent restaurant. I'm just hoping to keep going until most of my patients don't have any teeth left." He laughed, slapping himself on the knee.

"Hmm…well. Would you consider letting me be your assistant?" Matt asked. "I wouldn't be available until the middle of October, but I've been thinking that maybe Niederbipp would be a nice place to put down roots."

The old man glanced at his wife then turned back to Matt. "Are you pulling my leg, son?"

"No, sir. I been traveling for a couple of years, and I don't have a practice to go back to. I was just planning on finding work wherever it made sense at the end of the summer, but this…well…this might make as much sense as anywhere else."

The old man leaned forward, extending his hand to Matt. "You're hired. In fact, I'll do you one better. Why don't you just take over the whole thing?"

Matt laughed. "Now you're pulling my leg."

"I don't think I am."

"What about…I mean…how…what? Are you serious?"

"I am if you are."

"But you don't even know me. Are you sure you don't want to think about it and get back to me?"

The old man looked at his wife, who was smiling from ear to ear. "Nope, I think we're good. Why don't we call it a deal before you change your mind?"

"Our son's been trying to get us to move to Austin for years," Patsy said, a smile filling her face. "It's never felt right, ditching out on the patients who've fed our family for all these years. But if you're serious, we'll give our son a call right now and tell him to expect us for Christmas."

"Well, uh, yeah…my only hesitation is money. This is so sudden, but we should probably discuss how much you'd want for your practice. I…most of the work I've been doing over the last ten years doesn't pay much. I don't have much in savings."

Barney laughed, glancing at his wife. "We inherited this house and practice when Patsy's uncle retired and moved to California. We've made our living and saved our money for retirement. As frugal as we are, we've never needed to dip into it yet. It would seem greedy to make a profit on something that's cost us nothing and has provided a lifetime of fulfillment and financial support. I think Elwin O'Shannon, God rest his soul, would much rather see the home and practice he built go to someone who cares about it than to see it sold to the highest bidder."

Matt looked at the old woman then turned back to the old man. "This is the craziest thing I've ever heard of. You're not playing with me, are you? You don't even know me."

"Barney Cummings," the old man said, extending his hand.

Matt glanced at Genevieve and laughed, extending his own hand. "Matthew Owens. And I really can't believe this is happening."

"Neither can I," Patsy said, putting her hand on top of the men's hands and looking like she was about to erupt with joy. "Christmas in Austin! I wonder if that will be as beautiful as autumn in Niederbipp?"

"It'll be better," Barney said. "We'll be with our family, and we won't have to worry about shoveling the walks."

CHAPTER 62

Expiation

There are no rewards or punishments—only consequences.
—William Inge

"What just happened?" Matt asked as he nearly floated off the porch and down the front walk toward the library.

"I don't know for sure, but I think you've just experienced a very unique case of being at the right place at the right time."

Matt laughed. "That might be the understatement of my lifetime. I can't believe I actually get to stay here at the end of the summer!" He jumped up and kicked his heels. "Can you believe this?"

"No, I honestly can't. If I hadn't been there and seen it, I'd have no other option than to claim that you're bonkers."

"Yeah. Do you think we should tell the others?"

"I don't know why not. You should definitely tell Pops and Ruby. They'd want to know."

"Yeah, I think you're right." He laughed, turning around to look at the old house. Patsy and Barney were just closing the door behind them when he let out a whoop. "I actually get to live here!" he yelled. He ran his hands through his hair, making it all stand up so that he looked like a wild man. He let out a second whoop.

"Calm down," Genevieve said. "You're going to frighten your new neighbors and scare off your patients."

"Genevieve," he said, grabbing her by her shoulders. "*I get to spend the rest of my life in Niederbipp!*"

She laughed. "Yes, I heard you the first time, and I was there, remember? I'm happy for you."

"Thank you for bringing me here today! I wouldn't have been here if it weren't for you." He hugged her and held on for a moment. "Sorry," he said, pulling back. "This is awkward. I'm just so excited to have all of this to look forward to!"

"Isn't there a part of you that's at least a little bit worried or hesitant?"

"I don't think so. Why?"

"Matt, as your friend, maybe I need to remind you that you've been a ship without an anchor for…I don't even know how many years. What if you get sick of it? What if you decide you want to go on an assignment with Dentists Without Borders and never come back? What if the grass really is greener on the other side of the world?"

He nodded as he listened to her. "I guess there's always that risk, but I've seen half the world already. It's been exciting roaming from place to place, but I can't think of another place I'd rather be. I mean, yeah, I don't know if it would get me any closer to finding a wife, but…" he faded out. "Yeah, that's still gonna be a problem. I mean, I love what I've seen so far, but I came here for something else." He kicked a small rock, sending it skittering fifty feet down the road. "That could be a deal breaker."

"Not being able to find a wife?"

"Yeah. I mean, I can't imagine that a lot of women in my age bracket live around here. What if I…what if I never meet anyone? Then it wouldn't be worth it at all."

"Matt, you're a nice guy. You're going to meet someone. What about Susan? She's pretty close to your age, and she was telling me the other night how much she likes being here. What about her?"

Matt shrugged. "I don't know. I really don't know her that well."

"Well, you've got a whole summer to figure it out. I'm obviously not a matchmaker, but I think you should get to know Susan better."

"Really?"

"Sure. You've got nothing to lose, right?"

"Okay. Do you have any other advice?"

"Maybe. I know you're excited, but this is a really big decision. I'd hate to see you put all your eggs in this one basket and then for whatever reason have the bottom fall out of it."

He nodded but looked distracted.

"Maybe…maybe you should just focus on why you came here for the summer. You can't take over the dental practice until October anyway, and it seems like it could be a major distraction from what you want most."

He nodded again. "Yeah…that's really good advice. Hey, uh… maybe it would be better to keep this dental-practice thing a secret for now. I mean, I'll tell Ruby and Pops, but maybe it'd be better if we didn't tell anyone else."

"Sure," Genevieve responded.

He took a deep breath, calming himself down after his rush of excitement. "Let's go take that book back," he said, pointing to the Niederbipp Semi-Public Library sign.

As they walked up the sidewalk, Genevieve could tell that something was very different about the place today. There were actually people inside. She turned to see that cars were parked along the street in front. As Matt held open the door for her, out came two young mothers with four children. The women schlepped bags of books while carrying on an animated conversation, barely acknowledging Matt and Genevieve as they passed. Genevieve stopped just inside the door and looked over the room at all the people, some using the computers, others searching through the stacks. Most of the tables and chairs were occupied by patrons ranging widely in age.

"Oh, hello there," Thomas said from behind the front desk.

"Wait—you work here?" Genevieve responded, surprised.

"Yes, I thought I told you when you kids were in my backyard a week ago. I'm here only a couple of days a week—Tuesdays, Thursdays, and occasionally Saturdays."

Matt brushed past Genevieve and approached the wraparound counter. "It's good to see you again," he said, extending his hand to the priest.

"Yes, and you as well. How can I help you?"

"Genevieve needs to return a book," Matt said, motioning to her.

She approached the desk, feeling dumb. "I, uhh…I was in yesterday and borrowed this book without checking it out."

Thomas looked at her for a moment before smiling. "I heard about you," he said, looking down at the desk. He lifted a piece of paper with a sketch on it and held it next to Genevieve's face. "It's not even close," he said, laying the crudely drawn image on the counter in front of her. She looked down and read the writing scrawled across the top of the paper:

STOP BOOK THEFT NOW!

Her eyes moved down to the sketch, which was done in blue ink and looked like it might have been produced by a ten-year-old. From the long hair and big lips, she could tell it was supposed to be a woman. But other than the heavy blue patches under the figure's eyes, the drawing bore Genevieve little resemblance. More words were written across the bottom of the page:

$100 REWARD FOR THE APPREHENSION AND CONVICTION OF THIS BOOK THIEF. CAUTION—SHE IS A KNOWN BRAWLER AND MAY BE PRONE TO VIOLENT OUTBURSTS! REPORT ANY INFORMATION DIRECTLY TO THE SHERIFF.

"It looks like they nailed you," Matt said, looking over her shoulder.

"What should I do?" Genevieve asked, looking up at Thomas and trying not to laugh.

"I'll cut you a deal," Thomas said, looking very serious. "Turn yourself in now and we'll split the reward."

Genevieve put her hands up. "Don't shoot. I'm sorry."

"That's good enough for me," Thomas said, picking up the book from the counter. He read the title on the cover before looking up. "This certainly is not what I expected."

Genevieve tried not to smile. "Do you mind me asking what you expected?"

"Well, when I found this wanted poster in the copier this morning, I suppose I was expecting more of a prank."

"A prank?"

"Yes. A few years back a group of teens would frequent the library under the guise of studying, and they'd slip books into the bags of unsuspecting patrons so the alarm would go off when they went to leave. It was really all a harmless prank, but it embarrassed a lot of people."

"It sounds like fun," Matt admitted. "Why was it embarrassing?"

Thomas laughed. "It mostly came down to the titles of the books—things like *The Mating Habits of African Apes*; *Castration: The Advantages and Disadvantages*; or, what seemed to be their favorite, *Natural Bust Enlargement with Total Mind Power*, which had some laughable subtitle like *How to Use the Other 90 Percent of Your Mind to Increase the Size of Your Breasts*."

Matt and Genevieve looked at each other and laughed.

"The covers alone were usually enough to embarrass anyone caught unknowingly smuggling them out of the library. Of course, the teens knew their pranks played out even more effectively with Roberta as library cop. But she caught on after a while and began gathering up all the books with questionable titles and locking them up in the special collections cabinet."

"Sounds like a great prank," Matt replied, holding back his laughter. "I wish I would have thought of that when I was a kid."

"Yeah, well, it didn't stop there. When their favorite books got locked up, the teens responded by using Roberta's own books from the romance wing, especially the ones with the particularly racy covers. This went on for weeks until the teens went a little too far and slipped a couple of the books into the bag of a nun who was in town visiting her brother. After the alarm went off and Roberta discovered the lewd books, the poor nun fainted right there on the floor. Roberta tried to press charges."

"Against the teens?" Matt asked incredulously.

Thomas shook his head. "Against the nun. Apparently one of the books was quite rare. The charges were eventually dropped, but to my knowledge, the nun has never been back to visit her brother."

Genevieve laughed out loud, covering her mouth when she remembered she was in a library.

"Yep, there's not often a lot of excitement around here, so Roberta finds ways to make it a little more entertaining. Apparently she went through the security system videotape after you left. You're lucky you were wearing a sun hat and glasses. The camera didn't capture your face, so the sheriff asked Roberta to put together a sketch for them."

Genevieve looked down at the wanted poster and smiled. "Can I have this? I've never been on a wanted poster before."

"Sure. Now that the book's back, I think we can let this go. There does, however, remain the matter of this overdue book." He reached for a card that Genevieve recognized as the one Roberta had taken from the card file the day before. He slid it across the counter. In red pencil and emphatically circled was the dollar figure from yesterday: $3,672.

She looked up, smiling. "This can't be real, right?"

"Well, Roberta's math is right on, but she missed an important note on the back side of the card."

Genevieve turned it over. It had been stamped with the words SOLD/ DECOMMISSIONED. She looked up to find the priest smiling.

"Library records indicate that this book was sold for fifty cents seven years ago at the annual book sale. If you'll put the card in that book of yours, Roberta Mancini ought to leave you alone."

"Thanks," Genevieve said.

"You're welcome." He picked up the book Genevieve had returned. "I thought you looked familiar when I watched the security tape of you sneaking behind the desk here. I saw you take the book from the counter over there, but I never would have guessed it was one of my books. I'll admit that I'm a little bit flattered."

"Flattered?" Genevieve tried not to smile. "I'm sorry. I'm really not a thief, and honestly, I would have checked it out if I'd been given the opportunity. But she was just so…"

"I understand," Thomas said, nodding. "Patrons have had trouble with Roberta ever since she paid for the romance wing. Accepting her donation was probably one of the worst decisions the town council has ever made. We've all learned the hard way that free gifts sometimes aren't worth what you pay for them. The woman thinks she owns the place now, and most folks who are in the know tend to plan their library visits for the days she's not here. I've heard her say that she'd like to slow down to only one day a week. But there just aren't enough volunteers to pick up the slack. We'd rather keep the doors open for the patrons even if they're met by a cantankerous woman."

Matt and Genevieve nodded.

"So you're just a volunteer too?" Matt asked.

"Yes, but it's been a good gig. You get to know a lot of people when you volunteer at a library. Seeing the books coming and going has helped me keep a pulse on the health and interests of the community. It also gives me a chance to research and write. I helped microfiche most of the town archives back in the seventies and eighties."

"Micro what?" Genevieve asked.

Thomas smiled at Matt and shook his head. "Technology changes quicker than I do. I started *digitizing* the microfiche a few years ago so people of your generation could appreciate the archives, but I'm not sure anyone cares about history anymore."

Genevieve glanced at Matt. "We do."

"Oh, go on," Thomas responded.

"No, really. I mean, probably not all history, but your book is really interesting."

"You actually read it?" he asked, looking surprised.

"Well, not all of it, but I'd like to," Genevieve replied.

"I would too," Matt added. "I've been reading the farm's copy in the evenings. I already knew Niederbipp was an unusual place, but you really made it come to life."

"You both have actually *read from* my book?" he asked incredulously.

"Yes," they both responded.

"I'd like to check it out if I can," Genevieve replied.

Thomas smiled. "I'll do you one better than that. Follow me."

He pushed open the swinging gate attached to the front counter and headed past the romance wing to the far wall, where a series of old wooden doors were camouflaged by the surrounding bookshelves. He pulled a key from his pocket, unlocked a door, and pushed it open before switching on the light. The small windowless room was lined on all four walls with shelves holding books that looked very old. A wooden table sat in the middle of the room, along with a leather-covered chair with brass tacks. The priest walked to the other side of the table and stooped down to the bottom shelf. Matt and Genevieve followed and saw that the entire bottom shelf of all the bookcases were filled two deep with what looked like hundreds of copies of the same book: *A Short History of Niederbipp* by Thomas O. Kelly. He pulled out two copies of the book and stood up.

"I received a grant from the Pennsylvania Historical Society to publish a thousand copies of this book. I would like to present you each with one of those copies."

"How many do you have left?" Genevieve asked.

"Roughly 680."

"Wait, what?" Matt asked. "I'd have guessed you'd be into multiple printings by now. It's a really great book."

"Thank you," he beamed. "I spent thousands of hours searching through all of these books and interviewing hundreds of people to compile the most important nuggets for this book. I knew I'd never get rich writing a book about a little town most people have never heard of, and I'll be the first to admit that being a published author is totally overrated." He laughed as he set the books on the desk and signed them before handing one to each of them. "I tried giving copies away as wedding gifts for a while—until I noticed that many of them were being donated to the library or the secondhand store."

"I'm sorry," Matt said. "That has to be discouraging."

Thomas nodded. "History can be a beautiful thing—as long as you care. But each successive generation has its own worries and interests, and so the wisdom of one generation often ends up lining the birdcages of the next."

Matt shook his head. "I wouldn't have pegged you as a cynic."

"Oh, I try not to be. I'd like to say that being a small-town historian is its own reward, but the truth is that it's usually a thankless obsession."

"Then I'd like to thank you," Matt said, stepping forward with an outstretched hand. "Genevieve and I might be your biggest fans."

Thomas smiled, shaking Matt's hand. "You're more likely my only fans."

"Pops said it's one of the most popular books in the farm library," Matt responded.

"Is that right?"

"That's what he said," Matt replied, turning to Genevieve to back him up.

"Yeah, he told us that this morning," she said.

"Well, if ever you hear from one of your comrades that they'd like a copy, let me know. I'd be happy to sign one for them too." He motioned for the door. "Sorry, I need to keep my eyes on the front desk. You never know when someone's going to want to steal a book and make a run for it. Is there anything else I can help you with?"

Matt looked at Genevieve then turned back to the priest. "We've just been reading about the Engelhart Ebenezer. Genevieve actually took me there on our way here."

Thomas smiled and nodded, encouraging him to continue.

"I know your book describes a ton of interesting places, but we don't have the chance to get away from the farm very often. I was just wondering if you might recommend any other places since we have some time today."

Thomas straightened up a little taller. "You could spend a solid month visiting all of the interesting places around here. Do you have any particular interests?"

Matt looked at Genevieve. "I think we both have some interest in places that are meaningful—places where there's both a spiritual as well as a historical background."

He took Matt's book and flipped through the pages slowly while trying to keep an eye on the front desk. "I can't think of a single site that wouldn't offer you what you're looking for," he said as he reached the end of the book.

"Really?"

The priest nodded. "You will find—if you look with an open heart—that all good things have a spiritual connection. If there's one lesson I've learned from all my research, that's it. If there is good in a place or an idea—if it makes you happy—there is something of the gods in it."

"Are you suggesting that God's in everything?" Genevieve asked.

Thomas shook his head. "I wondered the same thing when I first started the journey of discovery that became this book. But many years ago I learned from a friend that all that glitters isn't necessarily spiritual gold."

Matt nodded slowly. "So...how can you tell the difference?"

"That's the question seekers have been asking for generations."

"And do you know the answer?"

"I know enough to say that the answer has many parts and that each part orbits around one all-important truth. And until you understand that truth, none of the other parts of the answer can lead to the understanding and joy you're looking for."

Matt nodded thoughtfully. "I think I might know what that truth is," he offered, looking a little uncertain. "Is it written on the bench at the Ebenezer?"

Thomas smiled and nodded. "Very good."

Matt looked relieved. "So if that's the first answer, what are the others?"

Thomas smiled again. "Truth and wisdom are beautiful, powerful things that, if consumed too quickly, can prove to be confusing, even destructive. I will always be happy to share what I know, but I've learned by sad experience that we must have milk before meat. And when we have teeth sufficient to chew without choking, we are ready for more."

"That's fair," Matt replied.

"That being said, your answer and your interest suggest to me a thirst, maybe even a hunger, for understanding."

Matt nodded again.

Thomas took the book from Matt again, flipping through several pages before handing the book back. He pointed to the heading at the top of the page.

"The Niederbipp Cemetery?" Matt asked.

The priest nodded affirmatively. "In the center of the cemetery, you will find a unique grave marker—a bench marking the burial place of one of Niederbipp's most beloved residents, Isaac Bingham."

"He was the potter, right?" Genevieve asked.

"Impressive. You've been paying attention. Isaac was the torchbearer for a whole generation of Niederbippians. He understood many truths with an unparalleled depth. I could tell you the many things I learned from him, but I'm certain they would mean more to you if you gathered them from him yourselves."

Thomas looked up to see that a line had formed in front of the checkout desk. "I'm sorry, I have to go. But if you'll start there, you'll find a secret key to the laws of joy, which very few people understand."

CHAPTER 63

Croissant Therapy

You may think the grass is greener on the other side of the fence, but if you took the time to water your own grass, yours would be just as green.
—Aunt Ann

"Did you get that?" Genevieve asked as they walked down the front sidewalk of the library.

Matt shrugged. "Not entirely, but I think he told us where to look, right?"

"Yeah, but…do we have time?" she asked as he set his eyes on the steeple of the church.

"We don't have to be back till milking time, right?"

"I guess not, but aren't you hungry? It's gotta be close to two."

"Oh...yeah...sorry about that. This is the first time in my life that I've consistently eaten three meals a day. What would you like to eat?"

"I don't care. I just know I better eat something before I get hangry."

"Thanks for the warning," he laughed. "Lead the way."

They walked back to Hauptstrasse, and Genevieve took the lead, looking for edible options. After passing several clothing and shoe stores, they came to a grocery store, Braun's Market.

"Is this where we're supposed to shop for the Ruby?" Matt asked.

"Yeah, but I'm not sure I want to carry the stuff around with me. Let's come back."

They kept walking until they came to a huge fountain in the middle of the cobbled street. Carved out of what looked like granite, the pool for the fountain was four feet high and had a diameter of at least seven feet. While Genevieve was distracted by the scents wafting about from Robintino's on one side of the street and The House of Kabobs on the other, Matt was distracted by a different muse. On top of a tall stone pedestal in the center of the fountain, a woman draped in flowing robes rose high above the cobblestones. At first glance, Matt wondered if it were a saint or a martyr, but then he remembered he wasn't in Europe and this was not a Catholic town. He stepped closer, looking up into the statue's serene face. She was smiling pleasantly, one balled fist on her hip, the other hand holding a strangely shaped tool that looked almost like a small sickle.

"I'm sure we don't have enough money for Robintino's, and I'm not in the mood for a kabob gut bomb," Genevieve said, interrupting his thoughts. "There's a bakery over there. I'm gonna go check it out. Do you want anything?"

"Uh, sure. Whatever you're having," Matt replied, distracted.

Remembering the book he had in his hand, he immediately wondered if it might contain something within its pages about the fountain and the statue.

He sat down on a bench carved out of the side of the fountain, and he opened the book to the table of contents, scanning it for references to anything that sounded like a fountain. He found something promising halfway down the second page and quickly leafed through until he came to the right page number. A small sketch of the fountain appeared in the middle of the page above the title:

FREIHEITSBRUNNEN—LIBERTY FOUNTAIN

Matt was anxious to begin reading, but he knew he should probably wait for Genevieve. While he waited, he walked around the entire fountain. Near a set of worn stone steps on the far side, he came upon a sign that said the water was potable. He climbed the stairs and drank deeply from a brass spigot.

"I got you a chocolate milk," Genevieve said before he had finished drinking.

"Thanks," he responded, wiping his mouth with the back of his hand. "You really should try this water. It's amazing."

"Amazing? It's water, right?" she responded sarcastically. "I've had that before."

"Not like this. Come on, taste it."

She rolled her eyes but climbed the narrow stairs and leaned over the fountain, extending her lips to meet the flowing water. "It's really cold," she said, recoiling. But she went back again, filling her mouth to overflowing. Water ran down the front of her neck and into her shirt. She squealed, pulling back and holding her damp shirt away from her chest.

"You know, of all the water I've ever tried, that was certainly some of the wettest."

Matt smiled. "But it's sweet, right?"

She licked her lips, making a funny face. "Yeah, I guess it's sweet. But did you notice how wet it is?" She grabbed a handful of water from the spigot and threw it at Matt. He responded quickly, dipping his hand into the fountain's pool and giving it right back to her. She squealed again, jumping back from the fountain and nearly landing on an innocent pedestrian.

"I'm so sorry," she said, turning to face the woman she'd nearly crushed. "Oh my gosh, Amy?" Genevieve said, pushing a wet strand of hair away from her eyes and trying to quickly wipe the smile off her face

"Genevieve?" Amy responded.

"Yeah, sorry to almost kill you. We were just...having a drinking fight—I mean, getting a drink...or something."

"Looks like fun," Amy replied. "It's weird bumping into you two days in a row. Did you run away from the farm?"

Genevieve laughed. "No, we had some time, and Ruby sent us down to pick up some things from the grocery store."

Amy nodded. "Well, I'll let you get back to it then. I was just on my way to the market myself. Maybe I'll see you again tomorrow."

"Who's this?" Matt asked, stepping down from the fountain's step.

"This is my old roommate Amy Eckstein," Genevieve offered. "And this is my friend, Matt."

"Nice to meet you," Amy said with a nod, her hands occupied with a colorful basket.

"Amy's an artist, and she's married to the potter of Niederbipp. They live right around the corner, right?" Genevieve looked around, trying to orient herself.

Amy nodded. "Well, it was nice to meet you and to see you again," she said, nodding to Genevieve. "We're having some friends to dinner, and I've got to pick up some things I forgot earlier."

"Umm, maybe we could stop in and meet your husband some time. He's the guy who rides around on the little red scooter, right?"

"Yeah," Amy responded, looking a little surprised or nervous or both.

"Oh," Matt responded quickly, recognizing her hesitation. "We were introduced to him when we first arrived. He was on a red scooter, and Lorenzo said he was the famous potter of Niederbipp, or something like that."

Amy smiled, obviously disarmed. "Come anytime. We're just around the corner and at the top of the street."

"Thanks," Matt replied, smiling and trying to disarm her even further.

Amy smiled and nodded to them both before continuing on her way.

"Is it just me, or was there some tension there?" Matt asked softly when Amy was beyond earshot.

Genevieve forced a smile. "No, it's probably real."

"Do you know why?"

Genevieve sat down on the bench and looked rather humble. "I... she...that was a really tough year, freshman year—away from home and dealing with all the stresses of..." She let out a long breath, shaking her head. "I'm sure I was a beast."

Matt looked surprised. "Why do you say that?"

"Because I'm sure it's true," she replied, laughing and shaking her head again. "I'm not a very nice person."

"What are you talking about?"

"You saw her jump back."

"Well, yeah. That's because you almost landed on her," he responded, laughing.

"I was talking about after that."

"I guess I didn't see it."

"No, but you sensed it. I did too." She shook her head, looking down at the paper bag in her hands. "I got this for you," she said handing the bag to him without looking up.

"Did you already eat yours?"

"No, I'm not really hungry anymore?"

"What?"

"Yeah, that water, it was really good—it filled me right up."

Matt laughed. "What's going on?"

"Nothing. I—I need to walk." She got up and grabbed the book Thomas had given her and walked back the way they'd come.

Matt grabbed his book as well and followed, catching up to her in a dozen steps. "Something's up."

She forced a smile but shook her head as she continued walking quickly.

"You don't want to talk about it?"

"There's nothing to talk about."

"Okay. Umm, do you want to hear about the fountain back there? I was waiting to read about it until you got back."

"Okay, sure," she responded without any enthusiasm. "But let's get out of here."

He nodded, looking concerned. "Follow me." He pulled a hard right, hurrying up some stairs that passed under a long tunneled arbor overgrown with fragrant purple wisteria. The stairs ended in the church's beautiful courtyard. Benches lined the promenade, trees trained over them to offer the greatest amount of shade. "Is this okay?" he asked, pointing to a bench.

She nodded and slumped into a seat, her eyes looking down at her clunky farm shoes.

Matt sat for a minute, not knowing what to do or say. "Uh, is this what hangry is for you?"

She looked up and smiled. "I'm sorry."

"You're okay."

"No, I'm really not okay. Give me one of those croissants, will you?" She reached into the bag, pulling out a bundle wrapped in grease-stained paper. She ripped it open and handed him a ham-and-cheese croissant. He took it, watching her closely as she ate nearly half of hers in one bite. He joined her, a little more slowly, savoring the flavor.

"This is *really* good," he said, reaching into the bag for the chocolate milks, handing Genevieve one. She opened it and drank half the bottle before sitting up straight and burping loudly.

Matt laughed, quickly taking a swig of his own chocolate milk and offering a burp to match hers.

She nodded, smiling and chewing with her mouth full.

"If we ever do this again, remind me to feed you before you turn into a..."

"Sorry, I tried to warn you," she said with her mouth full. She shook her head and looked away. She finished her croissant and emptied her chocolate milk before he was even half done.

"What's up?" he asked, nudging her with his shoulder.

She didn't respond right away, sitting there quietly. "I don't know what the hell's wrong with me."

He smiled and put his hand on her shoulder, rocking her slightly. "That's exactly what James said last night."

"Uhh, are you trying to make me feel better?"

"No, honest. That's exactly what he said. He had some kind of crazy meltdown, mumbling something about how much money he was missing out on. We finally picked him up off his bed and tossed him into the cold shower with his clothes on."

Genevieve laughed. "No wonder he was in such a bad mood this morning."

"Yeah, well, it was Greg's idea—said it helped sober him up when he was trying to quit drinking. Said it would be a good shock to the system."

"That's insane. There's no way that made things better."

"It did for a while. He stopped his bellyachin', but I guess it was back this morning, wasn't it?"

She smiled and nodded, looking back down at her shoes.

"Actually, maybe you and James should both avoid cold water. It doesn't seem to bring out the best in you."

Genevieve smiled, patting her wet shirt, but she didn't look up.

"Are you sure you don't want to talk about it?"

She didn't respond. And Matt didn't push her, finishing his lunch quietly.

"She makes me feel like a failure," Genevieve spoke softly after more than a minute of silence.

"I don't understand," Matt responded, leaning forward so he could see her face. "Who?"

"Amy...she's always had her crap together. She's always known who she is and has been on the road to get there. I've *always* been intimidated by her."

Matt nodded, encouraging her to continue.

"She was the only one of our roommates who didn't party every weekend. We'd all be coming out of our comas on Sunday afternoons, and she'd come back to the apartment, all happy and carefree after she'd been out painting or going on her nature walks. She was always put together and happy, and somehow she always stayed out of the drama. It's like she was never concerned about impressing anyone—she was just… Perfect Amy. I kind of hoped I'd never see her again after I transferred to Syracuse. And then I found out she was here—Perfect Amy living in a perfectly cute little town."

Genevieve shook her head. "I hated this place before I even knew anything about it. I hoped I'd find her shacked up in a trailer park, living on canned beans and Twinkies and weighing eight hundred pounds. But Perfect Amy lives in a perfect world with her perfectly handsome husband, and she's still cute even though she's twenty months pregnant. It just doesn't seem fair. I've got way more money than her. I'm living in a swanky New York loft and working my dream job. I get to travel first class and interview all the hippest people on the planet, wining and dining them with my expense account. And then I come here, thinking my life couldn't be more awesome, and I see this girl I learned to loathe ten years ago who has none of the perks I have. And she's still living a perfect little life, following her dreams, married for eight years to a really nice guy, ready to start a family—it just feels like there's no justice in the world, and I hate myself for wanting her life to suck. I hate myself for thinking she doesn't deserve it. I hate myself for…"

Matt put his hand on her shoulder again and rocked her back and forth.

"Am I a terrible person for hating her?" she asked.

"I guess it depends on why you hate her."

"Pfff, because she's so infuriating."

"I…I obviously don't know her like you do, but she seemed like a really nice girl to me."

Genevieve shook her head. "That's just it—she is! She's sweet and patient and kind."

"So why do you hate her again?"

She took a deep breath. "Because I want her life. I've always wanted her life—her confidence—her ability to be kind and sweet and beautiful without even trying. The girl doesn't even wear makeup! Back in college, she'd pull herself out of bed and brush her teeth and leave our apartment with all the confidence in the world, while the rest of us were probably spending too much time standing in front of the mirror, worried if our eyeliner was straight or if our jeans accentuated our muffin tops too much or if our boobs were perky enough to draw attention from the stupid boys. She didn't care about any of that, and those stupid boys were going crazy about her—and she either didn't notice or didn't care! She's a freaking ginger with a million freckles all over her. It's like she doesn't even know she's supposed to be self-conscious. She just goes on being her beautiful self like she didn't get the memo that she has red hair and freckles and is too tall and too damn…perfect."

Matt laughed. "How do you really feel?"

Genevieve smiled and leaned back against the tree behind them.

"So what are you going to do about it?" he asked

"What do you mean? What *can* I do about it?"

He shrugged. "Recognizing you've got an issue or a problem is an important step, but it doesn't seem like hating her for having the life you want has been a very good use of time and energy."

"You wouldn't do the same thing?" she asked defensively.

"I can't say what I'd do. I mean, yeah, I understand the feelings of jealousy. I told you, right, about running into my classmate at the airport? The one who was traveling with his beautiful wife of twenty-five years to meet their first grandchild?"

Genevieve nodded.

"It was hard not to be jealous of him and what he had. I mean, pfff… it made me feel like I'd wasted a ton of time. Had I really just blown almost two decades drifting around and getting sucked up in things that didn't matter? He already had two daughters by the time we graduated from dental school! I remember thinking he was nuts at the time—like he was missing out on life and fun and everything the world had to offer. It was a different story when I saw him at the airport on my way home from Nepal. I realized I was the one who'd missed out on life."

Matt sat back against the tree, touching shoulders with Genevieve. Neither of them spoke for a minute. "You know, my mom used to always tell me when I was a kid, 'if you don't like it, change it.' I learned to hate hearing that through most of my teenage years. It's true what they say: 'the truth will set you free, but first it will really tick you off.'"

Genevieve laughed out loud. "I've never heard that before. It's so true, right?"

Matt nodded, smiling back at her. "Genevieve, I'm here because I realized that my mom's advice was the only thing that could change my future. It really sucked to realize that I didn't like what I'd done with my first forty-three years. But that dang truth in my mom's nagging voice in the back of my head made me realize that the next forty-three years could be different—if I made them different. I know you're not looking for advice, but…maybe…if you want a life that looks like Perfect Amy's, maybe you could join me—and the rest of the campers—in making sure the future is brighter than the past."

She let out a long sigh. "Where do we start?"

"I think we already have."

"Huh?"

"We're at the farm, aren't we? Maybe for different reasons, but we both have a desire to make our lives better. And it seems like we've both come to the conclusion that inviting the Creator of the universe to the party is a wise and hopeful decision. It feels like we're on the right path, doesn't it?"

She nodded slowly.

"And it feels like we have a bit of a road map, right?" he asked, holding up Thomas's book.

She nodded again.

"And Ruby and Pops—it seems like they're willing to do anything to help us, right?"

"Okay, okay, I get it. This is a pretty good place to start."

"And...we've each got a friend to help us fly straight."

Genevieve nodded. She leaned forward and patted his knee awkwardly. "Thanks," she whispered.

"Sorry, what was that?" Matt shook his head, cupping his right ear. "You're going to have to speak up. My old ears can't hear you."

She rolled her eyes. "Thank you," she said, turning to face him. "Thank you for being my friend. This would be a really crappy summer without you here."

He nodded and smiled. "You're welcome. I'm grateful to have someone to talk to—to figure all of this out with."

"Me too. Let's hurry up and figure it out. I hate feeling this way."

"Yeah, Thomas seemed to make it pretty clear that we can't just hit fast-forward and be where we want to be. We have to take small steps."

Genevieve ran her fingers through her hair, her eyes closed as she breathed loudly. "Maybe that's part of my problem."

"Impatience?"

"How'd you know?"

"It takes one to know one. Patience has always been tough for me. Even now, I feel like it would be so much easier if I could just see the big picture and know it's all going to work out."

Genevieve nodded. "Why don't we just decide that it will?"

"What?"

"Why don't we just decide right now that our future's going to look awesome and that everything is going to work out and that we're going to be insanely happy?"

A smile spread across his face. "Do you think it will work?"

She shrugged. "Have you ever tried it before?"

He thought for a moment before shaking his head. "I hate to admit it, but I think I've always had more fear of the future than any *real* belief that I had the power to make it awesome."

"Maybe that's been our problem."

Matt nodded thoughtfully. "So what does your future awesomeness look like?"

She smiled, taking a deep breath. "That feels like a lot of pressure. I think I'm going to have to get back to you on that."

"Yeah," he agreed. He looked down at the book lying on the bench next to his leg. "In the meantime, do you want to hear about Niederbipp's famous Liberty Fountain?"

CHAPTER 64

Niederbipp's Liberty Fountain

Love is an adventure and a conquest.
It survives and develops, like the universe itself,
only by perpetual discovery.
—Pierre Teilhard de Chardin

    The combination of Genevieve being agreeable and Matt being curious sent them both deeper into the history of Niederbipp. He flipped through the pages of Thomas's book until he found the fountain page again.

"Are you ready?" he asked, looking up.

"Almost," she replied, smiling playfully. She situated her still-damp hair on her shoulders and leaned against the trunk of the tree before raising a knee against her chest and wrapping her arms around her leg. "Ready."

Matt laughed and turned back to the book, extending his arm as far as possible so his eyes could focus on the words.

Freiheitsbrunnen—Liberty Fountain

When Niederbipp's first settlers arrived in the spring of 1717, they quickly discovered a natural spring of sweet water bubbling up through the ground near their encampment. This became their main water source and remained so for many years until the town's needs exceeded the spring's ability to produce. By that time, most of the buildings and homes in what is now referred to as Old Town had been built, most of them within a short walking distance of the spring. The majority of the town's water now comes from the Allegheny through a publicly sponsored utility, but the spring still flows through the Liberty Fountain and continues to produce unusually cold, clean, and sweet water year-round to the delight and charm of residents and visitors alike.

The design of the current fountain, with its circular catch basin, was patterned after the original wooden basin built by Wilhelm Schnecken, the first cooper in Niederbipp. He ran his Küferei on Müllerstrasse (see pages 117–18). Schnecken's fountain was still in use in 1725, when the women of Niederbipp rallied together to petition the town council to pave the streets with cobblestone to help keep the dirt and dust out of their homes. They proposed that the new cobblestones first be installed around the fountain; the townsfolk gathered at the fountain daily to collect water for household use, so the surrounding streets were often quite muddy and thus a steady source of dirt tracked into dwellings. The fulfillment of the women's request created a powerful, yet subtle, expression of the stonemasons' faith. Whatever your persuasion, no one who observes the fine work these craftsmen left behind can deny its beauty.

Though at street level it may be difficult to recognize any clear pattern in the cobbles, the first aerial photos of the town, taken in the late 1960s, reveal two clear patterns in the streets of Niederbipp. The first of these patterns radiates in all directions from the Liberty Fountain. The second pattern emanates from the Niederbipp Chapel's front steps in a similar way and runs through the courtyard with ever-expanding concentric rings supported by horizontal arches. Resembling the circles left on the surface of a glassy pond when a stone is thrown into it, these expanding patterns in the cobblestones suggest at least two potentially meaningful concepts: 1) the path of truth's dispersion and expansion and 2) the path that invites the wanderer back to the source of all truth and righteousness. Some believe that both patterns subliminally draw residents and visitors toward the town's spiritual center.

Matt paused to look down at the stones beneath his feet realizing he had completely missed the pattern before, emanating from the church's front steps as described. He looked up to see that Genevieve was acknowledging their shared blindness. He shook his head, amazed by the symbolism right under his nose, and turned back to the book.

These aerial photos as well as a colonial-period journal discovered in the town archives make it unquestionably clear that Niederbipp's early stonemasons hoped to convey their understanding of humanity's need for constant nourishment to both body and spirit. Now, more than 250 years later, the patterns in the cobblestones continue to draw people toward symbols of life, hope, and peace, as well as the two most powerful symbols of purification: water and the fire of faith.

Matt looked up at Genevieve. "This goes a lot deeper than I could have guessed."

"Yeah! Is that all there is?"

He looked back at the book. "No, there are still a couple of pages. Do you want to read?"

"Sure," she said, taking the book from him.

In 1817, to celebrate the one hundredth anniversary of Niederbipp's founding, the current granite fountain was commissioned. It would replace a sandstone fountain that had replaced the wooden basin more than eighty years earlier. Sponsors hoped that the Liberty Fountain, covering the same footprint as the original, would help maintain the natural flow of the spring while adding the longevity that only a harder stone like granite could promise. Twelve large granite blocks cut from a quarry twelve miles north of town were sledged onto Hauptstrasse by oxcart, and over the next two weeks, a small team of skilled stonemasons carved and fit the blocks together so tightly that no mortar was required. A local sculptor, Ellie Rügner, was commissioned to carve the sculpture that crowns the fountain.

Taking for her muse the embodiment of Liberty, a common theme in the decades following the Revolutionary War, Ms. Rügner spent many weeks working on clay models before beginning her work in stone. Sketches found in the town archives suggest that she cycled through nearly a dozen ideas before settling on one. A faded article in the Niederbipp Sentinel (see pages 42–44) from the time of the fountain's dedication reported that "knowing this would stand as a symbol of our town's values for many generations to come, Ms. E. Rügner approached the project very deliberately, spending time in prayer and meditation. It was during a meditative vision that she reportedly saw the statue she would carve."

Following her vision, she produced a unique and beautiful symbol of liberty at the very heart of Niederbipp. The sculpture, now more than 150 years old, no longer presents all of its original symbolism, the details of which may have been lost to history had it not been for an interview I was fortunate enough to conduct with Alfred Rügner, Ellie Rügner's great-great-grandson, shortly before his death in 1972. We met at the fountain in May of that year, and I conducted the interview there.

The influence of Quakerism cannot be overstated in Niederbipp's long and fabled history, and the same is true of Ms. Rügner's sculpture. Pacifists through and through, the Quakers not only preach peace and brotherly love, but they do their best to live those concepts. Early Quaker leaders taught that spiritual liberty, offered by God to all mankind through Jesus Christ, also included physical compulsions, which were meant to be implemented and observed by peaceful means such as extending love where there is hate and winning over the sorrowful and fearful by means of gentleness, meekness, and charity.

Many depictions of Liberty show a woman who is masculine in her features; she also often wields a sword. Others portray a woman with strong arms and bare breasts, suggesting a balance or combination of masculine and feminine characteristics. Ms. Rügner's Liberty, though much more feminine than many, shows no sign of weakness. According to Alfred Rügner, his great-great-grandmother intended this Liberty to embody the virtues of modesty, meekness, and humility and to illustrate what it looks like when someone puts her faith and trust in the arm of God rather than rely on her own strength for defense.

Ever hopeful and vigilant in promoting the cause of peace, Niederbipp's Quaker settlers surrounded themselves with meaningful symbols that would regularly remind them of their ultimate goals. Such a symbol was the pruning knife held in the left hand of Ms. Rügner's Liberty. It comes from the latter part of this passage in the second chapter of Isaiah:

In the last days the mountain of the Lord's house will be established at the top of the mountains and will be raised above the hills. All nations will stream to it, and many peoples will come and say, "Come, let us go up to the mountain of the Lord, to the house of the God of Jacob. He will teach us about his ways so that we may walk in his paths."

For instruction will go out of Zion and the word of the Lord from Jerusalem. He will settle disputes among the nations and provide arbitration for many peoples. They will beat their swords into plows and their spears into pruning knives. Nation will not take up the sword against nation, and they will never again train for war.

    According to historical data—including early photographs— Ms. Rügner's Liberty held in her right hand a ring of five keys for more than 125 years. If you stand in front of Ms. Rügner's statue in the right light, you can still see the hole through which the ring once passed. Further evidence of the keys can be found in a slight green stain on Liberty's right hip. More than a century's worth of rain dripped over the brass keys and onto the hip, leaving behind a streak of oxidized metal. No one knows for certain what happened to these keys, though many older residents date their disappearance to roughly the same time that the first Niederbippian men relinquished their conscientious-objector status and were shipped off to Europe to fight in the Second World War. None of them returned alive. Six government-issue crosses in the Niederbipp Cemetery now mark the final resting places of these six young men who left their families to fight for the cause of peace (see page 117).

    Alfred Rügner told me that, according to family legend, each of the five keys was inscribed with a virtue. These five virtues, if understood and practiced, would unlock the power of God's greatest joys. At the time of our interview, Mr. Rügner, in his advanced years, could not recall any of the virtues reportedly inscribed on the keys. After an extensive search of the archives, I regretfully confess that I have found no mention of the keys or the forgotten virtues. Only a charcoal sketch and a few black-and-white photographs serve to confirm the keys' existence.

    Genevieve turned the page, looking for more, but looked up at Matt, disappointed. "I guess that's it."

    "Really? There's nothing else about those keys?"

    She looked again, quickly shaking her head. "What are you thinking?"

    "'Unlock the powers of God's greatest joys'? Are you kidding? I'm thinking I want to know what's on those keys!"

"Yeah, well, it sounds like that's going to be a challenge unless things have changed since this book was written. Thomas had access to the town's archives and couldn't come up with the answers."

"At least not answers he was willing to give away."

"What do you mean?"

"Didn't you get the feeling at the library that he knows more than he wrote in the book?"

She thought for a moment and then nodded. "That seems a little strange, right?"

"Which part?"

"I mean, if you knew the keys to the greatest joys, wouldn't you want to tell everyone you knew?"

Matt nodded. "But would that information have any value if you just gave it all away?"

"I don't understand the question. Does money not have value if it's given away?"

"Sure it does, but doesn't it have even more value if you've put in some sweat to earn it—if you've got some skin in game? Isn't that what he was saying about milk before meat—you need to learn to chew before meat has any value?"

"You think that's what he was talking about?"

"You don't?"

"I don't know. I guess I was confused. Maybe I still am."

Matt nodded. "I don't know if he wanted it to be like some kind of treasure hunt, but he told us where to look for at least one clue, right?"

She nodded slowly. "The cemetery."

"Yeah. We still have time, right?"

Genevieve nodded. "I think so, but we better hurry."

CHAPTER 65

Searching for Joy

It does not matter how slowly you go
as long as you do not stop.
—Confucius

The cemetery's rusty iron gate swung open with a groan as Matt and Genevieve entered, their eyes wide.

"It's beautiful," Matt said, looking around at all of the gravestones and the flowers that grew between the gravel paths. He pointed to the six white crosses they'd just read about, pulling Genevieve's attention away from the bench under the crabapple tree, where she'd fled after church on Sunday.

He started toward the crosses when Genevieve reminded him why they were there. Though seven benches were scattered across the yard, only two were anywhere near the center, where Thomas had said they would find Isaac Bingham's bench. Genevieve led off toward the middle of the graveyard, Matt following close behind.

"Which bench do you think Thomas was talking about?" Matt asked as they came near.

"He said the one built for Isaac, right?"

"That's right. It must be this one," he suggested, pointing to the newer-looking of the two benches. He stood over it, looking down at the colorful surface mosaicked with tiles and potsherds. The tile in the center of the bench confirmed Matt's guess; the name Isaac Aaron Bingham was carved into a clay tile that had been etched and glazed to look like a candlestick. They walked around the bench, observing the tiles on the bench's two solid legs. Many tiles had words carved into them. In each corner of the seat was a tile featuring a simple blue flower with five petals and a yellow center.

"Do you know what we're looking for?" Genevieve asked.

"Not exactly. What did Thomas say? Something about learning from Isaac himself?"

"Yeah, but there was also that part about finding joy, right?"

Matt nodded, pointing to the tile at one of the of the bench. "'I have no greater joy than to hear my children walk in truth,'" he read aloud. "Do you think that's what he was talking about?"

"I don't know. What does that that one say?" she asked, pointing to a tile on the opposite end of the bench.

"'My greatest wish is that you will come to know the love of God.'"

She glanced up at Matt before turning back to the bench, where several other tiles called out for attention.

Matt sat down on the bench that stood just a couple of feet away from Isaac's bench. "Both of those are meaningful. How do we know we which one Thomas was talking about?"

"Or maybe it was this one," Genevieve said, pointing to a smaller tile. "'Where your treasure is, there will your heart be also.'"

"That's from the Bible," Matt said, "and I'm pretty sure that one about children walking in truth is in there too." He thought for a moment before looking up at Genevieve. "All of those things could have ties to joy, right?"

She shrugged. "I guess so. This one might also," she said, pointing. "'Sweet is the peace the gospel brings.'"

Matt nodded. "What does that tile there say?" he asked, leaning forward to take a closer look. "'We are all beggars.'" He looked up, confused. "I'm not sure how that one ties in."

Genevieve looked blank, taking a seat next to Matt. She cocked her head sideways, realizing that the bench seat's narrow front face contained writing as well. She pointed as she read. "'Joy, in all its glory, can only be obtained through unselfishness.'" She looked up at Matt. "Is that from the Bible too?"

"I don't think so," he replied, looking more closely at it. He leaned forward and ran his thumb over the bright green tile, lingering over the word *joy*. "I think this might be it," he said, getting to his feet and walking around to the other side of the bench. He stooped over to read the writing on the seat's rear face. He looked up and smiled at Genevieve. "I think that's definitely it."

"Why? What does it say over there?"

"You want to guess?"

She shrugged.

"It says, '"Be still, and know that I am God."'"

"Seriously?" she responded, hurrying to his side.

She walked back around to the other side, sitting again on the bench across from Isaac's. "'Joy, in all its glory, can only be obtained through unselfishness,'" she repeated aloud. She looked up to find Matt smiling. "You think this is what Thomas wanted us to find?"

"I think so."

She looked down, reading it again before looking back up. "You think it's that easy?"

He walked back around and sat down next to her. "Really? You think being unselfish is easy?"

She laughed. "Maybe not."

"Yeah, it seems like selfishness might be the cause of many of the world's problems—both the big ones and the small ones."

Genevieve nodded slowly. "So its opposite—unselfishness—is maybe one of the keys Thomas was talking about."

"It could be, right?" Matt said, nodding. "It pretty basic in theory, but in practice...it seems like unselfishness pushes against the natural grain of almost everyone. It almost seems like to be truly unselfish we would have to be constantly at battle against our lesser natures."

Genevieve nodded again. "What was that word you and Pops were talking about earlier this week? Magna-something?"

"Magnanimous?"

"Yeah. Unselfishness—that's basically the same thing as being magnanimous, isn't it?"

Matt nodded after thinking a moment. "I think so. Maybe choosing to be unselfish is one of the first steps to becoming magnanimous."

Genevieve stared at the bench for a moment. "And, at least according to the wisdom of the bench, it's one of the keys to finding joy."

The church bells above them chimed four times, and they turned to see the ornate clock hands indicating four o'clock.

"We should probably get going, huh?" Matt said when the bells stopped.

"Yeah." Genevieve stood, walking around the bench and taking it all in before looking across the cemetery at the other benches. "I think we need to come back here."

"Sure. When?"

"I guess Sunday will probably be the next time we can, right?"

"I guess so." He looked down again at the bench, the details of a large tile on the right leg catching his eye for the first time. He knelt down to more closely examine it. "Did you see this?" he asked, looking up at Genevieve.

"No, what is it?" She knelt down next to him. "Hey, that's a yoke he's holding," she said, pointing to the tile, which featured a folksy carving of a robed and bearded man holding a double yoke like the one in the dining hall. "Do you think that's supposed to be Jesus?"

"Considering the content of the rest of these tiles, it seems likely, right?"

She nodded.

"I think we need to talk to Amy's husband. I'm betting he'd know something about all of this."

She nodded but didn't respond verbally. "I guess we better get those things for Ruby before we head out," Genevieve said, getting to her feet before dusting off her knees.

Matt followed her through the cemetery gate and across the courtyard. "You're upset, aren't you?" he said as they reached the top of the wisteria-arched stairs.

She didn't stop, continuing down the stairs. "Why would I be upset?"

"Aren't you? I only mentioned Amy's name and things turned chilly. Maybe it's time to be done being jealous."

"Maybe it's time to mind your own freakin' business."

He laughed out loud but stopped when she glared at him. "If you decide you want to talk about it, let me know. I'll be here all summer. And if I'm going to be the new dentist around here, it's likely that I'll get to know them."

"By that time I'll be back in New York, and I won't have to worry about any of this."

"*Really*? This jealousy has bugged you since your freshman year but you think it's just going to go away?" he asked incredulously.

"You've got a solution that doesn't include interacting with her?"

"Uh, probably not. Studies have shown that talking is still the most effective means of communicating."

She shook her head but smiled as they turned back onto Hauptstrasse, which was still busy with afternoon shoppers.

"Good afternoon, folks," a friendly male voice said from the registers as they walked through the doors of Braun's Market.

"Hi there," Matt responded. He noticed that Genevieve kept her head down.

The man at the register finished with his customer before wandering over to help them. "Welcome to Braun's Market. Is there anything I can help you find?"

"Oh, maybe," Matt said, turning to face the tall, slender man. Matt noticed that the man's red Braun's Market apron half concealed a faded aloha shirt.

"You look like you might be new in town. My name's Kai."

"Nice to meet you. I'm Matt. Genevieve and I, we're working up at the Swarovskis' farm this summer."

"Oh right—Ruby and Lorenzo's place. Great people. I probably would have ended up there myself had my wife not taken pity on me and agreed to marry me. It's hard to believe we've been married more than ten years already. Time flies when you're having fun."

"That's great," Matt responded. "Is this your shop?"

"It is now. We just finished paying off Molly's dad two months ago."

"Congratulations!"

"Thanks," Kai said, following Matt, who was trying to keep up with Genevieve. "Say, I bet you're looking for salt, aren't you?"

"Yeah, as a matter of fact we are," Matt said, turning around. "How'd you know?"

Kai smiled. "Well, being the lone grocer in town, I've got to know my customers, right? I know Ruby and Lorenzo try to raise most everything you folks eat up there, but I always meet a few of their summer hands when they come in for the things you can't raise. Salt is often on that list. And then of course there's always that one guy—usually a dude, but some chicks too—who wanders in looking winded, searching for a bag of flour because they couldn't figure out how to make the mill work. As a matter of fact, Molly was saying we had a guy in here earlier today who was looking for a fifty-pound sack of flour. That wouldn't have been one of your guys, would it?"

Matt glanced at Genevieve and replied. "Yeah, maybe. Tall guy, all business?"

"That's the one. The biggest bag we carry is only twenty pounds, so she sent him up to the mill on Müllerstrasse. She said he seemed to be having a bad day."

"Yeah, well, I guess this is a big adjustment for some of us," Matt responded.

"Oh, I totally get it. But I suppose it's good practice for marriage though, right? I'll tell you, marriage is a lot of work but totally worth it." He walked past them and picked up two types of salt packages. "This," he said, lifting a five-pound bag, "is the stuff they usually get for making cheese. And this"—holding up a smaller round carton—"is the stuff they use in the kitchen."

"Thanks," Genevieve said. "We need both."

"Cool. I'll drop them at the counter unless you wanna schlepp them around. I see you didn't grab a basket. Your list must be short today."

"Thanks. Yeah, it is short," Genevieve said.

"Let me guess. It's still early in the season, but I'd guess you need matches, toilet paper, and mmm…how about marshmallows, graham crackers, and chocolate?"

Genevieve looked down at her list. "I guess you really *do* know your customers. Toilet paper's not on the list, but we might as well get some while we're here. I'd hate to run out so far from town."

Kai nodded, offering a goofy grin. "I see s'mores in your future," he responded in his best fortune-teller voice. He walked them quickly through the aisles, picking up the items for them until his arms were full, then he pointed with his foot to the items they needed.

"It's not every day you get help like this from your neighborhood grocer," Matt said as they walked to the register.

"It's not every day you're in Niederbipp either. I'm glad to help." He rang them up and dropped their items into paper bags. "I hope I get to see you guys again. Good luck."

"Thanks," Matt responded. "I know I need all the luck I can get." He looked around the store and noticed that the few customers milling around didn't seem to need any help. He decided he was probably safe to ask Kai more. "Say, uh, I hope you don't mind me asking, but what's it like actually living here?"

Kai smiled. "Are you thinking about becoming a Niederbippian?"

"Actually, yeah, I am."

"We get that a lot," Kai responded. "I'll tell you what I tell everyone. It's a great place to be, a great community, a great place to raise kids, a great place to enjoy nature and quiet."

"Uh-oh. I sense a *but* coming," Matt said, bracing himself.

Kai shrugged. "Okay, maybe it's not for everyone. Lots of folks fall in love with Niederbipp over a weekend visit. They walk the charming streets and check out our unique shops and eat one of Sam's pastries and think they've found nirvana. We often see weekenders looking at the offerings in the windows at the real-estate office or overhear couples talking at Mancini's Ice Café about buying a cute little place where they can come and unwind. But at the end of the weekend, most folks go back to the cities or wherever they came from, and they get busy and forget about living in a dream like this, so far away from reality that the internet hasn't even made it out here yet. And every year at least one Swarovski kid asks me what it's like to live here, saying they'd maybe like to hang around when the season's over."

"You make it sound like no one ends up staying."

"Well, not many of them do, at least not long term. There was a couple that met at the Swarovskis' a few years back and got married at the end of the summer. Brian and Emily—really great couple. Molly and I actually got pretty close to them when they rented an apartment over the toy shop for six months while they figured out where to land. But they decided to move on to a place that was better for business. They still spend a week or two here every summer—they say to find their bearings and unplug and remember what it's like to breathe fresh air and forget about traffic. They keep threatening to buy a place and come more often, but it hasn't happened yet. And now with a couple of kids—well, you know. Things get complicated."

"Would you do it again? Buy a grocery store and stick around?" Matt asked.

"Oh heck yes! Any day of the week," Kai said with a big smile. "To be part of a community that cares, to be able to love and serve, to feel like you're making a difference and like life has purpose and meaning—I wouldn't trade it for anything. Yeah, it's hard work, and we're resigned to the fact that we'll never have a lot of money. But there are lots of things that money can't buy. Molly and I can't think of a place we'd rather raise our kids. So, yeah—stick around at the end of the summer. We could always use a few more families to be part of our village."

"Thank you for your time and honesty," Matt said, extending his hand to Kai as a customer rolled her cart up to the counter. "I'll be back."

CHAPTER 66

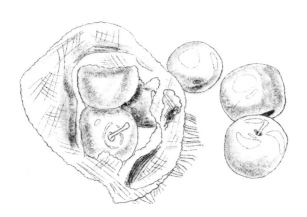

Two Paths Home

At the end of the day, you are solely responsible for your success and your failure.
And the sooner you realize that, you accept that, and integrate that into your work ethic,
you will start being successful. As long as you blame others for the reason you aren't where you want to be, you will always be a failure.
—Erin Cummings

"So, you're really gonna do it?" Genevieve asked as they began their walk back up Hauptstrasse.

"It's an exciting idea, isn't it?"

"You're not worried at all that you'll get bored?"

He didn't answer right away. "I don't know. It's a big decision. And I hope it won't be mine alone to make."

"What do you mean?"

"Well, I hope I'll have a wife to weigh in on the question of where to live and work and hopefully raise a family. I guess I didn't think about it when I was talking to Barney and Patsy, but I guess I really should have my future wife—whoever she is—weigh in on it too."

"That's probably a good idea. She might really hate Niederbipp."

"Yeah, I guess that's possible, but…what's there to hate?"

She realized she didn't have an immediate answer, all of her quibbles and issues with this quirky town having slowly sloughed off in the last two weeks.

They passed the open doors of a shop they'd missed before, calliope music now pouring out onto the streets.

"Come on in, folks!" said a teenaged boy wearing a top hat with a plastic pudding mold glued to its crown. "Happy hour—two-for-one entrance to the famous Mancini International Museum of Pudding Molds." He handed Matt a flyer printed on bright pink paper.

"Thanks," Matt said, looking confused as they kept walking.

Genevieve looked the flyer over quickly before turning back to the teen. "Maybe another day. We gotta get home to milk the cows."

The boy waved as he hurried to hand a flyer to another potential customer.

"Now there's an excuse you can't use every day," Matt responded.

She laughed out loud when she realized what she'd just said.

"Hey, did what that guy Kai say strike a chord with you?" Matt asked.

"Which part?"

"Oh, the part about feeling like his life had purpose, like he was making a difference, like he was part of a community. I'd love to be able to say any of those things."

"Don't your humanitarian trips give you some of that?"

"Yeah, they do. But then I come home, and life is…less than that. I feel like there's meaning to my life when I'm serving people."

"Maybe you could just give away your dental services here too," she joked.

"Sometimes I wish I could—just take the whole money thing out of equation and help people who need it. But I gotta eat and live. I always have to work to pay for that next humanitarian trip. Nothing in life is free."

"What are you talking about?" she laughed. "Just a couple of hours ago you were given a dental practice and a place to live."

He smiled, placing the heavier of the two grocery bags into the basket of his bicycle and handing the other to Genevieve. "I know, right? This might be the best day of my life so far."

She nodded, squeezing the grocery bag into her basket and stepping over the bar of her bicycle. "I'm happy for you."

"But…?" he asked, sensing a counterargument.

"But aren't you a little bit worried that you could be missing out on something even better?"

"Sounds like FOMO to me."

"It probably is," she admitted. "But if you moved here, you'd basically have to say goodbye to most of the conveniences of modern life."

They pushed off onto the blacktop and were soon riding side by side back to the farm.

"Have you missed those conveniences in these last two weeks?" he asked.

"Haven't you? To be able to walk to the corner shop and get a latté or go shopping during lunch break or wander around Central Park in the evening?"

"Are you kidding?" Matt asked, smiling. "This whole place is like a big Central Park, isn't it? Minus the panhandlers and the homeless folks sleeping on the benches."

"Yeah, well," she responded, acknowledging that he was right. "But what about the art and culture you find in the city? There's no way you could find anything like that around here."

"No, I guess not. But we do have the Mancini International Museum of Pudding Molds! I'm pretty sure you'd never find one of those in the city."

Genevieve smiled.

"So maybe I'd have to learn to appreciate the community theater," Matt continued, "or join a bowling league or take some art classes to scratch that itch. But here's my question: you have all of that culture at your fingertips in the city, but how often do you really take advantage of it?"

"Pfff. Not as often as I should—actually not very often at all. I'm always meaning to, but work gets in the way. Usually by the time I'm done for the day, all I want to do is hit the bar on the way home for a couple of cocktails. Speaking of which, I haven't had a cocktail in two weeks!"

"Have you missed drinking?"

She realized that this was the first time she'd even thought about a drink since Sunday. "I'm sure I normally would have, but we've been really busy, right? How about you?"

He shook his head. "I've never been much of a drinker. I don't like feeling out of control. I could probably live the rest of my life without a drink."

"It sounds like you're a pretty good candidate to become the newest Niederbippian."

"I'll consider that a compliment," he said, flashing a smile.

They continued talking until the road steepened and they had to focus their energy on making their bikes go. Matt took the lead again but pulled to the side after a hundred yards and cheered her on as she passed him. She pedaled for another twenty feet before dismounting, breathing like she was going to die.

"Do you think this ever gets easier?" she managed to ask as she tried to catch her breath.

"Maybe by the end of the summer," he responded, distracted by something in the road thirty feet ahead. "Is that a rabbit?" he asked, squinting.

Her eyes followed his to the white object. "I don't think so."

They pushed their bikes toward it. Genevieve reached it first and poked it with her foot.

"What is it?" Matt asked.

She turned around and smiled. "It's flour!"

"What the…?"

"Do you think it's from James?"

Matt smiled as he imagined James trying to balance a bicycle while wrestling with a fifty-pound bag of flour. "There's got to be an easier way to get flour back to the farm," he said, panting under his own burden.

"There's got to be at least ten easier ways, including pushing a wheelbarrow all the way to town and back," Genevieve responded.

They laughed together.

"Do you think he's okay?" Genevieve asked.

Matt shook his head as he continued to push his bike up the hill. "He's a tough one, isn't he?"

"You have no idea. You've never had to do the laundry with him."

"No, but I've had to bunk with him. I'm not sure what his problem is, but he seems to be making life really hard on himself."

"And everyone else, too! Would you have let him out of his contract?"

Matt shook his head after a moment. "I think Ruby was right. As difficult as he is to work with, it would be even tougher to have to work around the hole he'd leave."

"So what would you do with him?"

Matt thought for a moment, not knowing how to answer. But the answer came when he looked ahead and noticed a second clump of flour in the road, followed by a twenty-foot streak of the white powder. "I think I'd let him figure it out on his own," he said, pointing to the trail James had left behind. "Maybe Hildegard had it right."

"Which part?"

"Maybe he needs to get out of his own way. *It's in you*," he said in a perfect old woman voice, pointing to Genevieve's chest.

She laughed. "Do you think that's true? Do you think everyone can find the answers to their problems in their own hearts?"

"I'm still trying to figure that out," he admitted. "I think I mentioned my friend Mr. Reeve, the neighbor who took me under his wing when my parents divorced…"

"Yeah?"

"He told me once that the answers to many of the hardest questions in life are a little bit like the pinecones that stay closed up and don't spread their seeds until forest fires are raging all around them—that's when they know there's finally room for them to grow."

"Pfff. I don't know if I like that metaphor," Genevieve admitted.

"Why not?"

"Because it's too…true."

"Yeah. I know what you mean."

"Do you think that ever changes?" she asked.

"Huh?"

"Do you think you ever get to the point where you can just accept the truth the first time you see it rather than ignoring it until it has to smack you upside the head?"

Matt nodded. "I hope so. It seems like Ruby and Pops have that dialed in. And Hildegard. And Thomas. They get it, I think. None of them look like they've been smacked around by a two-by-four lately."

"Yeah, but they're all old. Do we really have to wait that long before any of this gets easier?"

"It seems like a lot of people have to wait until they're old, but I don't know if there's really an age requirement."

"No?"

Matt shook his head, turning to look at Genevieve. "Isn't that what Pops and Ruby are trying to teach us? Isn't that what this is all about? I mean, it seems like most of us have a few things to iron out before we're really ready for marriage, right? I thought I was ready before I came here, but, man...I've got a lot of things to figure out before I'd want to be married to me."

She nodded, smiling as they approached another white trail, this one stretching up and around the next bend. "Do you think he had any flour left in his sack by the time he got back?"

Matt smiled. "In my mind's eye, I can see him getting back to the house with only five pounds left in his sack and realizing he either has to go back to town again tomorrow or learn how to work with Crystal."

"Ooh, poor Crystal."

"I think maybe they've both met their match."

"What do you mean?"

"Like Ruby said, she's not exactly a picnic on a summer's day either."

"Really? I mean, I heard Ruby say that, and I know Crystal's a bit uppity and sometimes grumpy. But I still feel sorry for her—it sounds miserable to work with James for who knows how many days in a row."

Matt smiled. "It seems like maybe that's a lesson we all have to learn about marriage—how to work things out even when it's difficult or miserable."

"Okay, but this is different. They're *not* married. They don't even like each other."

"I get that, but they're still adults. We all have to deal with people we don't agree with, right? It seems like really great practice for marriage—learning to work things out with people when the stakes aren't as critical as they are in marriage. I can't help but wonder how that kind of practice might have helped my parents learn to work through their disagreements. It's been impossible for me to forget some of those *seriously* loud fights."

"Really? When my parents fight, they just avoid each other for weeks at a time."

"How's that any more effective?"

Genevieve shrugged. "It's probably not."

"It seems like both scenarios lead to unhappiness and discontent. What would your parents do if they had to cook and grind flour together for a couple of days every time they got so upset they stopped talking?"

"Are you kidding? They'd probably kill each other with their expert passive-aggressive jabs."

"Is that something like a pillow fight?"

She smiled, sweat beading up on her forehead as they labored to push their bikes up the hill. "Do you realize all the trouble we're avoiding by staying single?" Genevieve responded with a laugh. "Maybe this little lesson will backfire. Maybe everyone will mutiny and we'll all get to go home early."

"Is that what you want?" Matt asked, looking surprised.

She shook her head. "I just don't like the looming sense of conflict hovering over the farm right now."

"Me neither. How long do you think it will take for James and Crystal to figure it out?"

"Hmmm, James is tough. I could see it taking a few months."

"It probably would be better for all of us if they were on laundry duty rather than KP. They could poison us."

"I think they already tried this morning. I'm still burping burnt," Genevieve said.

"You mean kind of like your mesquite French toast?"

She laughed and shook her head as they rounded the curve and saw that the line of flour continued up the road as far as they could see.

"You'd think he would have noticed," Genevieve said, pointing to the line of flour that seemed to grow thicker the closer they got to the farm.

"Have you ever been so mad that you became blind to what was right in front of you?"

"I don't know. The night I came here was pretty upsetting, but what are you thinking of?"

"I remember pulling weeds at my grandma's house with my cousins when I was eleven or twelve. The other kids were teasing me about something stupid, and after a couple of hours of feeling bullied, I totally snapped. I picked up a shovel and threw it so hard that I'm sure it would have severed a limb had it hit anyone. I felt like I was drunk with anger.

It scared me. I decided that day that I'd never let my temper get the best of me again. I don't think James has reached that point."

"But just imagine the damage he could do with a shovel—he's a grown man. Do you think Crystal's even safe?"

"I guess I have to trust that Ruby knows what she's doing. I can imagine that over the course of fifty-six years, she's probably seen far worse. I think it's going to be okay."

They continued to follow the trail of flour all the way up Harmony Hill, imagining how James may have reacted when he finally realized that his flight to town had been for naught. They didn't have to imagine anymore once they reached the summit. Flour was scattered all over the entrance to the farm's drive, and the flour sack lay in the grass, shredded and torn to bits. James's bike lay in the middle of the drive, dusted with flour and looking like it had been stomped on; the frame was bent, and broken spokes hung from the wheel.

"Looks like he went ballistic!" Genevieve said with wide eyes. "Do you think everyone's okay?"

Matt looked down at the farm. He could see many of the campers sitting on the porch and two more playing with Rex on the lawn. "It looks like everything's okay."

"Do you see James?"

"No, but…I can hear him. It sounds like he's over there," he said, pointing to the phone booth.

The phone booth was empty, but they both could hear James's muffled voice coming from somewhere below the summit. They listened for a moment, realizing that they could also hear Crystal. The two didn't seem to be yelling like they had in the morning, but Genevieve and Matt could tell that things weren't settled yet.

Genevieve could tell he was troubled. "Are you okay?" she asked.

He shook his head. "Do you know where the road goes?" he asked, pointing to where it continued past the farm's turnout.

Genevieve had been that way before. "Yeah, the Cartwright's farm is up there. Why?"

"I need to get away from this," he said, looking at James's bike and the mess he'd made. He pushed off and pedaled hard down the road. Genevieve followed, but she struggled to catch up with him until he stopped pedaling and started coasting.

"Are you okay?" she asked when she noticed that his eyes were focused on the lines dotting the middle of the road.

He didn't answer or look up for a nearly a minute. "Sorry," he finally responded. "I…it just hit a little too close to home."

"Do you want to talk about it?"

He shook his head but coasted to a stop under the shade of a tree. Genevieve followed him and dismounted under the tree. Looking around, she saw that they'd nearly reached the Cartwright farm, where she'd met an Amish horse trainer the week before. She and Matt both leaned their bikes against the tree and sat down in the shady crabgrass.

"What's up?" Genevieve asked, seeing that his eyes were closed.

"I thought I was past all of this. But I…guess there's still some heavy stuff there I'd forgotten about." He lay back on the grass and looked up into the branches above them.

"You don't want to talk about it?"

"I'd rather just forget it, but that never seems to work for very long. I didn't realize that I'm still so sensitive to angry words and voices. It's hard for me to be around it without feeling the panic I used to feel when I was a child."

"Uh, I'm pretty sure that's called PTSD."

He nodded. "I had a therapist tell me the same thing. But knowing what it's called hardly makes it any easier to deal with."

"How do you deal with it?"

"I usually walk away—or, in some cases, pedal away." He forced a smile before closing his eyes. "It's stupid that things that happened so long ago still affect me this way. But when I hear the kind of anger we did this morning or see senseless destruction like with James's bike, I'm right back there, seeing the world with my nine-year-old eyes, watching my father tear things apart and yell at my mother that it's all her fault. It's been almost thirty-five years since the last time I really felt threatened, but the panic I feel in my chest is just as raw as it ever was. I hate it. It makes me feel weak and helpless and...afraid."

Genevieve didn't know what to say. This revelation surprised her. He had appeared so solid and unflinching, carrying no outward signs of whatever abuse he'd endured. But it was obvious that his scars were deep and painful. "I'm sorry," she said softly. "I wouldn't have guessed that this was a part of your history."

"Yeah, well, growing up in a dysfunctional family is hardly something to brag about. Seeing his bike and the flour sack torn to bits—it's so stupid that that was a trigger. I'm freakin' forty-three years old! There's no reason for any of this to still be affecting me this way."

"Isn't that the way PTSD works? You relive the trauma in your head even decades later. My grandfather still had flashbacks from World War II almost sixty years after. I know it's a real thing."

Matt took a deep breath but didn't open his eyes. "I didn't go to war. It just makes me feel like I'm weak, like I can't control my emotions."

"You may not have gone to war, but it sounds like you were living in a combat zone, right? And you were just a kid. There's no weakness in that. It sucks that you were exposed to the trauma, but walking away from triggers doesn't feel like a weakness to me. You know what that trauma is and you know you don't want any part of it. There's no shame in that."

He shook his head. "I couldn't protect her. I couldn't make it end. There was nothing I could do to make it better."

"Matt, I obviously don't know the details, but of course you couldn't do anything. You were a kid!"

"I know. I know. I know! If I could just go back and..."

"Do you really want to go back?"

"No. No, I...I just want to move forward and forget about it all."

"What's stopping you?"

"Fear. Fear of repeating history—fear of becoming...that. You know the statistics. Kids from abusive homes often become abusers. They get into stressful situations and turn into the very thing they hate most. I don't...I can't do that. I don't want to be my father."

"Matt, you're a gentle soul. I don't think you have it in you."

"I have two fists and a short fuse. The potential is always there."

"But isn't that the case with everyone? Don't we all have the potential to be monsters?"

"Sure, but I worry that my history—my exposure to all that ugliness—has served to stack the deck against me. You never know what stress can do, what nastiness it can trigger. I can't even handle watching it from a distance."

"Do you think that's one of the reasons you haven't married?"

"Yes," he said softly, his eyes still closed. "The last thing I want is for the Owens curse to continue on to another generation. I used to think that if I could just take myself out of the gene pool, the madness would end."

"Do you think that's the only way to end the madness?"

"I don't know. I've always wanted to believe I could be different, that I would respond differently with my own kids—that I'd have more patience and self-control. But the fact is, I'm weak. And my history combined with my genetics—it just feels like it all has the potential to be a lethal cocktail. That's one of the reasons I hate alcohol—why I hate the feeling of being out of control."

"Hey, I'm no expert, but I think that's what's going to save you. You know what you want, and you know what you absolutely don't want. You're aware of your triggers, and you know your weaknesses and natural inclinations. I wouldn't worry about you, Matt. You're thoughtful and kind and patient. I feel like your life is going to work out just fine."

"I wish I had the same confidence."

Genevieve was distracted by the neighing of a horse behind them. She turned to see the yellow stallion from last week kicking up dust in the corral. The Amish man stood near the fence.

"Come with me," she said, tapping Matt's ribs as she got to her feet.

"Where are you going?"

"Come see this."

He followed her, looking rather reluctant at first but quickly catching up as she led him down the Cartwrights' drive. She explained what she had seen the week before and told him about the discussion she'd had with the Amish man, who'd been hired to break the horse so it could be ridden. She also recounted how the Cartwrights had adopted the stallion from a wild herd in New Mexico, saving it from being culled. Matt and Genevieve reached the corral's pipe fence and leaned against it, watching the man use a long pole to lead the horse in a circle.

"Nice to see you again," the man said, nodding as the horse galloped past them.

"Yes, you, too!" Genevieve responded. "It looks like you've made some good progress."

"He's coming along, finally learning to trust a little bit. But we've got a way to go yet."

After the horse circled one more time, the man walked toward them. "It occurred to me after we last saw each other that I never introduced myself. I'm David Stoltzfus." He reached out his hand to Genevieve.

"Genevieve Patterson," she said. "And this is my friend, Matt."

"It's nice to meet you," Matt replied, taking the man's firm, calloused hand.

"How are things at Ruby's?"

She glanced at Matt before turning back. "They're good enough."

David nodded, turning to watch the horse. "I noticed on my way up here a line of what looked like flour along the road and a wrecked bike at the top of the drive. Is everything okay?"

"We're not sure," Genevieve said. "We just got back from town and missed whatever happened."

David nodded. "I suppose that's the way it goes, right?"

"Does it?"

"Well, sure. I mean, bringing twelve nonfarmers here for the summer and expecting them to learn how to navigate a new space with new chores and different personalities—it's gotta be a shock to your whole system, right?"

Matt nodded. "It takes some getting used to."

"Yeah. I feel fortunate to only have to deal with one horse at a time. I can't even imagine trying to train twelve new stallions and mares in the same corral at once, dealing with twelve personalities and their habits and hormones. It's amazing Ruby and Lorenzo don't have more trouble. I don't think I'd have the patience for it."

Genevieve smiled. "I saw that stallion last week. He was *not* happy to be here. You seem to have plenty of patience for that. And look how tame he's becoming! I'm impressed."

"Thank you. In another couple of months, I think he'll be ready to ride."

"*A couple of months?*" Matt asked, looking surprised as he watched the horse roll onto its side and play in the dirt.

"Yeah, well, can you imagine him doing that with a rider on his back? I might be able to ride him in a week or two, but I wouldn't want to put anyone else in danger until he's figured things out. We won't even be able to shoe him for at least a month. And after seeing that," he said, nodding toward a mangled horse trailer, "I wouldn't want to get him around the Cartwrights' grandkids until we've worked all the wild out of him."

"He did *that* to the trailer?" Matt asked, looking at the dented door, which even from a distance looked like it had been bashed at by a dozen angry bulls.

David nodded. "He obviously was dealing with some angst."

"Yeah, I guess. It's gotta scare you to be in the same pen as him," Genevieve said.

"Oh, it's not so bad. The first thing a horseman has to learn is that you've gotta respect the horse if you ever want him to respect you. My father taught me how to work with horses. He never liked the idea of *breaking* them—always taught me it was better to teach them to *bend* to your expectations."

"What's the difference?" Matt asked.

"The method. Some trainers feel like it's necessary to absolutely reduce a horse to a quivering sack of flesh and bones by beating and whipping it into submission. Then they slowly rebuild the horse into what they want it to be. My father taught me to honor a horse and teach it that it can trust me—that I've got its best interest at heart. That's why I might spend a couple of weeks in a corral like this one, talking to the horse, getting to know it, helping it see that it can trust me, showing it that there's nothing to be afraid of. I'm sure it takes longer this way, but our family believes a horse, if treated right, can become a friend—even a part of the family."

Matt nodded thoughtfully. He watched the horse gallop from one side of the corral to the other before it nudged the fence with its side as if trying to push the barrier over.

"He's still got a ways to go, obviously, but he's learning that cooperation has its rewards. Follow me if you want. It's time for his treat."

They followed David to a small horse cart that consisted of little more than two wheels and a bench seat. A beautiful reddish-brown horse, tied to an adjacent fence, stood patiently at the front of the cart. David spoke softly to the horse before walking along its side, patting its rump as he reached for a lumpy gunnysack on the floor of the cart. He stuck his arm deep into the sack and pulled out an old apple, offering it to Genevieve. "Would you like to feed Charlie?"

"Is it safe?" she asked, hesitating.

David smiled. "This is Charlie," he said, patting his horse again. "I'll take care of Duke."

Genevieve accepted the apple and moved to Charlie's head. The horse turned and looked at her like it knew what was coming, extending its lips and then its tongue to try to reach the apple. Genevieve was skittish, gripping the withered apple stem with only her thumb and forefinger as if she were worried the horse might mistake her fingers for the fruit. But she didn't need to worry. The horse was gentle and rather talented at plucking fruit from a human hand.

David smiled and nodded from his perch atop the fence. He turned and whistled to Duke. He lifted the gunnysack above his head before jumping down to the ground. He walked five paces toward the horse and, with exaggerated motions, pulled an apple from the sack, set it on the ground, and backed up to the fence. They all watched as Duke sauntered slowly toward the old apple. When the horse got within a few feet of the apple, he slowed, looking from side to side and inching his way forward. As he extended his neck and head, he kept his eyes on David as if expecting an ambush. But David just smiled as Duke snatched the apple and bounded away to enjoy it.

"He's getting braver," David said, reaching into the sack again and handing Charlie another apple, which he appeared to enjoy.

"Why didn't you try to feed Duke out of your hand?" Matt asked.

"Because I need my fingers," David said with a laugh. "The time will come, but I've got a lot more work to do to earn his trust and help him feel comfortable. Last week when we started, he wouldn't even look at the apple I offered him until I was on my way out of the drive. We'll get there. With any luck, he'll be eating out of my hand by the end of next month."

"Is it worth it?" Matt asked, watching the yellow stallion bucking and galloping at the far end of the corral, looking like he was in no hurry to do anything tame.

"You tell me," David said, gesturing to Charlie.

"Was *he* ever the same way?" Matt asked doubtfully.

"Yes. A man down in Franklin sold him to me for twenty dollars— said he'd been trying to break him for six months and finally decided to give up. I found him tied to a pole behind a barn, emaciated, standing in his own waste, angry, and full of fire. Broke my heart to see him like that. But I took him home and fed him and treated him with respect. It took a few months before he learned to trust me, but that was the best twenty dollars I ever spent. He's the horse I most trust with my wife and kids," he said, rubbing Charlie's nose before giving him another apple. "Yep, patience and kindness go a long way in creating trust and loyalty. It takes time and a few sacks of apples, but the investment's always worth it."

Matt nodded thoughtfully. "I'd love to stay and watch, but Genevieve and I are on milk duty tonight. Do you mind if I stop by again sometime?"

"Not at all. It's good for Duke to be around other people. I'm just heading home to dinner myself, but I'll be here most evenings for the next few months."

As Matt and Genevieve walked back to their bikes, Matt couldn't help but wonder what else he could learn from watching horses.

CHAPTER 67

History and Cheese

We can never obtain peace in the outer world until we make peace with ourselves.
—The 14th Dalai Lama

The broken bicycle was gone when Matt and Genevieve reached the drive, though the flour mess remained. They coasted down the bumpy drive, relieved to see several of their fellow campers on the porch and lawn. They had just parked the bikes in the shed when Pops found them.

"I was beginning to wonder if you two had gone AWOL," he said with a broad smile. "Mom assured me she hadn't given you enough money to make it past the county line, but with all the excitement around here today, I had to worry."

"Sorry. It's my fault," Matt responded. "I lost track of time."

"It's all good and fine. Just glad you're back. The cows are ready when you are. And I hope you were able to get the salt. We'll be needing that for the second half of the cheese lesson."

"Yes, right here," Matt said, holding up his grocery bag.

"Very good. Mom says dinner's gonna be late tonight. I'm sure you're probably hungry, but there's not a lot to eat right now."

"I think Matt and I can wait," Genevieve said. "Are things working out okay with James and Crystal?"

Pops shook his head as he led the way to the barn. "It's tougher for some kids to get used to the pace and rhythm of the farm. Everything always works out by the end of the summer, but we've never had a summer that didn't include a few hiccups. We're down a bike, but it's not the first time that's happened."

"Really? You've had someone destroy a bike before?" Matt asked, surprised.

"Yes, and you've ridden it at least a couple of times."

"I have?"

"Yes, and so have you," he said, nodding to Genevieve. "Bessie used to run on two wheels until Joel and Linda ended up in a bit of a tiff one afternoon down at the farm stand. In that case it was Linda who took her frustrations out on the bike when Joel was being less than cooperative. She ended up bending his bike beyond repair by repeatedly dropping a rock on it while he was in the outhouse. By the time he'd finished up, she'd taken off on a little joy ride on her own bike. She was gone most of the day, as I recall, blowing off steam."

Genevieve laughed nervously, considering her own experience at the farm stand with an uncooperative man.

"It all ended up being good for both of them. In her absence, Joel spent the day realizing he was being a turd muffin, and she came to the conclusion that her impatience and stubbornness were keeping her from experiencing a fullness of joy. Mom assigned them to work the farm stand together the whole next week to give them a chance to figure things out. They had to keep themselves busy somehow, so they patched things up and put their nerdy brains together. That's when they turned the wrecked bike into Bessie. It took them the rest of the summer to figure out that they'd learned to love each other in the process. Last we heard, they've been married almost twenty years and have invented all sorts of other contraptions. But Bessie the Niederbipp Neutralizer has always been my favorite for obvious reasons," he said, patting his belly.

"I don't condone violence or destruction in any form or for any reason, but I suppose a wrecked bike was a small price to pay for improving two lives. Among the good that came from that spat is the nearly 250 kids who've sat on Bessie's saddle and laughed and cried as they've churned out ice cream. Of course, things don't always work out that way when two kids get their undies in a bunch. But more often than not, when given the chance to figure things out, they come up with solutions that are better than anything we could have planned. It's sometimes tough to step back and let things happen, when what you really want to do is grab people by the collar and shake some sense into 'em, but the results of Mom's laissez-faire approach to discipline continue to surprise me."

While they milked the cows, Pops continued to share examples of bad behavior that resulted in eventual positive outcomes, though many of them proved to be far less immediate than Joel and Linda Hashimoto's tale. As they walked back to the big house to check on the timing of dinner, Pops said that during the second half of the cheese lesson, he would share his own story, which Ruby had alluded to earlier.

They found the campers on the front porch, looking tired and hungry as they wrote in their journals or flipped through scrapbooks filled with wedding announcements. Greg did his best to improve the morale by serenading them with classic folk tunes. While Pops slipped into the kitchen to check on the KP staff, Genevieve and Matt probed the group to see what they knew about the events of the afternoon. Pops returned before anyone could say much. He informed them that the kitchen staff needed a little more time and that part two of the cheese lesson would begin immediately.

Everyone seemed pleased to have a diversion from the stress of the afternoon, and their spirits lifted significantly by the time they reached the barn. Pops led them all back to the far wall of the creamery, where the cheese presses had done their work, expelling the last of the whey and creating six fresh cheese wheels. As Pops showed them how to lift the tender cheeses from their forms, tugging on the cheesecloth, he shared with them the story, now fifty-seven years old, of how he and Ruby had found their peace after working in the kitchen three days in a row at the demand of Millie Smurthwaite, the farm's previous matchmaker. He admitted he had been immature and rowdy that day, having already worked with Ruby a few times and finding her to be a self-righteous, cynical, and anything-but-pleasant killjoy.

Pops explained that he had taken her heat when she had criticized the inconsistent sizes of his pancakes. He had bitten his tongue when she had complained about his performance on the flour mill. He had even swallowed his pride when she found syrup on the underside of a plate he'd just washed and put it back in the sink for him to wash again. But he reached his limit when she dissed his mother for not teaching him better skills, not knowing that his mother had been dead for nearly twenty years. That was all he could take, and he'd turned on Ruby, calling her several unsavory words while suggesting he'd already identified at least a handful of obvious reasons why she was still single. The insults were personal and pointed, and he knew they'd struck a very atonal chord when she went ballistic, tossing flour into his eyes and mouth.

He said he could hear her talking to Millie on the front porch, demanding that he be either forced to apologize or kicked off the farm. He stayed in the kitchen, admittedly cowering, and continued to work on the bread while he listened to Ruby carry on about the injustice of having to work with such incompetent imbeciles as the six men Millie had brought to the farm that summer. He said that Millie listened patiently as Ruby had carried on for at least fifteen minutes. By the time she ran out of grievances, Pops had decided he'd rather be done with the farm than ever have to work with such a mean, cantankerous, wet blanket of woman like Ruby Johnson ever again.

Pops paused his story when the group had unwrapped the last of the six cheeses. Leaving them all hanging, he directed Matt and Spencer to use cool water to fill the big copper pot. To this, Pops added seven overflowing handfuls of the noniodized salt Matt and Genevieve had picked up from town. While Genevieve stirred the mixture until the salt dissolved, Pops continued his story, picking up right where he'd left off.

Ruby didn't return to the kitchen that day, he said, and Millie didn't appear to be in any hurry to offer a reprimand. So Pops had just kept on working, mixing the bread dough, cleaning up the kitchen, taking care of the things he was supposed to, and enjoying the peace and quiet that finally came with Ruby gone. But while the quiet remained, the peace didn't last long. As he reviewed their conversations, echoes of the things they'd said and the names they'd called each other bounced off the kitchen walls, hitting him in the chest with all the ugliness he'd felt before. And in that ugliness, he recognized how his words had solved nothing, making him feel better neither about himself nor the situation. In fact, in the silence Ruby and Millie had given him, he began to feel ashamed that he had lost control of himself. He feared he would never be able to consider himself a gentleman again.

Pops's bread came out of the oven that day looking good, but in the commotion, he had forgotten the salt, creating something that looked right but tasted blah. He had served it up to his fellow campers with a saltshaker, grateful that Ruby wasn't there to rub his nose in yet another failure. But while he was cleaning up the kitchen after lunch, Millie suggested to him that the only way he could find peace was to make the time and space for it. And so, after his work was done, he wandered off in search of his own peace. On a bench behind the phone booth at the top of the drive, he came to the realization that he'd been a jerk and that much of the trouble he felt was self-inflicted. As that became clear, he immediately wanted to apologize. Despite the way Ruby had treated him, he wanted to clear his conscience of his own failings in the matter and seek her forgiveness.

Pops paused his story again when he saw that the salt was fully dissolved in the water. He taught the campers the important technique of brining, which would harden the outer skin and help preserve the fresh cheese. Without measuring, he poured a heavy splash of white vinegar into the pot, added a handful of calcium chloride from a jar, and stirred in a couple of cups of expelled whey from the presses. He directed a few of the campers to help him line up the six cheese wheels in the brine. He said they'd let them soak while he continued his story.

After recognizing his own part in the situation with Ruby, Pops went looking for her and found her on the bench overlooking the orchard. In the hours that had passed since that morning's tumult, she had spent some time thinking about the mean things he had called her and told her. He tried to apologize, but she stopped him, having recognized that he was right about many of his points. To his surprise, she acknowledged being a cynical killjoy. She even recognized that she *was* self-righteous. And she admitted that she was unhappy and depressed and wanted to change. Pops admitted that her reaction had surprised him and inspired even more contrition on his part. He apologized for being an immature jerk, promising to try harder to be patient, respectful, and kind. Before they walked back to the house to make dinner, they promised each other that they would put aside their petty differences and focus their efforts on trying to be friends.

Pops explained that at Millie's insistence, they spent the next three days working together. The following day enabled them to lay a new foundation, and by the third day, they began building a strong friendship. After they got back into the normal rotation, they looked forward to the one day each week they could work together. This led to them checking in on each other throughout the week to see how the other one was doing.

As the weeks and months passed, Pops recognized that the feelings of friendship he had for Ruby were turning into something more. The differences they'd experienced early on had melted away, leaving behind sincere understanding and compassion, an open dialogue, and a tested and proven friendship. He smiled as he admitted that by the end of that summer, he'd begun to dread the passage of each day, knowing it would soon be over. In his last interview with Millie, just a few days before he was supposed to go home, he told her that he wanted to stick around and find a way to make Niederbipp his permanent residence. Millie suggested he check the flour mill in town. The mill offered him a job, and he'd begin as soon as his responsibilities on the farm ended. Pops admitted that having a job was nice. Being able to stay in Niederbipp was better. But the problem he'd come here with remained—he was still single.

The night before he was to leave the farm, he struggled to find peace. After everybody had gone to bed, he took a flashlight and wandered back to the bench that overlooked the orchard to spend some time in prayer, seeking answers about his future. To his surprise, Ruby arrived a few minutes later with the same intentions. They talked through the night, and as they watched the sun rising over the farm, they came to the mutual conclusion that for Ruby to go home to Ohio was not the best option for either of them. They admitted to each other what they both had known in their hearts for some time—that they loved each other and didn't want to see that love end. Pops proposed right there, and they went to the big house together to tell Millie and George of their plans to marry at the soonest possible date.

Millie and George received the news with great enthusiasm. A quiet ceremony was held that Sunday, and Pops and Ruby spent three days honeymooning in Erie, where they worked out a proposition for Millie and George. They would work as the Smurthwaites' assistants for one year and take over the farm at the end of the next summer. Upon Pops and Ruby's return to Niederbipp, however, Millie and George met them at the train station with a proposition of their own. The old couple explained that they'd been wanting to retire for several years but that the time and circumstances hadn't made such a plan possible. They invited Pops and Ruby to consider taking over right away. Overwhelmed by the prospect,

Ruby and Pops suggested a compromise: Millie and George would stay through New Year, sharing and teaching all of the skills that Ruby and Pops would need. Millie and George agreed. Before they departed for retirement in Florida, the Smurthwaites left the farm to the Swarovskis in the same way it had been left to them decades earlier—without any strings attached or anyone looking over their shoulders.

"So that was it?" Susan asked. "You just dropped everything you'd been doing before and reinvented yourselves as farmers and matchmakers?"

"That's right," Pops said in a very matter-of-fact way. He then drew their attention back to the brining cheese. He fished the soft yellow cheese wheels out of the brine one by one, handing each to a different camper. Josh lifted the trapdoor to the cheese cave, and everyone followed Pops down the stairs. They stowed the cheese on a board and slid it into place on the racks to allow the aging process to begin.

Matt and Spencer carefully carried the pot of brine into the cave, Pops explaining that the brine would be kept in the cave and used for each new batch of cheese. Before they climbed the stairs, he taught them the importance of record keeping and showed them a logbook designed for documenting the dates and numbers of cheeses. Genevieve noticed that the elephant in the room was the question of how long *these* cheeses would age. With the unknown future of the farm on their minds, they all scurried up the steep stairs to clean up the mess they'd left behind. While some rinsed the cheesecloths, others washed the floors or rinsed the forms; everyone found a place to help.

"I'm starving," Spencer moaned as he stacked the last of the wooden cheese forms on the shelf. "When's dinner?"

Many of the others grumbled as if they all wanted to know the same thing.

"I recognize that patience is hard sometimes, especially on an empty belly, but Mom and I discovered long ago that there are many reasons patience is considered a virtue." As he led them all back to the big house, Pops regaled them with more stories of campers who'd had to learn to work together for several days in a row while they overcame challenges.

"You almost make it sound like this happens every year," Holly said as they gathered on the front porch to wait for the dinner bell.

Pops nodded. "Sometimes it happens the very first week, and sometimes it doesn't happen for a month or two. But it always happens at least once, and occasionally it can happen a second time—if particularly slow learners are involved."

"I propose we don't do this again," Spencer said.

Many of the others agreed.

Pops smiled. "As Ruby is keen to say, 'that will depend entirely on you.' I'll go check on them. I'm guessing they must be getting close now." He walked into the house, leaving them to relax.

Holly, who was sitting next to Genevieve on a wicker loveseat, picked up the scrapbook she'd been looking through before the cheese lesson and continued to flip through wedding announcements and photos of happy couples. Intrigued, Genevieve joined her. They shifted the scrapbook to lie across both their laps. As they laughed together at the hair and dress styles of days past, others gathered around them. Greg was particularly interested to find a photo of his own parents, taken just months after his mother had spent the summer with Ruby and Pops. His reaction to his mother's big bangs and his father's mullet, along with their matching denim shirts, got all the campers interested. They gathered around as Holly and Genevieve flipped through the rest of the scrapbook, everyone commenting on and laughing at the styles of a bygone era.

While they continued to wait for the dinner bell, Holly went into the library and returned with another scrapbook filled with wedding announcements. This scrapbook was filled with photos that were at least a few years newer, the styles dramatically different from those exhibited in the previous scrapbook. But the laughter continued as they flipped through pages of men with dated haircuts wearing double-breasted suits and women with huge puffed sleeves, shoulder pads, and terribly big hairdos, crimps, and bangs.

As the others laughed and commented on the photos, Genevieve began to feel once again a pang of realization that her work in the fashion industry had such limited longevity when it came to meaning and relevance. Her discomfort grew slowly with each turn of the page and with each fit of laughter the photos inspired, taking her deeper into a place of self-doubt. She of course had witnessed styles changing from year to year as she'd studied fashion magazines since the time she was in her midteens. Stumbling upon dated materials had often left her feeling grateful for progress and evolution. But as she had consciously watched styles change, it had often left her wondering what was being lost in the name of progress. Models she had followed and even known personally became short-lived pawns in the hands of an industry that was marked by insatiable greed chasing after ever-fading beauty. Early on in her chosen career, Genevieve learned to push aside the feelings of doubt that cropped up whenever she witnessed the obliterative steamrolling of respect and decency. She knew that her work fed the inner critics of women who already suffered from self-doubt and body-image issues. And seeing these dated photos and listening to the others' laughter and commentary shook her conscience as she considered how quickly what was once stylish and en vogue become a laughingstock.

She found herself remembering the conversation she'd just witnessed between Matt and the grocer. Kai had said he felt…what were his words? *Like he was making a difference…that his life had purpose and meaning.* As she and Holly continued turning the scrapbook pages, Genevieve juxtaposed Kai's sense of purpose with her own. How long had it been since she'd felt that way? *Had she ever felt that way?*

Her job had been exciting and offered her a chance to see the world, but had it ever once given her a sense of *real* purpose? As she thought back on the list of people she'd interviewed and the recent articles she'd written, she felt almost empty inside, but with a twinge of shame and remorse. She knew in her heart that what she wrote—what her industry produced—ultimately objectified women, reducing them to two dimensions that relied solely on skin-deep beauty that was doomed to become a joke to future generations.

She had often justified her line of work by telling herself it was better

History and Cheese

than the porn industry. But even though the models in her magazine were clothed, she knew they were still being harmfully objectified; models and their viewers alike fell into unhealthy patterns in pursuit of the unrealistic and unsustainable beauty that the fashion industry espoused. Feeling agitated and claustrophobic as the campers huddled ever closer around the scrapbook, she was about to excuse herself when Pops returned to the porch to inform them that dinner was served.

As the others peeled back and began trailing Pops into the house, Genevieve's eyes fell on the open scrapbook in her lap. A familiar face stared back at her, catching her off guard. She looked closer, feeling shocked and confused. The woman in the photo was beautiful, clothed in a fashionable-for-the-time wraparound dress that accentuated her figure. Her hair and makeup, though dated, were done to the nines. The handsome man at her side was dressed in an equally fashionable double-breasted suit and tie. They looked so young compared to how she knew them now.

She read the accompanying embossed wedding announcement just to make sure she wasn't hallucinating.

Mr. and Mrs. Zachery P. Somerset
are pleased to announce the marriage of daughter,
Julia Marie
to
Lawrence Bradley Galiveto
son of Mr. and Mrs. Christopher B. Galiveto
on the twelfth day of June, nineteen hundred ninety-four
at the National United Methodist Church
3401 Nebraska Ave NW
Washington, District of Columbia

The pleasure of your company is requested
at a reception in their honor that evening from six thirty to nine o'clock
Columbia Country Club
7900 Connecticut Ave
Chevy Chase, Maryland

Genevieve took a deep breath and shook her head.

"Are you okay?" Matt asked, turning back from the front doorway. She looked up, surprised. "I don't know."

He walked back to her and looked over her shoulder. "What's up?"

Genevieve shook her head again, but her face was unreadable. "I just found a picture of my boss."

CHAPTER 68

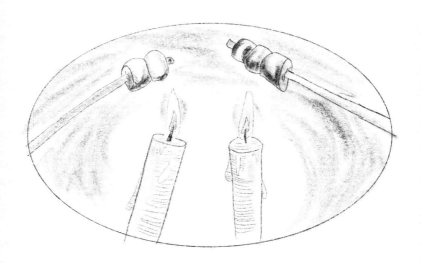

The First Key of Joy

If a man loses his reverence for any part of life, he will lose his reverence for all of life.
—Albert Schweitzer

Dinner was on the table when Matt and Genevieve entered the dining hall. Six beeswax candles flickered, filling the dimly lit room with sweet aroma; soft light; and warm, solemn ambiance. They slid into the two remaining spots at the long table, ending up across from each other and not realizing that the others were watching them curiously.

Susan offered to say grace, thanking God for a warm meal and a sense of peace at the end of a long day, but Genevieve hardly heard the words; she was preoccupied with what she had just seen. As the food was passed around, Genevieve's mind continued to buzz, searching for meaning. The presence of the wedding announcement meant that Julia Galiveto had either spent the summer here herself or had married someone who had. Either way, this revelation suggested a scenario that was much different from the one Ruby had told Genevieve about in the beginning. It suggested planning, timing…perhaps even collusion.

Startled from her contemplation by James's voice, Genevieve looked up, watching his mouth move but not hearing his words as he pointed to a heaping bowl of what looked like pasta. Genevieve felt lost, reeling under the weight of this new evidence as she considered its many ramifications. She had given Julia Galiveto seven of her best years; it was hard not to feel betrayed. Although she knew there had to be an explanation, she couldn't ask for one now—not here in front of everybody. But the burden of not knowing, of not being able to ask, felt concussive.

Greg, who sat to her right, was trying to be helpful, putting ravioli, French bread, and tossed salad onto her plate while she sat in a dazed silence. The food in front of her looked delicious, but she suddenly wasn't very hungry.

She felt someone kick her foot. She looked up to see Matt nodding and subtly pointing his fork at Crystal, who was standing at the opposite end of the table and addressing the group. Genevieve turned to look, but Crystal's words were meaningless. She heard the others clap and watched them smile as Crystal sat down. Late to the party, Genevieve joined in the applause without being sure why everyone was applauding. She felt lost as her mind tried to stitch all the facts together and reconcile them with a new and unruly set of suspicions.

Before she had eaten much of anything, she noticed that the plates were already being stacked in preparation to be cleared away. Panicking, she quickly stuffed her mouth full of lukewarm ravioli and was jolted by the pleasant flavor, which pulled her further out of her haze. As the plates were cleared, Ephraim circled the table and handed out Wisdom Cookies. Genevieve tried to be attentive as each camper read the wisdom they'd received, but her tired, disturbed mind felt like it was traveling through wormholes at lightning speed, catching only bits and pieces from which it would be impossible to form any semblance of intelligibility.

Genevieve was the last to share. She cracked open her cookie, unfolded the paper within, and read:

"'Reverence is the chief joy and power of life—reverence for that which is pure and bright in youth; for what is true and tried in age; for all that is gracious among the living, great among the dead,—and marvelous in the powers that cannot die.'"

Genevieve looked up, scanning the faces at the table until she came to Matt, who offered a gentle smile. She couldn't help but smile back.

"Any guesses on the author?" Ruby asked.

Matt shook his head, and the others looked clueless.

"That's John Ruskin, the English artist, writer, and thinker," said Ruby as she looked down the table at Pops, winking at him as if giving him a signal.

"And his quote is actually a great segue into something Mom and I wanted to talk to you all about tonight," Pops said. "We had hoped this would take place around a fire, but not knowing the exact timing of dinner, we decided to play it safe and opt for the candles instead."

"I hate to admit it, but I thought the candles were James's attempt to distract us from some ugly cooking," Spencer said.

"No, no, I assure you they are quite deliberate and don't have anything to do with distraction. If anything, they are here for quite the opposite reason," Pops said. "After campers leave at the end of every season, Mom and I eat most of our dinners by candlelight. There is something about a fire, even a small one, that invites those gathered around it to linger and enjoy a moment of closeness. Fire—and the stories it inspires—are two things that separate us from the animals. Long before television or radio, our ancestors gathered round fires at the close of day to make sense of the stars above them and give meaning to the world around them. As humanity evolved, they also came up with s'mores." He pulled one of the grocery bags from beneath his chair and opened it up, passing the bag of marshmallows, the box of graham crackers, and the bars of chocolate around the group, along with a Mason jar filled with a bouquet of hand-scraped sticks with pointy ends. Everyone responded joyfully.

"Improvisation and flexibility are two of the most helpful attributes to develop in order to maintain one's sanity in marriage and family life." Pops waited as the s'more fixings reached everyone. Holly didn't need any encouragement to begin roasting her marshmallow over the candle in front of her, and everyone else followed suit. As they shared the light and warmth of the six small flames positioned down the middle of the table, Pops cleared his throat and spoke again.

"There are some things we usually wait to share with our kids until we get a little further into the summer, when everyone has had a chance to experience the quiet magic that happens in the stillness of the farm. But Mom and I have recognized that you kids have already developed, both individually and collectively, a desire to know and learn things of great consequence. For some of you, what I am about to share may be slightly premature, but I hope you will understand our need to pass on these things now before…before we might not be able to. We hope you will use these concepts as a springboard into deeper knowledge and understanding." Pops pursed his lips as he nodded to Ruby.

"What I am about to share with you is not necessarily secret," Ruby began, "but Pops and I feel that it is sacred. Many of you have already come to understand that few of the lessons we learn on the farm have relevance only to marriage. We've been impressed with your desire to learn and apply what we like to call the *secrets of joy*. We have spoken of these things somewhat loosely as they have come up in conversations over the last two weeks. The quote Genevieve just read references what we have come to know as *the first key of joy*."

Matt tapped Genevieve's foot under the table, glancing at her before turning his attention back to Ruby. Distracted by the flame and the marshmallow at the end of her stick, she wondered what he meant by his glance, but she turned her attention to Ruby as well.

"This first key of joy has also been called *the first key of peace* or *the first key of liberty*. Before the end of the summer, we hope to share with you all five keys, which, if understood and applied, can unlock all the secrets to joy, peace, and liberty."

Suddenly much more alert, Genevieve glanced again at Matt, whose face reflected back her own surprise and intrigue. He seemed to be making the same connections she was.

"Many of you have recognized a unique sense of peace here on the farm and in the town of Niederbipp," Ruby continued.

Most of the campers bobbed their heads in agreement.

"This is a unique place, to be sure. The principles upon which this town was founded are equally unique, especially in today's world, where many of them have been neglected and forgotten. We have shared with you our hope that when you leave this farm and return home at the end of the summer, you will take with you a sense of responsibility to leaven your homes, families, and communities—lifting, inspiring, and improving wherever you can. The five keys we will share with you over the coming months can, if used with wisdom and prudence, offer knowledge and direction that lead to greater happiness and fulfillment. Each key builds upon the one before it, and if you wish to fully appreciate the value of the five keys, it will be important for you to put them to work in how you act, think, and speak. Pops and I will know it's time to share the next key when we see the previous key coming alive in all of you."

"So...these five keys," Matt began, "do they have anything to do with the five keys that were part of the Liberty Fountain on Hauptstrasse?"

Ruby smiled, nodding. "They are one and the same."

"Wait, what are you talking about?" asked Ephraim.

"It's a long story, but there's a sculpture of a woman that stands above a fountain—the Liberty Fountain—right in the heart of town."

"I remember seeing that our first Sunday here," Greg said.

Matt nodded. "In her left hand is a pruning knife, a symbol of peace. Her right hand, from what we've read, used to hold a ring of five keys that supposedly opened the doors of joy. But, at least according to Thomas's book, the keys went missing more than seventy years ago, and no one seems to remember the details about them."

All eyes turned to Ruby.

"You've been reading," she said with a smile. "I congratulate you on making good use of your time." She winked at Matt before looking into the expectant faces on both sides of the table. "What Matt just said is true. The keys that once hung from the statue did in fact go missing in 1943, but what very few people know is that the keys returned to Niederbipp less than a year later."

"Do you know where they are?" Matt asked.

"I do, but the keys are only symbols—physical representations of the principles that many of us try to always carry with us in our hearts."

"And on our hands," Pops said, raising his right hand, his fingers extended. "I've read Thomas's book. It was printed before he could talk to the people who have—or had—answers to the right questions. I'm certain he's discovered the keys by now, as we hope each of you will by the end of the summer. Mom and I learned these principles during our first summer on the farm. As Mom said, these keys are the foundation of our town and have always been the pillars of this farm. In the same way a finger is connected to each of its neighboring fingers as well as to the hand, everything we do here, every activity we participate in, every lesson we hope to share with you has ties to at least one of the keys."

"So what are these keys?" Spencer asked, sounding a little impatient.

"I remember my mom talking about these when I was just a kid," Greg said, holding out his hand.

"I'm glad to hear it," Ruby said. "Do you remember them?"

Greg looked down at his right hand and used his left index finger to point at each of his right digits. He looked up, disappointed. "I guess I forgot. Can you give me a hint?"

Ruby nodded. "If they're not practiced regularly, they're easy to forget. I'll give you a hint on the first one. The others, like I said, will come later. Once you know the first key, it may be easy to guess the second and the third. In the time between tonight and the next time we gather to share a key, Pops and I would like to encourage you to be thoughtful as you do your best to exercise the first key, which is directly tied to Genevieve's quote. Would you mind reading it again?"

Genevieve nodded. She looked down at her strip of paper and read: "'Reverence is the chief joy and power of life—reverence for that which is pure and bright in youth; for what is true and tried in age; for all that is gracious among the living, great among the dead,—and marvelous in the powers that cannot die.'"

Greg smiled as he lifted his hand in front of his face, wiggling his thumb. "That's right! Reverence!"

Pops nodded. "Reverence is the beginning of all wisdom and joy, tying us directly to the only sure foundation to build a house upon."

"'Except the Lord build the house, they labour in vain that build it,'" Matt whispered.

"Yes. Do you see the connection?" Pops asked.

Many of them nodded.

"'Be still, and know that I am God,'" Susan added.

"Excellent!" Pops said. "As you continue to look for connections and make time to be still, you will begin to see that these keys, as pure and simple as they are, form the foundation of all good things."

Greg nodded thoughtfully, still focused on his thumb. "I also remember my mom used to say that…that to love God was the first and most important commandment."

Ruby smiled. "Very good, Greg. I am glad to see that your mother shared those things with you."

"Yeah, and a lot of good it did me. I forgot them all!"

"And you will forget them again if you're not deliberate in remembering them. But they're in there," she said, tapping the side of her head. "And that which is once given meaning can always be drawn upon when it is sincerely needed or wanted. As it is with all things pertaining to wisdom, the table is laid before you. You must decide if you will nibble or indulge—or if you'll turn up your nose at what is offered and reject it altogether."

"Which is the reason why reverence is the first key," Pops said. "It's the reason twelve thinking benches are scattered across the farm. It's the reason we don't overschedule your days and the reason we offer a variety of activities throughout the week—so you can spend time considering your place in the universe and the connection you have to your Creator. Reverence begins with a conscious decision—a decision about what is important to you, what you will choose to revere, and who or what you decide will be your god. That is the decision of the ages."

"Are you talking about religion?" James asked.

Pops shook his head. "I suppose that can be part of it, but it's not the whole story. I know religion has a bad rap, especially among those under forty. We've watched spiritual trends change over the last five decades. It used to be that every single kid who came to the farm had grown up going to church on Sundays or temple on Saturdays. Now it's not uncommon for us to have only one or two kids who have attended church in the last year. Religion is what it is, and you'll have to decide which creed, if any, aligns with your spiritual sensitivities."

"Our desire is not to push religion on anyone," Ruby added, "but to promote a desire for a personal spiritual connection. We are far less concerned about whether you come out of this as a Christian or a Jew, a Muslim or a Buddhist, than we are about inviting you to experience the awe of recognizing that there's something bigger than yourself. Start there. Some of you already knew about this *something bigger* before you came here. Some of you have discovered it in the days since you arrived. None of us are likely to experience it regularly unless we want to—unless we invite God in and make room in our lives to experience the divine."

"Is reverence the same as recognizing something bigger?" Greg asked.

Ruby nodded. "It's a good place to start, but it expands from there. I don't believe you can have reverence for God without revering his creations: the world around you, the people you rub shoulders with, even the stars above your head. If you have eyes to see, you will find that these creations all bear the Creator's fingerprints—an orderly plan, a purpose, a design, and a cosmic balance that our brightest scientists are only beginning to understand. Let it begin with awe, and see where that leads you. Keep your mind and heart open. See if by honoring and loving your Creator, you do not experience at least an equal outpouring of love returning to you."

CHAPTER 69

Illumination

*Do all the good you can, by all the means you can,
in all the ways you can, in all the places you can,
at all the times you can, to all the people you can,
as long as ever you can.*
—John Wesley

The conversation continued as the campers polished off the last of the s'mores, but Genevieve's distraction persisted, leaving her feeling subdued and overwhelmed with questions. Julia's wedding announcement befuddled her, but with no hope of immediate answers, Genevieve turned her thoughts to the keys of joy. Several times in the last few days, she had felt what Ruby called *a sense of awe*, and Genevieve was eager to discover how to more consciously and deliberately exercise reverence.

At Ruby's suggestion, the campers gathered to help clean up the kitchen and wash and put away the dishes. As she swept the floor, Genevieve watched James and Crystal navigating around each other with a much different energy than she'd witnessed that morning. It wasn't exactly kindness, but there was a new level of respect between them. The cloud of negativity had parted, and she was surprised to find James smiling as he expressed sincere appreciation for the others' help. After the kitchen was clean, Ruby encouraged everyone to spend the last half hour of daylight writing in their journals at a bench of their choice. She didn't have to make the suggestion twice; most of the campers quickly poured out of the big house and scattered to the benches as the golden hour slowly faded away.

Unlike the others, Genevieve hung back. Walking out the front door, she noticed the open scrapbook and was once again confronted with feelings of betrayal. She sat down on the wicker loveseat, lay the scrapbook on her lap, and stared down at Julia's announcement. She tried to decide what this artifact ultimately meant for her, and she wondered which parts of this farm experience, if any, were real.

"Julia was a beautiful bride, wasn't she?" Ruby said from behind, resting her hands on Genevieve's shoulders.

Genevieve turned and looked up into the old woman's face, which glowed in the setting sun. As Genevieve looked into Ruby's gray-blue eyes, all suspicions of treachery were immediately subdued by a keen, overwhelming sense of love. "Yes, she was," Genevieve admitted, turning back to the scrapbook.

Ruby sat down beside her but didn't speak.

"Why didn't you tell me? Why didn't *she* tell me?" Genevieve asked.

"I'll take the blame for that. I asked her not to."

"Why?"

"Because I wanted you to be able to get to know me without any prejudices or preconceived notions. And I didn't want there to be any expectations that your experience here would be any different from the others'. I didn't know if it was the right decision, but I went with how I felt based on what little information I had about you."

"What information did you have about me?" Genevieve asked, looking surprised.

"Well, I knew two things. One, that you were a talented writer who had earned Julia's confidence; she believed you were up for the challenge."

"And two?" Genevieve asked.

Ruby took a deep breath. "And two, that you believed I was a fraud and were determined to find a way to smear my reputation."

"How? I...oh...Amy..." Genevieve said, looking embarrassed.

"If you haven't noticed, it's a mighty small town," Ruby said with an assuring smile. "Jake and Amy have been loyal friends, and they felt the need to protect me. But you don't need to worry. I hold no grudge against you. I've tried to treat you fairly, and I hope you'll do the same with me."

"I'm sorry," Genevieve said. "I...I didn't know who you were or what you were about."

"And now that you do, how have things changed?"

"I...wow. Uh, I guess everything's changed, hasn't it?"

Ruby nodded, patting the young woman's knee, drawing her attention back to the scrapbook.

"I knew the time would come when an explanation would be needed. To be honest, I'm relieved that the time is now. I'm not sure I'm prepared for all the questions you may have, but I'm willing to try."

Genevieve took a deep breath, shaking her head as she exhaled. "So, why am I here?"

"Well, the easy answer is that you're here at the request of Julia to write an article about the Matchmaker of Niederbipp, which is only the second article I've ever consented to be interviewed for. The first one was written by her," Ruby said, pointing to the picture.

"I don't understand. Why didn't she tell me?"

"Because she didn't want to influence what you would write or how your experience here would play out."

"But how…how did any of this get started, and how did I end up in the middle of it?"

"Do you want the long story or the short story?"

"I want the truth."

Ruby looked thoughtful for a moment. "Very well. The truth is a rather long story—more than fifty years long, as a matter of fact. Julia came here twenty-six years ago at the request of Shannon Ryder-Daniels, the dean of the School of Journalism at Columbia University. By then, Shannon had created a name for herself as a prominent thinker and gender-rights activist. But Pops and I had come to know and love Shannon as a gifted and spirited girl who'd joined us for our third summer on the farm, back when we were just getting our feet under us.

"We stayed in touch as she married and learned to balance three children and her lofty educational ambitions. When her youngest headed off to college, she landed a job at Columbia. She had a burning desire to help women find their voices and develop the courage to share them. Pops and I were among her first cheerleaders when her own parents thought she was foolish to believe she could break into a man's world. But Shannon never let the odds stacked against her stand in her way. Throughout her career, she maintained her determination to open doors for women around the world.

"Because of that, she was constantly on the lookout for determined women whose voices were strong enough to be heard. We kept in touch as her star continued to rise, and one day in early 1993, I got a letter from her. She asked me if I might consider taking on a coed graduate student who she believed showed promise. She proposed that Julia spend the summer working on the farm and then stay on through the winter to finish her dissertation on the changing roles of women.

"We were hesitant at first, worried that she might think herself above the chores, but we trusted Shannon. We knew she believed in the farm and what we were trying to accomplish here. So, Julia Somerset arrived on the bus with the recruits of 1993 and worked the farm, just the same as you are. Pops and I both took a liking to her. As you know, she's a strong but personable lady. She made a lot of friends here, but one stood out—Calvin Galiveto, a charming young man who was a few years younger than her and at least three inches shorter. When Calvin went home at the end of the summer and Julia stuck around to write, a whole lot of letters passed through that mailbox at the top of the hill. He invited her to join his family for Christmas. When she came back to the farm after her visit, she was in love with a different Galiveto." Ruby pointed to the picture, and Genevieve reread the name on the announcement, suddenly realizing it wasn't Calvin.

"What happened?"

"Well, the short answer is that she broke Calvin's heart, but there was no malice in it. We met Lawrence in the spring of that year when he dropped by for a surprise visit. He proposed before he left, and he and Julia were married three months later."

"Poor Calvin."

"Oh, there's nothing to be sorry about there. They each found the right person for them," Ruby said, flipping through several pages until she came to the announcement and photograph of another handsome couple. "Calvin and Felicity met at Julia and Lawrence's wedding. Felicity was actually Julia's maid of honor and former roommate. Things work out in interesting ways."

"So when did Julia write her article about you?"

"Oh, I'm not convinced she actually ever did, at least not on her own."

"What?"

Ruby shook her head but smiled. "Have you ever heard of Chelsea Banks?"

Genevieve laughed. "Yeah, that's a pen name that Julia's husband uses."

"That's right. However, as I understand it, it's also a pen name they use for their collaborative work. After they got married, Julia was busy getting ready to defend her dissertation, and Lawrence was her first editor. He was so impressed with what she'd learned here on the farm that he encouraged her to edit her dissertation down to an article-length snippet and submit it to a women's magazine. I'm not sure if it was Julia's or Chelsea's words that made the final cut, but a magazine printed the article, making the check out to Chelsea Banks." Ruby laughed. "I understand they had a heck of a time trying to cash it. That article caused a huge increase in camper applications for us. But it also motivated Julia and Lawrence to start a little business, Chelsea Banks Unlimited, where they focused on writing articles that promoted marriage and the principles behind the keys of joy."

"Wait! They wrote about the keys of joy?" Genevieve asked incredulously.

"Yes, though somewhat indirectly. That first article landed her a job with the magazine where you're now employed. She made a decent name for both herself and Chelsea Banks before she got pregnant with the twins and was confined to bed rest. But even bed rest and babies couldn't quench her fire. She continued to write and submit articles to several magazines and journals. And as her babies grew, Julia began teaching them the five keys of joy. Lawrence encouraged her to find ways to share the keys in her writing so that their kids might eventually have peers who shared similar values. The thought of helping to shape the world her children would grow into motivated her to continue writing throughout those chaotic and tumultuous child-rearing years. I have a scrapbook full of the articles she and Lawrence have written. They encourage women to honor themselves enough to demand respect, and they also focus on the need for men to stand up and be individuals of character and honor. Despite the trends away from such topics, Julia and Lawrence found magazines that not only bought their articles but also asked them to write more. They've always known that they're pushing against an incessant wave of degradation, but they've held on, bravely standing in defense of virtue."

Genevieve tried not to laugh. "Have you ever seen my magazine?"

"Yes. Julia gave me a subscription."

"Then you know it's not exactly a beacon of virtue."

"No, it's not. Change is hard. I know Julia's been frustrated that she hasn't been able to do more to change the culture there, but I'm sure you've noticed that things have changed significantly since she took the helm."

Genevieve nodded.

"She accepted the job as editor on the condition that the magazine's shareholders would give her license to make changes. The changes have been slower and subtler than she would have liked, but patience, as you will learn, plays a role in each of the five keys of joy. She's been encouraged by letters to the editor that ask for more of the positive and affirming messages that Chelsea Banks is known for. And from what I understand, readership is up under her direction. I know that where she wants the magazine to be is still a ways off, but Julia has always been a woman of vision. And she gained part of her vision here on the farm; that's why I agreed to let you come."

"I don't understand. Why me?"

Ruby looked down at her hands thoughtfully. "I'll admit I wondered the same thing when you arrived. I couldn't understand how your personality and passions could possibly align with the direction Julia wants to take the magazine. Two weeks in, though, I have to admit she may be a better judge of character than I am."

"What are you talking about?"

"Genevieve, it's my understanding that your article is part of a master plan to begin a new era of change for the magazine. You may be aware that Julia and Lawrence have been slowly acquiring more ownership shares, buying out the old guard who allowed the magazine's tenor to be shaped by society's ongoing race to the bottom. Julia wants to change the world for the better, and she believes that with the right training and experience, you have the power to help her."

"What?" Genevieve asked, confused.

"I questioned her sensibilities too when I first met you, but I've changed my mind after watching you more closely since Sunday."

"What do you mean?"

"Passion, Genevieve, is often in short supply. You can light fires under a lot of people's butts to get them moving, but passion—passion is something that comes from within. Anyone is capable of developing passion over time, but not the brand of passion you have. Julia is right; you've got it, and I have no doubt you were born with it. What many passionate people don't understand is that this rare gift comes with responsibilities."

Genevieve nodded but still looked confused. "I'm not sure I understand."

Ruby looked out over the farm, searching for the right words. "Many forces are at work in our world, and most of them, if not all, can be divided into forces of light and forces of darkness. That which is light cannot help but give off light and positivity, while that which is dark yields only shades of darkness and discouragement. Every day, each of us must decide which side of the line to walk on. We are all accountable for which path we choose and how we use our gifts. But those who are born with the gift of passion have an added measure of accountability."

"That hardly seems fair."

Ruby laughed. "You should know by now that life is never fair. I do believe, though, that it's all part of a brilliant master plan. I think we are given both gifts and challenges—along with the ability to take on the challenges and the desire to receive the gifts. But each gift is tied to responsibilities, and we cannot pick up one without picking up the other."

Genevieve nodded thoughtfully.

"I believe every person's gifts are unique and divinely inspired by a Creator who knows us intimately. The keys of joy can help each of us to unlock a personal understanding of our gifts and also help us to make sense of our challenges and trials. And I believe that at the day of reckoning, we will each be asked to give an accounting of how we used our gifts. For those who used their gifts to spread light, joy will be added upon their heads. But for those who used their gifts for darkness, there will be only sorrow and regret.

"How you use your passion is ultimately your decision, the same as each of the other gifts and talents you've developed or will yet develop. But the responsibility attached to passion, with its capacity to persuade and influence others, is great indeed. With your voice, your platform, and your passion, Genevieve, you have the ability to influence millions for good or ill. You can invite your readers to step closer to the light or to the darkness."

Genevieve nodded. "That's why I'm here, isn't it? That's why Julia sent me."

Ruby nodded. "Six years ago, when Julia first asked to send a writer, our campers had already been chosen for the year. We couldn't imagine the interruption, but we stayed in touch. In January of this year, as we began receiving applications, Pops and I decided that we would consider it if Julia contacted us again. When she wrote a few months later informing us that she had a brilliant young woman she wanted to send, we were sad to tell her that the bunks were already filled. But neither of us felt settled about it. When we received word that one of our girls had chosen to take a new job instead of coming to the farm, we felt like the heavens were opening. In all our years on this farm, we've never had a cancellation. It felt like this was the way it was supposed to be, and now we know why."

"You do?"

Ruby nodded. "This is the last summer I will be the Matchmaker of Niederbipp. I've done my job far longer than I expected. By the end of the season, the keys of joy will have been passed on to fifty-six sets of campers."

"That's quite an accomplishment."

"Thank you, but there's so much more I wish I could have done. It breaks my heart each year to turn so many away for lack of space. So many people could benefit from the things we share with you kids.

When we received my prognosis, we knew that all of the wisdom God has entrusted to us over the years would now be entirely in His hands. I wish I could look down the road and know that everything will work out, but faith has never worked that way. My previous trials of faith have always taught me to trust the Creator for all the things I can't see. But this much I do know: I can see far enough to take one more step. And tomorrow I will do the same— and the day after that and the day after that, until I go to sleep in the orchard and give my life back to God to do what He will with it."

Genevieve wiped a tear from her cheek, taking a deep breath and exhaling slowly. "So what does all of this mean for me?"

Ruby patted Genevieve on the knee. "That's entirely up to you."

To be continued!

About the Author

God. Family. Art. Stories. With his head, heart, and hands, Ben Behunin tries to bring his passions together to make the world a little more kind, thoughtful, and beautiful. A potter by day and a writer by night—and whenever he can get away with it, Ben maintains a studio just inches away from his home in Salt Lake City, Utah. He and his wife, Lynnette, are the happy parents of two teens, Isaac and Eve.

Information about studio visits and the Behunin's semi-annual home tours is available at www.potterboy.com.

Personalized books can be ordered
at www.potterboy.com.
There, you can register for the email mailing list
to receive updates about upcoming books, shows, and events.

Ben enjoys hearing from his readers.
You can reach him at benbehunin@comcast.net
or through snail mail at:

Abendmahl Press
P.O Box 581083
Salt Lake City, Utah 84158-1083

For speaking engagements including
book clubs, funerals and inaugurations
call 801-883-0146

See the short video Quin Boardman created about Ben at
www.hiveseries.com

For design information, contact
Bert Compton at bert@comptonds.com

 benbehunin

 niederbippboy

Join the Protopian Movement

 Protopians United    protopiansunited